CW00470404

EVERYMAN,

I WILL GO WITH THEE,

AND BE THY GUIDE,

IN THY MOST NEED

TO GO BY THY SIDE

Dec. 2018

To Chris

With thanks for your
friendship and my very best
wishes.

Paul,

STORIES OF ART AND ARTISTS

EDITED BY DIANA SECKER TESDELL

EVERYMAN'S POCKET CLASSICS

Alfred A. Knopf New York London Toronto

THIS IS A BORZOI BOOK
PUBLISHED BY ALFRED A. KNOPF

This selection by Diana Secker Tesdell first published in
Everyman's Library, 2014
Copyright © 2014 by Everyman's Library
A list of acknowledgments to copyright owners appears at the back
of this volume.

All rights reserved. Published in the United States by Alfred A. Knopf,
a division of Random House LLC, New York, and in Canada by
Random House of Canada Limited, Toronto, Penguin Random
House Companies. Distributed by Random House, LLC, New York.
Published in the United Kingdom by Everyman's Library,
Northburgh House, 10 Northburgh Street, London EC1V 0AT and
distributed by Random House (UK) Ltd.

www.randomhouse.com/everymans
www.everymanslibrary.co.uk

ISBN: 978-0-375-71249-4 (US)
978-1-84159-617-4 (UK)

A CIP catalogue reference for this book is available from the
British Library

Typography by Peter B. Willberg
Typeset in the UK by AccComputing, Wincanton, Somerset
Printed and bound in Germany by GGP Media GmbH, Pössneck

STORIES OF
ART AND
ARTISTS

CONTENTS

MARGUERITE YOURCENAR
How Wang-Fo Was Saved   9

EDGAR ALLAN POE
The Oval Portrait   25

GUY DE MAUPASSANT
A Portrait   31

PENELOPE FITZGERALD
The Red-Haired Girl   39

HENRY JAMES
The Real Thing   53

JULIAN BARNES
The Limner   87

WILLIAM BOYD
Varengeville   103

JOHN BERGER
A Brush   117

DORIS LESSING
Two Potters   131

A. S. BYATT
A Lamia in the Cévennes   151

BERNARD MALAMUD
Rembrandt's Hat   173

ALBERT CAMUS
Jonas, or The Artist at Work   187

HERMANN HESSE
The Painter   221

NATHANIEL HAWTHORNE
The Artist of the Beautiful   229

FRANZ KAFKA
A Hunger Artist   261

HONORÉ DE BALZAC
The Unknown Masterpiece   275

VALERIE MARTIN
His Blue Period   311

REBECCA LEE
Fialta   335

AIMEE BENDER
The Color Master   367

ORHAN PAMUK
I Am Red (from *My Name Is Red*)   389

ACKNOWLEDGMENTS   397

MARGUERITE YOURCENAR

HOW WANG-FO
WAS SAVED

Translated by Alberto Manguel

THE OLD PAINTER Wang-Fo and his disciple Ling were wandering along the roads of the Kingdom of Han.

They made slow progress because Wang-Fo would stop at night to watch the stars and during the day to observe the dragonflies. They carried hardly any luggage, because Wang-Fo loved the image of things and not the things themselves, and no object in the world seemed to him worth buying, except brushes, pots of lacquer and China ink, and rolls of silk and rice paper. They were poor, because Wang-Fo would exchange his paintings for a ration of boiled millet, and paid no attention to pieces of silver. Ling, his disciple, bent beneath the weight of a sack full of sketches, bowed his back with respect as if he were carrying the heavens' vault, because for Ling the sack was full of snow-covered mountains, torrents in spring, and the face of the summer moon.

Ling had not been born to trot down the roads, following an old man who seized the dawn and captured the dusk. His father had been a banker who dealt in gold, his mother the only child of a jade merchant who had left her all his worldly possessions, cursing her for not being a son. Ling had grown up in a house where wealth made him shy: he was afraid of insects, of thunder and the face of the dead. When Ling was fifteen, his father chose a bride for him, a very beautiful one because the thought of the happiness he was giving his son consoled him for having reached the age in which the night is meant for sleep. Ling's wife was as frail as a reed, childish as

II

milk, sweet as saliva, salty as tears. After the wedding, Ling's parents became discreet to the point of dying, and their son was left alone in a house painted vermilion, in the company of his young wife who never stopped smiling and a plum tree that blossomed every spring with pale-pink flowers. Ling loved this woman of a crystal-clear heart as one loves a mirror that will never tarnish, or a talisman that will protect one forever. He visited the teahouses to follow the dictates of fashion, and only moderately favored acrobats and dancers.

One night, in the tavern, Wang-Fo shared Ling's table. The old man had been drinking in order to better paint a drunkard, and he cocked his head to one side as if trying to measure the distance between his hand and his bowl. The rice wine undid the tongue of the taciturn craftsman, and that night Wang spoke as if silence were a wall and words the colors with which to cover it. Thanks to him, Ling got to know the beauty of the drunkards' faces blurred by the vapors of hot drink, the brown splendor of the roasts unevenly brushed by tongues of fire, and the exquisite blush of wine stains strewn on the tablecloths like withered petals. A gust of wind broke the window: the downpour entered the room. Wang-Fo leaned out to make Ling admire the livid zebra stripes of lightning, and Ling, spellbound, stopped being afraid of storms.

Ling paid the old painter's bill, and as Wang-Fo was both without money and without lodging, he humbly offered him a resting place. They walked away together; Ling held a lamp whose light projected unexpected fires in the puddles. That evening, Ling discovered with surprise that the walls of his house were not red, as he had always thought, but the color of an almost rotten orange. In the courtyard, Wang-Fo noticed the delicate shape of a bush to which no one had paid any attention until then, and compared it to a young woman letting down her hair to dry. In the passageway, he followed with delight the hesitant trail of an ant along the cracks in the wall, and Ling's horror of these creatures vanished into thin air. Realizing that Wang-Fo had just presented him with the gift of a new soul and a new vision of the world, Ling respectfully offered the old man the room in which his father and mother had died.

For many years now, Wang-Fo had dreamed of painting the portrait of a princess of olden days playing the lute under a willow. No woman was sufficiently unreal to be his model, but Ling would do because he was not a woman. Then Wang-Fo spoke of painting a young prince shooting an arrow at the foot of a large cedar tree. No young man of the present was sufficiently unreal to serve as his model, but Ling got his own wife to pose under the plum tree in the garden. Later on, Wang-Fo painted her in a fairy costume against the clouds of twilight, and the young woman wept because it was an omen of death. As Ling came to prefer the portraits painted by Wang-Fo to the young woman herself, her face began to fade, like a flower exposed to warm winds and summer rains. One morning, they found her hanging from the branches of the pink plum tree: the ends of the scarf that was strangling her floated in the wind, entangled with her hair. She looked even more delicate than usual, and as pure as the beauties celebrated by the poets of days gone by. Wang-Fo painted her one last time, because he loved the green hue that suffuses the face of the dead. His disciple Ling mixed the colors and the task needed such concentration that he forgot to shed tears.

One after the other, Ling sold his slaves, his jades, and the fish in his pond to buy his master pots of purple ink that came from the West. When the house was emptied, they left it, and Ling closed the door of his past behind him.

Wang-Fo felt weary of a city where the faces could no longer teach him secrets of ugliness or beauty, and the master and his disciple walked away together down the roads of the Kingdom of Han.

Their reputation preceded them into the villages, to the gateway of fortresses, and into the atrium of temples where restless pilgrims halt at dusk. It was murmured that Wang-Fo had the power to bring his paintings to life by adding a last touch of color to their eyes. Farmers would come and beg him to paint a watchdog, and the lords would ask him for portraits of their best warriors. The priests honored Wang-Fo as a sage; the people feared him as a sorcerer. Wang enjoyed these differences of opinion which gave him the chance to study expressions of gratitude, fear, and veneration.

Ling begged for food, watched over his master's rest, and took advantage of the old man's raptures to massage his feet. With the first rays of the sun, when the old man was still asleep, Ling went in pursuit of timid landscapes hidden behind bunches of reeds. In the evening, when the master, disheartened, threw down his brushes, he would carefully pick them up. When Wang became sad and spoke of his old age, Ling would smile and show him the solid trunk of an old oak; when Wang felt happy and made jokes, Ling would humbly pretend to listen.

One day, at sunset, they reached the outskirts of the Imperial City and Ling sought out and found an inn in which Wang-Fo could spend the night. The old man wrapped himself up in rags, and Ling lay down next to him to keep him warm because spring had only just begun and the floor of beaten earth was still frozen. At dawn, heavy steps echoed in the corridors of the inn; they heard the frightened whispers of the innkeeper and orders shouted in a foreign, barbaric tongue. Ling trembled, remembering that the night before, he had stolen a rice cake for his master's supper. Certain that they would come to take him to prison, he asked himself who would help Wang-Fo ford the next river on the following day.

The soldiers entered carrying lanterns. The flames gleaming through the motley paper cast red and blue lights on their leather helmets. The string of a bow quivered over their shoulders, and the fiercest among them suddenly let out a roar for no reason at all. A heavy hand fell on Wang-Fo's neck, and the painter could not help noticing that the soldiers' sleeves did not match the color of their coats.

Helped by his disciple, Wang-Fo followed the soldiers, stumbling along uneven roads. The passing crowds made fun of these two criminals who were certainly going to be beheaded. The soldiers answered Wang's questions with savage scowls. His bound hands hurt him, and Ling in despair looked smiling at his master, which for him was a gentler way of crying.

They reached the threshold of the Imperial Palace, whose purple walls rose in broad daylight like a sweep of sunset. The soldiers led Wang-Fo through countless square and circular rooms whose shapes symbolized the seasons, the cardinal points, the male and the female, longevity, and the prerogatives of power. The doors swung on their hinges with a musical note, and were placed in such a manner that one followed the entire scale when crossing the palace from east to west. Everything combined to give an impression of superhuman power and subtlety, and one could feel that here the simplest orders were as final and as terrible as the wisdom of the ancients. At last, the air became thin and the silence so deep that not even a man under torture would have dared to scream. A eunuch lifted a tapestry; the soldiers began to tremble like women, and the small troop entered

15

the chamber in which the Son of Heaven sat on a high throne.

It was a room without walls, held up by thick columns of blue stone. A garden spread out on the far side of the marble shafts, and each and every flower blooming in the greenery belonged to a rare species brought here from across the oceans. But none of them had any perfume, so that the Celestial Dragon's meditations would not be troubled by fine smells. Out of respect for the silence in which his thoughts evolved, no bird had been allowed within the enclosure, and even the bees had been driven away. An enormous wall separated the garden from the rest of the world, so that the wind that sweeps over dead dogs and corpses on the battlefield would not dare brush the Emperor's sleeve.

The Celestial Master sat on a throne of jade, and his hands were wrinkled like those of an old man, though he had scarcely reached the age of twenty. His robe was blue to symbolize winter, and green to remind one of spring. His face was beautiful but blank, like a looking glass placed too high, reflecting nothing except the stars and the immutable heavens. To his right stood his Minister of Perfect Pleasures, and to his left his Counselor of Just Torments. Because his courtiers, lined along the base of the columns, always lent a keen ear to the slightest sound from his lips, he had adopted the habit of speaking in a low voice.

'Celestial Dragon,' said Wang-Fo, bowing low, 'I am old, I am poor, I am weak. You are like summer; I am like winter. You have Ten Thousand Lives; I have but one, and it is near its close. What have I done to you? My hands have been tied, these hands that never harmed you.'

'You ask what you have done to me, old Wang-Fo?' said the Emperor.

His voice was so melodious that it made one want to cry.

He raised his right hand, to which the reflections from the jade pavement gave a pale sea-green hue like that of an underwater plant, and Wang-Fo marveled at the length of those thin fingers, and hunted among his memories to discover whether he had not at some time painted a mediocre portrait of either the Emperor or one of his ancestors that would now merit a sentence of death. But it seemed unlikely because Wang-Fo had not been an assiduous visitor at the Imperial Court. He preferred the farmers' huts or, in the cities, the courtesans' quarters and the taverns along the harbor where the dockers liked to quarrel.

'You ask me what it is you have done, old Wang-Fo?' repeated the Emperor, inclining his slender neck toward the old man waiting attentively. 'I will tell you. But, as another man's poison cannot enter our veins except through our nine openings, in order to show you your offenses I must take you with me down the corridors of my memory and tell you the story of my life. My father had assembled a collection of your work and hidden it in the most secret chamber in the palace, because he judged that the people in your paintings should be concealed from the world since they cannot lower their eyes in the presence of profane viewers. It was in those same rooms that I was brought up, old Wang-Fo, surrounded by solitude. To prevent my innocence from being sullied by other human souls, the restless crowd of my future subjects had been driven away from me, and no one was allowed to pass my threshold, for fear that his or her shadow would stretch out and touch me. The few aged servants that were placed in my service showed themselves as little as possible; the hours turned in circles; the colors of your paintings bloomed in the first hours of the morning and grew pale at dusk. At night, when I was unable to sleep, I gazed at them, and for nearly ten years I gazed at them every night. During the day, sitting on a carpet whose design I knew by heart, I dreamed of the joys the future had in store for me. I imagined the world, with the Kingdom of Han at the center, to be like the flat palm of my hand crossed by the fatal lines of the Five Rivers. Around it lay the sea in which monsters are born, and farther away the mountains that hold up the heavens. And to help me visualize these things I used your paintings. You made me believe that the sea looked like the vast sheet of water spread across your scrolls, so blue that if a stone were to fall into it, it would become a sapphire; that women opened and closed like flowers, like the creatures that come forward, pushed by the wind, along the paths of your painted gardens; and that the young, slim-waisted warriors who mount guard in the fortresses along the frontier were themselves like arrows that could pierce my heart. At sixteen I saw the doors that separated me from the world open once again; I climbed onto the balcony of my palace to look at the clouds, but they were far less beautiful than those in your sunsets. I ordered my litter; bounced along roads on which I had not foreseen either mud or stones, I traveled across the provinces of the Empire without ever finding your gardens full of women like fireflies, or a woman whose body was in itself a garden. The pebbles on the beach spoiled my taste for oceans; the blood of the tortured is less red than the pomegranates in your paintings; the village vermin prevented me from seeing the beauty of the rice fields; the flesh of mortal women disgusted me like the dead meat hanging from the butcher's hook, and the coarse laughter of my soldiers made me sick. You lied, Wang-Fo, you old impostor. The world is nothing but a mass of muddled colors thrown into the void by an insane painter, and smudged by our tears. The Kingdom of Han is not the most beautiful of kingdoms, and I am not the Emperor. The only empire which is worth reigning over is that which you alone can enter, old Wang, by the road of One Thousand Curves and Ten Thousand Colors. You alone reign peacefully over mountains covered in snow that cannot melt, and over fields of daffodils that cannot die. And that is why, Wang-Fo, I have conceived a punishment for you, for you whose enchantment has filled me with disgust at everything I own, and with desire for everything I shall never possess. And in order to lock you up in the only cell from which there is no escape, I have decided to have your eyes burned out, because your eyes, Wang-Fo, are the two magic gates that open onto your kingdom. And as your hands are the two roads of ten forking paths that lead to the heart of your kingdom, I have decided to have your hands cut off. Have you understood, old Wang-Fo?'

Hearing the sentence, Ling, the disciple, tore from his belt an old knife and leaped toward the Emperor. Two guards immediately seized him. The Son of Heaven smiled and added, with a sigh: 'And I also hate you, old Wang-Fo, because you have known how to make yourself beloved. Kill that dog.'

Ling jumped to one side so that his blood would not stain his master's robe. One of the soldiers lifted his sword and Ling's head fell from his neck like a cut flower. The servants carried away the remains, and Wang-Fo, in despair, admired the beautiful scarlet stain that his disciple's blood made on the green stone floor.

The Emperor made a sign and two eunuchs wiped Wang's eyes.

'Listen, old Wang-Fo,' said the Emperor, 'and dry your tears, because this is not the time to weep. Your eyes must be clear so that the little light that is left to them is not clouded by your weeping. Because it is not only the grudge I bear you that makes me desire your death; it is not only the cruelty in my heart that makes me want to see you suffer. I have other plans, old Wang-Fo. I possess among your works a remarkable painting in which the mountains, the river estuary, and the sea reflect each other, on a very small scale certainly, but with a clarity that surpasses the real landscapes themselves, like objects reflected on the walls of a metal sphere. But that painting is unfinished, Wang-Fo; your masterpiece is but a sketch. No doubt, when you began your work, sitting in a solitary valley, you noticed a passing bird, or a child running after the bird. And the bird's beak or the child's cheeks made you forget the blue eyelids of the sea. You never finished the frills of the water's cloak, or the seaweed hair of the rocks. Wang-Fo, I want you to use the few hours of light that are left to you to finish this painting, which will thus contain the final secrets amassed during your long life. I know that your hands, about to fall, will not tremble on the silken cloth, and infinity will enter your work through those unhappy cuts. I know that your eyes, about to be put out, will discover bearings far beyond all human senses. This is my plan, old Wang-Fo, and I can force you to fulfill it. If you refuse, before blinding you, I will have all your paintings burned, and you will be like a father whose children are slaughtered and all hopes of posterity extinguished. However, believe, if you wish, that this last order stems from nothing but my kindness, because I know that the silken scroll is the only mistress you ever deigned to touch. And to offer you brushes, paints, and inks to occupy your last hours is like offering the favors of a harlot to a man condemned to death.'

Upon a sign from the Emperor's little finger, two eunuchs respectfully brought forward the unfinished scroll on which Wang-Fo had outlined the image of the sea and the sky. Wang-Fo dried his tears and smiled, because that small sketch reminded him of his youth. Everything in it spoke of a fresh new spirit which Wang-Fo could no longer claim as his, and yet something was missing from it, because when Wang had painted it he had not yet looked long enough at the mountains or at the rocks bathing their naked flanks in the sea, and he had not yet penetrated deep enough into the sadness of the evening twilight. Wang-Fo selected one of the brushes which a slave held ready for him and began spreading wide strokes of blue onto the unfinished sea. A eunuch crouched by his feet, mixing the colors; he carried out his task with little skill, and more than ever Wang-Fo lamented the loss of his disciple Ling.

Wang began by adding a touch of pink to the tip of the wing of a cloud perched on a mountain. Then he painted onto the surface of the sea a few small lines that deepened the perfect feeling of calm. The jade floor became increasingly damp, but Wang-Fo, absorbed as he was in his painting, did not seem to notice that he was working with his feet in water.

The fragile rowboat grew under the strokes of the painter's brush and now occupied the entire foreground of the silken scroll. The rhythmic sound of the oars rose suddenly in the distance, quick and eager like the beating of wings. The sound came nearer, gently filling the whole room, then ceased, and a few trembling drops appeared on the boatman's oars. The red iron intended for Wang's eyes lay extinguished on the executioner's coals. The courtiers, motionless as etiquette required, stood in water up to their shoulders, trying to lift themselves onto the tips of their toes. The water finally reached the level of the imperial heart. The silence was so deep one could have heard a tear drop.

It was Ling. He wore his everyday robe, and his right sleeve still had a hole that he had not had time to mend that morning before the soldiers' arrival. But around his neck was tied a strange red scarf.

Wang-Fo said to him softly, while he continued painting, 'I thought you were dead.'

'You being alive,' said Ling respectfully, 'how could I have died?'

And he helped his master into the boat. The jade ceiling reflected itself in the water, so that Ling seemed to be inside a cave. The pigtails of submerged courtiers rippled up toward the surface like snakes, and the pale head of the Emperor floated like a lotus.

'Look at them,' said Wang-Fo sadly. 'These wretches will die, if they are not dead already. I never thought there was enough water in the sea to drown an Emperor. What are we to do?'

'Master, have no fear,' murmured the disciple. 'They will soon be dry again and will not even remember that their sleeves were ever wet. Only the Emperor will keep in his heart a little of the bitterness of the sea. These people are not the kind to lose themselves inside a painting.'

And he added: 'The sea is calm, the wind high, the sea-birds fly to their nests. Let us leave, Master, and sail to the land beyond the waves.'

'Let us leave,' said the old painter.

Wang-Fo took hold of the helm, and Ling bent over the oars. The sound of rowing filled the room again, strong and steady like the beating of a heart. The level of the water dropped unnoticed around the large vertical rocks that became columns once more. Soon only a few puddles glistened in the hollows of the jade floor. The courtiers' robes were dry, but a few wisps of foam still clung to the hem of the Emperor's cloak.

The painting finished by Wang-Fo was leaning against a

tapestry. A rowboat occupied the entire foreground. It drifted away little by little, leaving behind it a thin wake that smoothed out into the quiet sea. One could no longer make out the faces of the two men sitting in the boat, but one could still see Ling's red scarf and Wang-Fo's beard waving in the breeze.

The beating of the oars grew fainter, then ceased, blotted out by the distance. The Emperor, leaning forward, a hand above his eyes, watched Wang's boat sail away till it was nothing but an imperceptible dot in the paleness of the twilight. A golden mist rose and spread over the water. Finally the boat veered around a rock that stood at the gateway to the ocean; the shadow of a cliff fell across it; its wake disappeared from the deserted surface, and the painter Wang-Fo and his disciple Ling vanished forever on the jade-blue sea that Wang-Fo had just created.

EDGAR ALLAN POE

THE OVAL
PORTRAIT

THE CHÂTEAU INTO which my valet had ventured to make forcible entrance, rather than permit me, in my desperately wounded condition, to pass a night in the open air, was one of those piles of commingled gloom and grandeur which have so long frowned among the Apennines, not less in fact than in the fancy of Mrs Radcliffe. To all appearance it had been temporarily and very lately abandoned. We established ourselves in one of the smallest and least sumptuously furnished apartments. It lay in a remote turret of the building. Its decorations were rich, yet tattered and antique. Its walls were hung with tapestry and bedecked with manifold and multiform armorial trophies, together with an unusually great number of very spirited modern paintings in frames of rich golden arabesque. In these paintings, which depended from the walls not only in their main surfaces, but in very many nooks which the bizarre architecture of the château rendered necessary – in these paintings my incipient delirium, perhaps, had caused me to take deep interest; so that I bade Pedro to close the heavy shutters of the room – since it was already night, – to light the tongues of a tall candelabrum which stood by the head of my bed, and to throw open far and wide the fringed curtains of black velvet which enveloped the bed itself. I wished all this done that I might resign myself, if not to sleep, at least alternately to the contemplation of these pictures, and the perusal of a small volume which had been found upon the pillow, and which purported to criticize and describe them.

Long, long I read – and devoutly, devoutly I gazed. Rapidly and gloriously the hours flew by and the deep midnight came. The position of the candelabrum displeased me, and outreaching my hand with difficulty, rather than disturb my slumbering valet, I placed it so as to throw its rays more fully upon the book.

But the action produced an effect altogether unanticipated. The rays of the numerous candles (for there were many) now fell within a niche of the room which had hitherto been thrown into deep shade by one of the bedposts. I thus saw in vivid light a picture all unnoticed before. It was the portrait of a young girl just ripening into womanhood. I glanced at the painting hurriedly, and then closed my eyes. Why I did this was not at first apparent even to my own perception. But while my lids remained thus shut, I ran over in mind my reason for so shutting them. It was an impulsive movement to gain time for thought – to make sure that my vision had not deceived me – to calm and subdue my fancy for a more sober and more certain gaze. In a very few moments I again looked fixedly at the painting.

That I now saw aright I could not and would not doubt; for the first flashing of the candles upon that canvas had seemed to dissipate the dreamy stupor which was stealing over my senses, and to startle me at once into waking life.

The portrait, I have already said, was that of a young girl. It was a mere head and shoulders, done in what is technically termed a *vignette* manner; much in the style of the favorite heads of Sully. The arms, the bosom, and even the ends of the radiant hair melted imperceptibly into the vague yet deep shadow which formed the background of the whole. The frame was oval, richly gilded and filigreed in *Moresque*. As a thing of art nothing could be more admirable than the painting itself. But it could have been neither the execution of the work, nor the immortal beauty of the countenance, which had so suddenly and so vehemently moved me. Least of all, could it have been that my fancy, shaken from its half slumber, had mistaken the head for that of a living person. I saw at once that the peculiarities of the design, of the *vignetting*, and of the frame, must have instantly dispelled such idea – must have prevented even its momentary entertainment. Thinking earnestly upon these points, I remained, for an hour perhaps, half sitting, half reclining, with my vision riveted upon the portrait. At length, satisfied with the true secret of its effect, I fell back within the bed. I had found the spell of the picture in an absolute *life-likeliness* of expression, which, at first startling, finally confounded, subdued, and appalled me. With deep and reverent awe I replaced the candelabrum in its former position. The cause of my deep agitation being thus shut from view, I sought eagerly the volume which discussed the paintings and their histories. Turning to the number which designated the oval portrait, I there read the vague and quaint words which follow:

'She was a maiden of rarest beauty, and not more lovely than full of glee. And evil was the hour when she saw, and loved, and wedded the painter. He, passionate, studious, austere, and having already a bride in his Art: she a maiden of rarest beauty, and not more lovely than full of glee; all light and smiles, and frolicsome as the young fawn; loving and cherishing all things; hating only the Art which was her rival; dreading only the pallet and brushes and other untoward instruments which deprived her of the countenance of her lover. It was thus a terrible thing for this lady to hear the painter speak of his desire to portray even his young bride. But she was humble and obedient, and sat meekly for many weeks in the dark high turret-chamber where the light dripped upon the pale canvas only from overhead. But he, the painter, took glory in his work, which went on from hour to hour, and from day to day. And he was a passionate, and wild, and moody man, who became lost in reveries; so that he *would* not see that the light which fell so ghastly in that lone turret withered the health and the spirits of his bride, who pined visibly to all but him. Yet she smiled on and still on, uncomplainingly, because she saw that the painter (who had high renown) took a fervid and burning pleasure in his task, and wrought day and night to depict her who so loved him, yet who grew daily more dispirited and weak. And in sooth some who beheld the portrait spoke of its resemblance in low words, as of a mighty marvel, and a proof not less of the power of the painter than of his deep love for her whom he depicted so surpassingly well. But at length, as the labor drew nearer to its conclusion, there were admitted none into the turret; for the painter had grown wild with the ardor of his work, and turned his eyes from the canvas rarely, even to regard the countenance of his wife. And he *would* not see that the tints which he spread upon the canvas were drawn from the cheeks of her who sat beside him. And when many weeks had passed, and but little remained to do, save one brush upon the mouth and one tint upon the eye, the spirit of the lady again flickered up as the flame within the socket of the lamp. And then the brush was given, and then the tint was placed; and, for one moment, the painter stood entranced before the work which he had wrought; but in the next, while he yet gazed, he grew tremulous and very pallid, and aghast, and crying with a loud voice, "This is indeed *Life* itself!" turned suddenly to regard his beloved: – *She was dead!*'

GUY DE MAUPASSANT

A PORTRAIT

'HELLO! THERE'S MILIAL!' said somebody near me. I looked at the man who had been pointed out as I had been wishing for a long time to meet this Don Juan.

He was no longer young. His gray hair looked a little like those fur bonnets worn by certain Northern peoples, and his long beard, which fell down over his chest, had also somewhat the appearance of fur. He was talking to a lady, leaning toward her, speaking in a low voice and looking at her with an expression full of respect and tenderness.

I knew his life, or at least as much as was known of it. He had loved madly several times, and there had been certain tragedies with which his name had been connected. When I spoke to women who were the loudest in his praise, and asked them whence came this power, they always answered, after thinking for a while: 'I don't know – he has a certain charm about him.'

He was certainly not handsome. He had none of the elegance that we ascribe to conquerors of feminine hearts. I wondered what might be his hidden charm. Was it mental? I never had heard of a clever saying of his. In his glance? Perhaps. Or in his voice? The voices of some beings have a certain irresistible attraction, almost suggesting the flavor of things good to eat. One is hungry for them, and the sound of their words penetrates us like a dainty morsel. A friend was passing. I asked him: 'Do you know Monsieur Milial?'

'Yes.'

'Introduce us.'

A minute later we were shaking hands and talking in the doorway. What he said was correct, agreeable to hear; it contained no irritable thought. The voice was sweet, soft, caressing, musical; but I had heard others much more attractive, much more moving. One listened to him with pleasure, just as one would look at a pretty little brook. No tension of the mind was necessary in order to follow him, no hidden meaning aroused curiosity, no expectation awoke interest. His conversation was rather restful, but it did not awaken in one either a desire to answer, to contradict or to approve, and it was as easy to answer him as it was to listen to him. The response came to the lips of its own accord, as soon as he had finished talking, and phrases turned toward him as if he had naturally aroused them.

One thought soon struck me. I had known him for a quarter of an hour, and it seemed as if he were already one of my old friends, that I had known all about him for a long time; his face, his gestures, his voice, his ideas. Suddenly, after a few minutes of conversation, he seemed already to be installed in my intimacy. All constraint disappeared between us, and, had he so desired, I might have confided in him as one confides only in old friends.

Certainly there was some mystery about him. Those barriers that are closed between most people and that are lowered with time when sympathy, similar tastes, equal intellectual culture and constant intercourse remove constraint – those barriers seemed not to exist between him and me, and no doubt this was the case between him and all people, both men and women, whom fate threw in his path.

After half an hour we parted, promising to see each other often, and he gave me his address after inviting me to take luncheon with him in two days.

I forgot what hour he had stated, and I arrived too soon; he was not yet home. A correct and silent domestic showed me into a beautiful, quiet, softly lighted parlor. I felt comfortable there, at home. How often I have noticed the influence of apartments on the character and on the mind! There are some which make one feel foolish; in others, on the contrary, one always feels lively. Some make us sad, although well lighted and decorated in light-colored furniture; others cheer us up, although hung with sombre material. Our eye, like our heart, has its likes and dislikes, of which it does not inform us, and which it secretly imposes on our temperament. The harmony of furniture, walls, the style of an ensemble, act immediately on our mental state, just as the air from the woods, the sea or the mountains modifies our physical natures.

I sat down on a cushion-covered divan and felt myself suddenly carried and supported by these little silk bags of feathers, as if the outline of my body had been marked out beforehand on this couch.

Then I looked about. There was nothing striking about the room; everywhere were beautiful and modest things, simple and rare furniture, Oriental curtains which did not seem to come from a department store but from the interior of a harem; and exactly opposite me hung the portrait of a woman. It was a portrait of medium size, showing the head and the upper part of the body, and the hands, which were holding a book. She was young, bareheaded; ribbons were woven in her hair; she was smiling sadly. Was it because she was bareheaded, was it merely her natural expression? I never have seen a portrait of a lady which seemed so much in its place as that one in that dwelling. Of all those I knew I have seen nothing like that one. All those that I know are on exhibition, whether the lady be dressed in her gaudiest gown, with an attractive headdress and a look which shows that she is posing first of all before the artist and then before those who will look at her or whether they have taken a comfortable attitude in an ordinary gown. Some are standing majestically in all their beauty, which is not at all natural to them in life. All of them have something, a flower or a jewel, a crease in the dress or a curve of the lip, which one feels to have been placed there for effect by the artist. Whether they wear a hat or merely their hair one can immediately notice that they are not entirely natural. Why? One cannot say without knowing them, but the effect is there. They seem to be calling somewhere, on people whom they wish to please and to whom they wish to appear at their best advantage; and they have studied their attitudes, sometimes modest, sometimes haughty.

What could one say about this one? She was at home and alone. Yes, she was alone, for she was smiling as one smiles when thinking in solitude of something sad or sweet, and not as one smiles when one is being watched. She seemed so much alone and so much at home that she made the whole large apartment seem absolutely empty. She alone lived in it, filled it, gave it life. Many people might come in and converse, laugh, even sing; she would still be alone with a solitary smile, and she alone would give it life with her pictured gaze.

That look also was unique. It fell directly on me, fixed and caressing, without seeing me. All portraits know that they are being watched, and they answer with their eyes, which see, think, follow us without leaving us, from the very moment we enter the apartment they inhabit. This one did not see me; it saw nothing, although its look was fixed directly on me. I remembered the surprising verse of Baudelaire:

'And your eyes, attractive as those of a portrait.'

They did indeed attract me in an irresistible manner; those

painted eyes which had lived, or which were perhaps still living, threw over me a strange, powerful spell. Oh, what an infinite and tender charm, like a passing breeze, like a dying sunset of lilac, rose, and blue, a little sad like the approaching night, which comes behind the sombre frame and out of those impenetrable eyes! Those eyes, created by a few strokes from a brush, hide behind them the mystery of that which seems to be and which does not exist, which can appear in the eyes of a woman, which can make love blossom within us.

The door opened and M. Milial entered. He excused himself for being late. I excused myself for being ahead of time. Then I said: 'Might I ask you who is this lady?'

He answered: 'That is my mother. She died very young.'

Then I understood whence came the inexplicable attraction of this man.

PENELOPE FITZGERALD

THE
RED-HAIRED GIRL

HACKETT, HOLLAND, PARSONS, Charrington and Dubois all studied in Paris, in the atelier of Vincent Bonvin. Dubois, although his name sounded French, wasn't, and didn't speak any either. None of them did except Hackett.

In the summer of 1882 they made up a party to go to Brittany. That was because they admired Bastien-Lepage, which old Bonvin definitely didn't, and because they wanted somewhere cheap, somewhere with characteristic types, absolutely natural, busy with picturesque occupations and, above all, plein air. 'Your work cannot be really good unless you have caught a cold doing it,' said Hackett.

They were poor enough, but they took a certain quantity of luggage – only the necessities. Their canvases needed rigging like small craft putting out of harbor, and the artists themselves, for plein air work, had brought overcoats, knickerbockers, gaiters, boots, wide-awakes, broad straw hats for sunny days. They tried, to begin with, St Briac-sur-Mer, which had been recommended to them in Paris, but it didn't suit. On, then, to Palourde, on the coast near Cancale. All resented the time spent moving about. It wasn't in the spirit of the thing – they were artists, not sightseers.

At Palourde, although it looked, and was, larger than St Briac, there was, if anything, less room. The Palourdais had never come across artists before, considered them as rich rather than poor, and wondered why they did not go to St Malo. Holland, Parsons, Charrington and Dubois, however, each found a room of sorts. What about their possessions? There were sail lofts and potato cellars in Palourde, but, it seemed, not an inch of room to spare. Their clothes, books and painting materials had to go in some boats pulled up above the foreshore, awaiting repairs. They were covered with a piece of tarred sailcloth and roped down. Half the morning would have to be spent getting out what was wanted. Hackett, as interpreter, was obliged to ask whether there was any risk of their being stolen. The reply was that no one in Palourde wanted such things.

It was agreed that Hackett should take what appeared to be the only room in the constricted Hotel du Port. 'Right under the rafters,' he wrote to his intended, 'a bed, a chair, a basin, a broc of cold water brought up once a day, no view from the window, but I shan't of course paint in my room anyway. I have propped up the canvases I brought with me against the wall. That gives me the sensation of having done something. The food, so far, you wouldn't approve of. Black porridge, later on pieces of black porridge left over from the morning and fried, fish soup with onions, onion soup with fish. The thing is to understand these people well, try to share their devotion to onions, and above all to secure a good model' – he decided not to add 'who must be a young girl, otherwise I haven't much chance of any of the London exhibitions.'

The Hotel du Port was inconveniently placed at the top of the village. It had no restaurant, but Hackett was told that he could be served, if he wanted it, at half past six o'clock. The ground floor was taken up with the bar, so this service would be in a very small room at the back, opening off the kitchen.

After Hackett had sat for some time at a narrow table covered with rose-patterned oilcloth, the door opened

42

sufficiently for a second person to edge into the room. It was a red-haired girl, built for hard use and hard wear, who without speaking put down a bowl of fish soup. She and the soup between them filled the room with a sharp, cloudy odor, not quite disagreeable, but it wasn't possible for her to get in and out, concentrating always on not spilling anything, without knocking the back of the chair and the door itself, first with her elbows, then with her rump. The spoons and the saltbox on the table trembled as though in a railway carriage. Then the same maneuver again, this time bringing a loaf of dark bread and a carafe of cider. No more need to worry after that; there was no more to come.

'I think I've found rather a jolly-looking model already,' Hackett told the others. They, too, had not done so badly. They had set up their easels on the quay; been asked, as far as they could make out, to move them farther away from the moorings; done so 'with a friendly smile,' said Charrington – 'we find that goes a long way.' They hadn't risked asking anyone to model for them, just started some sea pieces between the handfuls of wind and rain. 'We might come up to the hotel tonight and dine with you. There's nothing but fish soup in our digs.'

Hackett discouraged them.

The hotelier's wife, when he had made the right preliminary inquiries to her about the red-haired girl, had answered – as she did on all subjects – largely with silences. He didn't learn who her parents were, or even her family name. Her given name was Annik. She worked an all-day job at the Hotel du Port, but she had one and a half hours free after her lunch, and if she wanted to spend that time being drawn or painted, well, there were no objections. Not in the hotel, however, where, as he could see, there was no room.

'I paint en plein air,' said Hackett.

43

'You'll find plenty of that.'

'I shall pay her, of course.'

'You must make your own arrangements.'

He spoke to the girl at dinner, during the few moments when she was conveniently trapped. When she had quite skillfully allowed the door to shut behind her and, soup dish in hand, was recovering her balance, he said: 'Anny, I want to ask you something.'

'I'm called Annik,' she said. It was the first time he had heard her speak.

'All the girls are called that. I shall call you Anny. I've spoken about you to the patronne.'

'Yes, she told me.'

Anny was a heavy breather, and the whole tiny room seemed to expand and deflate as she stood pondering.

'I shall want you to come to the back door of the hotel, I mean the back steps down to the Rue de Dol. Let us say tomorrow, at twelve forty-five.'

'I don't know about the forty-five,' she said. 'I can't be sure about that.'

'How do you usually know the time?' She was silent. He thought it was probably a matter of pride and she did not want to agree to anything too easily. But possibly she couldn't tell the time. She might be stupid to the degree of idiocy.

The Hotel du Port had no courtyard. Like every other house in the street, it had a flight of stone steps to adapt to the change of level. After lunch the shops shut for an hour and the women of Palourde sat or stood, according to their age, on the top step and knitted or did crochet. They didn't wear costume anymore, they wore white linen caps and jackets, long skirts, and, if they weren't going far, carpet slippers.

Anny was punctual to the minute. 'I shall want you to

44

stand quite still on the top step, with your back to the door. I've asked them not to open it.'

Anny also was wearing carpet slippers. 'I can't just stand here doing nothing.'

He allowed her to fetch her crochet. Give a little, take a little. He was relieved, possibly a bit disappointed, to find how little interest they caused in the Rue de Dol. He was used to being watched, quite openly, over his shoulder, as if he were giving a comic performance. Here even the children didn't stop to look.

'They don't care about our picture,' he said, trying to amuse her. He would have liked a somewhat gentler expression. Certainly she was not a beauty. She hadn't the white skin of the dreamed-of red-haired girl. In fact, her face and neck were covered with a faint but noticeable hairy down, as though proof against all weathers.

'How long will it take?' she asked.

'I don't know. As God disposes! An hour will do for today.'

'And then you'll pay me?' 'No,' he said, 'I shan't do that. I shall pay you when the whole thing's finished. I shall keep a record of the time you've worked, and if you like you can keep one as well.'

As he was packing up his box of charcoals he added, 'I shall want to make a few color notes tomorrow, and I should like you to wear a red shawl.' It seemed that she hadn't one. 'But you could borrow one, my dear. You could borrow one, since I ask you particularly.'

She looked at him as though he were an imbecile.

'You shouldn't have said "since I ask you particularly," ' Parsons told him that evening. 'That will have turned her head.'

'It can't have done,' said Hackett.

'Did you call her "my dear"?'

'I don't know, I don't think so.'

'I've noticed you say "particularly" with a peculiar intonation, which may well have become a matter of habit,' said Parsons, nodding sagely.

This is driving me crazy, thought Hackett. He began to feel a division which he had never so much as imagined of in Paris between himself and his fellow students. They had been working all day, having managed to rent a disused and indeed almost unusable shed on the quay. It had once been part of the market where the fishermen's wives did the triage, sorting out the catch by size. Hackett, as before, had done the interpreting. He had plenty of time, since Anny could only be spared for such short intervals. But at least he had been true to his principles. Holland, Parsons, Charrington and Dubois weren't working in the open air at all. Difficulties about models forgotten, they were sketching each other in the shed. The background of Palourde's not very picturesque jetty could be dashed in later.

Anny appeared promptly for the next three days to stand, with her crochet, on the back steps. Hackett didn't mind her blank expression, having accepted from the first that she was never likely to smile. The red shawl, though – that hadn't appeared. He could, perhaps, buy one in St Malo. He ached for the contrast between the copper-colored hair and the scarlet shawl. But he felt it wrong to introduce something from outside Palourde.

'Anny, I have to tell you that you've disappointed me.'

'I told you I had no red shawl.'

'You could have borrowed one.'

Charrington, who was supposed to understand women, and even to have had a great quarrel with Parsons about some woman or other, only said, 'She can't borrow what isn't there. I've been trying ever since we came here to borrow a decent tin opener. I've tried to make it clear that I'd give it back.'

Best to leave the subject alone. But the moment Anny turned up next day he found himself saying, 'You could borrow one from a friend, that was what I meant.'

'I haven't any friends,' said Anny. Hackett paused in the business of lighting his pipe. 'An empty life for you, then, Anny.'

'You don't know what I want,' she said, very low.

'Oh, everybody wants the same things. The only difference is what they will do to get them.'

'You don't know what I want, and you don't know what I feel,' she said, still in the same mutter. There was, however, a faint note of something more than the contradiction that came so naturally to her, and Hackett was a good-natured man.

'I'm sorry I said you disappointed me, Anny. The truth is I find it rather a taxing business, standing here drawing in the street.'

'I don't know why you came here in the first place. There's nothing here, nothing at all. If it's oysters you want, they're better at Cancale. There's nothing here to tell one morning from another, except to see if it's raining ... Once they brought in three drowned bodies, two men and a boy, a whole boat's crew, and laid them out on the tables in the fish market, and you could see blood and water running out of their mouths ... You can spend your whole life here, wash, pray, do your work, and all the time you might just as well not have been born.'

She was still speaking so that she could scarcely be heard. The passersby went unnoticing down Palourde's badly paved street. Hackett felt disturbed. It had never occurred to him that she would speak, without prompting, at such length.

'I've received a telegram from Paris,' said Parsons, who was standing at the shed door. 'It's taken its time about getting here. They gave it me, at the post office.'

'What does it say?' asked Hackett, feeling it was likely to be about money.

'Well, that he's coming – Bonvin, I mean. "As is my custom every summer, I am touring the coasts." It's a kind of informal inspection, you see. "Expect me, then, on the twenty-seventh for dinner at the Hotel du Port." '

'It's impossible.' Parsons suggested that, since Dubois had brought his banjo with him, they might get up some kind of impromptu entertainment. But he had to agree that one didn't associate old Bonvin with entertainment.

He couldn't, surely, be expected from Paris before six. But when they arrived, all of them except Hackett carrying their portfolios, at the hotel's front door, they recognized, from the moment it opened, the voice of Bonvin. Hackett looked round and felt his head swim. The bar – dark, faded, pickled in its own long-standing odors, crowded with stools and barrels, with the air of being older than Palourde, as though Palourde had been built round it without daring to disturb it – was swept and empty now except for a central table and chairs such as Hackett had never seen in the hotel. At the head of the table sat old Bonvin. 'Sit down, gentlemen! I am your host!' The everyday malicious dry voice, but a different Bonvin, in splendid seaside dress, a yellow waistcoat, a cravat. Palourde was indifferent to artists, but Bonvin had imposed himself as a professor.

'They are used to me here. They keep a room for me which I think is not available to other guests, and they are always ready to take a little trouble for me when I come.'

The artists sat meekly down while the patronne herself served them with a small glass of greenish-white Muscadet.

'I am your host,' repeated Bonvin. 'I can only say that I am delighted to see pupils, for the first time, in Palourde, but I assure you I have others as far away as Corsica. Once a teacher, always a teacher! I sometimes think it is a passion which outlasts even art itself.'

In Paris, they had all assured each other that old Bonvin was incapable of teaching anything. Time spent in his atelier was squandered. But here, in the strangely transformed bar of the Hotel du Port, with a quite inadequate drink in front of them, they felt overtaken by destiny. The patronne shut and locked the front door to keep out the world who might disturb the professor. Bonvin – not, after all, looking so old – called upon them to show their portfolios.

Hackett had to excuse himself to go up to his room and fetch the four drawings which he had made so far. He felt it an injustice that he had to show his things last.

Bonvin asked him to hold them up one by one, then to lay them out on the table. To Hackett he spoke magniloquently in French.

'Yes, they are bad,' he said, 'but, Monsieur Hackett, they are bad for two distinct reasons. In the first place, you should not draw the view from the top of a street if you cannot manage the perspective, which even a child, following simple mechanical rules, can do. The relationship in scale of the main figure to those lower down is quite, quite wrong. But there is something else amiss.

'You are an admirer, I know, of Bastien-Lepage, who has said, "There is nothing really lasting, nothing that will endure, except the sincere expression of the actual conditions of life." Conditions in the potato patch, in the hayfield, at the washtub, in the open street! That is pernicious nonsense. Look at this girl of yours. Evidently she is not a professional model, for she doesn't know how to hold herself. I see you have made a note that the color of the hair is red, but that is the only thing I know about her. She's standing against the door like a beast waiting to be put back in its stall. It's your intention, I am sure, to do the finished version in the same way, in the dust of the street. Well, your picture will say nothing and it will be nothing. It is only in the studio that you can bring out the heart of the subject, and that is what we are sent into this world to do, Monsieur Hackett, to paint the experiences of the heart.'

– Gibbering dotard, you can talk till your teeth fall out. I shall go on precisely as I have been doing, even if I can only paint her for an hour and a quarter a day. – An evening of nameless embarrassment, with Hackett's friends coughing, shuffling, eating noisily, asking questions to which they knew the answers, and telling anecdotes of which they forgot the endings. Anny had not appeared, evidently she was considered unworthy. The patronne came in again, bringing not soup but the very height of Brittany's grand-occasion cuisine, a fricassee of chicken. Who would have thought there were chickens in Palourde?

Hackett woke in what he supposed were the small hours. So far he had slept dreamlessly in Palourde, had never so much as lighted his bedside candle. – Probably, he thought, Bonvin made the same unpleasant speech wherever he went. The old impostor was drunk with power, not with anything else, only half a bottle of Muscadet and, later, a bottle of Gros-Plant among the six of them. – The sky had begun to thin and pale. It came to him that what had been keeping him awake was not an injustice of Bonvin's, but of his own. What had been the experiences of Anny's heart?

Bonvin, with his dressing cases and book boxes, left early. The horse omnibus stopped once a week in the little Place François-René de Chateaubriand, at the entrance to the village. Having made his formal farewells, Bonvin caught the omnibus. Hackett was left in good time for his appointment with Anny.

She did not come that day, nor the next day, nor the day after. On the first evening he was served by the bootboy, pitifully worried about getting in and out of the door, on the second by the hotel laundrywoman, on the third by the patronne. 'Where is Anny?' The patronne did not answer. For that in itself Hackett was prepared, but he tried again. 'Is she ill?' 'No, not ill.' 'Has she taken another job?' 'No.' He was beginning, he realized, in the matter of this plain and sullen girl, to sound like an anxious lover. 'Shall I see her again?' He got no answer.

Had she drowned herself? The question reared up in his mind like a savage dog, getting up from its sleep. She had hardly seemed to engage herself enough with life, hardly seemed to take enough interest in it to wish no more of it. Boredom, though, and the withering sense of insignificance can bring one as low as grief. He had felt the breath of it at his ear when Bonvin had told him – for that was what it came to – that there was no hope of his becoming an artist. Anny was stupid, but no one is too stupid to despair.

There was no police station in Palourde, and if Anny were truly drowned, they would say nothing about it at the Hotel du Port. Hackett had been in enough small hotels to know that they did not discuss anything that was bad for business. The red-haired body might drift anywhere, might be washed ashore anywhere between Pointe du Grouin and Cap Prehel.

That night it was the laundrywoman's turn to dish up the fish soup. Hackett thought of confiding in her, but did not need to. She said to him, 'You mustn't keep asking the patronne about Anny, it disturbs her.' Anny, it turned out, had been dismissed for stealing from the hotel – some money and a watch. 'You had better have a look through your things,' the laundrywoman said, 'and see there's nothing missing. One often doesn't notice till a good while afterwards.'

HENRY JAMES

THE REAL THING

I

WHEN THE PORTER'S wife (she used to answer the house-bell) announced 'A gentleman – with a lady, sir,' I had, as I often had in those days, for the wish was father to the thought, an immediate vision of sitters. Sitters my visitors in this case proved to be; but not in the sense I should have preferred. However, there was nothing at first to indicate that they might not have come for a portrait. The gentleman, a man of fifty, very high and very straight, with a moustache slightly grizzled and a dark grey walking-coat admirably fitted, both of which I noted professionally – I don't mean as a barber or yet as a tailor – would have struck me as a celebrity if celebrities often were striking. It was a truth of which I had for some time been conscious that a figure with a good deal of frontage was, as one might say, almost never a public institution. A glance at the lady helped to remind me of this paradoxical law: she also looked too distinguished to be a 'personality'. Moreover one would scarcely come across two variations together.

Neither of the pair spoke immediately – they only prolonged the preliminary gaze which suggested that each wished to give the other a chance. They were visibly shy; they stood there letting me take them in – which, as I afterwards perceived, was the most practical thing they could have done. In this way their embarrassment served their cause. I had seen people painfully reluctant to mention that they desired anything so gross as to be represented on canvas; but the scruples of my new friends appeared almost insurmountable. Yet the gentleman might have said 'I should like a portrait of my wife,' and the lady might have said 'I should like a portrait of my husband.' Perhaps they were not husband and wife – this naturally would make the matter more delicate. Perhaps they wished to be done together – in which case they ought to have brought a third person to break the news.

'We come from Mr Rivet,' the lady said at last, with a dim smile which had the effect of a moist sponge passed over a 'sunk' piece of painting, as well as of a vague allusion to vanished beauty. She was as tall and straight, in her degree, as her companion, and with ten years less to carry. She looked as sad as a woman could look whose face was not charged with expression; that is her tinted oval mask showed friction as an exposed surface shows it. The hand of time had played over her freely, but only to simplify. She was slim and stiff, and so well-dressed, in dark blue cloth, with lappets and pockets and buttons, that it was clear she employed the same tailor as her husband. The couple had an indefinable air of prosperous thrift – they evidently got a good deal of luxury for their money. If I was to be one of their luxuries it would behove me to consider my terms.

'Ah, Claude Rivet recommended me?' I inquired; and I added that it was very kind of him, though I could reflect that, as he only painted landscape, this was not a sacrifice.

The lady looked very hard at the gentleman, and the gentleman looked round the room. Then staring at the floor a moment and stroking his moustache, he rested his pleasant eyes on me with the remark: 'He said you were the right one.'

'I try to be, when people want to sit.'

'Yes, we should like to,' said the lady anxiously.

'Do you mean together?'

My visitors exchanged a glance. 'If you could do any-thing with *me*, I suppose it would be double,' the gentleman stammered.

'Oh yes, there's naturally a higher charge for two figures than for one.'

'We should like to make it pay,' the husband confessed.

'That's very good of you,' I returned, appreciating so un-wonted a sympathy – for I supposed he meant pay the artist.

A sense of strangeness seemed to dawn on the lady. 'We mean for the illustrations – Mr Rivet said you might put one in.'

'Put one in – an illustration?' I was equally confused.

'Sketch her off, you know,' said the gentleman, colouring.

It was only then that I understood the service Claude Rivet had rendered me; he had told them that I worked in black and white, for magazines, for story-books, for sketches of contemporary life, and consequently had frequent em-ployment for models. These things were true, but it was not less true (I may confess it now – whether because the aspira-tion was to lead to everything or to nothing I leave the reader to guess), that I couldn't get the honours, to say nothing of the emoluments, of a great painter of portraits out of my head. My 'illustrations' were my pot-boilers; I looked to a different branch of art (far and away the most interesting it had always seemed to me) to perpetuate my fame. There was no shame in looking to it also to make my fortune; but that fortune was by so much further from being made from the moment my visitors wished to be 'done' for nothing. I was disappointed; for in the pictorial sense I had immediately *seen* them. I had seized their type – I had already settled what I would do with it. Something that wouldn't absolutely have pleased them, I afterwards reflected.

'Ah, you're – you're – a –?' I began, as soon as I had mastered my surprise. I couldn't bring out the dingy word 'models'; it seemed to fit the case so little.

'We haven't had much practice,' said the lady.

'We've got to *do* something, and we've thought that an artist in your line might perhaps make something of us,' her husband threw off. He further mentioned that they didn't know many artists and that they had gone first, on the off-chance (he painted views of course, but sometimes put in figures – perhaps I remembered), to Mr Rivet, whom they had met a few years before at a place in Norfolk where he was sketching.

'We used to sketch a little ourselves,' the lady hinted.

'It's very awkward, but we absolutely *must* do something,' her husband went on.

'Of course, we're not so very young,' she admitted, with a wan smile.

With the remark that I might as well know something more about them, the husband had handed me a card extracted from a neat new pocket-book (their appurtenances were all of the freshest) and inscribed with the words 'Major Monarch'. Impressive as these words were they didn't carry my knowledge much further; but my visitor presently added: 'I've left the army, and we've had the misfortune to lose our money. In fact our means are dreadfully small.'

'It's an awful bore,' said Mrs Monarch.

They evidently wished to be discreet – to take care not to swagger because they were gentlefolks. I perceived they would have been willing to recognize this as something of a drawback, at the same time that I guessed at an underlying sense – their consolation in adversity – that they *had* their points. They certainly had; but these advantages struck me as preponderantly social; such for instance as would help to make a drawing-room look well. However, a drawing-room was always, or ought to be, a picture.

In consequence of his wife's allusion to their age Major Monarch observed: 'Naturally, it's more for the figure that we thought of going in. We can still hold ourselves up.' On the instant I saw that the figure was indeed their strong point. His 'naturally' didn't sound vain, but it lighted up the question. '*She* has got the best,' he continued, nodding at his wife, with a pleasant after-dinner absence of circumlocution. I could only reply, as if we were in fact sitting over our wine, that this didn't prevent his own from being very good; which led him in turn to rejoin: 'We thought that if you ever have to do people like us, we might be something like it. *She*, particularly – for a lady in a book, you know.'

I was so amused by them that, to get more of it, I did my best to take their point of view; and though it was an embarrassment to find myself appraising physically, as if they were animals on hire or useful blacks, a pair whom I should have expected to meet only in one of the relations in which criticism is tacit, I looked at Mrs Monarch judicially enough to be able to exclaim, after a moment, with conviction: 'Oh yes, a lady in a book!' She was singularly like a bad illustration.

'We'll stand up, if you like,' said the Major; and he raised himself before me with a really grand air.

I could take his measure at a glance – he was six feet two and a perfect gentleman. It would have paid any club in process of formation and in want of a stamp to engage him at a salary to stand in the principal window. What struck me immediately was that in coming to me they had rather missed their vocation; they could surely have been turned to better account for advertising purposes. I couldn't of course see the thing in detail, but I could see them make someone's fortune – I don't mean their own. There was something in them for a waistcoat-maker, an hotel-keeper or a soap-vendor. I could imagine 'We always use it' pinned on their bosoms with the greatest effect; I had a vision of the promptitude with which they would launch a *table d'hôte*.

Mrs Monarch sat still, not from pride but from shyness, and presently her husband said to her: 'Get up my dear and show how smart you are.' She obeyed, but she had no need to get up to show it. She walked to the end of the studio, and then she came back blushing, with her fluttered eyes on her husband. I was reminded of an incident I had accidentally had a glimpse of in Paris – being with a friend there, a dramatist about to produce a play – when an actress came to him to ask to be entrusted with a part. She went through her paces before him, walked up and down as Mrs Monarch was doing. Mrs Monarch did it quite as well, but I abstained from applauding. It was very odd to see such people apply for such poor pay. She looked as if she had ten thousand a year. Her husband had used the word that described her: she was, in the London current jargon, essentially and typically 'smart'. Her figure was, in the same order of ideas, conspicuously and irreproachably 'good'. For a woman of her age her waist was surprisingly small; her elbow moreover had the orthodox crook. She held her head at the conventional angle; but why did she come to *me*? She ought to have tried on jackets at a big shop. I feared my visitors were not only destitute, but 'artistic' – which would be a great complication. When she sat down again I thanked her, observing that what a draughtsman most valued in his model was the faculty of keeping quiet.

'Oh, *she* can keep quiet,' said Major Monarch. Then he added, jocosely: 'I've always kept her quiet.'

'I'm not a nasty fidget, am I?' Mrs Monarch appealed to her husband.

He addressed his answer to me. 'Perhaps it isn't out of place to mention – because we ought to be quite business-like, oughtn't we? – that when I married her she was known as the Beautiful Statue.'

'Oh dear!' said Mrs Monarch, ruefully.

'Of course I should want a certain amount of expression,' I rejoined.

'Of *course*!' they both exclaimed.

'And then I suppose you know that you'll get awfully tired.'

'Oh, we *never* get tired!' they eagerly cried.

'Have you had any kind of practice?'

They hesitated – they looked at each other. 'We've been photographed, *immensely*,' said Mrs Monarch.

'She means the fellows have asked us,' added the Major.

'I see – because you're so good-looking.'

'I don't know what they thought, but they were always after us.'

'We always got our photographs for nothing,' smiled Mrs Monarch.

'We might have brought some, my dear,' her husband remarked.

'I'm not sure we have any left. We've given quantities away,' she explained to me.

'With our autographs and that sort of thing,' said the Major.

'Are they to be got in the shops?' I inquired, as a harmless pleasantry.

'Oh, yes; *hers* – they used to be.'

'Not now,' said Mrs Monarch, with her eyes on the floor.

II

I could fancy the 'sort of thing' they put on the presentation-
copies of their photographs, and I was sure they wrote a
beautiful hand. It was odd how quickly I was sure of every-
thing that concerned them. If they were now so poor as to
have to earn shillings and pence, they never had had much
of a margin. Their good looks had been their capital, and
they had good-humouredly made the most of the career that
this resource marked out for them. It was in their faces, the
blankness, the deep intellectual repose of the twenty years
of country-house visiting which had given them pleasant
intonations. I could see the sunny drawing-rooms, sprinkled
with periodicals she didn't read, in which Mrs Monarch had
continuously sat; I could see the wet shrubberies in which
she had walked, equipped to admiration for either exercise.
I could see the rich covers the Major had helped to shoot and
the wonderful garments in which, late at night, he repaired
to the smoking-room to talk about them. I could imagine
their leggings and waterproofs, their knowing tweeds and
rugs, their rolls of sticks and cases of tackle and neat
umbrellas; and I could evoke the exact appearance of their
servants and the compact variety of their luggage on the plat-
forms of country stations.

They gave small tips, but they were liked; they didn't do
anything themselves, but they were welcome. They looked
so well everywhere; they gratified the general relish for
stature, complexion and 'form'. They knew it without fatuity
or vulgarity, and they respected themelves in consequence.
They were not superficial; they were thorough and kept
themselves up – it had been their line. People with such a
taste for activity had to have some line. I could feel how, even

in a dull house, they could have been counted upon for cheerfulness. At present something had happened – it didn't matter what, their little income had grown less, it had grown least – and they had to do something for pocket-money. Their friends liked them, but didn't like to support them. There was something about them that represented credit – their clothes, their manners, their type; but if credit is a large empty pocket in which an occasional chink reverberates, the chink at least must be audible. What they wanted of me was to help to make it so. Fortunately they had no children – I soon divined that. They would also perhaps wish our relations to be kept secret: this was why it was 'for the figure' – the reproduction of the face would betray them.

I liked them – they were so simple; and I had no objection to them if they would suit. But, somehow, with all their perfections I didn't easily believe in them. After all they were amateurs, and the ruling passion of my life was the detestation of the amateur. Combined with this was another perversity – an innate preference for the represented subject over the real one: the defect of the real one was so apt to be a lack of representation. I liked things that appeared; then one was sure. Whether they *were* or not was a subordinate and almost always a profitless question. There were other considerations, the first of which was that I already had two or three people in use, notably a young person with big feet, in alpaca, from Kilburn, who for a couple of years had come to me regularly for my illustrations and with whom I was still – perhaps ignobly – satisfied. I frankly explained to my visitors how the case stood; but they had taken more precautions than I supposed. They had reasoned out their opportunity, for Claude Rivet had told them of the projected *édition de luxe* of one of the writers of our day – the rarest of the novelists – who, long neglected by the multitudinous vulgar and dearly prized by the attentive (need I mention Philip Vincent?) had had the happy fortune of seeing, late in life, the dawn and then the full light of a higher criticism – an estimate in which, on the part of the public, there was something really of expiation. The edition in question, planned by a publisher of taste, was practically an act of high reparation; the woodcuts with which it was to be enriched were the homage of English art to one of the most independent representatives of English letters. Major and Mrs Monarch confessed to me that they had hoped I might be able to work *them* into my share of the enterprise. They knew I was to do the first of the books, 'Rutland Ramsay', but I had to make clear to them that my participation in the rest of the affair – this first book was to be a test – was to depend on the satisfaction I should give. If this should be limited my employers would drop me without a scruple. It was therefore a crisis for me, and naturally I was making special preparations, looking about for new people, if they should be necessary, and securing the best types. I admitted however that I should like to settle down to two or three good models who would do for everything.

'Should we have often to – a – put on special clothes?' Mrs Monarch timidly demanded.

'Dear, yes – that's half the business.'

'And should we be expected to supply our own costumes?'

'Oh, no; I've got a lot of things. A painter's models put on – or put off – anything he likes.'

'And do you mean – a – the same?'

'The same?'

Mrs Monarch looked at her husband again.

'Oh, she was just wondering,' he explained, 'if the costumes are in *general* use.' I had to confess that they were, and I mentioned further that some of them (I had a lot of genuine, greasy last-century things) had served their time, a hundred years ago, on living, world-stained men and women. 'We'll put on anything that *fits*,' said the Major.

'Oh, I arrange that – they fit in the pictures.'

'I'm afraid I should do better for the modern books. I would come as you like,' said Mrs Monarch.

'She has got a lot of clothes at home: they might do for contemporary life,' her husband continued.

'Oh, I can fancy scenes in which you'd be quite natural.' And indeed I could see the slipshod rearrangements of stale properties – the stories I tried to produce pictures for without the exasperation of reading them – whose sandy tracts the good lady might help to people. But I had to return to the fact that for this sort of work – the daily mechanical grind – I was already equipped; the people I was working with were fully adequate.

'We only thought we might be more like *some* characters,' said Mrs Monarch mildly, getting up.

Her husband also rose; he stood looking at me with a dim wistfulness that was touching in so fine a man. 'Wouldn't it be rather a pull sometimes to have – a – to have –?' He hung fire; he wanted me to help him by phrasing what he meant. But I couldn't – I didn't know. So he brought it out, awkwardly: 'The *real* thing; a gentleman, you know, or a lady.' I was quite ready to give a general assent – I admitted that there was a great deal in that. This encouraged Major Monarch to say, following up his appeal with an unacted gulp: 'It's awfully hard – we've tried everything.' The gulp was communicative; it proved too much for his wife. Before I knew it Mrs Monarch had dropped again upon a divan and burst into tears. Her husband sat down beside her, holding one of her hands; whereupon she quickly dried her eyes with the other, while I felt embarrassed as she looked up at me.

'There isn't a confounded job I haven't applied for – waited for – prayed for. You can fancy we'd be pretty bad first. Secretaryships and that sort of thing? You might as well ask for a peerage. I'd be *anything* – I'm strong; a messenger or a coalheaver. I'd put on a gold-laced cap and open carriage-doors in front of the haberdasher's; I'd hang about a station, to carry portmanteaus; I'd be a postman. But they won't *look* at you; there are thousands, as good as yourself, already on the ground. *Gentlemen*, poor beggars, who have drunk their wine, who have kept their hunters!'

I was as reassuring as I knew how to be, and my visitors were presently on their feet again while, for the experiment, we agreed on an hour. We were discussing it when the door opened and Miss Churm came in with a wet umbrella. Miss Churm had to take the omnibus to Maida Vale and then walk half-a-mile. She looked a trifle blowsy and slightly splashed. I scarcely ever saw her come in without thinking afresh how odd it was that, being so little in herself, she should yet be so much in others. She was a meagre little Miss Churm, but she was an ample heroine of romance. She was only a freckled cockney, but she could represent everything, from a fine lady to a shepherdess; she had the faculty, as she might have had a fine voice or long hair. She couldn't spell, and she loved beer, but she had two or three 'points', and practice, and a knack, and mother-wit, and a kind of whim-sical sensibility, and a love of the theatre, and seven sisters, and not an ounce of respect, especially for the *h*. The first thing my visitors saw was that her umbrella was wet, and in their spotless perfection they visibly winced at it. The rain had come on since their arrival.

'I'm all in a soak; there *was* a mess of people in the 'bus. I wish you lived near a stytion,' said Miss Churm. I requested her to get ready as quickly as possible, and she passed into the room in which she always changed her dress. But before going out she asked me what she was to get into this time.

'It's the Russian princess, don't you know?' I answered; 'the one with the "golden eyes", in black velvet, for the long thing in the *Cheapside*.'

'Golden eyes? I *say*!' cried Miss Churm, while my companions watched her with intensity as she withdrew. She always arranged herself, when she was late, before I could turn round; and I kept my visitors a little, on purpose, so that they might get an idea, from seeing her, what would be expected of themselves. I mentioned that she was quite my notion of an excellent model – she was really very clever.

'Do you think she looks like a Russian princess?' Major Monarch asked, with lurking alarm.

'When I make her, yes.'

'Oh, if you have to *make* her –!' he reasoned, acutely.

'That's the most you can ask. There are so many that are not makeable.'

'Well now, *here's* a lady' – and with a persuasive smile he passed his arm into his wife's – 'who's already made!'

'Oh, I'm not a Russian princess,' Mrs Monarch protested, a little coldly. I could see that she had known some and didn't like them. There, immediately, was a complication of a kind that I never had to fear with Miss Churm.

This young lady came back in black velvet – the gown was rather rusty and very low on her lean shoulders – and with a Japanese fan in her red hands. I reminded her that in the scene I was doing she had to look over someone's head. 'I forget whose it is; but it doesn't matter. Just look over a head.'

'I'd rather look over a stove,' said Miss Churm; and she took her station near the fire. She fell into position, settled herself into a tall attitude, gave a certain backward inclination to her head and a certain forward droop to her fan, and looked, at least to my prejudiced sense, distinguished and charming, foreign and dangerous. We left her looking so, while I went downstairs with Major and Mrs Monarch.

'I think I could come about as near it as that,' said Mrs Monarch.

'Oh, you think she's shabby, but you must allow for the alchemy of art.'

However, they went off with an evident increase of comfort, founded on their demonstrable advantage in being the real thing. I could fancy them shuddering over Miss Churm. She was very droll about them when I went back, for I told her what they wanted.

'Well, if *she* can sit I'll tyke to bookkeeping,' said my model.

'She's very lady-like,' I replied, as an innocent form of aggravation.

'So much the worse for *you*. That means she can't turn round.'

'She'll do for the fashionable novels.'

'Oh yes, she'll *do* for them!' my model humorously declared. 'Ain't they bad enough without her?' I had often sociably denounced them to Miss Churm.

III

It was for the elucidation of a mystery in one of these works that I first tried Mrs Monarch. Her husband came with her, to be useful if necessary – it was sufficiently clear that as a general thing he would prefer to come with her. At first I wondered if this were for 'propriety's' sake – if he were going to be jealous and meddling. The idea was too tiresome, and if it had been confirmed it would speedily have brought our acquaintance to a close. But I soon saw there was nothing in it and that if he accompanied Mrs Monarch it was (in addition to the chance of being wanted), simply because he had nothing else to do. When she was away from him his occupation was gone – she never *had* been away from him. I judged, rightly, that in their awkward situation their close union was their main comfort and that this union had no weak spot. It was a real marriage, an encouragement to the hesitating, a nut for pessimists to crack. Their address was humble (I remember afterwards thinking it had been the only thing about them that was really professional), and I could fancy the lamentable lodgings in which the Major would have been left alone. He could bear them with his wife – he couldn't bear them without her.

He had too much tact to try and make himself agreeable when he couldn't be useful; so he simply sat and waited, when I was too absorbed in my work to talk. But I liked to make him talk – it made my work, when it didn't interrupt it, less sordid, less special. To listen to him was to combine the excitement of going out with the economy of staying at home. There was only one hindrance: that I seemed not to know any of the people he and his wife had known. I think he wondered extremely, during the term of our intercourse, whom the deuce I *did* know. He hadn't a stray sixpence of an idea to fumble for; so we didn't spin it very fine – we confined ourselves to questions of leather and even of liquor (saddlers and breeches-makers and how to get good claret cheap), and matters like 'good trains' and the habits of small game. His lore on these last subjects was astonishing, he managed to interweave the stationmaster with the ornithologist. When he couldn't talk about greater things he could talk cheerfully about smaller, and since I couldn't accompany him into reminiscences of the fashionable world he could lower the conversation without a visible effort to my level.

So earnest a desire to please was touching in a man who could so easily have knocked one down. He looked after the fire and had an opinion on the draught of the stove, without my asking him, and I could see that he thought many of my arrangements not half clever enough. I remember telling him that if I were only rich I would offer him a salary to come and teach me how to live. Sometimes he gave a random sigh, of which the essence was: 'Give me even such a bare old barrack as *this*, and I'd do something with it!' When I wanted to use him he came alone; which was an illustration of the superior courage of women. His wife could bear her solitary second floor, and she was in general more discreet; showing by various small reserves that she was alive to the propriety of keeping our relations markedly professional – not letting them slide into sociability. She wished it to remain clear that she and the Major were employed, not cultivated, and if she approved of me as a superior, who could be kept in his place, she never thought me quite good enough for an equal.

She sat with great intensity, giving the whole of her mind to it, and was capable of remaining for an hour almost as motionless as if she were before a photographer's lens. I could see she had been photographed often, but somehow the very habit that made her good for that purpose unfitted her for mine. At first I was extremely pleased with her lady-like air, and it was a satisfaction, on coming to follow her lines, to see how good they were and how far they could lead the pencil. But after a few times I began to find her too insurmountably stiff; do what I would with it my drawing looked like a photograph or a copy of a photograph. Her figure had no variety of expression – she herself had no sense of variety.

You may say that this was my business, was only a question of placing her. I placed her in every conceivable position, but she managed to obliterate their differences. She was always a lady certainly, and into the bargain was always the same lady. She was the real thing, but always the same thing. There were moments when I was oppressed by the serenity of her confidence that she *was* the real thing. All her dealings with me and all her husband's were an implication that this was lucky for *me*. Meanwhile I found myself trying to invent types that approached her own, instead of making her own transform itself – in the clever way that was not impossible, for instance, to poor Miss Churm. Arrange as I would and take the precautions I would, she always, in my pictures, came out too tall – landing me in the dilemma of having represented a fascinating woman as seven feet high, which, out of respect perhaps to my own very much scantier inches, was far from my idea of such a personage.

The case was worse with the Major – nothing I could do would keep *him* down, so that he became useful only for the representation of brawny giants. I adored variety and range, I cherished human accidents, the illustrative note; I wanted to characterize closely, and the thing in the world I most hated was the danger of being ridden by a type. I had quarrelled with some of my friends about it – I had parted company with them for maintaining that one *had* to be, and that if the type was beautiful (witness Raphael and Leonardo), the servitude was only a gain. I was neither Leonardo nor Raphael; I might only be a presumptuous young modern searcher, but I held that everything was to be sacrificed sooner than character. When they averred that the haunting type in question could easily *be* character, I retorted, perhaps superficially: 'Whose?' It couldn't be everybody's – it might end in being nobody's.

After I had drawn Mrs Monarch a dozen times I perceived more clearly than before that the value of such a model as Miss Churm resided precisely in the fact that she had no positive stamp, combined of course with the other fact that what she did have was a curious and inexplicable talent for imitation. Her usual appearance was like a curtain which she could draw up at request for a capital performance. This performance was simply suggestive; but it was a word to the wise – it was vivid and pretty. Sometimes, even, I thought it, though she was plain herself, too insipidly pretty; I made it a reproach to her that the figures drawn from her were monotonously (*bêtement*, as we used to say) graceful. Nothing made her more angry; it was so much her pride to feel that she could sit for characters that had nothing in common with each other. She would accuse me at such moments of taking away her 'reputytion'.

It suffered a certain shrinkage, this queer quantity, from the repeated visits of my new friends. Miss Churm was greatly in demand, never in want of employment, so I had no scruple in putting her off occasionally, to try them more at my ease. It was certainly amusing at first to do the real thing – it was amusing to do Major Monarch's trousers. They *were* the real thing, even if he did come out colossal. It was amusing to do his wife's back hair (it was so mathematically neat) and the particular 'smart' tension of her tight stays. She lent herself especially to positions in which the face was somewhat averted or blurred; she abounded in lady-like back views and *profils perdus*. When she stood erect she took naturally one of the attitudes in which court-painters represent queens and princesses; so that I found myself wondering whether, to draw out this accomplishment, I couldn't get the editor of the *Cheapside* to publish a really royal romance, 'A Tale of Buckingham Palace'. Sometimes, however, the real thing and the make-believe came into contact; by which I mean that Miss Churm, keeping an appointment or coming to make one on days when I had much work in hand, encountered her invidious rivals. The encounter was not on their part, for they noticed her no more than if she had been the housemaid; not from intentional loftiness, but simply because, as yet, professionally, they didn't know how to fraternize, as I could guess that they would have liked – or at least that the Major would. They couldn't talk about the omnibus – they always walked; and they didn't know what else to try – she wasn't interested in good trains or cheap claret. Besides, they must have felt – in the air – that she was amused at them, secretly derisive of their ever knowing how. She was not a person to conceal her scepticism, if she had had a chance to show it. On the other hand Mrs Monarch didn't think her tidy; for why else did she take pains to say to me (it was going out of the way, for Mrs Monarch) that she didn't like dirty women?

One day when my young lady happened to be present with my other sitters (she even dropped in, when it was convenient, for a chat), I asked her to be so good as to lend a hand in getting tea – a service with which she was familiar and which was one of a class that, living as I did in a small way, with slender domestic resources, I often appealed to my models to render. They liked to lay hands on my property, to break the sitting, and sometimes the china – I made them feel Bohemian. The next time I saw Miss Churm after this incident she surprised me greatly by making a scene about it – she accused me of having wished to humiliate her. She had not resented the outrage at the time, but had seemed obliging and amused, enjoying the comedy of asking Mrs Monarch, who sat vague and silent, whether she would have cream and sugar, and putting an exaggerated simper into the question.

She had tried intonations – as if she too wished to pass for the real thing; till I was afraid my other visitors would take offence.

Oh, *they* were determined not to do this; and their touching patience was the measure of their great need. They would sit by the hour, uncomplaining, till I was ready to use them; they would come back on the chance of being wanted and would walk away cheerfully if they were not. I used to go to the door with them to see in what magnificent order they retreated. I tried to find other employment for them – I introduced them to several artists. But they didn't 'take', for reasons I could appreciate, and I became conscious, rather anxiously, that after such disappointments they fell back upon me with a heavier weight. They did me the honour to think that it was I who was most *their* form. They were not picturesque enough for the painters, and in those days there were not so many serious workers in black and white. Besides, they had an eye to the great job I had mentioned to them – they had secretly set their hearts on supplying the right essence for my pictorial vindication of our fine novelist. They knew that for this undertaking I should want no costume-effects, none of the frippery of past ages – that it was a case in which everything would be contemporary and satirical and, presumably, genteel. If I could work them into it their future would be assured, for the labour would of course be long and the occupation steady.

One day Mrs Monarch came without her husband – she explained his absence by his having had to go to the City. While she sat there in her usual anxious stiffness there came, at the door, a knock which I immediately recognized as the subdued appeal of a model out of work. It was followed by the entrance of a young man whom I easily perceived to be a foreigner and who proved in fact an Italian acquainted with no English word but my name, which he uttered in a way that made it seem to include all others. I had not then visited his country, nor was I proficient in his tongue; but as he was not so meanly constituted – what Italian is? – as to depend only on that member for expression he conveyed to me, in familiar but graceful mimicry, that he was in search of exactly the employment in which the lady before me was engaged. I was not struck with him at first, and while I continued to draw I emitted rough sounds of discouragement and dismissal. He stood his ground, however, not importunately, but with a dumb, dog-like fidelity in his eyes which amounted to innocent impudence – the manner of a devoted servant (he might have been in the house for years), unjustly suspected. Suddenly I saw that this very attitude and expression made a picture, whereupon I told him to sit down and wait till I should be free. There was another picture in the way he obeyed me, and I observed as I worked that there were others still in the way he looked wonderingly, with his head thrown back, about the high studio. He might have been crossing himself in St Peter's. Before I finished I said to myself: 'The fellow's a bankrupt orange-monger, but he's a treasure.'

When Mrs Monarch withdrew he passed across the room like a flash to open the door for her, standing there with the rapt, pure gaze of the young Dante spellbound by the young Beatrice. As I never insisted, in such situations, on the blankness of the British domestic, I reflected that he had the making of a servant (and I needed one, but couldn't pay him to be only that), as well as of a model; in short I made up my mind to adopt my bright adventurer if he would agree to officiate in the double capacity. He jumped at my offer, and in the event my rashness (for I had known nothing about him), was not brought home to me. He proved a sympathetic though a desultory ministrant, and had in a wonderful degree the *sentiment de la pose*. It was uncultivated, instinctive; a part of the happy instinct which had guided him to my door and helped him to spell out my name on the card nailed to it. He had had no other introduction to me than a guess, from the shape of my high north window, seen outside, that my place was a studio, and that as a studio it would contain an artist. He had wandered to England in search of fortune, like other itinerants, and had embarked, with a partner and a small green handcart, on the sale of penny ices. The ices had melted away and the partner had dissolved in their train. My young man wore tight yellow trousers with reddish stripes and his name was Oronte. He was sallow but fair, and when I put him into some old clothes of my own he looked like an Englishman. He was as good as Miss Churm, who could look, when required, like an Italian.

IV

I thought Mrs Monarch's face slightly convulsed when, on her coming back with her husband, she found Oronte installed. It was strange to have to recognize in a scrap of a lazzarone a competitor to her magnificent Major. It was she who scented danger first, for the Major was anecdotically unconscious. But Oronte gave us tea, with a hundred eager confusions (he had never seen such a queer process), and I think she thought better of me for having at last an 'establishment'. They saw a couple of drawings that I had made of the establishment, and Mrs Monarch hinted that it never would have struck her that he had sat for them. 'Now the drawings you make from *us*, they look exactly like us,' she reminded me, smiling in triumph; and I recognized that this was indeed just their defect. When I drew the Monarchs

76

I couldn't, somehow, get away from them – get into the character I wanted to represent; and I had not the least desire my model should be discoverable in my picture. Miss Churm never was, and Mrs Monarch thought I hid her, very properly, because she was vulgar; whereas if she was lost it was only as the dead who go to heaven are lost – in the gain of an angel the more.

By this time I had got a certain start with 'Rutland Ramsay', the first novel in the great projected series; that is I had produced a dozen drawings, several with the help of the Major and his wife, and I had sent them in for approval. My understanding with the publishers, as I have already hinted, had been that I was to be left to do my work, in this particular case, as I liked, with the whole book committed to me; but my connection with the rest of the series was only contingent. There were moments when, frankly, it *was* a comfort to have the real thing under one's hand; for there were characters in 'Rutland Ramsay' that were very much like it. There were people presumably as straight as the Major and women of as good a fashion as Mrs Monarch. There was a great deal of country-house life – treated, it is true, in a fine, fanciful, ironical, generalized way – and there was a considerable implication of knickerbockers and kilts. There were certain things I had to settle at the outset; such things for instance as the exact appearance of the hero, the particular bloom of the heroine. The author of course gave me a lead, but there was a margin for interpretation. I took the Monarchs into my confidence. I told them frankly what I was about, I mentioned my embarrassments and alternatives. 'Oh, take *him*!' Mrs Monarch murmured sweetly, looking at her husband; and 'What could you want better than my wife?' the Major inquired, with the comfortable candour that now prevailed between us.

I was not obliged to answer these remarks – I was only obliged to place my sitters. I was not easy in mind, and I postponed, a little timidly perhaps, the solution of the question. The book was a large canvas, the other figures were numerous, and I worked off at first some of the episodes in which the hero and the heroine were not concerned. When once I had set *them* up I should have to stick to them – I couldn't make my young man seven feet high in one place and five feet nine in another. I inclined on the whole to the latter measurement, though the Major more than once reminded me that *he* looked about as young as anyone. It was indeed quite possible to arrange him, for the figure, so that it would have been difficult to detect his age. After the spontaneous Oronte had been with me a month, and after I had given him to understand several different times that his native exuberance would presently constitute an insurmountable barrier to our further intercourse, I waked to a sense of his heroic capacity. He was only five feet seven, but the remaining inches were latent. I tried him almost secretly at first, for I was really rather afraid of the judgement my other models would pass on such a choice. If they regarded Miss Churm as little better than a snare, what would they think of the representation by a person so little the real thing as an Italian street-vendor of a protagonist formed by a public school?

If I went a little in fear of them it was not because they bullied me, because they had got an oppressive foothold, but because in their really pathetic decorum and mysteriously permanent newness they counted on me so intensely. I was therefore very glad when Jack Hawley came home: he was always of such good counsel. He painted badly himself, but there was no one like him for putting his finger on the place. He had been absent from England for a year; he had been somewhere – I don't remember where – to get a fresh eye.

I was in a good deal of dread of any such organ, but we were old friends; he had been away for months and a sense of emptiness was creeping into my life. I hadn't dodged a missile for a year.

He came back with a fresh eye, but with the same old black velvet blouse, and the first evening he spent in my studio we smoked cigarettes till the small hours. He had done no work himself, he had only got the eye; so the field was clear for the production of my little things. He wanted to see what I had done for the *Cheapside*, but he was disappointed in the exhibition. That at least seemed the meaning of two or three comprehensive groans which, as he lounged on my big divan, on a folded leg, looking at my latest drawings, issued from his lips with the smoke of the cigarette.

'What's the matter with you?' I asked.

'What's the matter with *you*?'

'Nothing save that I'm mystified.'

'You are indeed. You're quite off the hinge. What's the meaning of this new fad?' And he tossed me, with visible irreverence, a drawing in which I happened to have depicted both my majestic models. I asked if he didn't think it good, and he replied that it struck him as execrable, given the sort of thing I had always represented myself to him as wishing to arrive at; but I let that pass, I was so anxious to see exactly what he meant. The two figures in the picture looked colossal, but I supposed this was *not* what he meant, inasmuch as, for aught he knew to the contrary, I might have been trying for that. I maintained that I was working exactly in the same way as when he last had done me the honour to commend me. 'Well, there's a big hole somewhere,' he answered; 'wait a bit and I'll discover it.' I depended upon him to do so: where else was the fresh eye? But he produced at last nothing more luminous than 'I don't know – I don't like your types.' This was lame, for a critic who had never consented to discuss with me anything but the question of execution, the direction of strokes and the mystery of values.

'In the drawings you've been looking at I think my types are very handsome.'

'Oh, they won't do!'

'I've had a couple of new models.'

'I see you have. *They* won't do.'

'Are you very sure of that?'

'Absolutely – they're stupid.'

'You mean *I* am – for I ought to get round that.'

'You *can't* – with such people. Who are they?'

I told him, as far as was necessary, and he declared, heartlessly: '*Ce sont des gens qu'il faut mettre à la porte.*'

'You've never seen them; they're awfully good,' I compassionately objected.

'Not seen them? Why, all this recent work of yours drops to pieces with them. It's all I want to see of them.'

'No one else has said anything against it – the *Cheapside* people are pleased.'

'Everyone else is an ass, and the *Cheapside* people the biggest asses of all. Come, don't pretend, at this time of day, to have pretty illusions about the public, especially about publishers and editors. It's not for *such* animals you work – it's for those who know, *coloro che sanno*; so keep straight for *me* if you can't keep straight for yourself. There's a certain sort of thing you tried for from the first – and a very good thing it is. But this twaddle isn't *in* it.' When I talked with Hawley later about 'Rutland Ramsay' and its possible successors he declared that I must get back into my boat again or I would go to the bottom. His voice in short was the voice of warning.

I noted the warning, but I didn't turn my friends out of

doors. They bored me a good deal; but the very fact that they bored me admonished me not to sacrifice them – if there was anything to be done with them – simply to irritation. As I look back at this phase they seem to me to have pervaded my life not a little. I have a vision of them as most of the time in my studio, seated, against the wall, on an old velvet bench to be out of the way, and looking like a pair of patient courtiers in a royal antechamber. I am convinced that during the coldest weeks of the winter they held their ground because it saved them fire. Their newness was losing its gloss, and it was impossible not to feel that they were objects of charity. Whenever Miss Churm arrived they went away, and after I was fairly launched in 'Rutland Ramsay' Miss Churm arrived pretty often. They managed to express to me tacitly that they supposed I wanted her for the low life of the book, and I let them suppose it, since they had attempted to study the work – it was lying about the studio – without discovering that it dealt only with the highest circles. They had dipped into the most brilliant of our novelists without deciphering many passages. I still took an hour from them, now and again, in spite of Jack Hawley's warning: it would be time enough to dismiss them, if dismissal should be necessary, when the rigour of the season was over. Hawley had made their acquaintance – he had met them at my fireside – and thought them a ridiculous pair. Learning that he was a painter they tried to approach him, to show him too that they were the real thing; but he looked at them, across the big room, as if they were miles away: they were a compendium of everything that he most objected to in the social system of his country. Such people as that, all convention and patent-leather, with ejaculations that stopped conversation, had no business in a studio. A studio was a place to learn to see, and how could you see through a pair of feather beds?

The main inconvenience I suffered at their hands was that, at first, I was shy of letting them discover how my artful little servant had begun to sit to me for 'Rutland Ramsay'. They knew that I had been odd enough (they were prepared by this time to allow oddity to artists) to pick a foreign vagabond out of the streets, when I might have had a person with whiskers and credentials; but it was some time before they learned how high I rated his accomplishments. They found him in an attitude more than once, but they never doubted I was doing him as an organ-grinder. There were several things they never guessed, and one of them was that for a striking scene in the novel, in which a footman briefly figured, it occurred to me to make use of Major Monarch as the menial. I kept putting this off, I didn't like to ask him to don the livery – besides the difficulty of finding a livery to fit him. At last, one day late in the winter, when I was at work on the despised Oronte (he caught one's idea in an instant), and was in the glow of feeling that I was going very straight, they came in, the Major and his wife, with their society laugh about nothing (there was less and less to laugh at), like country-callers – they always reminded me of that – who have walked across the park after church and are presently persuaded to stay to luncheon. Luncheon was over, but they could stay to tea – I knew they wanted it. The fit was on me, however, and I couldn't let my ardour cool and my work wait, with the fading daylight, while my model prepared it. So I asked Mrs Monarch if she would mind laying it out – a request which, for an instant, brought all the blood to her face. Her eyes were on her husband's for a second, and some mute telegraphy passed between them. Their folly was over the next instant; his cheerful shrewdness put an end to it. So far from pitying their wounded pride, I must add, I was moved to give it as complete a lesson as I could. They bustled about together and got out the cups and saucers and made the kettle boil. I know they felt as if they were waiting on my servant, and when the tea was prepared I said: 'He'll have a cup, please – he's tired.' Mrs Monarch brought him one where he stood, and he took it from her as if he had been a gentleman at a party, squeezing a crush-hat with an elbow.

Then it came over me that she had made a great effort for me – made it with a kind of nobleness – and that I owed her a compensation. Each time I saw her after this I wondered what the compensation could be. I couldn't go on doing the wrong thing to oblige them. Oh, it *was* the wrong thing, the stamp of the work for which they sat – Hawley was not the only person to say it now. I sent in a large number of the drawings I had made for 'Rutland Ramsay', and I received a warning that was more to the point than Hawley's. The artistic adviser of the house for which I was working was of opinion that many of my illustrations were not what had been looked for. Most of these illustrations were the subjects in which the Monarchs had figured. Without going into the question of what *had* been looked for, I saw at this rate I shouldn't get the other books to do. I hurled myself in despair upon Miss Churm, I put her through all her paces. I not only adopted Oronte publicly as my hero, but one morning when the Major looked in to see if I didn't require him to finish a figure for the *Cheapside*, for which he had begun to sit the week before, I told him that I had changed my mind – I would do the drawing from my man. At this my visitor turned pale and stood looking at me. 'Is *he* your idea of an English gentleman?' he asked.

I was disappointed, I was nervous, I wanted to get on with my work; so I replied with irritation: 'Oh, my dear Major – I can't be ruined for *you*!'

He stood another moment; then, without a word, he

quitted the studio. I drew a long breath when he was gone, for I said to myself that I shouldn't see him again. I had not told him definitely that I was in danger of having my work rejected, but I was vexed at his not having felt the catastrophe in the air, read with me the moral of our fruitless collaboration, the lesson that, in the deceptive atmosphere of art, even the highest respectability may fail of being plastic.

I didn't owe my friends money, but I did see them again. They reappeared together, three days later, and under the circumstances there was something tragic in the fact. It was a proof to me that they could find nothing else in life to do. They had threshed the matter out in a dismal conference – they had digested the bad news that they were not in for the series. If they were not useful to me even for the *Cheapside* their function seemed difficult to determine, and I could only judge at first that they had come, forgivingly, decorously, to take a last leave. This made me rejoice in secret that I had little leisure for a scene; for I had placed both my other models in position together and I was pegging away at a drawing from which I hoped to derive glory. It had been suggested by the passage in which Rutland Ramsay, drawing up a chair to Artemisia's piano-stool, says extraordinary things to her while she ostensibly fingers out a difficult piece of music. I had done Miss Churm at the piano before – it was an attitude in which she knew how to take on an absolutely poetic grace. I wished the two figures to 'compose' together, intensely, and my little Italian had entered perfectly into my conception. The pair were vividly before me, the piano had been pulled out; it was a charming picture of blended youth and murmured love, which I had only to catch and keep. My visitors stood and looked at it, and I was friendly to them over my shoulder.

They made no response, but I was used to silent company

and went on with my work, only a little disconcerted (even though exhilarated by the sense that *this* was at least the ideal thing) at not having got rid of them after all. Presently I heard Mrs Monarch's sweet voice beside, or rather above me: 'I wish her hair was a little better done.' I looked up and she was staring with a strange fixedness at Miss Churm, whose back was turned to her. 'Do you mind my just touching it?' she went on – a question which made me spring up for an instant, as with the instinctive fear that she might do the young lady a harm. But she quieted me with a glance I shall never forget – I confess I should like to have been able to paint *that* – and went for a moment to my model. She spoke to her softly, laying a hand upon her shoulder and bending over her; and as the girl, understanding, gratefully assented, she disposed her rough curls, with a few quick passes, in such a way as to make Miss Churm's head twice as charming. It was one of the most heroic personal services I have ever seen rendered. Then Mrs Monarch turned away with a low sigh and, looking about her as if for something to do, stooped to the floor with a noble humility and picked up a dirty rag that had dropped out of my paint-box.

The Major meanwhile had also been looking for something to do and, wandering to the other end of the studio, saw before him my breakfast things, neglected, unremoved. 'I say, can't I be useful *here*?' he called out to me with an irrepressible quaver. I assented with a laugh that I fear was awkward and for the next ten minutes, while I worked, I heard the light clatter of china and the tinkle of spoons and glass. Mrs Monarch assisted her husband – they washed up my crockery, they put it away. They wandered off into my little scullery, and I afterwards found that they had cleaned my knives and that my slender stock of plate had an unprecedented surface. When it came over me, the latent eloquence

85

of what they were doing, I confess that my drawing was blurred for a moment – the picture swam. They had accepted their failure, but they couldn't accept their fate. They had bowed their heads in bewilderment to the perverse and cruel law in virtue of which the real thing could be so much less precious than the unreal; but they didn't want to starve. If my servants were my models, my models might be my servants. They would reverse the parts – the others would sit for the ladies and gentlemen, and *they* would do the work. They would still be in the studio – it was an intense dumb appeal to me not to turn them out. 'Take us on,' they wanted to say – 'we'll do *anything*.'

When all this hung before me the *afflatus* vanished – my pencil dropped from my hand. My sitting was spoiled and I got rid of my sitters, who were also evidently rather mystified and awestruck. Then, alone with the Major and his wife, I had a most uncomfortable moment. He put their prayer into a single sentence: 'I say, you know – just let *us* do for you, can't you?' I couldn't – it was dreadful to see them emptying my slops; but I pretended I could, to oblige them, for about a week. Then I gave them a sum of money to go away; and I never saw them again. I obtained the remaining books, but my friend Hawley repeats that Major and Mrs Monarch did me a permanent harm, got me into a second-rate trick. If it be true I am content to have paid the price – for the memory.

JULIAN BARNES

THE LIMNER

MR TUTTLE HAD been argumentative from the beginning: about the fee – twelve dollars – the size of the canvas, and the prospect to be shown through the window. Fortunately, there had been swift accord about the pose and the costume. Over these, Wadsworth was happy to oblige the collector of customs; happy also to give him the appearance, as far as it was within his skill, of a gentleman. That was, after all, his business. He was a limner, but also an artisan, and paid at an artisan's rate to produce what suited the client. In thirty years, few would remember what the collector of customs had looked like; the only relic of his physical presence after he had met his Maker would be this portrait. And in Wadsworth's experience, clients held it more important to be pictured as sober, God-fearing men and women than they did to be offered a true likeness. This was not a matter that perturbed him.

From the edge of his eye, Wadsworth became aware that his client had spoken, but did not divert his gaze from the tip of his brush. Instead he pointed to the bound notebook in which so many sitters had written comments, expressed their praise and blame, wisdom and fatuity. He might as well open the book at any page and ask his client to identify a remark left by a predecessor ten or twenty years before. The opinions of this collector of customs so far had been as predictable as his waistcoat buttons, if less interesting. Fortunately, Wadsworth was paid to represent waistcoats rather than opinions. Of course, it was more complicated than this: to represent the waistcoat, and the wig, and the breeches, *was* to represent an opinion, indeed a whole corpus of them. The waistcoat and breeches showed the body beneath, as the wig and hat showed the brain beneath; though in some cases it was a pictorial exaggeration to suggest that any brains lay beneath.

He would be happy to leave this town, to pack his brushes and canvases, his pigments and palette, into the small cart, to saddle his mare and then take the forest trails which in three days would lead him home. There he would rest, and reflect, and perhaps decide to live differently, without this constant travail of the itinerant. A pedlar's life; also a supplicant's. As always, he had come to this town, taken lodgings by the night, and placed an advertisement in the newspaper, indicating his competence, his prices and his availability. 'If no application is made within six days,' the advertisement ended, 'Mr Wadsworth will quit the town.' He had painted the small daughter of a dry-goods salesman, and then Deacon Zebediah Harries, who had given him Christian hospitality in his house, and recommended him to the collector of customs.

Mr Tuttle had not offered lodging; but the limner willingly slept in the stable with his mare for company, and ate in the kitchen. And then there had been that incident on the third evening, against which he had failed – or felt unable – to protest. It had made him sleep uneasily. It had wounded him too, if the truth were known. He ought to have written the collector down for an oaf and a bully – he had painted enough in his years – and forgotten the matter. Perhaps he should indeed consider his retirement, let his mare grow fat, and live from what crops he could grow and what farmstock he could raise. He could always paint windows and doors for a trade instead of people; he would not judge this an indignity.

Late on the first morning, Wadsworth had been obliged to introduce the collector of customs to the notebook. The fellow, like many another, had imagined that merely opening his mouth wider might be enough to effect communication. Wadsworth had watched the pen travel across the page, and then the forefinger tap impatiently. 'If God is merciful,' the man wrote, 'perhaps in Heaven you will hear.' In reply, he had half smiled, and given a brief nod, from which surprise and gratitude might be inferred. He had read the thought many times before. Often it was a true expression of Christian feeling and sympathetic hope; occasionally, as now, it represented scarce-concealed dismay that the world contained those with such frustrating deformities. Mr Tuttle was among those masters who preferred their servants to be mute, deaf and blind – except when his convenience suited the matter otherwise. Of course, masters and servants had become citizens and hired help once the juster republic had declared itself. But masters and servants did not thereby die out; nor did the essential inclinations of man.

Wadsworth did not think he was judging the collector in an un-Christian manner. His opinion had been forged on first contact, and confirmed on that third evening. The incident had been the crueller in that it involved a child, a garden boy who had scarcely entered the years of understanding. The limner always felt tenderly towards children: for themselves, for the grateful fact that they overlooked his deformity, and also because he had no issue himself. He had never known the company of a wife. Perhaps he might yet do so, though he would have to ensure that she was beyond child-bearing years. He could not inflict his deformity on others. Some had tried explaining that his fears were unnecessary, since the affliction had arrived not at birth, but after an attack of the spotted fever when he was a boy of five. Further, they pressed, had he not made his way in the world, and might not a son of his, howsoever constructed, do likewise? Perhaps that would be the case, but what of a daughter? The notion of a girl living as an outcast was too much for him. True, she might stay at home, and there would be a shared sympathy between them. But what would happen to such a child after his death?

No, he would go home and paint his mare. This had always been his intention, and perhaps now he would execute it. She had been his companion for twelve years, understood him easily, and took no heed of the noises that issued from his mouth when they were alone in the forest. His plan had been this: to paint her, on the same size of canvas used for Mr Tuttle, though turned to make an oblong; and afterwards, to cast a blanket over the picture and uncover it only on the mare's death. It was presumptuous to compare the daily reality of God's living creation with a human simulacrum by an inadequate hand – even if this was the very purpose for which his clients employed him.

He did not expect it would be easy to paint the mare. She would lack the patience, and the vanity, to pose for him, with one hoof proudly advanced. But then, neither would his mare have the vanity to come round and examine the canvas even as he worked on it. The collector of customs was now doing so, leaning over his shoulder, peering and pointing. There was something he did not approve. Wadsworth glanced upwards, from the immobile face to the mobile one. Even though he had a distant memory of speaking and hearing, and had been taught his letters, he had never learnt the facility of reading words upon the tongue. Wadsworth raised the narrowest of his brushes from the waistcoat button's boss, and transferred his eye to the notebook as the collector dipped his pen. 'More dignity,' the man wrote, and then underlined the words.

Wadsworth felt that he had already given Mr Tuttle dignity enough. He had increased his height, reduced his belly, ignored the hairy moles on the fellow's neck, and generally attempted to represent surliness as diligence, irascibility as moral principle. And now he wanted more of it! This was an un-Christian demand, and it would be an un-Christian act on Wadsworth's part to accede to it. It would do the man no service in God's eyes if the limner allowed him to appear puffed up with all the dignity he demanded.

He had painted infants, children, men and women, and even corpses. Three times he had urged his mare to a deathbed where he was asked to perform resuscitation – to represent as living someone he had just met as dead. If he could do that, surely he should be able to render the quickness of his mare as she shook her tail against the flies, or impatiently raised her neck while he prepared the little painting cart, or pricked her ears as he made noises to the forest.

At one time he had tried to make himself understood to his fellow mortals by gesture and by sound. It was true that a few simple actions could be easily imitated: he could show, for example, how a client might wish to stand. But other gestures often resulted in humiliating games of guessing; while the sounds he was able to utter failed to establish either his requirements or his shared nature as a human being, part of the Almighty's work, if differently made. Women judged the noises he made embarrassing, children found them a source of benign interest, men a proof of imbecility. He had tried to advance in this way, but had not succeeded, and so he had retreated into the muteness they expected, and perhaps preferred. It was at this point that he purchased his calf-skin notebook, in which all human statement and opinion recurred. *'Do you think, Sir, there will be painting in Heaven?'* *'Do you think, Sir, there will be hearing in Heaven?'*

But his understanding of men, such as it had developed, came less from what they wrote down, more from his mute observation. Men – and women too – imagined that they could alter their voice and meaning without it showing in their face. In this they were much deceived. His own face, as he observed the human carnival, was as inexpressive as his tongue; but his eye told him more than they could guess. Formerly, he had carried, inside his notebook, a set of hand-written cards, bearing useful responses, necessary sugges-tions, and civil corrections to what was being proposed. He even had one special card, for when he was being condes-cended to by his interlocutor beyond what he found proper. It read: 'Sir, the understanding does not cease to function when the portals of the mind are blocked.' This was some-times accepted as a just rebuke, sometimes held to be an impertinence from a mere artisan who slept in the stable. Wadsworth had abandoned its use, not because of either such response, but because it admitted too much knowledge. Those in the world of tongue held all the advantages: they were his paymasters, they wielded authority, they entered society, they exchanged thoughts and opinions naturally. Though, for all this, Wadsworth did not see that speaking was in itself a promoter of virtue. His own advantages were only two: that he could represent on canvas those who spoke, and could silently observe their meaning. It would be foolish to give away this second advantage.

The business with the piano, for instance. Wadsworth had first enquired, by pointing to his fee scale, if the collector of customs wished for a portrait of the entire family, matching portraits of himself and his wife, or a joint portrait, with perhaps miniatures of the children. Mr Tuttle, without looking at his wife, had pointed to his own breast, and written on the fee sheet, 'Myself alone.' Then he had glanced at his wife, put one hand to his chin, and added, 'Beside the piano.' Wadsworth had noticed the handsome rosewood instrument and asked with a gesture if he might go across to it. Whereupon he demonstrated several poses: from sitting informally beside the open keyboard with a favourite song on display, to standing more formally beside the instrument. Tuttle had taken Wadsworth's place, arranged himself, advanced one foot, and then, after consideration, closed the lid of the keyboard. Wadsworth deduced from this that only Mrs Tuttle played the piano; further, that Tuttle's desire to include it was an indirect way of including her in the portrait. Indirect, and also less expensive.

The limner had shown the collector of customs some miniatures of children, hoping to change his mind, but Tuttle merely shook his head. Wadsworth was disappointed, partly for reasons of money, but more because his delight in painting children had increased as that in painting their progenitors had declined. Children were more mobile than adults, more deliquescent of shape, it was true. But they also looked him in the eye, and when you were deaf you heard with your eyes. Children held his gaze, and he thereby perceived their nature. Adults often looked away, whether from modesty or a desire for concealment; while some, like the collector, stared back challengingly, with a false honesty, as if to say, Of course my eyes are concealing things, but you lack the discernment to realize it. Such clients judged Wadsworth's affinity with children proof that he was as deficient in understanding as the children were. Whereas Wadsworth found in their affinity with him proof that they saw as clearly as he did.

When he had first taken up his trade, he had carried his brushes and pigments on his back, and walked the forest trails like a pedlar. He found himself on his own, reliant upon recommendation and advertisement. But he was industrious, and being possessed of a companionable nature, was grateful that his skill allowed him access to the lives of others. He would enter a household, and whether placed in the stable, quartered with the help, or, very occasionally, and only in the most Christian of dwellings, treated like a guest, he had, for those few days, a function and a recognition. This did not mean he was treated with any less condescension than other artisans; but at least he was being judged a normal human being, that is to say, one who merited condescension. He was happy, perhaps for the first time in his life.

And then, without any help beyond his own perceptions, he began to understand that he had more than just a function; he had strength of his own. This was not something those who employed him would admit; but his eyes told him that it was the case. Slowly he realized the truth of his craft: that the client was the master, except when he, James Wadsworth, was the client's master. For a start, he was the client's master when his eye discerned what the client would prefer him not to know. A husband's contempt. A wife's dissatisfaction. A deacon's hypocrisy. A child's suffering. A man's complacency at having his wife's money to spend. A husband's eye for the hired girl. Large matters in small kingdoms.

And beyond this, he realized that, when he rose in the stable and brushed the horsehair from his clothes, then crossed to the house and took up a brush made from the hair of another animal, he became more than he was taken for. Those who sat for him and paid him did not truly know what their money would buy. They knew what had been agreed – the size of the canvas, the pose and the decorative elements (the bowl of strawberries, the bird on a string, the piano, the view from a window) – and from this agreement they inferred mastery. But this was the very moment at which mastery passed to the other side of the canvas. Hitherto in their lives they had seen themselves in looking glasses and hand mirrors, in the backs of spoons, and, dimly, in clear still water. It was even said that lovers were able to see their reflections in each other's eyes; but the limner had no experience of this. Yet all such images depended upon the person in front of the glass, the spoon, the water, the eye. When Wadsworth provided his clients with their portraits, it was habitually the first time they had seen themselves as someone else saw them. Sometimes, when the picture was presented, the limner would detect a sudden chill passing over the subject's skin, as if he were thinking: so this is how I truly am? It was a moment of unaccountable seriousness: this image was how he would be remembered when he was dead. And then there was a seriousness beyond even this. Wadsworth did not think himself presumptuous when his eye told him that often the subject's next reflection was: and is this perhaps how the Almighty sees me too?

Those who did not have the modesty to be struck by such doubts tended to comport themselves as the collector now did: to ask for adjustments and improvements, to tell the limner that his hand and eye were faulty. Would they have the vanity to complain to God in His turn? 'More dignity, more dignity.' An instruction additionally repugnant given Mr Tuttle's behaviour in the kitchen two nights ago.

Wadsworth had been taking his supper, content with his day's labour. He had just finished the piano. The instrument's narrow leg, which ran parallel to Tuttle's more massive limb, ended in a gilt claw, which Wadsworth had had some trouble in rendering. But now he was able to refresh himself,

97

to stretch by the fire, to feed, and to observe the society of the help. There were more of these than expected. A collector of customs might earn fifteen dollars a week, enough to keep a hired girl. Yet Tuttle also kept a cook and a boy to work the garden. Since the collector did not appear to be a man lavish with his own money, Wadsworth deduced that it was Mrs Tuttle's portion which permitted such luxury of attention.

Once they became accustomed to his deformity, the help treated him easily, as if his deafness rendered him their equal. It was an equality Wadsworth was happy to concede. The garden boy, an elf with eyes of burnt umber, had taken to amusing him with tricks. It was as if he imagined that the limner, being shorn of words, thereby lacked amusement. This was not the case, but he indulged this indulgence of him and smiled as the boy turned cartwheels, stole up behind the cook while she bent to the bake oven, or played a guessing game with acorns hidden in his fists.

The limner had finished his broth and was warming himself before the fire – an element Mr Tuttle was not generous with elsewhere in the house – when an idea came to him. He drew a charred stick from the edge of the ashes, touched the garden boy on the shoulder to make him stay as he was, then pulled a drawing book from his pocket. The cook and the hired girl tried to watch what he was doing, but he held them away with a hand, as if to say that this particular trick, one he was offering in thanks for the boy's own tricks, would not work if observed. It was a rough sketch – it could only be so, given the crudeness of the implement – but it contained some part of a likeness. He tore the page from the book and handed it to the boy. The child looked up at him with astonishment and gratitude, placed the sketch on the table, took Wadsworth's drawing hand and kissed it. I should always paint children, the limner thought, looking the boy in the eye. He was almost unaware of the laughing tumult that broke out when the other two examined the drawing, and then of the silence which fell when the collector of customs, drawn by the sudden noise, entered the kitchen.

The limner watched as Tuttle stood there, one foot advanced, as in his portrait, his mouth opening and closing in a manner that did not suggest dignity. He watched as the cook and the girl rearranged themselves in more decorous attitudes. He watched as the boy, alert to his master's gaze, picked up the drawing and modestly, proudly, handed it over. He watched as Tuttle took the paper calmly, examined it, glanced at the boy, then at Wadsworth, nodded, deliberately tore the sketch in four, placed it in the fire, waited until it blazed, said something further when in quarter-profile to the limner, and made his exit. He watched as the boy wept.

The portrait was finished: both rosewood piano and collector of customs gleamed. The small white customs house filled the window at Mr Tuttle's elbow – not that there was any real window there, nor, if there had been, any customs house visible through it. Yet everyone understood this modest transcendence of reality. And perhaps the collector, in his own mind, was only asking for a similar transcendence of reality when he demanded more dignity. He was still leaning over Wadsworth, gesturing at the representation of his face, chest, leg. It did not matter in the least that the limner could not hear what he was saying. He knew exactly what was meant, and also how little it signified. Indeed, it was an advantage not to hear, for the particularities would doubtless have raised him to an even greater anger than that which he presently felt.

He reached for his notebook. 'Sir,' he wrote, 'we agreed upon five days for my labour. I must leave tomorrow morning by daybreak. We agreed that you would pay me tonight.

Pay me, give me three candles, and by the morning I shall work such improvement as you require.'

It was rare for him to treat a client with so little deference. It would be bad for his reputation in the county; but he no longer cared. He offered the pen in the direction of Mr Tuttle, who did not deign to receive it. Instead, he left the room. While waiting, the limner examined his work. It was well done: the proportions pleasing, the colours harmonious, and the likeness within the bounds of honesty. The collector ought to be satisfied, posterity impressed, and his Maker – always assuming he was vouchsafed Heaven – not too rebuking.

Tuttle returned and handed over six dollars – half the fee – and two candles. Doubtless their cost would be deducted from the second half of the fee when it came to be paid. If it came to be paid. Wadsworth looked long at the portrait, which had come to assume for him equal reality with its fleshly subject, and then he made several decisions.

He took his supper as usual in the kitchen. His companions had been subdued the previous night. He did not think they blamed him for the incident with the garden boy; at most, they thought his presence had led to their own misjudgement, and so they were chastened. This, at any rate, was how Wadsworth saw matters, and he did not think their meaning would be clearer if he could hear speech or read lips; indeed, perhaps the opposite. If his notebook of men's thoughts and observations was anything to judge by, the world's knowledge of itself, when spoken and written down, did not amount to much.

This time, he selected a piece of charcoal more carefully, and with his pocketknife scraped its end to a semblance of sharpness. Then, as the boy sat opposite him, immobile more through apprehension than a sitter's sense of duty, the limner drew him again. When he had finished, he tore out the sheet and, with the boy's eyes upon him, mimed the act of concealing it beneath his shirt, and handed it across the table. The boy immediately did as he had seen, and smiled for the first time that evening. Next, sharpening his piece of charcoal before each task, Wadsworth drew the cook and the hired girl. Each took the sheet and concealed it without looking. Then he rose, shook their hands, embraced the garden boy, and returned to his night's work.

More dignity, he repeated to himself as he lit the candles and took up his brush. Well then, a dignified man is one whose appearance implies a lifetime of thought; one whose brow expresses it. Yes, there was an improvement to be made there. He measured the distance between the eyebrow and the hairline, and at the midpoint, in line with the right eyeball, he developed the brow: an enlargement, a small mound, almost as if something was beginning to grow. Then he did the same above the left eye. Yes, that was better. But dignity was also to be inferred from the state of a man's chin. Not that there was anything patently insufficient about Tuttle's jawline. But perhaps the discernible beginnings of a beard might help – a few touches on each point of the chin. Nothing to cause immediate remark, let alone offence, merely an indication.

And perhaps another indication was required. He followed the collector's sturdily dignified leg down its stockinged calf to the buckled shoe. Then he followed the parallel leg of the piano down from the closed keyboard lid to the gilt claw which had so delayed him. Perhaps that trouble could have been avoided? The collector had not specified that the piano be rendered exactly. If a little transcendence had been applied to the window and the customs house, why not to the piano as well? The more so, since the spectacle of a claw beside a customs man might suggest a grasping and rapacious nature, which no client would wish implied, whether there was evidence for it or no. Wadsworth therefore painted out the feline paw and replaced it with a quieter hoof, grey in colour and lightly bifurcated.

Habit and prudence urged him to snuff out the two candles he had been awarded; but the limner decided to leave them burning. They were his now – or at least, he would have paid for them soon. He washed his brushes in the kitchen, packed his painting box, saddled his mare and harnessed the little cart to her. She seemed as happy to leave as he. As they walked from the stable, he saw windows outlined by candle-light. He hauled himself into the saddle, the mare moved beneath him, and he began to feel cold air on his face. At daybreak, an hour from now, his penultimate portrait would be examined by the hired girl pinching out wasteful candles. He hoped that there would be painting in Heaven, but more than this he hoped that there would be deafness in Heaven. The mare, soon to be the subject of his final portrait, found her own way to the trail. After a while, with Mr Tuttle's house now far behind them, Wadsworth shouted into the silence of the forest.

WILLIAM BOYD

VARENGEVILLE

OLIVER FROWNED DARKLY and pushed his spectacles back up to the bridge of his nose, taking in his mother's suspiciously bright smile and trying to ignore Lucien's almost sneering, almost leering grimace of pride and self-satisfaction. Lucien was his mother's 'friend': Oliver had decided he did not particularly like Lucien.

'What exactly is it?' Oliver said, playing for time.

'I believe people call it a bicycle,' Lucien said. Oliver noticed that his mother thought this sally was amusing.

'I know that,' Oliver said patiently, 'but why are *you* giving *me* a bicycle?'

'It's a present,' his mother said. 'It's a gift for you – you can go exploring. Say thank you to Uncle Lucien. Really, you're intolerably spoilt.'

'Thank you, Lucien,' Oliver said. 'You are most kind.'

The bicycle was solid, a little too big for him, black, with three gears and lights and possessed – Oliver admitted he was pleased by this gadget – a small folding-down support that allowed the bike to stand free when it was parked.

However, it did not take long for the real purpose of the gift to become evident. Oliver wondered if his mother thought he was really that stupid. Every time Lucien motored over from Deauville, always after lunch (always leaving before six), his mother would turn to Oliver and say, 'Oliver, darling, why don't you cycle into Varengeville and post this letter for me.' She would give him a hundred francs and tell him to have a *diabolo menthe* at the café in the square. 'Explore,' she would further enjoin, vaguely, waving her arms about. 'Wander here and there. Wonderful countryside, beaches, trees. The freedom of the open road. Fill your lungs, my darling, fill your lungs.'

And Oliver would wearily mount the big black bicycle and pedal off down the road to Varengeville, the letter tucked into his belt. He had a good idea what his mother and Lucien would be doing in his absence – he knew, in fact he was absolutely convinced, that it would involve a lot of kissing – and he was sure his father would not be pleased. He had discovered his mother and Lucien in a kiss on one occasion and had watched them silently, slightly disturbed at the violence, the audible suction with which their mouths fed on each other. Then they had broken apart and his mother had seen him watching. She took him at once into the next room and explained that Maman had been unhappy and Uncle Lucien was simply being kind and had been trying to cheer her up but that it would be best if he didn't tell Papa. They were both instantly aware – Oliver's eyes narrowing – that this explanation was laughably inept, that it did not even begin to undermine the blatant deceit. So she changed tactics and instead made him promise to her: she extracted one of her most severe and terrifying and implacable promises from him. Oliver knew he would never dare tell Papa.

Lucien came two or three times a week, always in the afternoon. Once he came with some other friends on a Sunday for lunch, accompanied by a nervy, febrile woman with strange coppery hair, who was introduced as his wife. It was early August, and Oliver was beginning doggedly to count the days before he would go back to school in England, to count the days before he would see his father again, conscious all the while that the summer was only half done and that there would be many more cycle trips into Varengeville.

It was on his sixth or seventh journey into the village that he spotted the old painter. Oliver always took the same route: up the sloping drive to the gates, turning down the farm lane to the road; then there was an exhilarating swift downhill freewheel along the hedgerow to the D.75, then right along the cliff road toward Varengeville, with the brilliant ocean, restless and refulgent, on his left, his eyes screwed up behind his spectacle lenses, half blinded by the glare of the afternoon sun.

It was the odd shape of the canvas that attracted his attention first: it was long and thin, almost like a short plank, screwed into a small easel. The old painter sat absolutely still on a collapsible canvas stool, his arms folded across his breast, staring out to sea, his brushes and paints resting on his knees. Oliver noticed his shock of completely white hair, neatly combed, and, even though the man was sitting, he knew he must be tall and thin.

In Varengeville he posted his mother's letter and then went to the café for his *diabolo*. The café was always quiet in mid-afternoon, and the surly young waiter, with a new downy mustache on his top lip, listened to his order, served him his drink, accepted his payment, tossed down the change, tore a corner off the receipt, and wandered off, loudly straightening already straight chairs, without a word.

Oliver looked out at the little square and thought about things: his mother and Lucien, for a start; then the scab that was hardening nicely on his elbow; his desire to have a pet of some sort, mammal or reptile, he couldn't decide; the film that his father was making in London ... Then he would observe, covertly but closely, the rare customers that came and went, and from time to time admire the perfect stolidity of his parked bicycle – canted over somewhat, but resolutely firm on its stand – and note how the slightly elliptical shadow version of it, angled flat on the pavement, shadow wheels touching real rubber wheels, was both absolutely exact and yet undeniably distorted. The phrase 'as faithful as a shadow' came into his head, and he thought how true it was, but then wondered, Where did your shadow go when the sun wasn't shining? How could something be faithful if you couldn't see it? And then he found his thoughts were returning to his mother and Lucien and decided he would cycle back as slowly as possible, hoping Lucien would be gone by the time he arrived home and he would not have to encounter him, mysteriously washed and perfumed, a permanent smile on his lips and full of an unfamiliar and repugnant affection for Oliver.

The old painter was still sitting motionless in his field, still staring out at the sea and the coastline. The afternoon had turned hazy, the sky full of spilled-milk clouds, but still glary and dazzling. Coming from the other direction, Oliver could now see what was on the canvas, and as he approached he was surprised to note that it seemed almost black, full of murky blues and dark grays. For an absurd second, as he glanced at the silvered sea with its vast backdrop of sunlit cloud, he wondered if the painter might be blind. And then he wondered if he might be dead. People could die like that suddenly, sitting up, just stiffen into a posture like that – they could, he'd read about it.

'Are you all right, *Monsieur*?' Oliver asked softly.

The painter turned slowly around. He had a big rectangular face, its features powerfully present – the nose; the eyes; the thin, wide mouth; the absolutely white hair – yet in no way was it distinctive or handsome, just a strong, simple oblong face, Oliver thought, but somehow oddly memorable.

'But of course, young man,' the painter said. 'Many thanks for asking.'

Oliver had parked his bicycle and climbed over the fence and approached the painter without seeing any movement in him, aware now that he wasn't in fact dead, of course, but still curious about the man's impressive immobility.

'I thought,' Oliver began, 'because you weren't painting, that –'

'No, I was just refreshing my memory,' the painter said. 'I just needed to come out here again, in case I had got something wrong.'

Oliver looked at the murky canvas, which showed, as far as he could tell, a ship washed up on a shore in the night. He looked up at the bleached, blinding sky and back at the dark, thin canvas.

'This happened a long time ago,' the painter said in explanation, pointing at his painting.

He began to ask Oliver polite questions: What is your name? Oliver Feverall. How old are you? Almost twelve. Where do you live? Château Les Pruniers, but just for the summer.

'You speak very good French, but you have an English name,' the painter observed. Oliver told him that his mother was French and his father was English. His mother was an actress. She had appeared in half a dozen films, perhaps he knew of her – Fabienne Farde? The painter confessed he did not.

'Perhaps you've heard of my father. He's a famous film director – Denton Feverall?'

'I rarely go to the cinema,' the painter said, beginning to pack away his brushes and tubes. As far as Oliver could tell, he hadn't added a stroke of color to his grimy canvas, just come outside and stared at it for a couple of hours.

They walked back to the gate that led to the coast road. The painter admired Oliver's bicycle, admired the efficacy of its folding-down stand. Oliver tried once more.

'It was given to me by a singer, a famous singer. He's in Deauville for the summer, at the Casino – Lucien Navarro.'

'Lucien Navarro, Lucien Navarro . . .' the painter repeated, holding his forefinger erect on his right hand as if calling for silence. Oliver waited. Then, after a while: 'No, never heard of him.' Oliver shrugged, wondering what kind of reclusive life this man led, never having heard of Fabienne Farde, Denton Feverall, or Lucien Navarro.

They shook hands, formally, and the painter wished Oliver a good end to the afternoon and thanked him again for his solicitude. Oliver looked back as he cycled away and saw the old man striding down the road, his canvas and easel under one arm, the afternoon sun striking his silver hair, making it flame with light.

Lucien had a new car – a Lancia, with a roof that came down. Lucien and his Lancia, Oliver thought, a note of disgust coloring his reflections as he cycled off to Varengeville with his mother's letter. Lucien and his Lancia.

Lucien had not visited for some six days, and Oliver had noted his mother's mood steadily deteriorating. One morning she had not descended from her bedroom at all – only the maid was allowed access, bringing up all manner of curious drinks. Even Oliver's soft knock on her door in the afternoon produced only the moaned response 'Darling, *Maman* has one of her migraines,' and he did not see her at all, he calculated, for a further thirty-seven hours.

And then Lucien was coming and she was alert and

agitated, changing her clothes, shifting vases of flowers about the drawing room, her perfumes more noticeably pungent, her affection for Oliver falling upon him suddenly, with brusque, sore hugs and alarming cannonades of kisses and caresses. Oliver looked impassively out the library windows as Lucien's midnight-blue Lancia crunched dustily to a halt and, for the first time, felt relieved that he had to go to Varengeville and post a letter.

But in the village, standing in front of the pale yellow post-box, he felt a sudden flow of anger at his ritual banishment. He tore open the letter – always to his mother's sister in Paris – and, as he knew he would, discovered three perfectly blank sheets of paper. He folded them up, deliberately, slowly, and dropped them in a litter bin by a set of traffic lights. He cycled south out of Varengeville, toward the plateau, heading for Longeuil, not wanting a *diabolo menthe*, wondering how he was going to survive the two and a half weeks of August that were left, wondering how he could go through this pretense, this silly game, each time Lucien arrived. Why didn't she just say she wanted to be alone? He didn't care how long they kissed each other, or whatever else they got up to. He simply wanted summer to be over, he wanted to get back to school, he wanted his father to finish filming *Daughters of Dracula*.

The painter was walking along the road with his usual light burden of easel, folding stool, and long, thin canvas. Oliver slowed to a halt, and they greeted each other, Oliver noticing that although the day was hot the painter was wearing a tweed jacket with a shirt and tie and a curious knitted waistcoat. Old men felt the cold, Oliver remembered, even on the warmest days.

'Where are you going?' the painter asked. He gestured at

the flat, baking landscape inland. In the enormous sky a fleet of huge burly white clouds moved slowly along, northward, pushed by a warm southern breeze. A heavy flight of crows crossed the stubbly field beside them. 'It's hot out there,' the painter said.

'I'm not going anywhere in particular,' Oliver said, feeling unfamiliar tears sting his eyes.

'Is everything all right?'

'Yes, absolutely.'

'Come home with me,' the painter said. 'Have a cold drink.'

The painter showed Oliver into his studio: it was a large, tidy room with a Persian rug hanging on the wall. On an easel was a sizable painting of a blue bird shape against a slate-gray sky. On tables and on the floor were rows of cleaned brushes laid on palettes, and others stuffed into ceramic pots. Small tables held neat rows of tubes of oil paint, as well as jars of flowers, many of them dried. Oliver was impressed.

'You must have hundreds of brushes,' he said. 'Thousands.'

'You may be right,' said the painter, smiling, placing his small canvas on an empty easel and stepping back to contemplate it. Oliver circled around to stare at it, glancing at the picture of the bird and thinking that he, Oliver Feverall, could paint a better-looking bird than that.

The small canvas portrayed what looked like a sodden field beneath winter skies, three uneven stripes of brown, green, and gray, the paint thickly smeared but quite dry.

'I'm having real problems,' the painter said. 'I don't know what to do. I did one like this before and put a plow in it, and it seemed to work.'

'What about a man?'

'No. I don't want people in these pictures.'

'What about some crows?'

'It's an idea.'

As they were going outside to the terrace to have their cold drinks, Oliver heard a woman's voice call out, 'Georges? Are you back?' The painter excused himself and went upstairs, returning a minute later.

'It's my wife,' he said. 'She thinks she's getting flu.'

They sat outside at a metal table under a small canvas awning, which provided a neat square of shade, and sipped at their cold drinks, fetched for them by a plump, smiley housekeeper. Oliver was introduced as 'Monsieur Oliver, my English friend,' and his hand was shaken. The painter drank mineral water, Oliver an Orangina, and they both sat there silently for a while in the relentless afternoon heat, staring out at the big, solid clouds steaming toward them, north-ward. Oliver thought that the painter had a sad face and noticed how the lines that ran from his nose to his mouth were particularly marked, casting, even in this shade, dark sickle shadows.

'It's an interesting idea, that,' the painter said, 'crows.' He turned to Oliver and continued, 'So, when's your birthday?'

'Next week. Wednesday.'

'Come by. We'll have another drink. I'll drink your health. No, I mean it – if you've nothing better to do.'

Oliver thanked him. Wednesday was usually a Lucien day – Wednesday and Friday.

They were silent again for a while, together.

'Do you know what a love affair is?' Oliver asked.

'Yes,' the painter said, 'I certainly do.'

'Do you think that if you're married you should have a love affair with someone else?'

'I don't know,' the painter said.

'Isn't it wrong?'

'It depends.' The painter sipped at his mineral water. He held up his glass as if to look at the sky through it. 'Sometimes water is the best drink in the world, isn't it?'

He walked Oliver to the road and watched him as he crouched to undo the padlock on the chain that Oliver had threaded through the rear wheel as an antitheft device.

'Do you think someone will steal your bike?' the painter asked.

'You can't be too careful. In London I've had three bikes stolen.'

'But this is Varengeville, not London. Still, it is a splendid machine, isn't it, wonderfully built.'

'I wish it had drop handlebars,' Oliver said. 'I think it looks a bit old-fashioned.' He kicked up the stand with his left shoe. 'I'd better get home,' he said. 'My mother will be waiting.'

'See you on Wednesday,' the painter said.

On his birthday his mother gave Oliver a very crumpled ten-pound note and promised him a proper treat when they returned home. Oliver said he was going to see a friend in Varengeville and set off up the drive a good half hour before Lucien was due.

The housekeeper was watering some pots of geraniums by the front door as Oliver approached.

'He's not here,' she said. 'They had to go back to Paris yesterday. Madame has bronchitis, we think.'

Oliver pursed his lips and pushed his spectacles up to the bridge of his nose. Damn, he thought, bloody damn. He looked about him, hands on his hips, wondering resentfully what he would do for the rest of the day – maybe he should just go to the beach.

'He's left a present for you,' the housekeeper said, disappearing back into the house and reemerging with a long, thin brown-paper parcel. 'He was very insistent you should have this.'

Oliver sat on the beach below the small cliff and took his shoes and socks off. He looked at his watch – he'd better stay here for a couple of hours at least, to allow Lucien time to leave. It was annoying that the painter had been obliged to go to Paris – he had been looking forward to the visit. It would have solved the problem of the day.

Oliver allowed himself an audible sigh and looked about him idly. A stout dark girl in a yellow bikini sunbathed some feet away, her small Yorkshire terrier at her side, huddling under a bunched towel for shade. Farther along a group of kids sat in a circle around a transistor radio. Toddlers studiously dug in the wet sand at the gentle surf's edge. Oliver thought about his birthday – what could he get for ten pounds? Maybe Dad will call this evening. He's bound to give me ten pounds too, maybe more ... He mentally totaled all the potential fiscal gifts that he might receive from his assorted relatives and came up with a satisfyingly large figure. Not such a bad birthday after all, he thought, and unwrapped the painter's present.

It was the wet fields painting, Oliver was not too surprised to discover – and just what was he supposed to do with it, he wondered? It wasn't particularly well painted, Oliver thought, and also the painter himself had seemed dissatisfied with it. He felt a slight surge of irritation that the painter had given him a picture that even he had been unable to finish properly. What it needed was something else in it, not just fields and sky. Maybe, Oliver thought, he should paint his bike in one of the corners, have it leaning over on its stand . . .

The sunbathing girl in the bikini turned over suddenly and rolled onto her small dog, which gave an anguished yelp of pain and surprise. No, Oliver thought, inspired, if he painted the sky blue, then the field would look like a beach. Then he could paint the girl lying on the beach with her yellow bikini and her little dog. And then the painting would at least be finished – at least it would be about something. Oliver stared at the plump girl as she fussed and petted her discomfited dog. He found himself grinning, felt the laugh brim in his throat, and quickly covered his mouth with his hand in case she should see.

JOHN BERGER

A BRUSH

I WANT TO tell you the story of how I gave away this *Sho* Japanese brush. Where it happened and how. The brush had been given to me by an actor friend who had gone to work for a while with some Noh performers in Japan.

I drew often with it. It was made of the hairs of horse and sheep. These hairs once grew out of a skin. Maybe this is why when gathered together into a brush with a bamboo handle they transmit sensations so vividly. When I drew with it I had the impression that it and my fingers loosely holding it were touching not paper but a skin. The notion that a paper being drawn on is like a skin is there in the very word: *brushstroke*. The one and only touch of the brush! as the great draftsman Shitao termed it.

The setting for the story was a municipal swimming pool in a popular, not chic, Paris suburb, where, from time to time, I was something of an habitué. I would go there every day at 1:00 p.m., when most people were eating, and so the pool was not crowded.

The building is long and squat, and its walls are of glass and brick. It was built in the late 1960s, and it opened in 1971. It's situated in a small park where there are a few silver birches and weeping willows.

From the pool when swimming you can see the willows high up through the glass walls. The ceiling above the pool is paneled, and now, forty years later, several of the panels are missing. How many times when swimming on my back have I noticed this, while being aware of the water holding up both me and whatever story I'm puzzling over?

There's an eighteenth-century drawing by Huang Shen of a cicada singing on the branch of a weeping willow. Each leaf in it is a single brushstroke.

Seen from the outside, it's an urban not a rural building, and if you didn't know it was a swimming pool and you forgot about the trees you might suppose it was some kind of railway building, a cleaning shed for coaches, a loading bay.

There's nothing written above the entrance, just a small blazon containing the three colors of the tricolor. Emblem of the Republic. The entrance doors are of glass with the instruction POUSSEZ stenciled on them.

When you push one of these doors open and step inside you are in another realm that has little to do with the streets outside, the parked cars, or the shopping street.

The air smells slightly of chlorine. Everything is lit from below rather than from above as a consequence of the light reflected off the water of the two pools. The acoustics are distinct: every sound has its slight echo. Everywhere the horizontal, as distinct from the vertical, dominates. Most people are swimming, swimming from one end of the large pool to the other, length after length. Those standing have just taken off their clothes or are getting out of them, so there's little sense of rank or hierarchy. Instead, everywhere, there's this sense of an odd horizontal equality.

There are many printed notices, all of them employing a distinctive bureaucratic syntax and vocabulary.

THE HAIR DRYER WILL STOP 5 MINUTES BEFORE CLOSING TIME.

BATHING CAPS OBLIGATORY. COUNCIL DECREE AS FROM MONDAY JAN. 5, 1981.

ENTRY THROUGH THIS DOOR FORBIDDEN TO ANY
PERSON WHO IS NOT A MEMBER OF STAFF. THANK YOU.

The voice embodied in such announcements is insepar-
able from the long political struggle during the Third
Republic for the recognition of citizens' rights and duties.
A measured, impersonal committee voice – with somewhere
in the distance a child laughing.

Around 1945 Fernand Léger painted a series of canvases
about *plongeurs* – divers in a swimming pool. With their
primary colors and their simple, relaxed outlines these paint-
ings celebrated the dream and the plan of workers enjoying
leisure and, because they were workers, transforming leisure
into something that had not yet been named.

Today the realization of this dream is further away than
ever. Yet sometimes while putting my clothes in a locker in
the men's changing room and attaching the key to my wrist,
and taking the obligatory hot shower before walking through
the footbath, and going to the edge of the large pool and
diving in, I remember these paintings.

Most of the swimmers wear, as well as the obligatory
bathing cap, dark goggles to protect their eyes from the
chlorine. There's little eye contact between us, and if a swim-
mer's foot accidentally touches another swimmer, he or
she immediately apologizes. The atmosphere is not that of
the Côte d'Azur! Here each one privately pursues her or his
own target.

I first noticed her because she swam differently. The move-
ments of her arms and legs were curiously slow, like those of
a frog, and at the same time her speed was not dramatically
reduced. She had a different relationship to the element
of water.

The Chinese master Qi Baishe (1863–1957) loved drawing

frogs, and he made the tops of their heads very black, as if they were wearing bathing caps. In the Far East the frog is a symbol of freedom.

Her bathing cap was ginger-colored and she was wearing a costume with a floral pattern, a little like English chintz. She was in her late fifties and I assumed was Vietnamese. Later I discovered my mistake. She is Cambodian.

Every day she swam, length after length, for almost an hour. As I did too. When she decided it was time to climb up one of the corner ladders and leave the pool, a man, who was himself swimming several tracks away, came to help her. He was also Southeast Asian, a little thinner than she, a little shorter, with a face that was more carved than hers; her face was moonlike.

He came up behind her in the water and put his hands under her arse so that she, facing the edge of the pool, sat on them and he bore a little of her weight when they climbed out together.

Once on the solid floor she walked away from the corner of the pool toward the footbath and the entrance to the women's changing room, alone and without any discernible limp. Having noticed this ritual a number of times, I could see, however, that, when walking, her body was taut, as if stretched on tenterhooks.

The man with the brave carved face was presumably her husband. I don't know why I had a slight doubt about this. Was it his deference? Or her aloofness?

When she first came to the pool and wanted to enter the water, he would climb halfway down the ladder and she would sit on one of his shoulders, and then he would prudently descend until the water was over his hips and she could launch herself to swim away.

Both of them knew these rituals of immersion and extraction by heart, and perhaps both recognized that in the ritual the water played a more important role than either of them. This might explain why they appeared more like fellow performers than man and wife.

Time went by. The days passed repetitively. Eventually when she and I, swimming our lengths, crossed each other for the first time going in opposite directions, with only a meter or two between us, we lifted our heads and nodded at each other. And when, about to leave the pool, we crossed for the last time that day, we signaled Au Revoir.

How to describe that particular signal? It involves raising the eyebrows, tossing the head as if to throw back the hair, and then screwing up the eyes in a smile. Very discreetly. Goggles pushed up onto the bathing cap.

One day while I was taking a hot shower after my swim – there are eight showers for men, and to switch one on there are no taps, you press an old-fashioned button like a door-knob, and the trick is that among the eight there's some variation in the duration of the flow of hot water until the button has to be pressed again, so by now I knew exactly which shower had the hot jet that lasted longest, and, if it was free, I always chose it – one day while I was taking a hot shower after my swim, the man from Southeast Asia came under the shower next to mine and we shook hands.

Afterwards we exchanged a few words and agreed to meet outside in the little park after we'd dressed. And this is what we did, and his wife joined us.

It was then that I learned they were from Cambodia. She is very distantly related to the family of the famous Prince Sihanouk. She had fled to Europe when she was twenty,

123

in the mid-seventies. Prior to that she had studied art in Phnom Penh.

It was she who talked and I who asked the questions. Again I had the impression that his role was that of a body-guard or assistant. We were standing near the birch trees beside their parked two-seater Citroën C15 with a seatless space behind. A vehicle much the worse for wear. Do you still paint? I asked. She lifted her left hand into the air, making a gesture of releasing a bird, and nodded. Often she's in pain, he said. I read a lot too, she added, in Khmer and in Chinese. Then he indicated it was perhaps time for them to climb into their C15. Hanging from the rear mirror above the wind-shield I noticed a tiny Buddhist dharma wheel, like a ship's helm in miniature.

After they had driven off I lay on the grass – it was the month of May – beneath the weeping willows and found myself thinking about pain. She'd left Cambodia after Siha-nouk had been ousted with the probable help of the CIA and in the year when the Khmer Rouge under Pol Pot had taken over the capital and begun the enforced deportation of its two million inhabitants to the countryside, where, living in communities with no individual property, they had to learn to become New Khmers! Nearly a million of them didn't survive. In the preceding years Phnom Penh and its surround-ing villages had been systematically bombarded by U.S. B-52s. At least a hundred thousand people died.

The Khmer people, with their mighty past of Angkor Wat and its gigantic, impassive stone statues that later were abandoned, damaged, marauded, and so acquired a look of suffering. The Khmer were, at the moment she left her coun-try, surrounded by enemies – Vietnamese, Laotians, Thais – and were on the point of being tyrannized and massacred by their own political visionaries, who transformed themselves into fanatics so that they could inflict vengeance on reality itself, so they could reduce reality to a single dimension. Such reduction brings with it as many pains as there are cells in a heart.

Gazing at the willows, I watched their leaves trailing in the wind. Each leaf a small brushstroke.

Today Cambodia is one of the poorest countries in Southeast Asia, and 75 percent of its exports are manufactured in sweatshops producing garments for the brand-name rag trade multinationals of the West.

A group of four-year-old kids ran past me up the steps and through the glass doors. They were going to their swimming lessons.

The next time I saw her and her husband in the pool I approached her when she had finished one of her lengths and asked if she could tell me what it was that caused her pain. She answered immediately as if naming a place: polyarthritis. It came when I was young, when I knew I had to leave. It's kind of you to ask.

The left half of her forehead is a little discolored, browner than the rest, as if the leaf of a frond, once placed on her skin there, had slightly stained it. When her head is thrown back floating on the water, and her face looks moonlike, you could compare this little discoloring to one of the so-called seas on the moon's surface.

We both trod water and she smiled. When I'm in water, she said, I weigh less, and after a little while my joints stop hurting.

I nodded. And then we went on swimming. Swimming on her front, as I have said, she moved her legs and arms as slowly as a frog sometimes does. On her back she swam like an otter.

*   *   *

Cambodia is a land that has a unique osmotic relationship with freshwater. The Khmer word for homeland is *Teuk-Dey*, which means Water-Land. Framed by mountains, its flat, horizontal, alluvial plain – about a quarter of the size of France – is crossed by six major rivers including the vast Mekong. During and after the summer monsoon rains, the flow of this river multiplies by fifty! And in Phnom Penh, the river's level rises systematically by eight meters. At the same time, to the north, the lake of Tonle Sap overflows each summer to five times its 'normal' winter size to become an immense reservoir, and the river of Tonle Sap turns round to run in the opposite direction, its downstream becoming upstream.

Small wonder then that this plain offered some of the most varied and abundant freshwater fishing in the world, and that for centuries its peasants lived off rice and the fish of these waters.

It was on that day while swimming during the lunch hour at the municipal swimming pool, after she had said the word *polyarthritis*, pronouncing it as if it were a place, that I thought of giving her my *Sho* brush.

The same evening I put it into a box and wrapped it. And each time I went to the pool I took it with me until they turned up again. Then I placed the little box on one of the benches behind the diving boards and told her husband so he could pick it up when they left. I left before they did.

Months passed without my seeing them because I was else-where. When I returned to the pool, I looked for them but could not see them. I adjusted my goggles and dived in. Several kids were jumping in feetfirst, holding their noses. Others on the edge were adjusting flippers on their feet.

It was noisier and more animated than usual because by now it was the month of July, school was over, and the kids, whose families couldn't afford to leave Paris, were coming to play for hours in the water. The special entrance fee for them was minimal, and the lifesaving swimming instructors maintained an easygoing discipline. A few regulars, with their strict routines and personal targets, were still there.

I had done nearly twenty lengths and was about to start another when – to my astonishment – I felt a hand firmly placed on my right shoulder from behind. I turned my head and saw the stained moon face of the onetime art student from Phnom Penh. She was wearing the same ginger-colored bathing cap and she was smiling a wide smile.

You're here!

She nods, and while we are treading water she comes close and kisses me twice on both cheeks.

Then she asks: Bird or flower?

Bird!

Thereupon she lays her head back on the water and laughs. I wish I could let you hear her laugh. Compared with the splashing and cries of the kids around us, it is low-keyed, slow, and persistent. Her face is more moonlike than ever, moonlike and timeless. The laugh of this woman, who will soon be sixty, continues. It is unaccountably the laugh of a child – that same child whom I imagined laughing somewhere behind the committee voices.

A few days later her husband swims towards me, asks after my health, and whispers: On the bench by the diving boards. Then they leave the pool. He comes up behind her, puts his hands under her arse, and she, facing the edge of the pool, sits on them while he bears a little of her weight, and they climb up and out together.

Neither of them waves back to me as they have on other

127

occasions. A question of modesty. Gestural modesty. No gift can be accompanied by a claim.

On the bench is a large envelope, which I take. Inside is a painting on rice paper. The painting of the bird I chose when she asked me what I wanted. The painting shows a bamboo, and perched on one of its stems a blue tit. The bamboo is drawn according to all the rules of the art. A single brush-stroke beginning at the top of the stalk, stopping at each section, descending and becoming slightly wider. The branches, narrow as matches, drawn with the tip of the brush. The dark leaves rendered in single strokes like darting fish. And last the horizontal nodes, brushed from left to right, between each section of the hollow stalk.

The bird with its blue cap, its yellow breast, its grayish tail, and its claws like the letter W, from which it can hang upside down when necessary, is depicted differently. Whereas the bamboo is liquid, the bird looks embroidered, its colors applied with a brush as pointed as a needle.

Together, on the surface of the rice paper, bamboo and bird have the elegance of a single image, with the discrete stencil of the artist's name stamped below and to the left of the bird. Her name is L—.

When you enter the drawing, however, and let its air touch the back of your head, you sense how this bird is homeless. Inexplicably homeless.

I framed the drawing like a scroll, without a mount, and with great pleasure chose a place to hang it. Then one day, many months later, I needed to look up something in one of the Larousse illustrated encyclopedias. And, turning the pages, I happened to fall upon the little illustration it contained of a *mésange bleue* (blue tit). I was puzzled. It looked oddly familiar. Then I realized that, in this standard encyclopedia, I was looking at the model – the two Ws of the blue tit's claws were, for instance, at precisely the same angle, as were also the head and beak – the exact model that L— had taken for the bird perched on the bamboo.

And again I understood a little more about homelessness.

DORIS LESSING

TWO POTTERS

I HAVE ONLY known one potter in this country, Mary Tawnish, and she lives out of London in a village where her husband is a school-teacher. She seldom comes to town, and I seldom leave it, so we write.

The making of pots is not a thing I often think of, so when I dreamed about the old potter it was natural to think of Mary. But it was difficult to tell her; there are two kinds of humanity, those who dream and those who don't, and both tend to despise, or to tolerate, the other. Mary Tawnish says, when others relate their dreams: 'I've never had a dream in my life.' And adds, to soften or placate: 'At least, I don't remember. They say it's a question of remembering?'

I would have guessed her to be a person who would dream a good deal, I don't know why.

A tall woman, and rather large, she has bright brown clustering hair, and brown eyes that give the impression of light, though not from their surface: it is not a 'bright' or 'brilliant' glance. She looks at you, smiling or not, but always calm, and there is an impression of light, which seems caught in the structure of colour in the iris, so sometimes her eyes look yellow, set off by smooth brown eyebrows.

A large, slow-moving woman, with large white slow hands. And a silent one – she is a listener.

Her life has been a series of dramas: a childhood on the move, with erratic parents, a bad first marriage, a child that died, lovers, but none lasting; then a second marriage to

133

William Tawnish who teaches physics and biology. He is a quick, biting, bitter little man with whom she has three half-grown children.

More than once I have told her story, without comment, in order to observe the silent judgement: another misfit, another unhappy soul, only to see the judger confounded on meeting her, for there was never a woman less fitted by nature for discord or miseries. Or so it would seem. So it seems she feels herself, for she disapproves of other people's collisions with themselves, just as if her own life had nothing to do with her.

The first dream about the potter was simple and short. Once upon a time . . . there was a village or a settlement, not in England, that was certain, for the scene was of a baked red-dust bareness. Low rectangular structures, of simple baked mud, also reddish-brown, were set evenly on the baked soil, yet because some were roofless and others in the process of crumbling, and others half-built, there was nothing finished or formed about this place. And for leagues and leagues, in all directions, the great plain, of reddish earth, and in the middle of the plain the settlement that looked as if it were hastily moulded by a great hand out of wet clay, allowed to dry, and left there. It seemed uninhabited, but in an empty space among the huts, all by himself, working away on a primitive potter's wheel turned by foot, was an old man. He wore a garment of coarse sacking over yellowish and dusty limbs. One bare foot was set in the dust near me, the cracked toes spread and curled. He had a bit of yellow straw stuck in close grizzling hair.

When I woke from this dream I was rested and excited, in spite of the great dried-up plain and the empty settlement one precarious stage from the dust. In the end I sat down and wrote to Mary Tawnish, although I could hear her flat comment very clearly: Well, that's interesting. Our letters are usually of the kind known as 'keeping in touch'. First I enquired about her children, and about William, and then I told the dream: 'For some reason I thought of you. I did know a man who made pots in Africa. The farmer he worked for discovered he had a talent for pot-making (it seemed his tribe were potters by tradition), because when they made bricks for the farm, this man, Elija, slipped little dishes and bowls into the kiln to bake with the bricks. The farmer used to pay him a couple of shillings a week extra, and sold the dishes to a dealer in the city. He made simple things, not like yours. He had no wheel, of course. He didn't use colour. His things were a darkish yellow, because of the kind of soil on that farm. A bit monotonous after a bit. And they broke easily. If you come up to London give me a ring...'

She didn't come, but soon I had a letter with a postscript: 'What an interesting dream, thanks so much for telling me.'

I dreamed about the old potter again. There was the great, flat, dust-beaten reddish plain, ringed by very distant blue-hazed mountains, so far away they were like mirages, or clouds, or low-lying smoke. There was the settlement. And there the old potter, sitting on one of his own upturned pots, one foot set firmly in the dust, and the other moving the wheel; one palm shaping the clay, the other shedding water which glittered in the low sullen glare in flashes of moving light on its way to the turning wet clay. He was extremely old, his eyes faded and of the same deceiving blue as the mountains. All around him, drying in rows on a thin scatter-ing of yellow straw, were pots of different sizes. They were all round. The huts were rectangular, the pots round. I looked at these two different manifestations of the earth, separated by shape; and then through a gap in the huts to the plain. No one in sight. It seemed no one lived there. Yet there sat the old man, with the hundreds of pots and dishes drying in rows on the straw, dipping his hand into an enormous jar of water and scattering drops that smelled sweet as they hit the dust and pitted it.

Again I thought of Mary. But they had nothing in common, that poor old potter who had no one to buy his work, and Mary who sold her strange coloured bowls and jugs to the big shops in London. I wondered what the old potter would think of Mary's work – particularly what he'd think of a square flat dish I'd bought from her, coloured a greenish-yellow. The square had, as it were, slipped out of whack, and the surface is rough, with finger marks left showing. I serve cheese on it. The old man's jars were for millet, I knew that, or for soured milk.

I wrote and told Mary the second dream, thinking: Well, if it bores or irritates her, it's too bad. This time she rang me up. She wanted me to go down to one of the shops which had been slow in making a new order. Weren't her things selling? she wanted to know. She added she was getting a fellow feeling for the old potter; he didn't have any customers either, from the size of his stock. But it turned out that the shop had sold all Mary's things, and had simply forgotten to order more.

I waited, with patient excitement, for the next instalment, or unfolding, of the dream.

The settlement was now populated, indeed, teeming, and it was much bigger. The low flat rooms of dull earth had spread over an area of some miles. They were not separated now, but linked. I walked through a system of these rooms. They were roughly the same size, but set at all angles to each other so that, standing in one, it might have one, two, three doors, leading to a corresponding number of mud rooms. I walked for something like half a mile through low dark rooms without once needing to cross a roofless space, and when I emerged in the daylight, there was the potter, and beyond him a marketplace. But a poor one. From out of his great jars, women, wearing the same sort of yellowish sacking as he, sold grain and milk to dusty, smallish, rather listless people. The potter worked on, under heavy sunlight, with his rows and rows of clay vessels drying on the glinting yellow straw. A very small boy crouched by him, watching every movement he made. I saw how the water shaken from the old fingers on the whirling pot flew past it and spattered the small intent poverty-shaped face with its narrowed watching eyes. But the face received the water unflinching, probably unnoticed.

Beyond the settlement stretched the plain. Beyond that, the thin, illusory mountains. Over the red flat plain drifted small shadows: they were from great birds wheeling and banking and turning.

I wrote to Mary and she wrote back that she was glad the old man had some customers at last, she had been worried about him. As for her, she thought it was time he used some colour, all that red dust was depressing. She said she could see the settlement was short of water, since I hadn't mentioned a well, let alone a river, only the potter's great brimming jar which reflected the blue sky, the sun, the great birds. Wasn't a diet of milk and millet bad for people? Here she broke off to say she supposed I couldn't help all this, it was my nature, and 'Apropos, isn't it time your poor village had a storyteller at least? How bored the poor things must be!'

I wrote back to say I was not responsible for this settlement, and whereas if I had my way, it would be set in groves of fruit trees and surrounded by whitening cornfields, with a river full of splashing brown children. I couldn't help it, that's how things were in this place, wherever it was.

One day in a shop I saw a shelf of her work and noticed that some of them were of smooth, dully shining brown, like polished skin – jars, and flat round plates. Our village potter would have known these, nothing to surprise him here. All the same, there was a difference between Mary's consciously simple vessels and the simplicity of the old potter. I looked at them and thought: Well, my dear, that's not going to get you very far . . . But I would have found it hard to say exactly what I meant, and in fact I bought a plate and a jar, and they gave me great pleasure, thinking of Mary and the old potter linked in them, between my hands.

Quite a long time passed. When I dreamed again, all the plain was populated. The mountains had come closer in, reaching up tall and blue into blue sky, circumscribing the plain. The settlements, looked at from the height of the mountain tops, seemed like patches of slightly raised surface on the plain. I understood their nature and substance: a slight raising of the dust here and there, like the frail patterning of raindrops hitting dry dust, pitting it, then the sun coming out swiftly to dry the dust. The resulting tiny fragile patterned crust of dried dust – that gives, as near as I can, the feeling the settlements gave me, viewed from the mountains. Except that the raised dried crusts were patterned in rectangles. I could see the tiny patternings all over the plain. I let myself down from the mountains, through the great birds that wheeled and floated, and descended to the settlement I knew. There sat the potter, the clay curving under his left hand as he flicked water over it from his right. It was all going on as usual – I was reassured by his being there, creating his pots. Nothing much had changed, though so much time had passed. The low flat monotonous dwellings were the same, though they had crumbled to dust and raised themselves from it a hundred times since I had been here last. No green yet, no river. A scum-covered creek had goats grazing beside it, and the millet grew in straggly patches, flattened and brown from drought. In the marketplace were pinkish fruits, lying in heaps by the soft piles of millet, on woven straw mats. I didn't know the fruit: it was small, about plum-size, smooth-skinned, and I felt it had a sharp pulpy taste. Pinky-yellow skins lay scattered in the dust. A man passed me, with a low slinking movement of the hips, holding his sack-like garment in position at his side with the pressure of an elbow, staring in front of him over the pink fruit which he pressed against sharp yellow teeth.

I wrote and told Mary the plain was more populated, but that things hadn't improved much, except for the fruit. But it was astringent, I wouldn't care for it myself.

She wrote back to say she was glad she slept so soundly, she would find such dreams depressing.

I said there was nothing depressing about it. I entered the dream with pleasure, as if listening to a storyteller say: Once upon a time...

But the next was discouraging, I woke depressed. I stood by the old potter in the marketplace, and for once his hands were still, the wheel at rest. His eyes followed the movements of the people buying and selling, and his mouth was bitter. Beside him, his vessels stood in rows on the warm glinting straw. From time to time a woman came picking her way along the rows, bending to narrow her eyes at the pots. Then she chose one, dropped a coin in the potter's hand, and bore it off over her shoulder.

I was inside the potter's mind and I knew what he was thinking. He said: 'Just once, Lord, just once, just once!' He put his hand down into a patch of hot shade under the wheel and lifted on his palm a small clay rabbit which he held out to the ground. He sat motionless, looking at the sky, then at the rabbit, praying: 'Please, Lord, just once.' But nothing happened.

I wrote Mary that the old man was tired with long centuries of making pots whose life was so short: the litter of broken pots under the settlement had raised its level twenty feet by now, and every pot had come off his wheel. He wanted God to breathe life into his clay rabbit. He had hoped to see it lift up its long red-veined ears, to feel its furry feet on his palm, and watch it hop down and off among the great earthenware pots, sniffing at them and twitching its ears – a live thing among the forms of clay.

Mary said the old man was getting above himself. She said further: 'Why a *rabbit*? I simply don't *see* a rabbit. What use would a rabbit be? Do you realize that apart from goats (you say they have milk), and those vultures overhead, they have no animals at all? Wouldn't a cow be better than a rabbit?'

I wrote: 'I can't do anything about that place when I'm dreaming it, but when I'm awake, why not? Right then, the rabbit hopped off the old man's hand into the dust. It sat twitching its nose and throbbing all over, the way rabbits do. Then it sprang slowly off and began nibbling at the straw, while the old man wept with happiness. Now what have you to say? If I say there was a rabbit, a rabbit there was. Besides, that poor old man deserves one, after so long. God could have done so much, it wouldn't have cost Him anything.'

I had no reply to that letter, and I stopped dreaming about the settlement. I knew it was because of my effrontery in creating that rabbit, inserting myself into the story. Very well, then ... I wrote to Mary: 'I've been thinking: suppose it had been you who'd dreamed about the potter – all right, all right, just suppose it. Now. Next morning you sat at the breakfast table, your William at one end, and the children between eating cornflakes and drinking milk. You were rather silent. (Of course you usually are.) You looked at your husband and you thought: What on earth would he say if I told him what I'm going to do? You said nothing, presiding at the table; then you sent the children off to school, and your husband to his classes. Then you were alone and when you'd washed the dishes and put them away, you went secretly into the stone-floored room where your wheel and the kiln are, and you took some clay and you made a small rabbit and you set it on a high shelf behind some finished vases to dry. You didn't want anyone to see that rabbit. One day, a week later, when it was dry, you waited until your family was out of the house, then you put your rabbit on your palm, and you went into a field, and you knelt down and held the rabbit out to the grass, and you waited. You didn't pray, because you don't believe in God, but you wouldn't have been in the least surprised if that rabbit's nose had started to twitch and its long soft ears stood up ...'

Mary wrote: 'There aren't any rabbits any more, had you forgotten myxomatosis? Actually I did make some small rabbits recently, for the children, in blue and green glaze, because it occurred to me the two youngest haven't seen a rabbit out of a picture book. Still, they're coming back in some parts, I hear. The farmers will be angry.'

I wrote: 'Yes, I had forgotten. Well then ... sometimes at evening, when you walk in the fields, you think: How nice to see a rabbit lift his paws and look at us. You remember the rotting little corpses of a few years back. You think: *I'll try again*. Meantime, you're nervous of what William will say, he's such a rationalist. Well of course, so are we, but he wouldn't even play a little. I may be wrong, but I think you're afraid of William catching you out, and you are careful not to be caught. One sunny morning you take it out on to the field and ... all right, all right then, it *doesn't* hop away. You

141

can't decide whether to lay your clay rabbit down among the warm grasses (it's a sunny day) and let it crumble back into the earth, or whether to bake it in your kiln. You haven't baked it, it's even rather damp still: the old potter's rabbit was wet, just before he held it out into the sun he sprinkled water on it, I saw him.

'Later you decide to tell your husband. Out of curiosity? The children are in the garden, you can hear their voices and William sits opposite you reading the newspaper. You have a crazy impulse to say: I'm going to take my rabbit into the field tonight and pray for God to breathe life into it, a field without rabbits is empty. Instead you say: "William, I had a dream last night . . ." First he frowns, a quick frown, then he turns those small quick sandy-lashed intelligent eyes on you, taking it all in. To your surprise, instead of saying: "I don't remember your ever dreaming," he says: "Mary, I didn't know you disapproved of the farmers killing off their rabbits." You say: "I didn't disapprove. I'd have done the same, I suppose." The fact that he's not reacted with sarcasm or impatience, as he might very well, makes you feel guilty when you lift the clay rabbit down, take it out to a field and set it in a hedge, its nose pointing out towards some fresh grass. That night William says, casual: "You'll be glad to hear the rabbits are back. Basil Smith shot one in his field – the first for eight years, he says. Well, I'm glad myself, I've missed the little beggars." You are delighted. You slip secretly into a cold misty moonlight and you run to the hedge and of course the rabbit is gone. You stand, clutching your thick green stole around you, because it's cold, shivering, but delighted, delighted! Though you know quite well one of your children, or someone else's child, has slipped along this hedge, seen the rabbit, and taken it off to play with.'

Mary wrote: 'Oh all right, if you say so, so it is. But I must tell you, if you are interested in *facts*, that the only thing that has happened is that Dennis (the middle one) put his blue rabbit out in a hedge for a joke near the Smiths' gate, and Basil Smith shot it to smithereens one dusk thinking it was real. He used to lose a small fortune every year to rabbits, he didn't think it was a funny joke at all. Anyway, why don't you come down for a weekend?'

The Tawnishes live in an old farmhouse on the edge of the village. There is a great garden, with fruit trees, roses – everything. The big house and the three boys mean a lot of work, but Mary spends all the time she can in the shed that used to be a dairy where she pots. I arrived to find them in the kitchen, having lunch. Mary nodded to me to sit down. William was in conflict with the middle boy, Dennis, who was, as the other two boys kept saying, 'showing off'. Or, rather, he was in that torment of writhing self-consciousness that afflicts small boys sometimes, rolling his eyes while he stuttered and wriggled, his whole sandy freckled person scarlet and miserable.

'Well I did I did I did I did I did . . .' He paused for breath, his eyes popping, and his older brother chanted: 'No you didn't, you didn't, you didn't.'

'Yes I did I did I did I did . . .'

And the father said, brisk but irritated: 'Now then, Dennis, use your loaf, you couldn't have, because it is obvious you have *not*.'

'But I did I did I did I did . . .'

'Well, then, you had better go out of the room until you come to your senses and are fit company for rational people,' said his father, triumphantly in the right.

The child choked on his battling breath, and ran howling out into the garden. Where, after a minute, the older boy followed, ostensibly to control him.

'He did what?' I asked.

'Who knows?' said Mary. There she sat, at the head of the table, bright-eyed and smiling, serving apple pie and custard, a dark changeling in the middle of her gingery, freckled family.

Her husband said, brisk: 'What do you mean, who knows? You know quite well.'

'It's his battle with Basil Smith,' said Mary to me. 'Ever since Basil Smith shot at his blue rabbit and broke it, there's been evil feeling on both sides. Dennis claims that he set fire to the Smith farmhouse last night.'

'*What?*'

Mary pointed through a low window, where the Smiths' house showed, two fields away, like a picture in a frame.

William said: 'He's hysterical and he's got to stop it.'

'Well,' said Mary, 'if Basil shot my blue rabbit I'd want to burn his house down too. It seems quite reasonable to me.'

William let out an exclamation of rage, checked himself because of my presence, shot fiery glances all round, and went out, taking the youngest boy with him.

'Well,' said Mary. 'Well . . .' She smiled. 'Come into the pottery, I've got something to show you.' She went ahead along a stone passage, a tall, lazy-moving woman, her bright brown hair catching the light. As we passed an open window, there was a fearful row of shrieks, yells, blows; and we saw the three boys rolling and tussling in the grass, while William danced futilely around them shouting: 'Stop it, stop it at once!' Their mother proceeded, apparently uninterested, into the potting room.

This held the potting apparatus, and a great many jars, plates, and jugs of all colours and kinds, ranged on shelves. She lifted down a creature from a high shelf, and set it before

144

me. Then she left it with me, while she bent to attend to the kiln.

It was yellowish-brown, a sort of rabbit or hare, but with ears like neither – narrower, sharp, short, like the pointed unfolding shoots of a plant. It had a muzzle more like a dog's than a rabbit's; it looked as if it did not eat grass – perhaps insects and beetles? Yellowish eyes were set on the front of its head. Its hind legs were less powerful than a rabbit's, or hare's; and I saw its talents were for concealment, not for escaping enemies in great pistoning leaps. It rested on short, stubby hind legs, with front paws held up in a queer, twisted, almost affected posture, head turned to one side, and ears furled around each other. It looked as if it had been wound up like a spring, and had half-unwound. It looked like a strangely shaped rock, or like the harsh twisted plants that sometimes grow on rocks.

Mary came back and stood by me, her head slightly on one side, with her characteristic small patient smile that nevertheless held a sweet concealed exasperation.

'Well,' she said, 'there it is.'

I hesitated, because it was not the creature I had seen on the old potter's palm.

'What was an English rabbit doing there at all?' she asked.

'I didn't say it was an English rabbit.'

But of course, she was right: this animal was far more in keeping with the dried mud houses, the dusty plain, than the pretty furry rabbit I had dreamed.

I smiled at Mary, because she was humouring me, as she humoured her husband and her children. For some reason I thought of her first husband and her lovers, two of whom I had known. At moments of painful crisis, or at parting, had she stood thus – a calm, pretty woman, smiling her sweetly satirical smile, as if to say: 'Well, make a fuss if you like, it's got nothing at all to do with me'? If so, I'm surprised that one of them didn't murder her.

'Well,' I said at last, 'thanks. Can I take this thing, whatever it is?'

'Of course. I made it for you. You must admit, it may not be pretty, but it's more likely to be *true*.'

I accepted this, as I had to; and I said: 'Well, thanks for coming down to our level long enough to play games with us.'

At which there was a flash of yellow light from her luminous eyes, while her face remained grave, as if amusement, or acknowledgement of the *truth*, could only be focused in her thus, through a change of light in her irises.

A few minutes later, the three boys and the father came round this part of the house in a whirlwind of quarrelling energy. The aggrieved Dennis was in tears, and the father almost beside himself. Mary, who until now had remained apart from it all, gave an exclamation, slipped on a coat, and said: 'I can't stand this. I'm going to talk to Basil Smith.'

She went out, and I watched her cross the fields to the other house.

Meanwhile Dennis, scarlet and suffering, came into the pottery in search of his mother. He whirled about, looking for her, then grabbed my creature, said: 'Is that for me?', snatched it possessively to him when I said: 'No, it's for me,' set it down when I told him to, and stood breathing like a furnace, his freckles like tea leaves against his skin.

'Your mother's gone to see Mr Smith,' I said.

'He shot my rabbit,' he said.

'It wasn't a real rabbit.'

'But he thought it was a real rabbit.'

'Yes, but you knew he would think so, and that he'd shoot at it.'

'He killed it!'

'You wanted him to!'

At which he let out a scream and danced up and down like a mad boy, shouting: 'I didn't I didn't I didn't I didn't . . .'

His father, entering on this scene, grabbed him by his flailing arms, fought the child into a position of tensed stillness, and held him there, saying, in a frenzy of incredulous commonsense: 'I've never – in – my – life – heard – such – lunacy!'

Now Mary came in, accompanied by Mr Smith, a large, fair, youngish man, with a sweet open face, which was uncomfortable now, because of what he had agreed to do.

'Let that child go,' said Mary to her husband. Dennis dropped to the floor, rolled over, and lay face down, heaving with sobs.

'Call the others!'

Resignation itself, William went to the window, and shouted: 'Harry, John, Harry, John, come here at once, your mother wants you!' He then stood, with folded arms, a defeated philosopher, grinning angrily while the two other children came in and stood waiting by the door.

'Now,' said Mary. 'Get up, Dennis.'

Dennis got up, his face battered with suffering, and looked with hope towards his mother.

Mary looked at Basil Smith.

Who said, careful to get the words right: 'I am very sorry that I killed your rabbit.'

The father let out a sharp outraged breath, but kept quiet at a glance from his wife.

The chest of Dennis swelled and sank – in one moment there would be a storm of tears.

'Dennis,' said Mary, 'say after me: "Mr Smith, I'm very sorry I set fire to your house." '

Dennis said in a rush, to get it out in time: 'Mr Smith I'm very sorry I set fire to your ... to your ... to your ...' He sniffed and heaved, and Mary said firmly: '*House*, Dennis.'

'House,' said Dennis, in a wail. He then rushed at his mother, buried his head in her waist, and stood howling and wrestling, while she laid large hands on his ginger head and smiled over it at Mr Basil Smith.

'Dear God,' said her husband, letting his folded arms drop dramatically, now the ridiculous play was over. 'Come and have a drink, Basil.'

The men went off. The two other children stood silent and abashed, because of the force of Dennis's emotion, for which they clearly felt partly responsible. Then they slipped out to play. The house was tranquil again, save for Dennis's quietening sobs. Soon Mary took the boy up to his room to sleep it off. I stayed in the great, stone-floored pottery, looking at my strange twisted animal, and at the blues and greens of Mary's work all around the walls.

Supper was early and soon over. The boys were silent, Dennis too limp to eat. Bed was prescribed for everyone. William kept looking at his wife, his mouth set under his ginger moustache, and he could positively be heard thinking: Filling them full of this nonsense while I try to bring them up reasonable human beings! But she avoided his eyes, and sat calm and remote, serving mashed potatoes and brown stew. It was only when we had finished the washing-up that she smiled at him – her sweet, amused smile. It was clear they needed to be alone. I said I wanted an early night and left them: he had gone to touch her before I was out of the room.

Next day, a warm summer Sunday, everyone was relaxed, the old house peaceful. I left that evening, with my clay creature, and Mary said smiling, humouring me: 'Let me know how things go on with your place, wherever it is.' But I had her beautiful animal in my suitcase, so I did not mind being humoured.

That night, at home, I went into the marketplace, and up to the old potter, who stilled his wheel when he saw me coming. The small boy lifted his frowning attentive eyes from the potter's hands and smiled at me. I held out Mary's creature. The old man took it, screwed up his eyes to examine it, nodded. He held it in his left hand, scattered water on it with his right, held his palm down towards the littered dust, and the creature jumped off it and away, with quick, jerky movements, not stopping until it was through the huts, clear of the settlement, and against a small outcrop of jagged brown rocks where it raised its front paws and froze in the posture Mary had created for it. Overhead an eagle or a hawk floated by, looked down, but failed to see Mary's creature, and floated on, up and away into the great blue spaces over the flat dry plain to the mountains. I heard the wheel creak; the old man was back at work. The small boy crouched, watching, and the water flung by the potter's right hand sprayed the bowl he was making and the child's face, in a beautiful curving spray of glittering light.

A. S. BYATT

A LAMIA IN THE CÉVENNES

IN THE MID-1980s Bernard Lycett-Kean decided that Thatcher's Britain was uninhabitable, a land of dog-eat-dog, lung-corroding ozone and floating money, of which there was at once far too much and far too little. He sold his West Hampstead flat and bought a small stone house on a Cévenol hillside. He had three rooms, and a large barn, which he weatherproofed, using it as a studio in winter and a storehouse in summer. He did not know how he would take to solitude, and laid in a large quantity of red wine, of which he drank a good deal at first, and afterwards much less. He discovered that the effect of the air and the light and the extremes of heat and cold were enough, indeed too much, without alcohol. He stood on the terrace in front of his house and battled with these things, with mistral and tramontane and thunderbolts and howling clouds. The Cévennes is a place of extreme weather. There were also days of white heat, and days of yellow heat, and days of burning blue heat. He produced some paintings of heat and light, with very little else in them, and some other paintings of the small river which ran along the foot of the steep, terraced hill on which his house stood; these were dark green and dotted with the bright blue of the kingfisher and the electric blue of the dragonflies.

These paintings he packed in his van and took to London and sold for largish sums of the despised money. He went to his own Private View and found he had lost the habit of conversation. He stared and snorted. He was a big man, a burly man, his stare seemed aggressive when it was largely baffled. His old friends were annoyed. He himself found London just as rushing and evil-smelling and unreal as he had been imagining it. He hurried back to the Cévennes. With his earnings, he built himself a swimming-pool, where once there had been a patch of baked mud and a few bushes.

It is not quite right to say he built it. It was built by the Jardinerie Émeraude, two enterprising young men, who dug and lined and carried mud and monstrous stones, and built a humming power-house full of taps and pipes and a swirling cauldron of filter-sand. The pool was blue, a swimming-pool blue, lined with a glittering tile mosaic, and with a mosaic dolphin cavorting amiably in its depths, a dark blue dolphin with a pale blue eye. It was not a boring rectangular pool, but an irregular oval triangle, hugging the contour of the terrace on which it lay. It had a white stone rim, moulded to the hand, delightful to touch when it was hot in the sun.

The two young men were surprised that Bernard wanted it blue. Blue was a little *moche*, they thought. People now were making pools steel-grey or emerald-green, or even dark wine-red. But Bernard's mind was full of blue dots now visible across the southern mountains when you travelled from Paris to Montpellier by air. It was a recalcitrant blue, a blue that asked to be painted by David Hockney and only by David Hockney. He felt something else could and must be done with that blue. It was a blue he needed to know and fight. His painting was combative painting. That blue, that amiable, non-natural aquamarine was different in the un-compromising mountains from what it was in Hollywood. There were no naked male backsides by his pool, no umbrellas, no tennis-courts. The river-water was sombre and weedy, full of little shoals of needle-fishes and their shadows, of curling water-snakes and the triangular divisions of flow around pebbles and boulders. This mild blue, here, was to be seen in *that* terrain.

He swam more and more, trying to understand the blue, which was different when it was under the nose, ahead of the eyes, over and around the sweeping hands and the flickering toes and the groin and the armpits and the hairs of his chest, which held bubbles of air for a time. His shadow in the blue moved over a pale eggshell mosaic, a darker blue, with huge paddle-shaped hands. The light changed, and with it, everything. The best days were under racing cloud, when the aquamarine took on a cool grey tone, which was then chased back, or rolled away, by the flickering gold-in-blue of yellow light in liquid. In front of his prow or chin in the brightest lights moved a mesh of hexagonal threads, flashing rainbow colours, flashing liquid silver-gilt, with a hint of molten glass; on such days liquid fire, rosy and yellow and clear, ran across the dolphin, who lent it a thread of intense blue. But the surface could be a reflective plane, with the trees hanging in it, with two white diagonals where the aluminium steps entered. The shadows of the sides were a deeper blue but not a deep blue, a blue not reflective and yet lying flatly *under* reflections. The pool was deep, for the Émeraude young men envisaged much diving. The wind changed the surface, frilled and furred it, flecked it with diamond drops, shirred it and made a witless patchwork of its plane. His own motion changed the surface – the longer he swam, the faster he swam, the more the glassy hills and valleys chopped and changed and ran back on each other.

Swimming was *volupté* – he used the French word, because of Matisse. *Luxe, calme et volupté.* Swimming was a strenuous battle with immense problems, of geometry, of chemistry, of apprehension, of style, of other colours. He put pots of petunias and geraniums near the pool. The bright hot pinks and purples were dangerous. They did something to that blue.

The stone was easy. Almost too blandly easy. He could paint chalky white and creamy sand and cool grey and paradoxical hot grey; he could understand the shadows in the high rough wall of monstrous cobblestones that bounded his land.

The problem was the sky. Swimming in one direction, he was headed towards a great rounded green mountain, thick with the bright yellow-green of dense chestnut trees, making a slightly innocent, simple arc against the sky. Whereas the other way, he swam towards crags, towards a bowl of bald crags, with a few pines and lines of dark shale. And against the green hump the blue sky was one blue, and against the bald stone another, even when for a brief few hours it was uniformly blue overhead, that rich blue, that cobalt, deep-washed blue of the South, which fought all the blues of the pool, all the green-tinged, duck-egg-tinged blues of the shifting water. But the sky had also its greenish days, and its powdery-hazed days, and its theatrical louring days, and none of these blues and whites and golds and ultramarines and faded washes harmonized in any way with the pool blues, though they all went through their changes and splendours in the same world, in which he and his shadow swam, in which he and his shadow stood in the sun and struggled to record them.

He muttered to himself. Why bother. Why does this *matter* so much. *What difference does it make to anything if I solve this blue* and just start again. I could just sit down and drink wine. I could go and be useful in a cholera-camp in Colombia or Ethiopia. *Why bother to render the transparency in solid paint or air on a bit of board?* I could *just stop.*

He could not.

He tried oil paint and acrylic, watercolour and gouache, large designs and small plain planes and complicated juxtaposed planes. He tried trapping light on thick impasto and tried also glazing his surfaces flat and glossy, like seventeenth-century Dutch or Spanish paintings of silk. One of these almost pleased him, done at night, with the lights under the water and the dark round the stone, on an oval bit of board. But then he thought it was sentimental. He tried veils of watery blues on white in watercolour, he tried Matisse-like patches of blue and petunia – pool blue, sky blue, petunia – he tried Bonnard's mixtures of pastel and gouache.

His brain hurt, and his eyes stared, and he felt whipped by winds and dried by suns.

He was happy, in one of the ways human beings have found in which to be happy.

One day he got up as usual and as usual flung himself naked into the water to watch the dawn in the sky and the blue come out of the black and grey in the water.

There was a hissing in his ears, and a stench in his nostrils, perhaps a sulphurous stench, he was not sure; his eyes were sharp but his profession, with spirits and turpentine, had dulled his nostrils. As he moved through the sluggish surface he stirred up bubbles, which broke, foamed, frothed and crusted. He began to leave a trail of white, which reminded him of polluted rivers, of the waste-pipes of tanneries, of deserted mines. He came out rapidly and showered. He sent a fax to the Jardinerie Émeraude. What was Paradise is become the Infernal Pit. Where once I smelled lavender and salt, now I have a mephitic stench. What have you done to my water? Undo it, undo it. I cannot coexist with these exhalations. His French was more florid than his English.

I am polluted, my work is polluted, *I cannot go on*. How could the two young men be brought to recognize the extent of the insult? He paced the terrace like an angry panther. The sickly smell crept like marsh-grass over the flower-pots, through the lavender bushes. An emerald-green van drew up, with a painted swimming-pool and a painted palm tree. Every time he saw the van, he was pleased and irritated that this commercial emerald-and-blue had found an exact balance for the difficult aquamarine without admitting any difficulty.

The young men ran along the edge of the pool, peering in, their muscular legs brown under their shorts, their plimsolls padding. The sun came up over the green hill and showed the plague-stricken water-skin, ashy and suppurating. It is all OK, said the young men, this is a product we put in to fight algae, not because you *have* algae, M. Bernard, but in case algae might appear, as a precaution. It will all be exhaled in a week or two, the mousse will go, the water will clear.

'Empty the pool,' said Bernard. '*Now*. Empty it now. I will not coexist for two weeks with this vapour. Give me back my clean salty water. *This water is my life-work*. Empty it *now*.'

'It will take days to fill,' said one young man, with a French acceptance of Bernard's desperation. 'Also there is the question of the allocation of water, of how much you are permitted to take.'

'We could fetch it up from the river,' said the other. In French this is literally, we could draw it in the river, *puiser dans le ruisseau*, like fishing. 'It will be cold, ice-cold from the Source, up the mountain,' said the Émeraude young men.

'Do it,' said Bernard. 'Fill it from the river. I am an Englishman, I swim in the North Sea, I like cold water. Do it. *Now*.'

The young men ran up and down. They turned huge taps in the grey plastic pipes that debouched in the side of the mountain. The swimming-pool soughed and sighed and began, still sighing, to sink, whilst down below, on the hillside, a frothing flood spread and laughed and pranced and curled and divided and swept into the river. Bernard stalked behind the young men, admonishing them. 'Look at that froth. We are polluting the river.'

'It is only two litres. It is perfectly safe. Everyone has it in his pool, M. Bernard. It is tried and tested, it is a product for *purifying water*.' It is only you, his pleasant voice implied, who is pig-headed enough to insist on voiding it.

The pool became a pit. The mosaic sparkled a little in the sun, but it was a sad sight. It was a deep blue pit of an entirely unproblematic dull texture. Almost like a bathroom floor. The dolphin lost his movement and his fire, and his curvetting ripples, and became a stolid fish in two dimensions. Bernard peered in from the deep end and from the shallow end, and looked over the terrace wall at the hillside where froth was expiring on nettles and brambles. It took almost all day to empty and began to make sounds like a gigantic version of the bath-plug terrors of Bernard's infant dreams.

The two young men appeared carrying an immense boa-constrictor of heavy black plastic pipe, and an implement that looked like a torpedo, or a diver's oxygen pack. The mountainside was steep, and the river ran green and chuckling at its foot. Bernard stood and watched. The coil of pipe was uncoiled, the electricity was connected in his humming pumphouse, and a strange sound began, a regular boum-boum, like the beat of a giant heart, echoing off the green mountain. Water began to gush from the mouth of the pipe into the sad dry depths of his pool-pit. Where it trickled upwards, the mosaic took on a little life again, like crystals glinting.

'It will take all night to fill,' said the young men. 'But do not be afraid, even if the pool overflows, it will not come in your house, the slope is too steep, it will run away back to the river. And tomorrow we will come and regulate it and filter it and you may swim. But it will be very cold.'

'*Tant pis*,' said Bernard.

All night the black tube on the hillside wailed like a monstrous bullfrog, boum-boum, boum-boum. All night the water rose, silent and powerful. Bernard could not sleep; he paced his terrace and watched the silver line creep up the sides of the pit, watched the greenish water sway. Finally he slept, and in the morning his world was awash with river-water, and the heart-beat machine was still howling on the river-bank, boum-boum, boum-boum. He watched a small fish skid and slide across his terrace, flow over the edge and slip in a stream of water down the hillside and back into the river. Everything smelt wet and lively, with no hint of sulphur and no clear smell of purified water. His friend Raymond Potter telephoned from London to say he might come on a visit; Bernard, who could not cope with visitors, was non-committal, and tried to describe his delicious flood as a minor disaster.

'You don't want river-water,' said Raymond Potter. 'What about liver-flukes and things, and bilharzia?'

'They don't have bilharzia in the Cévennes,' said Bernard.

The Émeraude young men came and turned off the machine, which groaned, made a sipping sound and relapsed into silence. The water in the pool had a grassy depth it hadn't had. It was a lovely colour, a natural colour, a colour that harmonized with the hills, and it was not the problem Bernard was preoccupied with. It would clear, the young men assured him, once the filtration was working again.

* * *

Bernard went swimming in the green water. His body slipped into its usual movements. He looked down for his shadow and thought he saw out of the corner of his eye a swirling movement in the depths, a shadowy coiling. It would be strange, he said to himself, if there were a big snake down there, moving around. The dolphin was blue in green gloom. Bernard spread his arms and legs and floated. He heard a rippling sound of movement, turned his head, and found he was swimming alongside a yellow-green frog with a salmon patch on its cheek and another on its butt, the colour of the roes of scallops. It made vigorous thrusts with its hind legs, and vanished into the skimmer, from the mouth of which it peered out at Bernard. The underside of its throat beat, beat, cream-coloured. When it emerged, Bernard cupped his hands under its cool wet body and lifted it over the edge: it clung to his fingers with its own tiny fingers, and then went away, in long hops. Bernard went on swimming. There was still a kind of movement in the depths that was not his own.

This persisted for some days, although the young men set the filter in motion, tipped in sacks of white salt, and did indeed restore the aquamarine transparency, as promised. Now and then he saw a shadow that was not his, now and then something moved behind him; he felt the water swirl and tug. This did not alarm him, because he both believed and disbelieved his senses. He liked to imagine a snake. Bernard liked snakes. He liked the darting river-snakes, and the long silver-brown grass snakes who travelled the grasses beside the river.

Sometimes he swam at night, and it was at night that he first definitely saw the snake, only for a few moments, after he had switched on the underwater lights, which made the water look like turquoise milk. And there under the milk was something very large, something coiled in two intertwined figures of eight and like no snake he had ever seen, a velvety-black, it seemed, with long bars of crimson and peacock-eyed spots, gold, green, blue, mixed with silver moonshapes, all of which appeared to dim and brighten and breathe under the deep water. Bernard did not try to touch; he sat down cautiously and stared. He could see neither head nor tail; the form appeared to be a continuous coil like a Möbius strip. And the colours changed as he watched them: the gold and silver lit up and went out, like lamps, the eyes expanded and contracted, the bars and stripes flamed with electric vermilion and crimson and then changed to purple, to blue, to green, moving through the rainbow. He tried professionally to commit the forms and the colours to memory. He looked up for a moment at the night sky. The Plough hung very low, and the stars glittered white-gold in Orion's belt on thick midnight velvet. When he looked back, there was the pearly water, vacant.

Many men might have run roaring in terror; the courageous might have prodded with a pool-net, the extravagant might have reached for a shot-gun. What Bernard saw was a solution to his professional problem, at least a nocturnal solution. Between the night sky and the breathing, dissolving eyes and moons in the depths, the colour of the water was solved, dissolved, it became a medium to contain a darkness spangled with living colours. He went in and took notes in watercolour and gouache. He went out and stared and the pool was empty.

For several days he neither saw nor felt the snake. He tried to remember it, and to trace its markings into his pool-paintings, which became very tentative and watery. He swam

162

even more than usual, invoking the creature from time to time. 'Come back,' he said to the pleasant blue depths, to the twisting coiling lines of rainbow light. 'Come back, I need you.'

And then, one day, when a thunderstorm was gathering behind the crest of the mountains, when the sky loured and the pool was unreflective, he felt the alien tug of the other current again, and looked round quick, quick, to catch it. And there was a head, urging itself sinuously through the water beside his own, and there below his body coiled the miraculous black velvet rope or tube with its shimmering moons and stars, its peacock eyes, its crimson bands.

The head was a snake-head, diamond-shaped, half the size of his own head, swarthy and scaled, with a strange little crown of pale lights hanging above it like its own rainbow. He turned cautiously to look at it and saw that it had large eyes with fringed eyelashes, human eyes, very lustrous, very liquid, very black. He opened his mouth, swallowed water by accident, coughed. The creature watched him, and then opened its mouth, in turn, which was full of small, even, pearly human teeth. Between these protruded a flickering dark forked tongue, entirely serpentine. Bernard felt a prick of recognition. The creature sighed. It spoke. It spoke in Cévenol French, very sibilant, but comprehensible.

'I am so unhappy,' it said.

'I am sorry,' said Bernard stupidly, treading water. He felt the black coils slide against his naked legs, a tail-tip across his private parts.

'You are a very beautiful man,' said the snake in a languishing voice.

'You are a very beautiful snake,' replied Bernard courteously, watching the absurd eyelashes dip and lift.

'I am not entirely a snake. I am an enchanted spirit, a

Lamia. If you will kiss my mouth, I will become a most beautiful woman, and if you will marry me, I will be eternally faithful and gain an immortal soul. I will also bring you power, and riches, and knowledge you never dreamed of. But you must have faith in me.'

Bernard turned over on his side, and floated, disentangling his brown legs from the twining coloured coils. The snake sighed.

'You do not believe me. You find my present form too loathsome to touch. I love you. I have watched you for months and I love and worship your every movement, your powerful body, your formidable brow, the movements of your hands when you paint. Never in all my thousands of years have I seen so perfect a male being. I will do anything for you –'

'Anything?'

'Oh, *anything*. Ask. Do not reject me.'

'What I want,' said Bernard, swimming towards the craggy end of the pool, with the snake stretched out behind him, 'what I want, is to be able to paint your portrait, *as you are*, for certain reasons of my own, and because I find you very beautiful – if you would consent to remain here for a little time, as a snake – with all these amazing colours and lights – if I could paint you *in my pool* – just for a little time –'

'And then you will kiss me, and we will be married, and I shall have an immortal soul.'

'Nobody nowadays believes in immortal souls,' said Bernard.

'It does not matter if you believe in them or not,' said the snake. 'You have one and it will be horribly tormented if you break your pact with me.'

Bernard did not point out that he had not made a pact, not having answered her request yes or no. He wanted quite desperately that she should remain in his pool, in her present form, until he had solved the colours, and was almost prepared for a Faustian damnation.

There followed a few weeks of hectic activity. The Lamia lingered agreeably in the pool, disposing herself wherever she was asked, under or on the water, in figures of three or six or eight or O, in spirals and tight coils. Bernard painted and swam and painted and swam. He swam less since he found the Lamia's wreathing flirtatiousness oppressive, though occasionally to encourage her, he stroked her sleek sides, or wound her tail round his arm or his arm round her tail. He never painted her head, which he found hideous and repulsive. Bernard liked snakes but he did not like women. The Lamia with female intuition began to sense his lack of enthusiasm for this aspect of her. 'My teeth,' she told him, 'will be lovely in rosy lips, my eyes will be melting and mysterious in a human face. Kiss me, Bernard, and you will see.'

'Not yet, not yet,' said Bernard.

'I will not wait for ever,' said the Lamia.

Bernard remembered where he had, so to speak, seen her before. He looked her up one evening in Keats, and there she was, teeth, eyelashes, frecklings, streaks and bars, sapphires, greens, amethyst and rubious-argent. He had always found the teeth and eyelashes repulsive and had supposed Keats was as usual piling excess on excess. Now he decided Keats must have seen one himself, or read someone who had, and felt the same mixture of aesthetic frenzy and repulsion. Mary Douglas, the anthropologist, says that *mixed* things, neither flesh nor fowl, so to speak, always excite repulsion and prohibition. The poor Lamia was a mess, as far as her head went. Her beseeching eyes were horrible. He looked up from his reading and saw her snake-face peering sadly in at the window, her halo shimmering, her teeth shining like pearls. He saw to his locks: he was not about to be accidentally kissed in his sleep. They were each other's prisoners, he and she. He would paint his painting and think how to escape.

The painting was getting somewhere. The snake-colours were a fourth term in the equation pool > sky > mountains-trees > paint. Their movement in the aquamarines linked and divided delectably, firing the neurones in Bernard's brain to greater and greater activity, and thus causing the Lamia to become sulkier and eventually duller and less brilliant.

'I am *so sad*, Bernard. I want to be a woman.'

'You've had thousands of years already. Give me a few more days.'

'You see how kind I am, when I am in pain.'

What would have happened if Raymond Potter had not kept his word will never be known. Bernard had quite forgotten the liver-fluke conversation and Raymond's promised, or threatened, visit. But one day he heard wheels on his track, and saw Potter's dark red BMW creeping up its slope.

'Hide,' he said to the Lamia. 'Keep still. It's a dreadful Englishman of the fee-fi-fo-fum sort; he has a shouting voice, he *makes jokes*, he smokes cigars, he's bad news, *hide*.'

The Lamia slipped underwater in a flurry of bubbles like the Milky Way.

Raymond Potter came out of the car smiling and carried in a leg of wild boar and the ingredients of a *ratatouille*, a crate of red wine, and several bottles of *eau-de-vie Poire William*.

'Brought my own provisions. Show me the stove.'

He cooked. They ate on the terrace, in the evening. Bernard did not switch on the lights in the pool and did not suggest that Raymond might swim. Raymond in fact did not like swimming; he was too fat to wish to be seen, and preferred eating and smoking. Both men drank rather a lot of red wine and then rather a lot of eau-de-vie. The smell of the mountains was laced with the smells of pork crackling and cigar smoke. Raymond peered drunkenly at Bernard's current painting. He pronounced it rather sinister, very striking, a bit weird, not quite usual, funny-coloured, a bit over the top? Looking at Bernard each time for a response and getting none, as Bernard, exhausted and a little drunk, was largely asleep. They went to bed, and Bernard woke in the night to realize he had not shut his bedroom window as he usually did; a shutter was banging. But he was unkissed and solitary; he slid back into unconsciousness.

The next morning Bernard was up first. He made coffee, he cycled to the village and bought croissants, bread and peaches, he laid the table on the terrace and poured heated milk into a blue and white jug. The pool lay flat and still, quietly and incompatibly shining at the quiet sky.

Raymond made rather a noise coming downstairs. This was because his arm was round a young woman with a great deal of hennaed black hair, who wore a garment of that see-through cheesecloth from India which is sold in every southern French market. The garment was calf-length, clinging, with little shoulder-straps and dyed in a rather musty brownish-black, scattered with little round green spots like peas. It could have been a sundress or a nightdress; it was only too easy to see that the woman wore nothing at all underneath. The black triangle of her pubic hair swayed with her hips. Her breasts were large and thrusting, that was the word that sprang to Bernard's mind. The nipples stood out in the cheesecloth.

'This is Melanie,' Raymond said, pulling out a chair for her. She flung back her hair with an actressy gesture of her hands and sat down gracefully, pulling the cheesecloth round her knees and staring down at her ankles. She had long pale hairless legs with very pretty feet. Her toenails were varnished with a pink pearly varnish. She turned them this way and that, admiring them. She wore rather a lot of very pink lipstick and smiled in a satisfied way at her own toes.

'Do you want coffee?' said Bernard to Melanie.

'She doesn't speak English,' said Raymond. He leaned over and made a guzzling, kissing noise in the hollow of her collar-bone. 'Do you, darling?'

He was obviously going to make no attempt to explain her presence. It was not even quite clear that he knew that Bernard had a right to an explanation, or that he had himself any idea where she had come from. He was simply obsessed. His fingers were pulled towards her hair like needles to a magnet: he kept standing up and kissing her breasts, her shoulders, her ears. Bernard watched Raymond's fat tongue explore the coil of Melanie's ear with considerable distaste.

'Will you have coffee?' he said to Melanie in French. He indicated the coffee pot. She bent her head towards it with a quick curving movement, sniffed it, and then hovered briefly over the milk jug.

'This,' she said, indicating the hot milk. 'I will drink this.'

She looked at Bernard with huge black eyes under long lashes.

'I wish you joy,' said Bernard in Cévenol French, 'of your immortal soul.'

'Hey,' said Raymond, 'don't flirt with my girl in foreign languages.'

'I don't flirt,' said Bernard. 'I paint.'

'And we'll be off after breakfast and leave you to your

painting,' said Raymond. 'Won't we, my sweet darling? Melanie wants – Melanie hasn't got – she didn't exactly bring – you understand – all her clothes and things. We're going to go to Cannes and buy some real clothes. Melanie wants to see the film festival and the stars. You won't mind, old friend, you didn't want me in the first place. I don't want to interrupt your *painting. Chacun à sa boue*, as we used to say in the army, I know that much French.'

Melanie held out her pretty fat hands and turned them over and over with considerable satisfaction. They were pinkly pale and also ornamented with pearly nail-varnish. She did not look at Raymond, simply twisted her head about with what could have been pleasure at his little sallies of physical attention, or could have been irritation. She did not speak. She smiled a little, over her milk, like a satisfied cat, displaying two rows of sweet little pearly teeth between her glossy pink lips.

Raymond's packing did not take long. Melanie turned out to have one piece of luggage – a large green leather bag full of rattling coins, by the sound. Raymond saw her into the car like a princess, and came back to say goodbye to his friend.

'Have a good time,' said Bernard. 'Beware of philosophers.'

'Where would I find any philosophers?' asked Raymond, who had done theatre design at art school with Bernard and now designed sets for a successful children's TV programme called *The A-Mazing Maze of Monsters*. 'Philosophers are extinct. I think your wits are turning, old friend, with stomping around on your own. You need a girlfriend.'

'I don't,' said Bernard. 'Have a good holiday.'

'We're going to be married,' said Raymond, looking surprised, as though he himself had not known this until he said it. The face of Melanie swam at the car window, the pearly teeth visible inside the soft lips, the dark eyes staring. 'I must go,' said Raymond. 'Melanie's waiting.'

Left to himself, Bernard settled back into the bliss of solitude. He looked at his latest work and saw that it was good. Encouraged, he looked at his earlier work and saw that that was good, too. All those blues, all those curious questions, all those almost-answers. The only problem was, where to go now. He walked up and down, he remembered the philosopher and laughed. He got out his Keats. He reread the dreadful moment in *Lamia* where the bride vanished away under the coldly malevolent eye of the sage.

> Do not all charms fly
> At the mere touch of cold philosophy?
> There was an awful rainbow once in heaven:
> We know her woof, her texture; she is given
> In the dull catalogue of common things.
> Philosophy will clip an Angel's wings,
> Conquer all mysteries by rule and line,
> Empty the haunted air and gnomed mine –
> Unweave a rainbow, as it erewhile made
> The tender-personed Lamia melt into a shade.

Personally, Bernard said to himself, he had never gone along with Keats about all that stuff. By philosophy Keats seems to mean natural science, and personally he, Bernard, would rather have the optical mysteries of waves and particles in the water and light of the rainbow than any old gnome or fay. He had been at least as interested in the problems of reflection and refraction when he had had the lovely snake in his pool as he had been in its oddity – in its *otherness* – as snakes went. He hoped that no natural scientist would

170

come along and find Melanie's blood group to be that of some sort of herpes, or do an X-ray and see something odd in her spine. She made a very good blowzy sort of a woman, just right for Raymond. He wondered what sort of a woman she would have become for him, and dismissed the problem. He didn't want a woman. He wanted another visual idea. A mystery to be explained by rule and line. He looked around his breakfast table. A rather nondescript orange-brown butterfly was sipping the juice of the rejected peaches. It had a golden eye at the base of its wings and a rather lovely white streak, shaped like a tiny dragon-wing. It stood on the glistening rich yellow peach-flesh and manoeuvred its body to sip the sugary juices and suddenly it was not orange-brown at all, it was a rich, gleaming intense purple. And then it was both at once, orange-gold and purple-veiled, and then it was purple again, and then it folded its wings and the undersides had a purple eye and a soft green streak, and tan, and white edged with charcoal . . .

When he came back with his paintbox it was still turning and sipping. He mixed purple, he mixed orange, he made browns. It was done with a dusting of scales, with refractions of rays. The pigments were discovered and measured, the scales on the wings were noted and *seen*, everything was a mystery, serpents and water and light. He was off again. Exact study would not clip this creature's wings, it would dazzle his eyes with its brightness. Don't go, he begged it, watching and learning, don't go. Purple and orange is a terrible and violent fate. There is months of work in it. Bernard attacked it. He was happy, in one of the ways in which human beings are happy.

BERNARD MALAMUD

REMBRANDT'S
HAT

RUBIN, IN CARELESS white cloth hat, or visorless soft round cap, however one described it, wandered with unexpressed or inexpressive thoughts up the stairs from his studio in the basement of the New York art school where he made his sculpture, to a workshop on the second floor, where he taught. Arkin, the art historian, a hypertensive bachelor of thirty-four – a man often swept by strong feeling, he thought – about a dozen years younger than the sculptor, observed him through his open office door, wearing his cap amid a crowd of art students and teachers in the hall during a change of classes. In his white hat he stands out and apart, the art historian thought. It illumines a lonely inexpressiveness arrived at after years of experience. Though it was not entirely apt he imagined a lean white animal – hind, stag, goat? – staring steadfastly but despondently through trees of a dense wood. Their gazes momentarily interlocked and parted. Rubin hurried to his workshop class.

Arkin was friendly with Rubin though they were not really friends. Not his fault, he felt; the sculptor was a very private person. When they talked, he listened, looking away, as though guarding his impressions. Attentive, apparently, he seemed to be thinking of something else – his sad life no doubt, if saddened eyes, a faded green mistakable for gray, necessarily denote sad life. Sometimes he uttered an opinion, usually a flat statement about the nature of life, or art, never much about himself; and he said absolutely nothing about his work.

'Are you working, Rubin?' Arkin was reduced to.

'Of course I'm working.'

'What are you doing if I may ask?'

'I have a thing going.'

There Arkin let it lie.

Once, in the faculty cafeteria, listening to the art historian discourse on the work of Jackson Pollock, the sculptor's anger had flared.

'The world of art ain't necessarily in your eyes.'

'I have to believe that what I see is there,' Arkin had politely responded.

'Have you ever painted?'

'Painting is my life.'

Rubin, with dignity, reverted to silence. That evening, leaving the building, they tipped hats to each other over small smiles.

In recent years, after his wife had left him and costume and headdress became a mode among students, Rubin had taken to wearing various odd hats from time to time, and this white one was the newest, resembling Nehru's Congress Party cap, but rounded – a cross between a cantor's hat and a bloated yarmulke; or perhaps like a French judge's in Rouault, or working doctor's in a Daumier print. Rubin wore it like a crown. Maybe it kept his head warm under the cold skylight of his large studio.

When the sculptor again passed along the crowded hall on his way down to his studio that day he had first appeared in his white cap, Arkin, who had been reading an article on Giacometti, put it down and went into the hall. He was in an ebullient mood he could not explain to himself, and told Rubin he very much admired his hat.

'I'll tell you why I like it so much. It looks like Rembrandt's hat that he wears in one of the middle-aged self-portraits, the really profound ones. May it bring you the best of luck.'

Rubin, who had for a moment looked as though he was struggling to say something extraordinary, fixed Arkin in a strong stare and hurried downstairs. That ended the incident, though it did not diminish the art historian's pleasure in his observation.

Arkin later remembered that when he had come to the art school via an assistant curator's job in a museum in St Louis, seven years ago, Rubin had been working in wood; he now welded triangular pieces of scrap iron to construct his sculptures. Working at one time with a hatchet, later a modified small meat cleaver, he had reshaped driftwood pieces, out of which he had created some arresting forms. Dr Levis, the director of the art school, had talked the sculptor into giving an exhibition of his altered driftwood objects in one of the downtown galleries. Arkin, in his first term at the school, had gone on the subway to see the show one winter's day. This man is an original, he thought, maybe his work will be, too. Rubin had refused a gallery vernissage, and on the opening day the place was nearly deserted. The sculptor, as though escaping his hacked forms, had retreated into a storage room at the rear of the gallery and stayed there looking at pictures. Arkin, after reflecting whether he ought to, sought him out to say hello, but seeing Rubin seated on a crate with his back to him, examining a folio of somebody's prints, silently shut the door and departed. Although in time two notices of the show appeared, one bad, the other mildly favorable, the sculptor seemed unhappy about having exhibited his work, and after that didn't for years. Nor had there been any sales. Recently, when Arkin had suggested it might be a good idea to show what he was doing with his welded iron triangles, Rubin, after a wildly inexpressive moment, had answered, 'Don't bother playing around with that idea.'

The day after the art historian's remarks in the hall about Rubin's white cap, it disappeared from sight – gone totally; for a while he wore on his head nothing but his heavy reddish hair. And a week or two later, though he could momentarily not believe it, it seemed to Arkin that the sculptor was avoiding him. He guessed the man was no longer using the staircase to the right of his office but was coming up from the basement on the other side of the building, where his corner workshop room was anyway, so he wouldn't have to pass Arkin's open door. When he was certain of this Arkin felt uneasy, then experienced moments of anger.

Have I offended him in some way? he asked himself. If so, what did I say that's so offensive? All I did was remark on the hat in one of Rembrandt's self-portraits and say it looked like the cap he was wearing. How can that be offensive?

He then thought: No offense where none's intended. All I have is good will to him. He's shy and may have been embarrassed in some way – maybe my exuberant voice in the presence of students – if that's so it's no fault of mine. And if that's not it, I don't know what's the matter except his own nature. Maybe he hasn't been feeling well, or it's some momentary mishigas – nowadays there are more ways of insults without meaning to than ever before – so why raise up a sweat over it? I'll wait it out.

But as weeks, then months went by and Rubin continued to shun the art historian – he saw the sculptor only at faculty meetings when Rubin attended them; and once in a while glimpsed him going up or down the left staircase; or sitting in the Fine Arts secretary's office poring over inventory lists of supplies for sculpture – Arkin thought: Maybe the man is having a breakdown. He did not believe it. One day they met in the men's room and Rubin strode out without a word. Arkin felt for the sculptor surges of hatred. He didn't like people who didn't like him. Here I make a sociable, innocent remark to the son of a bitch – at worst it might be called innocuous – and to him it's an insult. I'll give him tit for tat. Two can play.

But when he had calmed down, Arkin continued to wonder and worry over what might have gone wrong. I've always thought I was fairly good in human relationships. Yet he had a worrisome nature and wore a thought ragged if in it lurked a fear the fault was his own. Arkin searched the past. He had always liked the sculptor, even though Rubin offered only his fingertip in friendship; yet Arkin had been friendly, courteous, interested in his work, and respectful of his dignity, almost visibly weighted with unspoken thoughts. Had it, he often wondered, something to do with his mentioning – suggesting – not long ago, the possibility of a new exhibition of his sculpture, to which Rubin had reacted as though his life was threatened?

It was then he recalled he had never told Rubin how he had felt about his hacked-driftwood show – never once commented on it, although he had signed the guest book. Arkin hadn't liked the show, yet he wanted to seek Rubin out to name one or two interesting pieces. But when he had located him in the storage room, intently involved with a folio of prints, lost in hangdog introspection so deeply he had been unwilling, or unable, to greet whoever was standing at his back – Arkin had said to himself, Better let it be. He had ducked out of the gallery. Nor had he mentioned the driftwood exhibition thereafter. Was this kindness cruel?

Still it's not very likely he's been avoiding me so long for that alone, Arkin reflected. If he was disappointed, or irritated, by my not mentioning his driftwood show, he would then and there have stopped talking to me, if he was going to stop. But he didn't. He seemed as friendly as ever, according to his measure, and he isn't a dissembler. And when I afterwards suggested the possibility of a new show he obviously wasn't eager to have – which touched him to torment on the spot – he wasn't at all impatient with me but only started staying out of my sight after the business of his white cap, whatever that meant to him. Maybe it wasn't my mention of the cap itself that's annoyed him. Maybe it's a cumulative thing – three minuses for me? Arkin felt it was probably cumulative; still it seemed that the cap remark had mysteriously wounded Rubin most, because nothing that had happened before had threatened their relationship, such as it was, and it was then at least amicable. Having thought it through to this point, Arkin had to admit he did not know why Rubin acted as strangely as he was now acting.

Off and on, the art historian considered going down to the sculptor's studio and there apologizing to him if he had said something inept, which he certainly hadn't meant to do. He would ask Rubin if he'd mind telling him what bothered him; if it was something *else* he had inadvertently said or done, he would apologize and clear things up. It would be mutually beneficial.

One early spring day he made up his mind to visit Rubin after his seminar that afternoon, but one of his students, a bearded printmaker, had found out it was Arkin's thirty-fifth birthday and presented the art historian with a white ten-gallon Stetson that the student's father, a traveling salesman, had brought back from Waco, Texas.

'Wear it in good health, Mr Arkin,' said the student. 'Now you're one of the good guys.'

Arkin was wearing the hat, going up the stairs to his office accompanied by the student who had given it to him, when they encountered the sculptor, who grimaced in disgust.

Arkin was upset, though he felt at once that the force of this uncalled-for reaction indicated that, indeed, the hat remark had been taken by Rubin as an insult. After the bearded student left Arkin he placed the Stetson on his work-table – it had seemed to him – before going to the men's room; and when he returned the cowboy hat was gone. The art historian searched for it in his office and even hurried back to his seminar room to see whether it could possibly have landed up there, someone having snatched it as a joke. It was not in the seminar room. Arkin thought of rushing down and confronting Rubin nose to nose in his studio, but could not bear the thought. What if he hadn't taken it?

Now both evaded each other. But after a period of rarely meeting they began, ironically, Arkin thought, to encounter one another everywhere – even in the streets, especially near galleries on Madison, or Fifty-seventh, or in SoHo; or on entering or leaving movie houses. Each then hastily crossed the street to skirt the other. In the art school both refused to serve together on committees. One, if he entered the lava-tory and saw the other, stepped outside and remained a dis-tance away till he had left. Each hurried to be first into the basement cafeteria at lunchtime because when one followed the other in and observed him standing on line, or already eating at a table, alone or in the company of colleagues, invariably he left and had his meal elsewhere.

Once, when they came in together they hurriedly depar-ted together. After often losing out to Rubin, who could get to the cafeteria easily from his studio, Arkin began to eat sandwiches in his office. Each had become a greater burden to the other, Arkin felt, than he would have been if only one was doing the shunning. Each was in the other's mind to a degree and extent that bored him. When they met unexpectedly in the building after turning a corner or opening a door, or had come face-to-face on the stairs, one glanced at the other's head to see what, if anything, adorned it; they then hurried away in opposite directions. Arkin as a rule wore no hat unless he had a cold; and Rubin lately affected a railroad engineer's cap. The art historian hated Rubin for hating him and beheld repugnance in Rubin's eyes.

'It's your doing,' he heard himself mutter. 'You brought me to this, it's on your head.'

After that came coldness. Each froze the other out of his life; or froze him in.

One early morning, neither looking where he was going as he rushed into the building to his first class, they bumped into each other in front of the arched art school entrance. Both started shouting. Rubin, his face flushed, called Arkin 'murderer,' and the art historian retaliated by calling the sculptor 'hat thief.' Rubin smiled in scorn, Arkin in pity; they then fled.

Afterwards Arkin felt faint and had to cancel his class. His weakness became nausea, so he went home and lay in bed, nursing a severe occipital headache. For a week he slept badly, felt tremors in his sleep, ate next to nothing. 'What has this bastard done to me?' Later he asked, 'What have I done to myself?' I'm in this against my will, he thought. It had occurred to him that he found it easier to judge paintings than to judge people. A woman had said this to him once but he denied it indignantly. Arkin answered neither question and fought off remorse. Then it went through him again that he ought to apologize, if only because if the other couldn't he could. Yet he feared an apology would cripple his craw.

Half a year later, on his thirty-sixth birthday, Arkin, thinking of his lost cowboy hat and having heard from the Fine

Arts secretary that Rubin was home sitting shiva for his dead mother, was drawn to the sculptor's studio – a jungle of stone and iron figures – to look around for the hat. He found a discarded welder's helmet but nothing he could call a cowboy hat. Arkin spent hours in the large skylighted studio, minutely inspecting the sculptor's work in welded triangular iron pieces, set amid broken stone statuary he had been collecting for years – decorative garden figures placed charmingly among iron flowers seeking daylight. Flowers were what Rubin was mostly into now, on long stalks with small corollas, on short stalks with petaled blooms. Some of the flowers were mosaics of triangles fixing white stones and broken pieces of thick colored glass in jeweled forms. Rubin had in the last several years come from abstract driftwood sculptures to figurative objects – the flowers, and some uncompleted, possibly abandoned, busts of men and women colleagues, including one that vaguely resembled Rubin in a cowboy hat. He had also done a lovely sculpture of a dwarf tree. In the far corner of the studio was a place for his welding torch and gas tanks as well as arc-welding apparatus, crowded by open heavy wooden boxes of iron triangles of assorted size and thickness. The art historian studied each sculpture and after a while thought he understood why talk of a new exhibition had threatened Rubin. There was perhaps one fine piece, the dwarf tree, in the iron jungle. Was this what he was afraid he might confess if he fully expressed himself?

Several days later, while preparing a lecture on Rembrandt's self-portraits, Arkin, examining the slides, observed that the portrait of the painter which he had remembered as the one he had seen in the Rijksmuseum in Amsterdam was probably hanging in Kenwood House in London. And neither hat the painter wore in either gallery, though both were white, was that much like Rubin's cap. The observation startled Arkin. The Amsterdam portrait was of Rembrandt in a white turban he had wound around his head; the London portrait was him in a studio cap or beret worn slightly cocked. Rubin's white thing, on the other hand, looked more like an assistant cook's cap in Sam's Diner than like either of Rembrandt's hats in the large oils, or in the other self-portraits Arkin was showing himself on slides. What those had in common was the unillusioned honesty of his gaze. In his self-created mirror the painter beheld distance, objectivity painted to stare out of his right eye; but the left looked out of bedrock, beyond quality. Yet the expression of each of the portraits seemed magisterially sad; or was this what life was if when Rembrandt painted he did not paint the sadness?

After studying the pictures projected on the small screen in his dark office, Arkin felt he had, in truth, made a referential error, confusing the two hats. Even so, what had Rubin, who no doubt was acquainted with the self-portraits, or may have had a recent look at them – at *what* had he taken offense?

Whether I was right or wrong, so what if his white cap made me think of Rembrandt's hat and I told him so? That's not throwing rocks at his head, so what bothered him? Arkin felt he ought to be able to figure it out. Therefore suppose Rubin was Arkin and Arkin Rubin – Suppose it was me in his hat: 'Here I am, an aging sculptor with only one show, which I never had confidence in and nobody saw. And standing close by, making critical pronouncements one way or another, is this art historian Arkin, a big-nosed, gawky, over-curious gent, friendly but no friend of mine because he doesn't know how to be. That's not his talent. An interest in art we have in common, but not much more. Anyway, Arkin, maybe not because it means anything in particular – who says he knows what he means? – mentions Rembrandt's hat on my head and wishes me good luck in my work. So say he meant well – but it's still more than I can take. In plain words it irritates me. The mention of Rembrandt, considering the quality of my own work, and what I am generally feeling about life, is a fat burden on my soul because it makes me ask myself once too often – why am I going on if this is the kind of sculptor I am going to be for the rest of my life? And since Arkin makes me think the same unhappy thing no matter what he says – or even what he doesn't say, as for instance about my driftwood show – who wants to hear more? From then on I avoid the guy – like forever.'

After staring in the mirror in the men's room, Arkin wandered on every floor of the building, and then wandered down to Rubin's studio. He knocked on the door. No one answered. After a moment he tested the knob; it gave, he thrust his head into the room and called Rubin's name. Night lay on the skylight. The studio was lit with many dusty bulbs but Rubin was not present. The forest of sculptures was. Arkin went among the iron flowers and broken stone garden pieces to see if he had been wrong in his judgment. After a while he felt he hadn't been.

He was staring at the dwarf tree when the door opened and Rubin, wearing his railroad engineer's cap, in astonishment entered.

'It's a beautiful sculpture,' Arkin got out, 'the best in the room I'd say.'

Rubin stared at him in flushed anger, his face lean; he had grown long reddish sideburns. His eyes were for once green rather than gray. His mouth worked nervously but he said nothing.

'Excuse me, Rubin, I came in to tell you I got those hats I mentioned to you some time ago mixed up.'

'Damn right you did.'

'Also for letting things get out of hand for a while.'

'Damn right.'

Rubin, though he tried not to, then began to cry. He wept silently, his shoulders shaking, tears seeping through his coarse fingers on his face. Arkin had taken off.

They stopped avoiding each other and spoke pleasantly when they met, which wasn't often. One day Arkin, when he went into the men's room, saw Rubin regarding himself in the mirror in his white cap, the one that seemed to resemble Rembrandt's hat. He wore it like a crown of failure and hope.

ALBERT CAMUS

JONAS, OR THE ARTIST AT WORK

Translated by Carol Cosman

Cast me into the sea...
For I know that for my sake
This great tempest is upon you.

JONAH I:I2

GILBERT JONAS, ARTIST and painter, believed in his star. Indeed, it was all he believed in, although he felt respect and even a kind of admiration for the religion of others. His own faith, however, had its virtues, since it consisted of admitting, somehow obscurely, that he had done nothing to merit what he had achieved. And when, around his thirty-fifth year, a dozen critics suddenly fought over the glory of discovering his talent, he showed not the slightest surprise. But his serenity, attributed by some to smugness, could on the contrary be entirely explained by a trusting modesty. Jonas gave credit to his star rather than his merits.

He showed rather more surprise when an art dealer offered him a monthly stipend that freed him from all cares. The architect Rateau, who had loved Jonas and his star since their school days, argued with him in vain that this monthly stipend was hardly a decent living, and that the art dealer had nothing to lose. 'All the same,' Jonas said. Rateau, who succeeded in everything he did by sheer hard work, goaded his friend. 'What's this "all the same"? You can negotiate.' This was useless. Deep down, Jonas thanked his star. 'As you like,' he told the art dealer. And he gave up his position in the family publishing house to devote himself entirely to painting. 'What luck!' he said.

In reality he was thinking: 'My luck goes on.' As far back as he could remember, he found this luck at work. He felt a fond gratitude toward his parents, first because they had raised him distractedly, which allowed him the leisure to day-dream, then because they had separated on grounds of adul-tery. At least that was the pretext claimed by his father, who forgot to specify that it was a rather peculiar sort of adultery: he could not stand his wife's good works. She was well nigh a secular saint who saw no malice in making a gift of herself to suffering humanity. But the husband insisted on being master of his wife's virtues. 'I've had enough,' this Othello said, 'of being cuckolded by the poor.'

This misunderstanding was to Jonas's advantage. Having read or heard of several sadistic murderers who were the off-spring of divorce, his parents vied to lavish him with treats and nip in the bud any such distressing development. Less apparent were the effects of the shock, according to them, to the child's consciousness, and so they worried even more, for invisible damage must be deepest. If Jonas announced that he was happy with himself or his day, his parents' usual anxiety verged on panic. Their attentions redoubled and the child then wanted for nothing.

His presumed misfortune finally earned Jonas a devoted brother in the person of his friend Rateau. Rateau's parents often invited his little school friend, pleading his unhappi-ness. Their pitying remarks inspired in their son, a vigorous sportsman, a desire to take under his protection the child whose effortless success he already admired. Admiration and condescension made a good mix in a friendship that Jonas received, like everything else, with encouraging simplicity.

When Jonas had completed his studies – without any

special effort – he again had the luck to join his father's publishing house, finding a position there and, indirectly, his vocation as painter. As the most prestigious publisher in France, Jonas's father was of the opinion that more than ever, and indeed owing to the cultural crisis, the book was the future. 'History shows,' he would say, 'that the less people read the more they buy books.' A trendsetter himself, he only rarely read the manuscripts submitted to him, decided to publish strictly on the basis of the author's personality or the timeliness of his subject (since in this view sex was the only ever-timely subject, the publisher eventually specialized), and was strictly interested in finding novelties and free publicity. Along with the manuscript department, then, Jonas took over a lot of spare time. That was how he came to painting.

For the first time he discovered an unexpected and in-exhaustible passion, soon devoted his days to painting, and – always effortlessly – excelled in that practice. Nothing else seemed to interest him, and it was unlikely that he would marry at a reasonable age, as painting entirely consumed him. For the beings and ordinary circumstances of life he had only a benevolent smile, which exempted him from concerning himself further. It took a motorcycle accident – Rateau was driving too fast, with his friend riding behind – for Jonas, his right hand immobilized in a cast, and feel-ing bored, to become interested in love. Here again he was inclined to see the good effects of his star in this serious accident. Without it, he would not have taken the time to notice Louise Poulin as she deserved.

According to Rateau, moreover, Louise did not deserve to be noticed. Short and stocky himself, he liked only tall women. 'I don't know what you see in that little ant,' he said. Louise was in fact petite, with dark complexion, hair, and eyes, but she had a nice shape and a pretty face. Jonas, tall and solid, felt tenderly toward the ant, especially because she was industrious. Louise's vocation was activity. Such a vocation happily complemented Jonas's taste for inertia, and for its advantages. Louise devoted herself first to literature, at least as long as she believed that publishing interested Jonas. She read everything indiscriminately, and in a matter of weeks became capable of talking about it all. Jonas admired her and decided that he was definitively exempt from reading since Louise kept him sufficiently informed and up-to-date on the basics of contemporary discoveries. 'You mustn't say,' Louise announced, 'that someone is bad or ugly but that he chooses to be bad or ugly.' The distinction was important and might well lead, at the very least, as Rateau pointed out, to the condemnation of the human race. But Louise settled the matter by pointing out that since this truth was supported by both the tabloid press and philosophical reviews, it was therefore universal and beyond dispute. 'As you like,' said Jonas, who immediately forgot this cruel discovery to dream on his star.

Louise deserted literature when she realized that Jonas was only interested in painting. She immediately devoted herself to the plastic arts, ran to museums and exhibitions, and dragged Jonas along, although he could hardly understand the painting of his contemporaries and in his artistic simplicity found it troubling. Yet he rejoiced at being so well informed on everything that concerned his art. It is true that the next day he would forget the name of the painter whose works he had just seen. But Louise was right when she peremptorily reminded him of one of the certainties she had preserved from her literary period, the knowledge that in reality, nothing is ever forgotten. His star certainly protected Jonas, who could in this way guiltlessly accumulate the certainties of memory and the conveniences of forgetting.

But the treasures of devotion Louise lavished upon him sparkled brightest in Jonas's daily life. This good angel spared him the purchases of shoes, clothing, and underwear that for any normal man shorten the days of an already brief life. She resolutely took charge of the thousand inventions of the time-killing machine, from the obscure paperwork involved in social security to endlessly multiplying fiscal arrangements. 'Yes, okay,' Rateau would say, 'but she can't go to the dentist for you.' She did not do that, but she telephoned and made appointments at the best times; she took care of oil changes for the car, hotel rentals for vacations, domestic heating; she bought whatever gifts Jonas wanted to give, chose and sent his flowers, and still found time on certain evenings to come by his place in his absence and make up the bed that he would not need to turn down that night before going to sleep.

With the same spirit, naturally, she got into this bed, then made the appointment at City Hall, led Jonas there two years before his talent was finally recognized, and organized the honeymoon so that they could visit all the museums. Not without first managing to find, in the midst of a housing crisis, a three-room apartment where they settled on their return. She then produced two children in quick succession, a boy and a girl, in accordance with her plan to have a total of three, which she completed shortly after Jonas had left the publishing house to devote himself to painting.

Once she had given birth, however, Louise devoted herself entirely to her child, then to her children. She still tried to help her husband, but she had no time. To be sure, she regretted neglecting Jonas, but her decisive character prevented her from lingering on these regrets. 'Oh well,' she often said, 'to each his own workbench.' An expression that seemed to delight Jonas, for like all the artists of his time, he wanted to be considered an artisan. So the artisan was a little neglected and had to buy his shoes himself. However, apart from the fact that this was in the nature of things, Jonas was tempted to congratulate himself. Certainly he had to make the effort to visit the shops, but this effort was rewarded by one of those hours of solitude that only enhances a couple's happiness.

The problem of usable space, however, prevailed over other household problems, for time and space were shrinking around them at the same rate. The birth of the children, Jonas's new profession, their cramped digs, and the modest stipend that ruled out the purchase of a larger apartment left only a narrow field for Louise and Jonas's respective activities. The apartment was on the second floor of what had been, in the eighteenth century, a private townhouse in an old quarter of the capital. Many artists lived in this part of the city, faithful to the principle that in art, the search for the new must be done within a framework of the old. Jonas, who shared this conviction, was delighted to be living in this quarter.

For old his apartment certainly was. But some very modern arrangements had given it an original character that consisted chiefly of offering its residents a great volume of air while occupying only a limited surface. The rooms, unusually high and graced with magnificent windows, had surely been intended – to judge by their majestic proportions – for grand receptions and ceremonial dress. But the necessities of urban crowding and real-estate profits had forced successive landlords to divide these vast rooms with partitions and so to multiply the stalls, which they rented at top dollar to their herd of tenants. They set particular value on what they called 'the important square footage of air.' The advantage was undeniable. This could only be attributed to the impossibility of partitioning the rooms' vertical space as well. Even so, the landlords did not hesitate to make the necessary sacrifices to offer some additional refuge to the upcoming generation, especially to the married and multiplying of that era. Besides, the square footage of air offered not only advantages; it offered the inconvenience of making the rooms difficult to heat in winter, and this unfortunately obliged the landlords to increase the heating bill. In summer, due to the vast glass surfaces, the apartment was literally violated by light: there were no blinds. The landlords had neglected to install them, no doubt discouraged by the height of the windows and the cost of carpentry. After all, thick curtains could perform the same function, and posed no problem as to cost since they were charged to the tenants. The landlords certainly did not refuse to help and provided curtains from their own stores at unbeatable prices. Indeed, philanthropic real estate was their hobby. In their ordinary lives these new princes sold percale and velvet.

Jonas was ecstatic at the apartment's advantages and had no trouble accepting its drawbacks. 'As you like,' he said to the landlord about the heating bill. As for the curtains, he agreed with Louise that it was enough to provide them for the only bedroom and leave the other windows bare. 'We have nothing to hide,' said that pure heart. Jonas had been especially charmed by the largest room, whose ceiling was so high that any lighting installation was out of the question. This room was entered directly from the outside, and connected by a narrow hallway to the two much smaller ones lined up behind it. At the end of the apartment was the kitchen, next to the WC, and a cubbyhole graced with the name of shower room. It could indeed pass as such, providing they installed the fixture vertically and were willing to stand absolutely still to receive its beneficial spray.

The truly extraordinary height of the ceilings and the

cramped nature of the rooms made this apartment an odd assemblage of almost entirely glassed-in parallelepipeds, all doors and windows, where furniture could find no supporting wall and human beings, lost in the white and violent light, seemed to float like bottled imps in a vertical aquarium. Furthermore, all the windows looked out onto the courtyard and – from scarcely any distance – onto other windows of the same style, behind which could be glimpsed the stately outline of new windows opening onto a second courtyard. 'It's a hall of mirrors,' said Jonas, thrilled. On Rateau's advice, they decided to place the marriage bed in one of the small rooms, the other being necessary to shelter the child that was already on its way. The large room served as Jonas's studio during the day, as living room in the evening and at mealtimes. Besides, they could eat in the kitchen if necessary, provided that Jonas or Louise was willing to stand. Rateau, for his part, had installed any number of ingenious devices. With sliding doors, retractable shelves, and folding tables, he had managed to compensate for the scarcity of furniture by accentuating this original apartment's resemblance to a set of Chinese boxes.

But when the rooms were full of pictures and children, they needed to think quickly about a new arrangement. Before the birth of their third child, Jonas worked in the large room, Louise knitted in their bedroom, while the two children occupied the last room, romping around in there, then tumbling freely through the rest of the apartment. So they decided to settle the newborn in a corner of the studio, which Jonas enclosed by making a screen of his canvases. This offered the advantage of having the baby within earshot so they could respond more readily to his cries. Besides, Jonas need never be disturbed, Louise told him. She would come into the studio before the baby cried, although with a thousand precautions and always on tiptoe. Jonas, touched by such discretion, one day assured Louise that he was not so sensitive, and that he could work quite well to the sound of her steps. Louise replied that she was also trying not to waken the baby. Full of admiration for her tender maternal instinct, Jonas laughed good-naturedly at his mistake. As a result, he dared not admit that Louise's prudent interventions were more disruptive than if she were to burst in openly. First because they lasted longer, then because they were done in pantomime: Louise, with her arms opened wide, her torso leaning back a little and her leg thrown up high in front of her, could hardly go unnoticed. This method even went counter to her avowed intentions, since at any moment Louise was liable to snag one of the canvases that filled the studio. Then the noise woke the baby, who expressed his discontent according to his own powerful means. The father, enchanted by his son's pulmonary capacity, would run to comfort him, then be immediately relieved by his wife. Jonas once again set up his canvases, then, brushes in hand, listened, charmed, to his son's insistent and sovereign voice.

This was about the time that Jonas's success earned him many friends. These friends materialized on the telephone or in unannounced visits. The telephone, which after due consideration had been placed in the studio, rang often, always to the detriment of the sleeping baby, who mingled his cries with the gadget's imperative ring. If Louise happened to be looking after the other children, she was forced to come running with one of them in tow, but most of the time she found Jonas holding the baby with one hand and with the other his paintbrushes and the telephone receiver, which would be transmitting a friendly invitation to lunch. Jonas was amazed that anyone would really want to have lunch with him, as his conversation was banal, but to keep his workday unbroken he preferred evening outings. Most of the time, unfortunately, the friend was free only for lunch, and for lunch that very day; he was reserving it for dear Jonas. Dear Jonas would accept: 'As you like!' hang up and say: 'What a good fellow!' and pass the baby to Louise. He would take up his work again, soon interrupted by lunch or dinner. Now he had to move his canvases out of the way, unfold the modified table, and sit down with the children. During the meal, Jonas would keep one eye on the painting in progress, and in the beginning at least, he found his children a little slow in chewing and swallowing, so that every meal seemed excessively drawn out. But he read in the paper that it was important to eat slowly in order to digest properly, and from then on found each meal an occasion to enjoy himself at length.

At other times his new friends would visit him. Rateau himself came only after dinner. He was at his office during the day, and besides, he knew that painters work during daylight. But Jonas's new friends almost all belonged to the species of artists or critics. Some had painted, others were going to paint, and the critics were busy with what had been or would be painted. All of them, of course, held artistic efforts in high esteem, and complained of the organization of the modern world that makes it so difficult to pursue those very efforts and the practice of meditation so indispensable to the artist. They complained through long afternoons, begging Jonas to continue working as if they were not there, and to treat them freely, after all, they weren't philistines and knew what an artist's time was worth. Jonas, content to have made friends capable of allowing him to work in their presence, would return to his painting but continue to answer their questions or laugh at their anecdotes.

Such simplicity put his friends more and more at ease.

Their good humor was so authentic that they forgot it was mealtime. The children, however, had better memories. They would rush about, mingle with the guests, shout, be taken in hand by the visitors, and bounced from knee to knee. At last the light would fade on the square of sky outlined by the courtyard, and Jonas would set down his paintbrushes. Naturally they had to invite the friends to take potluck and to go on talking late into the night, about art of course, but especially about painters without talent, plagiarists, or self-promoters, who were not there. Jonas himself liked to rise early to take advantage of the first hours of daylight. He knew that this would be difficult, that breakfast would not be ready on time, and that he himself would be tired. But he was also delighted to learn so many things in one evening that could not fail to be advantageous to him, in some invisible way, in his art. 'In art, as in nature, nothing is lost,' he would say. 'Because of the star.'

Sometimes the friends were joined by disciples: Jonas was now attracting a school. At first he had been surprised, not seeing what anyone could learn from him, since he still had everything to discover himself. The artist in him was groping in the dark; how could he teach the true paths? But he quickly understood that a disciple was not necessarily someone who aspired to learn something. More often, on the contrary, a person became a disciple for the disinterested pleasure of teaching his master. After that, Jonas could accept this surplus in honors with humility. The disciples explained to Jonas at length what he had painted, and why. Jonas thus discovered in his work many intentions that rather surprised him, and a host of things he had not put there. He thought he was poor and, thanks to his students, suddenly found he was rich. Sometimes, faced with such hitherto unknown riches, Jonas would feel a surge of pride. 'It's true, though,' he would say to himself. 'That face in the background really does stand out. I don't honestly understand what they mean by indirect humanization. Yet I've gone rather far with that technique.' But very soon he would shift this uncomfortable mastery to his star. 'It's the star,' he would say to himself, 'that's going far. As for me, I'm staying close to Louise and the children.'

The disciples, moreover, had another advantage: they forced Jonas to be stricter with himself. They ranked him so high in their conversation, particularly with regard to his conscience and his energy for work, that from now on no weakness was permissible. So he lost his old habit of nibbling on a piece of sugar or chocolate when he had finished a difficult passage, before getting back to work. Had he been alone, he might have secretly surrendered to this weakness. But he was aided in his moral progress by the nearly constant presence of his disciples and friends, with whom he would have been embarrassed to nibble some chocolate, and anyway, he could hardly interrupt the interesting conversation for such a trivial habit.

In addition, his disciples demanded that he remain faithful to his aesthetic. Jonas, who struggled long and hard to receive a moment of fleeting clarity now and then in which reality would suddenly appear in a fresh light, had only a vague idea of his own aesthetic. His disciples, on the other hand, had many contradictory and categorical ideas about it; and they were not joking. Jonas would sometimes have liked to invoke caprice, the artist's humble friend. But his disciples' frowns at certain canvases that departed from their idea forced him to reflect a little more on his art, which was all to the good.

Finally, the disciples helped Jonas in another way by obliging him to offer his opinion on their own production.

Indeed, not a day passed without someone bringing him some barely sketched-in canvas that its author would place between Jonas and his painting in progress, in order to take advantage of the best light. An opinion was required. Until this period, Jonas was always secretly ashamed of his utter inability to judge a work of art. Exception was made for a handful of paintings that transported him, and for obviously crude scribblings, all of which seemed to him equally interesting and indifferent. Consequently, he was forced to provide himself with an arsenal of judgments, and varied ones at that, because his disciples, like all the artists of the capital, had a certain talent, and when they were around, it was up to him to draw adequate distinctions to satisfy each of them. This happy obligation required him, then, to forge a vocabulary and opinions on his art. Yet his natural kindness was not soured by this effort. He quickly realized that his disciples were not asking him for criticism, for which they had no use, but only encouragement and, if possible, praise. Only the praise had to be different for each. Jonas was no longer content with being his usual amiable self. He was amiable with ingenuity.

So time went by as Jonas painted amidst friends and students settled on chairs, now arranged in concentric circles around the easel. Often neighbors would appear at the windows across the way and this would add to his public. He would discuss, exchange views, examine the paintings submitted to him, smile at Louise's comings and goings, soothe the children, and warmly answer telephone calls, without ever setting down his paintbrushes, with which he would add a touch now and then to the painting he had begun. In a sense, his life was very full, all his hours were occupied, and he gave thanks to the fate that spared him from boredom. In another sense, it took many brushstrokes to fill a painting, and he sometimes thought the good thing about boredom was that it could be avoided by unremitting work. Jonas's production, though, slowed down as his friends became more interesting. Even in the rare hours when he was by himself, he felt too tired to redouble his efforts. And in these hours he could only dream of a new arrangement that would reconcile the pleasures of friendship with the advantages of boredom.

He broached the subject with Louise, who was already worrying about the two older children outgrowing their cramped room. She proposed setting them up in the large room by screening off their beds, and moving the baby into the small room where the telephone would not wake him up. Since the baby took up no space to speak of, Jonas could turn the small room into his studio. The large one would then be used for daytime visitors, and Jonas could come and go, joining his friends or working, certain that his need for isolation would be understood. Moreover, the need to put the older children to bed would allow them to cut the evenings short. 'Wonderful,' said Jonas, after some reflection. 'And then,' said Louise, 'if your friends leave early, we'll see a little more of each other . . .' Jonas looked at her. A shadow of sadness passed over Louise's face. Touched, he held her and kissed her tenderly. She surrendered to him, and for a moment they were as happy as they had been at the beginning of their marriage. But she pulled herself away: perhaps the room was too small for Jonas. Louise grabbed a tape measure and they discovered that because of the crowding created by his canvases and his students', which were by far the most numerous, he was working anyway in a space that was scarcely bigger than the new one would be. Jonas began to move at once.

As luck would have it, the less he worked the greater his

reputation grew. Every exhibition was anticipated and cele-brated in advance. True, a small number of critics, among them two of the usual visitors to the studio, tempered the warmth of their reviews with a few reservations. But the dis-ciples' indignation more than compensated for this small misfortune. To be sure, the disciples would assert, they prized the canvases from the first period above all, but the current explorations were laying the groundwork for a real revolution. Jonas reproached himself for the slight irritation he felt whenever they exalted his early works and thanked them effusively. Only Rateau grumbled: 'Weird characters ... They want you to stand still, like a statue ... you're not allowed to live!' But Jonas defended his disciples: 'You can't understand,' he said to Rateau, 'you ... you like everything I do.' Rateau laughed: 'Damn it. It's not your pictures I like. It's your painting.'

The pictures continued to please in any event, and after one enthusiastically received exhibition, the dealer voluntar-ily proposed to increase the monthly stipend. Jonas accepted, protesting his gratitude. 'Listening to you,' said the dealer, 'anyone would think you actually care about money.' Such good nature won the painter's heart. However, when he asked the dealer for permission to donate a canvas to be sold for charity, the man was anxious to know if it was a charity 'that would pay.' Jonas did not know. The dealer then pro-posed that they respect the terms of the contract, which accorded him exclusive sales rights. 'A contract is a contract,' he said. In theirs, no clause was found to cover charity. 'As you like,' said the painter.

The new household arrangement gave Jonas nothing but satisfaction. He could, in fact, isolate himself often enough to answer the numerous letters he now received, which he was too courteous to leave unanswered. Some concerned

Jonas's art, others, the majority, concerned the correspond-ent, who wanted either to be encouraged in his vocation as painter or to ask for advice or financial aid. And the more Jonas's name appeared in the papers, the more he was soli-cited, like everyone else, to intervene and denounce grievous injustices. Jonas would answer, write about art, thank people, give his advice, forgo a new tie to send a little aid, and sign the high-minded protests submitted to him. 'You're in politics now? Leave that to the writers and to unattractive spinsters,' said Rateau. No, he signed only protests that claimed to be nonpartisan. But everyone claimed this worthy indepen-dence. For weeks at a time Jonas would drag around, his pockets sagging with correspondence constantly neglected and renewed. He would answer the most urgent, which gen-erally came from strangers, and kept for a better moment those that demanded a lengthier reply, namely letters from friends. So many obligations in any case prohibited idle strolling and a light heart. He always felt behind and always guilty, even when he was working, which still happened now and then.

Louise was more and more taken up with the children, and exhausted herself doing everything that in other circum-stances he had been able to do in the house. This made Jonas unhappy. After all, he was working for his own pleasure, whereas she was getting the worst of it. He noticed it clearly when she was out shopping. 'The telephone!' the eldest would call, and Jonas would set down his picture only to return to it, his heart at peace, with an additional invitation. 'Here to read the meter!' the gas man would yell at the door a child had opened for him. 'Coming! Coming!' When Jonas would leave the telephone or the door, a friend, a disciple, perhaps both, would follow him into the small room to finish the conversation they had begun. Gradually, they all became familiar with the hallway, where they congregated, gossiping among themselves, calling for Jonas to take sides from a distance, even bursting briefly into the small room. 'Here, at least,' those who entered exclaimed, 'we can see you a little, at leisure.' Jonas softened: 'It's true,' he said. 'We hardly see each other anymore.' He also felt that he was disappointing those he did not see, and this saddened him. Often these were friends he would have preferred to meet. But he had no time, he could not be everywhere at once.

His reputation suffered. 'He's gotten proud,' people said, 'since his success. He doesn't see anyone anymore.' Or: 'He cares only for himself.' No, he loved his painting, and Louise, his children, Rateau, a few others as well, and he had sympathy for everyone. But life is short, time goes by quickly, and his own energy had its limits. It was difficult to paint the world and men and to live with them at the same time. On the other hand, he could neither complain nor explain his difficulties. Because then someone would slap him on the back: 'Lucky bastard! That's the price of fame!'

So the mail accumulated, the disciples would not allow any relaxation, and now society people flocked to him. Jonas thought they were interested in painting when, like everyone else, they might have been equally fascinated by the English royal family or gourmet restaurants. In truth, they were society women in particular, but their manners had great simplicity. They did not buy any pictures themselves and brought their friends to the artist only in the hope, which was often disappointed, that the friends would buy instead. On the other hand, these ladies helped Louise, especially by serving tea to the visitors. The cups passed from hand to hand, traveled down the hallway from the kitchen to the large room, coming round again to rest in the small studio where Jonas, amidst a handful of friends and visitors who filled the room, continued to paint until he had to set down his paintbrushes to accept, with gratitude, the cup that a fascinating lady had filled specially for him.

He would drink his tea, look at the sketch that a disciple had just placed on his easel, laugh with his friends, interrupt himself to ask one of them to be so good as to post the packet of letters he had written the night before, set his second child back on her feet, pose for a photograph, and then: 'Jonas, the telephone!' He would brandish his cup, push his way apologetically through the crowd in the hall, return, paint in a corner of the picture, stop to answer the fascinating lady that yes, certainly he would do her portrait, and return to the easel. He was working, but: 'Jonas, a signature!' – 'What is it now?' he said, 'The mailman?' – 'No, the convicts in Kashmir.' – 'I'm coming, I'm coming!' Then he would run to the door to receive a young friend of humanity and his letter of protest, anxiously inquire if it was a political matter, sign after receiving complete assurance along with remonstrations on the duties of his privileged life as an artist, and reappear so that someone might introduce him to a new boxing champion or the greatest playwright from a foreign country, though he could not make out the name. The playwright would stand there for five minutes, expressing with emotional eye contact what his ignorance of French prevented him from saying more clearly, while Jonas would nod his head with sincere sympathy. Happily, this insoluble situation would be interrupted by the sudden entrance of the latest charmer who wanted to be introduced to the great painter. Jonas, so delighted to make his acquaintance, would say that was him, tap the letters in his pocket, grab his paintbrushes, and prepare to finish another passage, but would first have to thank someone for the pair of setters she had just brought him, park them in the bedroom, return to accept his benefactress's invitation to lunch, run out again at Louise's cries, venture to say that it was certainly possible the setters had not been trained to live in an apartment, and lead them to the shower room where they set up such a constant howling that in the end no one paid any attention. Now and then, above the visitors' heads, Jonas glimpsed the look in Louise's eyes and thought she seemed sad. The end of the day would arrive at last, the visitors would take their leave, others would linger in the large room and look on fondly as Louise put the children to bed, with the kind help of an elegant lady in a hat who was terribly sorry to have to return at once to her two-story town house, where life was so much less cozy and intimate than at the Jonas household.

One Saturday afternoon Rateau came to bring Louise an ingenious clothes dryer that could be attached to the kitchen ceiling. He found the apartment full to bursting and in the small room, surrounded by art lovers, Jonas was painting the lady of the dogs, while being painted himself by an official artist. This person, according to Louise, was executing a state commission. 'It will be called *The Artist at Work.*' Rateau withdrew to a corner of the room to watch his friend, visibly absorbed by his effort. One of the art lovers, who had never seen Rateau, leaned toward him: 'Hey,' he said, 'he looks good!' Rateau did not reply. 'You paint?' the other man continued. 'Me too. Ah well, believe me, he's on the way out.'

'Already?' Rateau asked.

'Yes. It's success. No one can resist success. He's finished.'

'He's on the way out or he's finished?'

'An artist who's on the way out is finished. Look, he has nothing to paint anymore. Now they're painting him and they'll hang him on the wall.'

Later, in the middle of the night, in the bedroom, Louise, Rateau, and Jonas, who stood while the other two sat on a corner of the bed, were quiet. The children were sleeping, the dogs were at a kennel in the country, Louise had just washed up all the dishes, which Jonas and Rateau had dried, and their fatigue felt good.

'Hire a housekeeper,' Rateau had said, looking at the pile of dishes. But Louise said sadly:

'Where would we put her?'

So they were quiet.

'Are you happy?' Rateau suddenly asked. Jonas smiled, but he looked weary.

'Yes. Everyone is kind to me.'

'No,' said Rateau. 'Watch out. They're not all good.'

'Who?'

'Your painter friends, for instance.'

'I know,' said Jonas. 'But many artists are like that. They're not sure they exist, even the greatest. So they look for proof, they judge, they condemn. It bolsters them, it's the beginning of existence. They're so alone!'

Rateau shook his head.

'Believe me,' Jonas said, 'I know them. You have to love them.'

'And what about you,' said Rateau, 'do you exist, then? You never speak ill of anyone.'

Jonas began to laugh:

'Oh, I often think ill of them. Only then I forget.' He grew serious:

'No, I'm not certain I exist. But one day I will, I'm sure of that.'

Rateau asked Louise what she thought. She emerged from her fatigue to say that Jonas was right: their visitors' opinions were not important. Only Jonas's work mattered. And she felt that the baby was in his way. Besides, he was growing, they needed to buy a little bed, and that would take up space.

What could be done until they found a larger apartment? Jonas looked around the bedroom. Of course it was not ideal; the bed was very big. But the room was empty all day. He said this to Louise, who thought for a moment. In this room at least Jonas would not be disturbed; surely visitors wouldn't dare stretch out on their bed. 'What do you think?' Louise asked Rateau. He looked at Jonas. Jonas was contemplating the windows across the way. Then he raised his eyes toward the starless sky and went to draw the curtains. When he returned, he smiled at Rateau and sat down beside him on the bed without saying anything. Louise, clearly exhausted, declared that she was going to take her shower. When the two friends were alone, Jonas felt Rateau's shoulder touch his. He did not look at him but said:

'I love to paint. I would like to paint all my life, day and night. Isn't that lucky?'

Rateau looked at him fondly:

'Yes,' he said, 'it's lucky.'

The children were growing up and Jonas was happy to see them cheerful and vigorous. They were now in school and returned at four o'clock. Jonas still had them on Saturday afternoons, Thursdays, and also whole days during the long and frequent vacations. They were not yet big enough to play quietly, but were sturdy enough to fill the apartment with their squabbles and their laughter. They needed to be calmed, warned, sometimes threatened with a slap. There was also underwear to keep clean, buttons to sew on; Louise could no longer manage alone. Since they couldn't have a live-in housekeeper, or even bring such a person into the close intimacy of their living quarters, Jonas suggested appealing for help to Louise's sister, Rose, who had been left a widow with a grown daughter.

'Yes,' said Louise, 'with Rose, we won't be inconvenienced. We can tell her to leave when we like.'

Jonas was pleased with this solution, which would relieve both Louise and his own conscience, as he was embarrassed by his wife's fatigue. The relief was even greater since the sister often brought her daughter along for reinforcement. The two of them were as good-hearted as could be: their decent natures radiated virtue and selflessness. They did whatever they could to come to the aid of the household, and never checked the clock. They were encouraged in this task by the tedium of their solitary lives and their pleasure in the ease they found at Louise's. As foreseen, indeed, no one was inconvenienced, and from the first day the two relatives felt at home. The large room became a common room, at once dining room, laundry room, and nursery. The small room, where the youngest child slept, served as a storeroom for canvases and a camp bed where Rose sometimes slept when she came without her daughter.

Jonas occupied the master bedroom and worked in the space that separated the bed from the window. He merely had to wait for the room to be made up in the morning, after the children's room was done. Then, no one would come to disturb him except to look for bed linen or towels, for the only armoire in the house was in this room. As for the visitors, although fewer in number, they already had their habits and, contrary to Louise's hope, did not hesitate to stretch out on the double bed, the better to chat with Jonas. The children would also come in to greet their father, saying, 'Show us the picture.' Jonas would show them the picture he was painting and kiss them fondly. Sending them off again, he felt that they took up all the space in his heart, fully, unconditionally. Deprived of them, he would find nothing but emptiness and solitude. He loved them as much as his painting because they alone in all the world were as alive as it was.

Yet Jonas was working less, without quite knowing why. He had always followed his routine, but now he had difficulty painting, even in moments of solitude. He would spend these moments looking at the sky. He had always been distracted and absorbed, but now he became a dreamer. He would think about painting, about his vocation, instead of painting. 'I love to paint,' he still said to himself, and the hand holding the paintbrush would hang at his side as he listened to a distant radio.

At the same time his reputation waned. People brought him articles that contained reservations, some that were plainly negative, and some that were so nasty his heart ached. But he told himself that there was also something to be gained from such attacks, which would incite him to work better. Those who continued to come treated him with less deference, like an old friend one needn't coddle. When he wanted to return to his work, they would say, 'Come on, you've got plenty of time!' Jonas felt that in a certain sense they were already assimilating him to their own failure. But in another sense this new solidarity was in some way beneficial. Rateau shrugged his shoulders: 'You're such a fool. They don't really love you.'

'They still love me a little,' Jonas replied. 'A little love is a great thing. It doesn't matter how you get it!'

He continued to talk this way, writing letters and painting as best he could. Now and then he really painted, especially on Sunday afternoons when the children went out with Louise and Rose. On those evenings he rejoiced at having made a little progress on the unfinished picture. During this period he was painting skies.

On the day the dealer told him that, much to his regret, a clear decline in sales obliged him to reduce the monthly stipend, Jonas agreed but Louise expressed some anxiety. It was the month of September, the children needed clothes for the new school year. She set to work with her customary courage, and was soon overwhelmed. Rose, who could mend and sew on buttons, was not really a seamstress. But her husband's cousin was; she came to help Louise. From time to time she would settle in Jonas's room, in a corner chair, where this silent lady kept very still. So still was she that Louise suggested Jonas do a painting: *Woman at Work*. 'Good idea,' said Jonas. He tried, ruined two canvases, then went back to a sky he had begun. The following day he walked back and forth in the apartment and meditated instead of painting. A disciple, all worked up, came to show him a long article he would not otherwise have read, in which he learned that his painting was at once overrated and outdated; the dealer telephoned again to express his concern at the decline in sales. Yet Jonas continued to dream and meditate. He told the disciple that there was some truth in the article, but that he, Jonas, could still count on many years of work. To the dealer he replied that he understood his concern, but did not share it. He had a great work to do, something truly new; everything was going to begin again. As he talked he felt that what he said was true, and that his star was still there. All he needed was a good household arrangement.

On the days that followed he first tried to work in the hall, the day after that in the shower room under electric light, the next day in the kitchen. But for the first time he was bothered by the people he encountered everywhere, those he hardly knew and his own family, whom he loved. He stopped working for a while and meditated. He would have painted a seasonal subject if the weather were better. Unfortunately,

winter was about to begin, it would be difficult to do a land-
scape before spring. He tried, however, and gave up: the
cold chilled him to the bone. He lived several days with
his canvases, most often sitting beside them, or standing
motionless in front of the window. He was not painting any-
more. Then he started going out in the morning. He would
devise a project to sketch a detail, a tree, a crooked house, a
profile glimpsed in passing. By the end of the day, he had
done nothing. The slightest temptation – the newspapers, a
chance meeting, the shop windows, the warmth of a café –
held him spellbound. By evening he had no good excuse to
assuage his lingering bad conscience. He was going to paint,
that was certain, and paint better, after this period of appa-
rent emptiness. The work was going on inside, that's all, the
star would emerge again, washed clean and sparkling, from
this dark fog. Meanwhile, he haunted the cafés. He had
discovered that alcohol gave him the same exaltation as
those days of good work when he used to think of his paint-
ing with that tenderness and warmth he had never felt for
anything but his children. With the second cognac he re-
discovered the poignant emotion that made him at once the
world's master and its servant. Simply he enjoyed it in a
vacuum, his hands idle, without putting it into a work. Still,
this was where he came closest to the joy he lived for, and he
now spent long hours sitting, dreaming in smoke-filled,
noisy places.

Yet he avoided the haunts and the neighborhoods fre-
quented by artists. When he met an acquaintance who spoke
to him about his painting he was seized with panic. He
wanted to flee, that was obvious, and he fled. He knew what
people were saying behind his back: 'He thinks he's Rem-
brandt,' and his discomfort grew. He did not smile anymore,
and his old friends drew an odd but inevitable conclusion

from this: 'If he doesn't smile anymore, it's because he's so pleased with himself.' Knowing this, he became more and more evasive and skittish. He had only to enter a café and feel that someone there recognized him, and everything would go black inside him. For a moment he would stand stock still, filled with helplessness and a strange sorrow, his closed face concealing his unease, as well as his avid and abiding need for friendship. He would think of Rateau's friendly gaze, and he would leave abruptly. 'Talk about a sad sack!' someone said one day, right next to him, as he was leaving.

He now visited only the outlying neighborhoods where no one knew him. There he could talk and smile, his benevolence was returned, no one asked anything of him. He made a few undemanding friends. He particularly liked the company of a waiter at a train station buffet where he often went. This waiter had asked him what he did for a living. 'Painter,' Jonas had replied. 'Artist painter or house painter?' – 'Artist.' – 'Ah well!' the man had said, 'that's hard.' And they never discussed the subject again. Yes it was hard, but Jonas was going to manage it once he had figured out how to organize his work.

Drinking day after day brought other chance encounters: women helped him. He could talk to them, before or after lovemaking, and above all boast a little, for they would understand him even if they were not convinced. Sometimes he felt his old strength returning. One day when he had been encouraged by one of his lady friends, he made a firm decision. He went home and tried to work again in the bedroom – the seamstress wasn't there. But after an hour he stowed his canvas, smiled at Louise without seeing her, and went out. He drank the entire day and spent the night at his friend's, without really feeling any desire for her. In the morning a living pain with its ravaged face received him in the person of Louise. She wanted to know if he had slept with this woman. And for the first time he saw on Louise's face that despair caused by surprise and an excess of pain, and it broke his heart. He discovered then that he had not thought about her all this time, and he was ashamed. He begged her forgiveness, it was over, tomorrow everything would begin again as before. Louise could not speak and turned away to hide her tears.

The next day Jonas went out very early. It was raining. When he came home, wet as a dog, he was loaded down with wooden boards. At his apartment two old friends, come for a visit, were drinking coffee in the large room. 'Jonas is changing his technique. He is going to paint on wood!' they said. Jonas smiled: 'It's not that. But I am beginning something new.' He reached the little hallway that led to the shower room, the toilets, and the kitchen. In the right angle where the halls joined, he stopped and considered at length the high walls that rose to the dark ceiling. He needed a stepladder, and went downstairs to borrow one from the concierge.

When he climbed back upstairs there were a few more people at his apartment, and he had to struggle against the affection of his visitors, delighted to find him in again, and against his family's questions, in order to reach the end of the hall. His wife was just coming out of the kitchen. Jonas, setting down his stepladder, hugged her close. Louise was looking at him: 'I beg you,' she said, 'don't do it again.'

'No, no,' said Jonas. 'I'm going to paint. I must paint.' But he seemed to be talking to himself, his gaze was elsewhere. He set to work. Halfway up the walls he built a floor to form a kind of narrow loft, both high and deep. By the end of the afternoon, everything was finished. With the help of the stepladder, Jonas hung on to the floor of the loft and, to test the solidity of his work, did a few pull-ups. Then he mingled with the others and everyone was delighted to find him so friendly again. That evening, when the house was relatively empty, Jonas took an oil lamp, a chair, a stool, and a frame. He took everything up to the loft before the bewildered gaze of three women and the children. 'There,' he said from the height of his perch. 'Now I'll work without bothering anyone.' Louise asked if he was sure about this. 'Yes, of course,' he said, 'I don't need much space. I'll be freer, there were great painters who painted by candlelight, and ...' 'Is the floor solid?' It was. 'Don't worry,' said Jonas, 'it's a very good solution.' And he came down again.

The next day, as early as possible, he climbed up to the loft, sat down, placed the frame on the stool against the wall, and waited without lighting the lamp. The only noises he heard clearly were coming from the kitchen or the toilet. Other sounds seemed distant, and the visits, the ringing of the doorbell or the telephone, the comings and goings, the conversations reached him half-muffled, as if they were coming from the street or from the other courtyard. Besides, when the whole apartment was flooded with a harsh light, the darkness here was restful. From time to time a friend would come and camp beneath the loft. 'What are you doing up there, Jonas?' – 'I'm working.' – 'Without light?' – 'Yes, for the time being.' He was not painting, but he was meditating. In the darkness and this half silence which, compared to his previous experience, seemed to him the silence of the desert or the grave, he was listening to his own heart. The sounds that reached the loft did not seem to concern him now, even if they were addressed to him. He was like those men who die at home alone in their sleep, and when morning comes the telephone rings and keeps ringing, urgent and insistent, in the deserted house, over a corpse forever deaf.

But he was alive, he was listening to this silence within himself, he was waiting for his star, still hidden but ready to rise again, to emerge at last, unchanged, above the disorder of these empty days. 'Shine, shine,' he would say. 'Don't deprive me of your light.' It would shine again, he was sure of it. But he still needed more time to meditate, since at last he had the chance to be alone without being separated from his family. He needed to discover what he had not yet clearly understood, although he had always known it, and had always painted as if he knew it. He had to grasp at long last that secret which was not merely the secret of art, he could see. That is why he did not light the lamp.

Each day now Jonas climbed back up to his loft. The visitors were fewer because Louise was preoccupied and rarely engaged in conversation. Jonas would come down for meals and climb back to his perch. There he sat still in the dark all day. At night, he rejoined his wife, who was already asleep. At the end of a few days, he asked Louise to please give him his lunch, which she did with a care that touched Jonas deeply. So as not to bother her on other occasions, he suggested she prepare some provisions that he could store in the loft. As time went by, he no longer came back down during the day. But he hardly touched his provisions.

One evening he called Louise and asked for some blankets: 'I'm going to spend the night here.' Louise looked at him, her head tilted back. She opened her mouth, then shut it. She merely examined Jonas with a sad and worried expression; he suddenly saw how much she had aged, and how deeply the wear and tear of their life had affected her too. He realized that he had never really helped her. But before he could speak, she smiled at him with a tenderness that wrung his heart. 'As you like, my dear,' she said.

Afterward, he spent his nights in the loft and almost never

came down. As a result, the apartment emptied of its visitors since they could no longer see Jonas, either day or night. Some said that he was in the country, others, tired of lying, that he had found a studio. Only Rateau came faithfully. He would climb up on the stepladder until his kind, intelligent face reached above the level of the floor: 'How are you?' he would say. – 'Couldn't be better.' – 'Are you working?' – 'It amounts to the same thing.' – 'But you have no canvas!' – 'I'm working anyway.' It was difficult to sustain this dialogue from stepladder to loft. Rateau would shake his head, climb back down, help Louise repair the plumbing or fix a lock, then, without climbing on the stepladder, say goodnight to Jonas, who would answer from the darkness: 'So long, my friend.' One evening, Jonas added a thanks to his farewell. 'Why thanks?' – 'Because you love me.' – 'Big news!' said Rateau and he left.

Another evening Jonas called Rateau, who came running. The lamp was lit for the first time. Jonas was leaning out of the loft with an anxious expression. 'Pass me a canvas,' he said. – 'But what's going on? You're so thin, you look like a ghost.' – 'I've hardly eaten for a couple of days. It's nothing, I must work.' – 'Eat first.' – 'No, I'm not hungry.' Rateau brought a canvas. As he was about to disappear into the loft, Jonas asked him: 'How are they?' – 'Who?' – 'Louise and the children.' – 'They're all right. They'd be better if you were with them.' – 'I'm not leaving them. Be sure to tell them, I'm not leaving them.' And he disappeared. Rateau came to tell Louise he was worried. She admitted that she had been tormenting herself for several days. 'What can we do? Oh, if only I could work in his place!' Miserable, she faced Rateau. 'I can't live without him,' she said. She looked like a young girl again, which surprised Rateau. Then he saw that she had blushed.

The lamp stayed lit all night and all morning the next day.

To those who came, Rateau or Louise, Jonas said only: 'Leave me alone, I'm working.' At noon he asked for kerosene. The flickering lamp shone brightly again until evening. Rateau stayed for dinner with Louise and the children. At midnight, he went to say goodnight to Jonas. He waited a moment below the lighted loft, then left without a word. On the morning of the second day, when Louise got up, the lamp was still lit.

A beautiful day was dawning, but Jonas did not notice. He had turned the canvas to the wall. Exhausted, he was waiting, sitting with his hands open on his knees. He told himself that now he would never work again, he was happy. He heard his children shouting, the water running, the dishes clinking. Louise was talking. The huge windows rattled as a truck passed on the boulevard. The world was still there, young, lovable: Jonas listened to the lovely murmur of humanity. From so far away it did not conflict with that joyful strength in him, his art, those thoughts that he could never express but that set him above all things, in an atmosphere that was free and alive. The children were running through the rooms, the little girl was laughing, and Louise, too – he hadn't heard her laughter for a long time. He loved them! How he loved them! He put out the lamp, and in the familiar darkness wasn't that his star still shining? It was, he recognized it, his heart full of gratitude, and he was still gazing at it when he fell, noiselessly.

'It's nothing,' the doctor who was called in declared some time later. 'He's working too much. He'll be on his feet in a week.' – 'He will get well, you're quite sure?' said Louise, her face haggard. – 'He will get well.' In the other room, Rateau was looking at the canvas. It was entirely blank, though in the center Jonas had written in very small characters one word, which could be deciphered, but it was hard to tell whether it should be read as *independent* or *interdependent*.

219

HERMANN HESSE

THE PAINTER

Translated by Jack Zipes

DURING HIS YOUTH a painter by the name of Albert did not manage to achieve the success and effect with his pictures that he desired. Therefore, he withdrew from society and decided just to satisfy himself. He tried this for many years, but it became more and more apparent that he could not do this either. One time, as he sat and painted the picture of a hero, he kept thinking, 'Is it really necessary to do what you're doing? Do these pictures have to be painted? Wouldn't it be just as well for you and everyone if you would merely take walks and drink wine? Aren't you just confusing yourself by painting, forgetting who you are, and passing the time away?'

These thoughts were not conducive to his work. In time Albert's painting stopped almost completely. He took walks. He drank wine. He read books. He took trips. But he was not satisfied by doing these things.

He was often compelled to think of how he had first begun painting with certain wishes and hopes. He recalled how he had felt and wished that a beautiful, powerful connection and current would develop between him and the world, that something strong and vigorous would vibrate incessantly between him and the world and generate soft music. He had wanted to express his innermost feelings and satisfy them with his heroes and heroic landscapes so that the outside world would judge and appreciate his pictures, and people would be grateful for and interested in his work.

Well, he had not found any of this. It had been a dream,

and even the dream had gradually faded and become hazy. Then, wherever Albert was, traveling through the world or living alone in remote places, sailing on ships or wandering over mountain passes, the dream began returning more and more frequently. It was different from before, but just as beautiful, just as powerful and alluring, just as desirable and glimmering as it originally had been.

Oh, how he yearned to feel the vibration between himself and everything in the world! To feel that his breath and the breath of the winds and seas were the same, that brotherhood and affinity, love and closeness, sound and harmony would be between him and everything!

He no longer desired to paint pictures in which he himself and his yearning would be portrayed, which would bring him understanding and love, pictures that were intended to explain, justify, and celebrate himself. He no longer thought about heroes and parades that were to express and describe his own existence as picture and smoke. He desired only to feel that vibration, that powerful stream, that fervor in which he himself would turn to nothing and sink, die, and be reborn. Just the new dream about this, the new, reinforced yearning for this, made his life bearable, endowed it with something like meaning, elevated it, rescued it.

Albert's friends, insofar as he still had some, did not understand these fantasies very well. They saw only that this man lived more and more within himself, that he spoke more quietly and strangely, that he was away a great deal, that he took no interest in what was lovely and important for other people, took no interest in politics or business, in shooting matches or dances, in clever conversations about art, or in anything that gave his friends pleasure. He had become an odd person, somewhat of a fool. He ran through the gray, cool winter air and breathed in the colors and

224

smells of this air. He ran after a little child who sang *la la* to himself. He stared for hours into green water, at a bed of flowers, or he absorbed himself, like a reader in his book, in reading the lines and cuts in a little piece of wood, in a root or turnip.

No one was concerned about Albert. At that time he lived in a small city in a foreign country, and one morning he took a walk down a street, and as he looked between the trees, he saw a small lazy river, a steep yellow clay bank, and bushes and thorny weeds that spread their dusty branches over landslides and bleak stones. All at once something sounded within him. He stood still. He felt an old song from legendary times strike up again in his soul. The yellow clay and dusty green, or the lazy river and steep parts of the bank, some combination of the colors or lines, some kind of sound, a uniqueness in the random picture was beautiful, was incredibly beautiful, moving, and upsetting, spoke to him, was related to him. And he felt vibrations and the most fervent connection between forest and river, between river and himself, between sky, earth, and plants. All things seemed to be set there unique and alone so that they could be reflected just at this moment, coming together as one in his eye and heart, so they could meet and greet each other. His heart was the place where river and grass, tree and air could unite, become one, enhance one another, and celebrate the festivals of love.

When this thrilling experience had repeated itself a few times, the painter found himself enveloped by a glorious feeling of happiness, thick and full, like a golden evening or a garden fragrance. He tasted it. It was sweet and thick, and he could no longer bear it. It was too rich. It became ripe and was filled with tension. It aroused him and made him almost anxious and furious. It was stronger than he was, tore him away. He was afraid that it would drag him down with it.

And he did not want that. He wanted to live, to live an eternity! Never, never had he wished to live as intensely as he did now.

One day he was silent and alone in his room as though he had just been intoxicated. He had a box of paints standing in front of him and had laid out a piece of cardboard. Now, for the first time in years, he was sitting and painting again.

And it stayed that way. The thought – 'Why am I doing this?' – did not return. He painted. He did nothing more except see and paint. Either he went outside and became lost in the pictures of the world, or he sat in his room and let the fullness stream away again. He composed picture after picture on cardboard, a rainbow sky with meadows, a garden wall, a bench in the woods, a country road, also people and animals, and things that he had never seen before, perhaps heroes or angels, who, however, became alive like wall and forest.

When he started circulating among people again, it became known that he had resumed painting. People found him quite crazy, but they were curious to see his paintings. He did not want to show them to anyone. Yet they did not leave him in peace. People pestered and forced him until he gave an acquaintance the key to his room. He himself departed on a journey. He did not want to be there when others saw the paintings.

People came, and soon there was a great hue and cry. They had discovered a spectacular genius, to be sure, an eccentric, but one who was blessed by God, and they began using sayings to describe him that are used by experts and speakers.

In the meantime Albert had arrived in a village, rented a room from farmers, and unpacked his paints and brush. Once again he went happily through valleys and mountains and later reflected all that he experienced and felt in his paintings.

One day he learned from a newspaper that many people had seen his paintings back home. In a tavern while drinking a glass of wine, he read a long, glowing report in the newspaper of the major city. His name was printed in big letters in the heading, and there were numerous fat words of praise throughout the article. But the more he read, the stranger he felt.

'How splendid the yellow of the background shines in the picture with the blue lady – a new, incredibly daring and enchanting harmony!'

'The art of the expressions in the still life with roses is also wonderful. Not to mention the series of self-portraits! We may place them alongside the great masterpieces of psychological portrait art.'

Strange, strange! He could not recall having ever painted a still life with roses, or a blue lady, and as far as he knew, he had never made a self-portrait. On the other hand, the article did not mention the clay bank or the angels, the rainbow sky or the other pictures that he loved so much.

Albert returned to the city. He went to his apartment dressed in his traveling clothes. People were going in and out. A man sat by the door, and Albert had to show a ticket in order to enter. Of course, he recognized his paintings. Someone had, however, hung placards on them, unknown to Albert. 'Self-portrait' could be read on many of them, and other titles. He stood contemplatively awhile before the paintings and their unfamiliar names. He saw it was possible to give these paintings completely different names than he had done. He saw that he had revealed something in the garden wall that seemed to be a cloud to some, and that the chasms of his rocky landscape could be the face of a person for others.

Ultimately, it was not all so important. But Albert desired

most of all to leave again quietly and to travel and never return to this city. He continued to paint many pictures and gave them many names, and he was happy with whatever he did. But he did not show his paintings to anyone.

NATHANIEL HAWTHORNE

THE ARTIST OF
THE BEAUTIFUL

AN ELDERLY MAN, with his pretty daughter on his arm, was passing along the street, and emerged from the gloom of the cloudy evening into the light that fell across the pavement from the window of a small shop. It was a projecting window; and on the inside were suspended a variety of watches, pinchbeck, silver, and one or two of gold, all with their faces turned from the streets, as if churlishly disinclined to inform the wayfarers what o'clock it was. Seated within the shop, sidelong to the window, with his pale face bent earnestly over some delicate piece of mechanism on which was thrown the concentrated lustre of a shade lamp, appeared a young man.

'What can Owen Warland be about?' muttered old Peter Hovenden, himself a retired watchmaker, and the former master of this same young man whose occupation he was now wondering at. 'What can the fellow be about? These six months past I have never come by his shop without seeing him just as steadily at work as now. It would be a flight beyond his usual foolery to seek for the perpetual motion; and yet I know enough of my old business to be certain that what he is now so busy with is no part of the machinery of a watch.'

'Perhaps, father,' said Annie, without showing much interest in the question, 'Owen is inventing a new kind of timekeeper. I am sure he has ingenuity enough.'

'Poh, child! He has not the sort of ingenuity to invent anything better than a Dutch toy,' answered her father, who had formerly been put to much vexation by Owen Warland's irregular genius. 'A plague on such ingenuity! All the effect that ever I knew of it was to spoil the accuracy of some of the best watches in my shop. He would turn the sun out of its orbit and derange the whole course of time, if, as I said before, his ingenuity could grasp anything bigger than a child's toy!'

'Hush, father! He hears you!' whispered Annie, pressing the old man's arm. 'His ears are as delicate as his feelings; and you know how easily disturbed they are. Do let us move on.'

So Peter Hovenden and his daughter Annie plodded on without further conversation, until in a by-street of the town they found themselves passing the open door of a blacksmith's shop. Within was seen the forge, now blazing up and illuminating the high and dusky roof, and now confining its lustre to a narrow precinct of the coal-strewn floor, according as the breath of the bellows was puffed forth or again inhaled into its vast leathern lungs. In the intervals of brightness it was easy to distinguish objects in remote corners of the shop and the horseshoes that hung upon the wall; in the momentary gloom the fire seemed to be glimmering amidst the vagueness of unenclosed space. Moving about in this red glare and alternate dusk was the figure of the blacksmith, well worthy to be viewed in so picturesque an aspect of light and shade, where the bright blaze struggled with the black night, as if each would have snatched his comely strength from the other. Anon he drew a white-hot bar of iron from the coals, laid it on the anvil, uplifted his arm of might, and was soon enveloped in the myriads of sparks which the strokes of his hammer scattered into the surrounding gloom.

'Now, that is a pleasant sight,' said the old watchmaker. 'I know what it is to work in gold; but give me the worker in iron after all is said and done. He spends his labor upon a reality. What say you, daughter Annie?'

'Pray don't speak so loud, father,' whispered Annie, 'Robert Danforth will hear you.'

'And what if he should hear me?' said Peter Hovenden. 'I say again, it is a good and a wholesome thing to depend upon main strength and reality, and to earn one's bread with the bare and brawny arm of a blacksmith. A watchmaker gets his brain puzzled by his wheels within a wheel, or loses his health or the nicety of his eyesight, as was my case, and finds himself at middle age, or a little after, past labor at his own trade and fit for nothing else, yet too poor to live at his ease. So I say once again, give me main strength for my money. And then, how it takes the nonsense out of a man! Did you ever hear of a blacksmith being such a fool as Owen Warland yonder?'

'Well said, uncle Hovenden!' shouted Robert Danforth from the forge, in a full, deep, merry voice, that made the roof reëcho. 'And what says Miss Annie to that doctrine? She, I suppose, will think it a genteeler business to tinker up a lady's watch than to forge a horseshoe or make a gridiron.'

Annie drew her father onward without giving him time for reply.

But we must return to Owen Warland's shop, and spend more meditation upon his history and character than either Peter Hovenden, or probably his daughter Annie, or Owen's old school-fellow, Robert Danforth, would have thought due to so slight a subject. From the time that his little fingers could grasp a penknife, Owen had been remarkable for a delicate ingenuity, which sometimes produced pretty shapes in wood, principally figures of flowers and birds, and sometimes seemed to aim at the hidden mysteries of mechanism.

But it was always for purposes of grace, and never with any mockery of the useful. He did not, like the crowd of schoolboy artisans, construct little windmills on the angle of a barn or watermills across the neighboring brook. Those who discovered such peculiarity in the boy as to think it worth their while to observe him closely, sometimes saw reason to suppose that he was attempting to imitate the beautiful movements of Nature as exemplified in the flight of birds or the activity of little animals. It seemed, in fact, a new development of the love of the beautiful, such as might have made him a poet, a painter, or a sculptor, and which was as completely refined from all utilitarian coarseness as it could have been in either of the fine arts. He looked with singular distaste at the stiff and regular processes of ordinary machinery. Being once carried to see a steam-engine, in the expectation that his intuitive comprehension of mechanical principles would be gratified, he turned pale and grew sick, as if something monstrous and unnatural had been presented to him. This horror was partly owing to the size and terrible energy of the iron laborer; for the character of Owen's mind was microscopic, and tended naturally to the minute, in accordance with his diminutive frame and the marvellous smallness and delicate power of his fingers. Not that his sense of beauty was thereby diminished into a sense of prettiness. The beautiful idea has no relation to size, and may be as perfectly developed in a space too minute for any but microscopic investigation as within the ample verge that is measured by the arc of the rainbow. But, at all events, this characteristic minuteness in his objects and accomplishments made the world even more incapable than it might otherwise have been of appreciating Owen Warland's genius. The boy's relatives saw nothing better to be done – as perhaps there was not – than to bind him apprentice to a watchmaker, hoping that his strange ingenuity might thus be regulated and put to utilitarian purposes.

Peter Hovenden's opinion of his apprentice has already been expressed. He could make nothing of the lad. Owen's apprehension of the professional mysteries, it is true, was inconceivably quick; but he altogether forgot or despised the grand object of a watchmaker's business, and cared no more for the measurement of time than if it had been merged into eternity. So long, however, as he remained under his old master's care, Owen's lack of sturdiness made it possible, by strict injunctions and sharp oversight, to restrain his creative eccentricity within bounds; but when his apprenticeship was served out, and he had taken the little shop which Peter Hovenden's failing eyesight compelled him to relinquish, then did people recognize how unfit a person was Owen Warland to lead old blind Father Time along his daily course. One of his most rational projects was to connect a musical operation with the machinery of his watches, so that all the harsh dissonances of life might be rendered tuneful, and each flitting moment fall into the abyss of the past in golden drops of harmony. If a family clock was intrusted to him for repair, – one of those tall, ancient clocks that have grown nearly allied to human nature by measuring out the lifetime of many generations, – he would take upon himself to arrange a dance or funeral procession of figures across its venerable face, representing twelve mirthful or melancholy hours. Several freaks of this kind quite destroyed the young watchmaker's credit with that steady and matter-of-fact class of people who hold the opinion that time is not to be trifled with, whether considered as the medium of advancement and prosperity in this world or preparation for the next. His custom rapidly diminished – a misfortune, however, that was probably reckoned among his better accidents by Owen

Warland, who was becoming more and more absorbed in a secret occupation which drew all his science and manual dexterity into itself, and likewise gave full employment to the characteristic tendencies of his genius. This pursuit had already consumed many months.

After the old watchmaker and his pretty daughter had gazed at him out of the obscurity of the street, Owen Warland was seized with a fluttering of the nerves, which made his hand tremble too violently to proceed with such delicate labor as he was now engaged upon.

'It was Annie herself!' murmured he. 'I should have known it, by this throbbing of my heart, before I heard her father's voice. Ah, how it throbs! I shall scarcely be able to work again on this exquisite mechanism tonight. Annie! dearest Annie! thou shouldst give firmness to my heart and hand, and not shake them thus; for if I strive to put the very spirit of beauty into form and give it motion, it is for thy sake alone. O throbbing heart, be quiet! If my labor be thus thwarted, there will come vague and unsatisfied dreams which will leave me spiritless tomorrow.'

As he was endeavoring to settle himself again to his task, the shop door opened and gave admittance to no other than the stalwart figure which Peter Hovenden had paused to admire, as seen amid the light and shadow of the blacksmith's shop. Robert Danforth had brought a little anvil of his own manufacture, and peculiarly constructed, which the young artist had recently bespoken. Owen examined the article and pronounced it fashioned according to his wish.

'Why, yes,' said Robert Danforth, his strong voice filling the shop as with the sound of a bass viol, 'I consider myself equal to anything in the way of my own trade; though I should have made but a poor figure at yours with such a fist as this,' added he, laughing, as he laid his vast hand beside the delicate one of Owen. 'But what then? I put more main strength into one blow of my sledge hammer than all that you have expended since you were a 'prentice. Is not that the truth?'

'Very probably,' answered the low and slender voice of Owen. 'Strength is an earthly monster. I make no pretensions to it. My force, whatever there may be of it, is altogether spiritual.'

'Well, but, Owen, what are you about?' asked his old school-fellow, still in such a hearty volume of tone that it made the artist shrink, especially as the question related to a subject so sacred as the absorbing dream of his imagination. 'Folks do say that you are trying to discover the perpetual motion.'

'The perpetual motion? Nonsense!' replied Owen Warland, with a movement of disgust; for he was full of little petulances. 'It can never be discovered. It is a dream that may delude men whose brains are mystified with matter, but not me. Besides, if such a discovery were possible, it would not be worth my while to make it only to have the secret turned to such purposes as are now effected by steam and water power. I am not ambitious to be honored with the paternity of a new kind of cotton machine.'

'That would be droll enough!' cried the blacksmith, breaking out into such an uproar of laughter that Owen himself and the bell glasses on his workboard quivered in unison. 'No, no, Owen! No child of yours will have iron joints and sinews. Well, I won't hinder you any more. Good night, Owen, and success, and if you need any assistance, so far as a downright blow of hammer upon anvil will answer the purpose, I'm your man.'

And with another laugh the man of main strength left the shop.

'How strange it is,' whispered Owen Warland to himself, leaning his head upon his hand, 'that all my musings, my purposes, my passion for the beautiful, my consciousness of power to create it, – a finer, more ethereal power, of which this earthly giant can have no conception, – all, all, look so vain and idle whenever my path is crossed by Robert Danforth! He would drive me mad were I to meet him often. His hard, brute force darkens and confuses the spiritual element within me; but I, too, will be strong in my own way. I will not yield to him.'

He took from beneath a glass a piece of minute machinery, which he set in the condensed light of his lamp, and, looking intently at it through a magnifying glass, proceeded to operate with a delicate instrument of steel. In an instant, however, he fell back in his chair and clasped his hands, with a look of horror on his face that made its small features as impressive as those of a giant would have been.

'Heaven! What have I done?' exclaimed he. 'The vapor, the influence of that brute force, – it has bewildered me and obscured my perception. I have made the very stroke – the fatal stroke – that I have dreaded from the first. It is all over – the toil of months, the object of my life. I am ruined!'

And there he sat, in strange despair, until his lamp flickered in the socket and left the Artist of the Beautiful in darkness.

Thus it is that ideas, which grow up within the imagination and appear so lovely to it and of a value beyond whatever men call valuable, are exposed to be shattered and annihilated by contact with the practical. It is requisite for the ideal artist to possess a force of character that seems hardly compatible with its delicacy; he must keep his faith in himself while the incredulous world assails him with its utter disbelief; he must stand up against mankind and be his own sole disciple, both as respects his genius and the objects to which it is directed.

For a time Owen Warland succumbed to this severe but inevitable test. He spent a few sluggish weeks with his head so continually resting in his hands that the towns-people had scarcely an opportunity to see his countenance. When at last it was again uplifted to the light of day, a cold, dull, nameless change was perceptible upon it. In the opinion of Peter Hovenden, however, and that order of sagacious understandings who think that life should be regulated, like clockwork, with leaden weights, the alteration was entirely for the better. Owen now, indeed, applied himself to business with dogged industry. It was marvellous to witness the obtuse gravity with which he would inspect the wheels of a great old silver watch; thereby delighting the owner, in whose fob it had been worn till he deemed it a portion of his own life, and was accordingly jealous of its treatment. In consequence of the good report thus acquired, Owen Warland was invited by the proper authorities to regulate the clock in the church steeple. He succeeded so admirably in this matter of public interest that the merchants gruffly acknowledged his merits on 'Change; the nurse whispered his praises as she gave the potion in the sick-chamber; the lover blessed him at the hour of appointed interview; and the town in general thanked Owen for the punctuality of dinner time. In a word, the heavy weight upon his spirits kept everything in order, not merely within his own system, but wheresoever the iron accents of the church clock were audible. It was a circumstance, though minute, yet characteristic of his present state, that, when employed to engrave names or initials on silver spoons, he now wrote the requisite letters in the plainest possible style, omitting a variety of fanciful flourishes that had heretofore distinguished his work in this kind.

One day, during the era of this happy transformation, old Peter Hovenden came to visit his former apprentice.

'Well, Owen,' said he, 'I am glad to hear such good accounts of you from all quarters, and especially from the town clock yonder, which speaks in your commendation every hour of the twenty-four. Only get rid altogether of your nonsensical trash about the beautiful, which I nor nobody else, nor yourself to boot, could ever understand, – only free yourself of that, and your success in life is as sure as daylight. Why, if you go on in this way, I should even venture to let you doctor this precious old watch of mine; though, except my daughter Annie, I have nothing else so valuable in the world.'

'I should hardly dare touch it, sir,' replied Owen, in a depressed tone; for he was weighed down by his old master's presence.

'In time,' said the latter, – 'in time, you will be capable of it.'

The old watchmaker, with the freedom naturally consequent on his former authority, went on inspecting the work which Owen had in hand at the moment, together with other matters that were in progress. The artist, meanwhile, could scarcely lift his head. There was nothing so antipodal to his nature as this man's cold, unimaginative sagacity, by contact with which everything was converted into a dream except the densest matter of the physical world. Owen groaned in spirit and prayed fervently to be delivered from him.

'But what is this?' cried Peter Hovenden abruptly, taking up a dusty bell glass, beneath which appeared a mechanical something, as delicate and minute as the system of a butterfly's anatomy. 'What have we here? Owen! Owen! there is witchcraft in these little chains, and wheels, and paddles. See! with one pinch of my finger and thumb I am going to deliver you from all future peril.'

'For Heaven's sake,' screamed Owen Warland, springing up with wonderful energy, 'as you would not drive me mad, do not touch it! The slightest pressure of your finger would ruin me forever.'

'Aha, young man! And is it so?' said the old watchmaker, looking at him with just enough of penetration to torture Owen's soul with the bitterness of worldly criticism. 'Well, take your own course; but I warn you again that in this small piece of mechanism lives your evil spirit. Shall I exorcise him?'

'You are my evil spirit,' answered Owen, much excited, – 'you and the hard, coarse world! The leaden thoughts and the despondency that you fling upon me are my clogs, else I should long ago have achieved the task that I was created for.'

Peter Hovenden shook his head, with the mixture of contempt and indignation which mankind, of whom he was partly a representative, deem themselves entitled to feel towards all simpletons who seek other prizes than the dusty one along the highway. He then took his leave, with an uplifted finger and a sneer upon his face that haunted the artist's dreams for many a night afterwards. At the time of his old master's visit, Owen was probably on the point of taking up the relinquished task; but, by this sinister event, he was thrown back into the state whence he had been slowly emerging.

But the innate tendency of his soul had only been accumulating fresh vigor during its apparent sluggishness. As the summer advanced he almost totally relinquished his business, and permitted Father Time, so far as the old gentleman was represented by the clocks and watches under his control, to stray at random through human life, making infinite confusion among the train of bewildered hours. He wasted the sunshine, as people said, in wandering through the woods and fields and along the banks of streams. There, like a child, he found amusement in chasing butterflies or watching the motions of water insects. There was something truly mysterious in the intentness with which he contemplated these living playthings as they sported on the breeze or examined the structure of an imperial insect whom he had imprisoned. The chase of butterflies was an apt emblem of the ideal pursuit in which he had spent so many golden hours; but would the beautiful idea ever be yielded to his hand like the butterfly that symbolized it? Sweet, doubtless, were these days, and congenial to the artist's soul. They were full of bright conceptions, which gleamed through his intellectual world as the butterflies gleamed through the outward atmosphere, and were real to him, for the instant, without the toil, and perplexity, and many disappointments of attempting to make them visible to the sensual eye. Alas that the artist, whether in poetry, or whatever other material, may not content himself with the inward enjoyment of the beautiful, but must chase the flitting mystery beyond the verge of his ethereal domain, and crush its frail being in seizing it with a material grasp. Owen Warland felt the impulse to give external reality to his ideas as irresistibly as any of the poets or painters who have arrayed the world in a dimmer and fainter beauty, imperfectly copied from the richness of their visions.

The night was now his time for the slow progress of recreating the one idea to which all his intellectual activity referred itself. Always at the approach of dusk he stole into the town, locked himself within his shop, and wrought with patient delicacy of touch for many hours. Sometimes he was startled by the rap of the watchman, who, when all the world should be asleep, had caught the gleam of lamplight through the crevices of Owen Warland's shutters. Daylight, to the morbid sensibility of his mind, seemed to have an intrusiveness that interfered with his pursuits. On cloudy and inclement days, therefore, he sat with his head upon his hands, muffling, as it were, his sensitive brain in a mist of indefinite musings; for it was a relief to escape from the sharp distinctness with which he was compelled to shape out his thoughts during his nightly toil.

From one of these fits of torpor he was aroused by the entrance of Annie Hovenden, who came into the shop with the freedom of a customer, and also with something of the familiarity of a childish friend. She had worn a hole through her silver thimble, and wanted Owen to repair it.

'But I don't know whether you will condescend to such a task,' said she, laughing, 'now that you are so taken up with the notion of putting spirit into machinery.'

'Where did you get that idea, Annie?' said Owen, starting in surprise.

'Oh, out of my own head,' answered she, 'and from something that I heard you say, long ago, when you were but a boy and I a little child. But come; will you mend this poor thimble of mine?'

'Anything for your sake, Annie,' said Owen Warland, – 'anything, even were it to work at Robert Danforth's forge.'

'And that would be a pretty sight!' retorted Annie, glancing with imperceptible slightness at the artist's small and slender frame. 'Well; here is the thimble.'

'But that is a strange idea of yours,' said Owen, 'about the spiritualization of matter.'

And then the thought stole into his mind that this young girl possessed the gift to comprehend him better than all the world besides. And what a help and strength would it be to him in his lonely toil if he could gain the sympathy of the only being whom he loved! To persons whose pursuits are insulated from the common business of life – who are either in advance of mankind or apart from it – there often comes a sensation of moral cold that makes the spirit shiver as if it had reached the frozen solitudes around the pole. What the prophet, the poet, the reformer, the criminal, or any other man with human yearnings, but separated from the multitude by a peculiar lot, might feel, poor Owen felt.

'Annie,' cried he, growing pale as death at the thought, 'how gladly would I tell you the secret of my pursuit! You, methinks, would estimate it rightly. You, I know, would hear it with a reverence that I must not expect from the harsh, material world.'

'Would I not? to be sure I would!' replied Annie Hovenden, lightly laughing. 'Come; explain to me quickly what is the meaning of this little whirligig, so delicately wrought, that it might be a plaything for Queen Mab. See! I will put it in motion.'

'Hold!' exclaimed Owen, 'hold!'

Annie had but given the slightest possible touch, with the point of a needle, to the same minute portion of complicated machinery which has been more than once mentioned, when the artist seized her by the wrist with a force that made her scream aloud. She was affrighted at the convulsion of intense rage and anguish that writhed across his features. The next instant he let his head sink upon his hands.

'Go, Annie,' murmured he; 'I have deceived myself, and must suffer for it. I yearned for sympathy and thought, and fancied, and dreamed that you might give it me; but you lack the talisman, Annie, that should admit you into my secrets. That touch has undone the toil of months and the thought of a lifetime! It was not your fault, Annie; but you have ruined me!'

Poor Owen Warland! He had indeed erred, yet pardonably; for if any human spirit could have sufficiently reverenced the processes so sacred in his eyes, it must have been a woman's. Even Annie Hovenden, possibly, might not have disappointed him had she been enlightened by the deep intelligence of love.

The artist spent the ensuing winter in a way that satisfied any persons who had hitherto retained a hopeful opinion of him that he was, in truth, irrevocably doomed to inutility as regarded the world, and to an evil destiny on his own part. The decease of a relative had put him in possession of a small inheritance. Thus freed from the necessity of toil, and having lost the steadfast influence of a great purpose, – great, at least, to him, – he abandoned himself to habits from which it might have been supposed the mere delicacy of his organization would have availed to secure him. But when the ethereal portion of a man of genius is obscured, the earthly part assumes an influence the more uncontrollable, because the character is now thrown off the balance to which Providence had so nicely adjusted it, and which, in coarser natures, is adjusted by some other method. Owen Warland made proof of whatever show of bliss may be found in riot. He looked at the world through the golden medium of wine, and contemplated the visions that bubble up so gayly around the brim of the glass, and that people the air with shapes of pleasant madness, which so soon grow ghostly and forlorn. Even when this dismal and inevitable change had taken place, the young man might still have continued to quaff the cup of enchantments, though its vapor did but shroud life in gloom and fill the gloom with spectres that mocked at him. There was a certain irksomeness of spirit, which, being real, and the deepest sensation of which the artist was now conscious, was more intolerable than any fantastic miseries and horrors that the abuse of wine could summon up. In the latter case he could remember, even out of the midst of his trouble, that all was but a delusion; in the former, the heavy anguish was his actual life.

From this perilous state he was redeemed by an incident which more than one person witnessed, but of which the shrewdest could not explain or conjecture the operation on Owen Warland's mind. It was very simple. On a warm afternoon of spring, as the artist sat among his riotous companions with a glass of wine before him, a splendid butterfly flew in at the open window and fluttered about his head.

'Ah,' exclaimed Owen, who had drank freely, 'are you alive again, child of the sun and playmate of the summer breeze, after your dismal winter's nap? Then it is time for me to be at work!'

And, leaving his unemptied glass upon the table, he departed and was never known to sip another drop of wine.

And now, again, he resumed his wanderings in the woods and fields. It might be fancied that the bright butterfly, which had come so spirit-like into the window as Owen sat with the rude revellers, was indeed a spirit commissioned to recall him to the pure, ideal life that had so etherealized him among men. It might be fancied that he went forth to seek this spirit in its sunny haunts; for still, as in the summer time gone by, he was seen to steal gently up wherever a butterfly had alighted, and lose himself in contemplation of it. When it took flight his eyes followed the winged vision, as if its airy track would show the path to heaven. But what could be the purpose of the unseasonable toil, which was again resumed, as the watchman knew by the lines of lamplight through the crevices of Owen Warland's shutters? The towns-people had one comprehensive explanation of all these singularities. Owen Warland had gone mad! How universally efficacious – how satisfactory, too, and soothing to the injured sensibility of narrowness and dulness – is this easy method of accounting for whatever lies beyond the world's most ordinary scope! From St Paul's days down to our poor little Artist of the

Beautiful, the same talisman had been applied to the elucidation of all mysteries in the words or deeds of men who spoke or acted too wisely or too well. In Owen Warland's case the judgment of his towns-people may have been correct. Perhaps he was mad. The lack of sympathy – that contrast between himself and his neighbors which took away the restraint of example – was enough to make him so. Or possibly he had caught just so much of ethereal radiance as served to bewilder him, in an earthly sense, by its intermixture with the common daylight.

One evening, when the artist had returned from a customary ramble and had just thrown the lustre of his lamp on the delicate piece of work so often interrupted, but still taken up again, as if his fate were embodied in its mechanism, he was surprised by the entrance of old Peter Hovenden. Owen never met this man without a shrinking of the heart. Of all the world he was most terrible, by reason of a keen understanding which saw so distinctly what it did see, and disbelieved so uncompromisingly in what it could not see. On this occasion the old watchmaker had merely a gracious word or two to say.

'Owen, my lad,' said he, 'we must see you at my house tomorrow night.'

The artist began to mutter some excuse.

'Oh, but it must be so,' quoth Peter Hovenden, 'for the sake of the days when you were one of the household. What, my boy! don't you know that my daughter Annie is engaged to Robert Danforth? We are making an entertainment, in our humble way, to celebrate the event.'

'Ah!' said Owen.

That little monosyllable was all he uttered; its tone seemed cold and unconcerned to an ear like Peter Hovenden's; and yet there was in it the stifled outcry of the poor artist's heart, which he compressed within him like a man holding down an evil spirit. One slight outbreak, however, imperceptible to the old watchmaker, he allowed himself. Raising the instrument with which he was about to begin his work, he let it fall upon the little system of machinery that had, anew, cost him months of thought and toil. It was shattered by the stroke!

Owen Warland's story would have been no tolerable representation of the troubled life of those who strive to create the beautiful, if, amid all other thwarting influences, love had not interposed to steal the cunning from his hand. Outwardly he had been no ardent or enterprising lover; the career of his passion had confined its tumults and vicissitudes so entirely within the artist's imagination that Annie herself had scarcely more than a woman's intuitive perception of it; but, in Owen's view, it covered the whole field of his life. Forgetful of the time when she had shown herself incapable of any deep response, he had persisted in connecting all his dreams of artistical success with Annie's image; she was the visible shape in which the spiritual power that he worshipped, and on whose altar he hoped to lay a not unworthy offering, was made manifest to him. Of course he had deceived himself; there were no such attributes in Annie Hovenden as his imagination had endowed her with. She, in the aspect which she wore to his inward vision, was as much a creature of his own as the mysterious piece of mechanism would be were it ever realized. Had he become convinced of his mistake through the medium of successful love, – had he won Annie to his bosom, and there beheld her fade from angel into ordinary woman, – the disappointment might have driven him back, with concentrated energy, upon his sole remaining object. On the other hand, had he found Annie what he fancied, his lot would have been so rich in beauty that out

248

of its mere redundancy he might have wrought the beautiful into many a worthier type than he had toiled for; but the guise in which his sorrow came to him, the sense that the angel of his life had been snatched away and given to a rude man of earth and iron, who could neither need nor appreciate her ministrations, – this was the very perversity of fate that makes human existence appear too absurd and contradictory to be the scene of one other hope or one other fear. There was nothing left for Owen Warland but to sit down like a man that had been stunned.

He went through a fit of illness. After his recovery his small and slender frame assumed an obtuser garniture of flesh than it had ever before worn. His thin cheeks became round; his delicate little hand, so spiritually fashioned to achieve fairy task-work, grew plumper than the hand of a thriving infant. His aspect had a childishness such as might have induced a stranger to pat him on the head – pausing, however, in the act, to wonder what manner of child was here. It was as if the spirit had gone out of him, leaving the body to flourish in a sort of vegetable existence. Not that Owen Warland was idiotic. He could talk, and not irrationally. Somewhat of a babbler, indeed, did people begin to think him; for he was apt to discourse at wearisome length of marvels of mechanism that he had read about in books, but which he had learned to consider as absolutely fabulous. Among them he enumerated the Man of Brass, constructed by Albertus Magnus, and the Brazen Head of Friar Bacon; and, coming down to later times, the automata of a little coach and horses, which it was pretended had been manu- factured for the Dauphin of France; together with an insect that buzzed about the ear like a living fly, and yet was but a contrivance of minute steel springs. There was a story, too, of a duck that waddled, and quacked, and ate; though, had

249

any honest citizen purchased it for dinner, he would have found himself cheated with the mere mechanical apparition of a duck.

'But all these accounts,' said Owen Warland, 'I am now satisfied are mere impositions.'

Then, in a mysterious way, he would confess that he once thought differently. In his idle and dreamy days he had considered it possible, in a certain sense, to spiritualize machinery, and to combine with the new species of life and motion thus produced a beauty that should attain to the ideal which Nature has proposed to herself in all her creatures, but has never taken pains to realize. He seemed, however, to retain no very distinct perception either of the process of achieving this object or of the design itself.

'I have thrown it all aside now,' he would say. 'It was a dream such as young men are always mystifying themselves with. Now that I have acquired a little common sense, it makes me laugh to think of it.'

Poor, poor and fallen Owen Warland! These were the symptoms that he had ceased to be an inhabitant of the better sphere that lies unseen around us. He had lost his faith in the invisible, and now prided himself, as such unfortunates invariably do, in the wisdom which rejected much that even his eye could see, and trusted confidently in nothing but what his hand could touch. This is the calamity of men whose spiritual part dies out of them and leaves the grosser understanding to assimilate them more and more to the things of which alone it can take cognizance; but in Owen Warland the spirit was not dead nor passed away; it only slept.

How it awoke again is not recorded. Perhaps the torpid slumber was broken by a convulsive pain. Perhaps, as in a former instance, the butterfly came and hovered about his head and reinspired him, – as indeed this creature of the sunshine had always a mysterious mission for the artist, – reinspired him with the former purpose of his life. Whether it were pain or happiness that thrilled through his veins, his first impulse was to thank Heaven for rendering him again the being of thought, imagination, and keenest sensibility that he had long ceased to be.

'Now for my task,' said he. 'Never did I feel such strength for it as now.'

Yet, strong as he felt himself, he was incited to toil the more diligently by an anxiety lest death should surprise him in the midst of his labors. This anxiety, perhaps, is common to all men who set their hearts upon anything so high, in their own view of it, that life becomes of importance only as conditional to its accomplishment. So long as we love life for itself, we seldom dread the losing it. When we desire life for the attainment of an object, we recognize the frailty of its texture. But, side by side with this sense of insecurity, there is a vital faith in our invulnerability to the shaft of death while engaged in any task that seems assigned by Providence as our proper thing to do, and which the world would have cause to mourn for should we leave it unaccomplished. Can the philosopher, big with the inspiration of an idea that is to reform mankind, believe that he is to be beckoned from this sensible existence at the very instant when he is mustering his breath to speak the word of light? Should he perish so, the weary ages may pass away – the world's, whose life sand may fall, drop by drop – before another intellect is prepared to develop the truth that might have been uttered then. But history affords many an example where the most precious spirit, at any particular epoch manifested in human shape, has gone hence untimely, without space allowed him, so far as mortal judgment could discern, to perform his mission on the earth. The prophet dies, and the man of torpid heart and sluggish brain lives on.

The poet leaves his song half sung, or finishes it, beyond the scope of mortal ears, in a celestial choir. The painter – as Allston did – leaves half his conception on the canvas to sadden us with its imperfect beauty, and goes to picture forth the whole, if it be no irreverence to say so, in the hues of heaven. But rather such incomplete designs of this life will be perfected nowhere. This so frequent abortion of man's dearest projects must be taken as a proof that the deeds of earth, however etherealized by piety or genius, are without value, except as exercises and manifestations of the spirit. In heaven, all ordinary thought is higher and more melodious than Milton's song. Then, would he add another verse to any strain that he had left unfinished here?

But to return to Owen Warland. It was his fortune, good or ill, to achieve the purpose of his life. Pass we over a long space of intense thought, yearning effort, minute toil, and wasting anxiety, succeeded by an instant of solitary triumph: let all this be imagined; and then behold the artist, on a winter evening, seeking admittance to Robert Danforth's fireside circle. There he found the man of iron, with his massive substance thoroughly warmed and attempered by domestic influences. And there was Annie, too, now transformed into a matron, with much of her husband's plain and sturdy nature, but imbued, as Owen Warland still believed, with a finer grace, that might enable her to be the interpreter between strength and beauty. It happened, likewise, that old Peter Hovenden was a guest this evening at his daughter's fireside, and it was his well-remembered expression of keen, cold criticism that first encountered the artist's glance.

'My old friend Owen!' cried Robert Danforth, starting up, and compressing the artist's delicate fingers within a hand that was accustomed to gripe bars of iron. 'This is kind and neighborly to come to us at last. I was afraid your perpetual motion had bewitched you out of the remembrance of old times.'

'We are glad to see you,' said Annie, while a blush reddened her matronly cheek. 'It was not like a friend to stay from us so long.'

'Well, Owen,' inquired the old watchmaker, as his first greeting, 'how comes on the beautiful? Have you created it at last?'

The artist did not immediately reply, being startled by the apparition of a young child of strength that was tumbling about on the carpet, – a little personage who had come mysteriously out of the infinite but with something so sturdy and real in his composition that he seemed moulded out of the densest substance which earth could supply. This hopeful infant crawled towards the newcomer, and setting himself on end, as Robert Danforth expressed the posture, stared at Owen with a look of such sagacious observation that the mother could not help exchanging a proud glance with her husband. But the artist was disturbed by the child's look, as imagining a resemblance between it and Peter Hovenden's habitual expression. He could have fancied that the old watchmaker was compressed into this baby shape, and looking out of those baby eyes, and repeating, as he now did, the malicious question: –

'The beautiful, Owen! How comes on the beautiful? Have you succeeded in creating the beautiful?'

'I have succeeded,' replied the artist, with a momentary light of triumph in his eyes and a smile of sunshine, yet steeped in such depth of thought that it was almost sadness. 'Yes, my friends, it is the truth. I have succeeded.'

'Indeed!' cried Annie, a look of maiden mirthfulness peeping out of her face again. 'And is it lawful, now, to inquire what the secret is?'

'Surely; it is to disclose it that I have come,' answered Owen Warland. 'You shall know, and see, and touch, and possess the secret! For, Annie, – if by that name I may still address the friend of my boyish years, – Annie, it is for your bridal gift that I have wrought this spiritualized mechanism, this harmony of motion, this mystery of beauty. It comes late, indeed; but it is as we go onward in life, when objects begin to lose their freshness of hue and our souls their delicacy of perception, that the spirit of beauty is most needed. If, – forgive me, Annie, – if you know how to value this gift, it can never come too late.'

He produced, as he spoke, what seemed a jewel box. It was carved richly out of ebony by his own hand, and inlaid with a fanciful tracery of pearl, representing a boy in pursuit of a butterfly, which, elsewhere, had become a winged spirit, and was flying heavenward; while the boy, or youth, had found such efficacy in his strong desire that he ascended from earth to cloud, and from cloud to celestial atmosphere, to win the beautiful. This case of ebony the artist opened, and bade Annie place her finger on its edge. She did so, but almost screamed as a butterfly fluttered forth, and, alighting on her finger's tip, sat waving the ample magnificence of its purple and gold-speckled wings, as if in prelude to a flight. It is impossible to express by words the glory, the splendor, the delicate gorgeousness which were softened into the beauty of this object. Nature's ideal butterfly was here realized in all its perfection; not in the pattern of such faded insects as flit among earthly flowers, but of those which hover across the meads of paradise for child-angels and the spirits of departed infants to disport themselves with. The rich down was visible upon its wings; the lustre of its eyes seemed instinct with spirit. The firelight glimmered around this wonder – the candles gleamed upon it; but it glistened apparently by its

254

own radiance, and illuminated the finger and outstretched hand on which it rested with a white gleam like that of precious stones. In its perfect beauty, the consideration of size was entirely lost. Had its wings overreached the firmament, the mind could not have been more filled or satisfied.

'Beautiful! beautiful!' exclaimed Annie. 'Is it alive? Is it alive?'

'Alive? To be sure it is,' answered her husband. 'Do you suppose any mortal has skill enough to make a butterfly, or would put himself to the trouble of making one, when any child may catch a score of them in a summer's afternoon? Alive? Certainly! But this pretty box is undoubtedly of our friend Owen's manufacture; and really it does him credit.'

At this moment the butterfly waved its wings anew, with a motion so absolutely lifelike that Annie was startled, and even awe-stricken; for, in spite of her husband's opinion, she could not satisfy herself whether it was indeed a living creature or a piece of wondrous mechanism.

'Is it alive?' she repeated, more earnestly than before.

'Judge for yourself,' said Owen Warland, who stood gazing in her face with fixed attention.

The butterfly now flung itself upon the air, fluttered round Annie's head, and soared into a distant region of the parlor, still making itself perceptible to sight by the starry gleam in which the motion of its wings enveloped it. The infant on the floor followed its course with his sagacious little eyes. After flying about the room, it returned in a spiral curve and settled again on Annie's finger.

'But is it alive?' exclaimed she again; and the finger on which the gorgeous mystery had alighted was so tremulous that the butterfly was forced to balance himself with his wings. 'Tell me if it be alive, or whether you created it.'

'Wherefore ask who created it, so it be beautiful?' replied

Owen Warland. 'Alive? Yes, Annie; it may well be said to possess life, for it has absorbed my own being into itself; and in the secret of that butterfly, and in its beauty, – which is not merely outward, but deep as its whole system, – is represented the intellect, the imagination, the sensibility, the soul of an Artist of the Beautiful! Yes; I created it. But' – and here his countenance somewhat changed – 'this butterfly is not now to me what it was when I beheld it afar off in the daydreams of my youth.'

'Be it what it may, it is a pretty plaything,' said the blacksmith, grinning with childlike delight. 'I wonder whether it would condescend to alight on such a great clumsy finger as mine? Hold it hither, Annie.'

By the artist's direction, Annie touched her finger's tip to that of her husband; and, after a momentary delay, the butterfly fluttered from one to the other. It preluded a second flight by a similar, yet not precisely the same, waving of wings as in the first experiment; then, ascending from the blacksmith's stalwart finger, it rose in a gradually enlarging curve to the ceiling, made one wide sweep around the room, and returned with an undulating movement to the point whence it had started.

'Well, that does beat all nature!' cried Robert Danforth, bestowing the heartiest praise that he could find expression for; and, indeed, had he paused there, a man of finer words and nicer perception could not easily have said more. 'That goes beyond me, I confess. But what then? There is more real use in one downright blow of my sledge hammer than in the whole five years' labor that our friend Owen has wasted on this butterfly.'

Here the child clapped his hands and made a great babble of indistinct utterance, apparently demanding that the butterfly should be given him for a plaything.

Owen Warland, meanwhile, glanced sidelong at Annie, to discover whether she sympathized in her husband's estimate of the comparative value of the beautiful and the practical. There was, amid all her kindness towards himself, amid all the wonder and admiration with which she contemplated the marvellous work of his hands and incarnation of his idea, a secret scorn – too secret, perhaps, for her own consciousness, and perceptible only to such intuitive discernment as that of the artist. But Owen, in the latter stages of his pursuit, had risen out of the region in which such a discovery might have been torture. He knew that the world, and Annie as the representative of the world, whatever praise might be bestowed, could never say the fitting word nor feel the fitting sentiment which should be the perfect recompense of an artist who, symbolizing a lofty moral by a material trifle, – converting what was earthly to spiritual gold, – had won the beautiful into his handiwork. Not at this latest moment was he to learn that the reward of all high performance must be sought within itself, or sought in vain. There was, however, a view of the matter which Annie and her husband, and even Peter Hovenden, might fully have understood, and which would have satisfied them that the toil of years had here been worthily bestowed. Owen Warland might have told them that this butterfly, this plaything, this bridal gift of a poor watchmaker to a blacksmith's wife, was, in truth, a gem of art that a monarch would have purchased with honors and abundant wealth, and have treasured it among the jewels of his kingdom as the most unique and wondrous of them all. But the artist smiled and kept the secret to himself.

'Father,' said Annie, thinking that a word of praise from the old watchmaker might gratify his former apprentice, 'do come and admire this pretty butterfly.'

'Let us see,' said Peter Hovenden, rising from his chair,

with a sneer upon his face that always made people doubt, as he himself did, in everything but a material existence. 'Here is my finger for it to alight upon. I shall understand it better when once I have touched it.'

But, to the increased astonishment of Annie, when the tip of her father's finger was pressed against that of her husband, on which the butterfly still rested, the insect drooped its wings and seemed on the point of falling to the floor. Even the bright spots of gold upon its wings and body, unless her eyes deceived her, grew dim, and the glowing purple took a dusky hue, and the starry lustre that gleamed around the blacksmith's hand became faint and vanished.

'It is dying! it is dying!' cried Annie, in alarm.

'It has been delicately wrought,' said the artist, calmly. 'As I told you, it has imbibed a spiritual essence – call it magnetism, or what you will. In an atmosphere of doubt and mockery its exquisite susceptibility suffers torture, as does the soul of him who instilled his own life into it. It has already lost its beauty; in a few moments more its mechanism would be irreparably injured.'

'Take away your hand, father!' entreated Annie, turning pale. 'Here is my child; let it rest on his innocent hand. There, perhaps, its life will revive and its colors grow brighter than ever.'

Her father, with an acrid smile, withdrew his finger. The butterfly then appeared to recover the power of voluntary motion, while its hues assumed much of their original lustre, and the gleam of starlight, which was its most ethereal attribute, again formed a halo round about it. At first, when transferred from Robert Danforth's hand to the small finger of the child, this radiance grew so powerful that it positively threw the little fellow's shadow back against the wall. He, meanwhile, extended his plump hand as he had seen his father and mother do, and watched the waving of the insect's wings with infantine delight. Nevertheless, there was a certain odd expression of sagacity that made Owen Warland feel as if here were old Peter Hovenden, partially, and but partially, redeemed from his hard scepticism into childish faith.

'How wise the little monkey looks!' whispered Robert Danforth to his wife.

'I never saw such a look on a child's face,' answered Annie, admiring her own infant, and with good reason, far more than the artistic butterfly. 'The darling knows more of the mystery than we do.'

As if the butterfly, like the artist, were conscious of something not entirely congenial in the child's nature, it alternately sparkled and grew dim. At length it arose from the small hand of the infant with an airy motion that seemed to bear it upward without an effort, as if the ethereal instincts with which its master's spirit had endowed it impelled this fair vision involuntarily to a higher sphere. Had there been no obstruction, it might have soared into the sky and grown immortal. But its lustre gleamed upon the ceiling; the exquisite texture of its wings brushed against that earthly medium; and a sparkle or two, as of stardust, floated downward and lay glimmering on the carpet. Then the butterfly came fluttering down, and, instead of returning to the infant, was apparently attracted towards the artist's hand.

'Not so! not so!' murmured Owen Warland, as if his handiwork could have understood him. 'Thou hast gone forth out of thy master's heart. There is no return for thee.'

With a wavering movement, and emitting a tremulous radiance, the butterfly struggled, as it were, towards the infant, and was about to alight upon his finger; but while it still hovered in the air, the little child of strength, with his grandsire's sharp and shrewd expression in his face, made a snatch at the marvellous insect and compressed it in his hand. Annie screamed. Old Peter Hovenden burst into a cold and scornful laugh. The blacksmith, by main force, unclosed the infant's hand, and found within the palm a small heap of glittering fragments, whence the mystery of beauty had fled forever. And as for Owen Warland, he looked placidly at what seemed the ruin of his life's labor, and which was yet no ruin. He had caught a far other butterfly than this. When the artist rose high enough to achieve the beautiful, the symbol by which he made it perceptible to mortal senses became of little value in his eyes while his spirit possessed itself in the enjoyment of the reality.

FRANZ KAFKA

A HUNGER ARTIST

Translated by Willa and Edwin Muir

DURING THESE LAST decades the interest in professional fasting has markedly diminished. It used to pay very well to stage such great performances under one's own management, but today that is quite impossible. We live in a different world now. At one time the whole town took a lively interest in the hunger artist; from day to day of his fast the excitement mounted; everybody wanted to see him at least once a day; there were people who bought season tickets for the last few days and sat from morning till night in front of his small barred cage; even in the nighttime there were visiting hours, when the whole effect was heightened by torch flares; on fine days the cage was set out in the open air, and then it was the children's special treat to see the hunger artist; for their elders he was often just a joke that happened to be in fashion, but the children stood openmouthed, holding each other's hands for greater security, marveling at him as he sat there pallid in black tights, with his ribs sticking out so prominently, not even on a seat but down among straw on the ground, sometimes giving a courteous nod, answering questions with a constrained smile, or perhaps stretching an arm through the bars so that one might feel how thin it was, and then again withdrawing deep into himself, paying no attention to anyone or anything, not even to the all-important striking of the clock that was the only piece of furniture in his cage, but merely staring into vacancy with half-shut eyes, now and then taking a sip from a tiny glass of water to moisten his lips.

Besides casual onlookers there were also relays of permanent watchers selected by the public, usually butchers, strangely enough, and it was their task to watch the hunger artist day and night, three of them at a time, in case he should have some secret recourse to nourishment. This was nothing but a formality, instituted to reassure the masses, for the initiates knew well enough that during his fast the artist would never in any circumstances, not even under forcible compulsion, swallow the smallest morsel of food; the honor of his profession forbade it. Not every watcher, of course, was capable of understanding this, there were often groups of night watchers who were very lax in carrying out their duties and deliberately huddled together in a retired corner to play cards with great absorption, obviously intending to give the hunger artist the chance of a little refreshment, which they supposed he could draw from some private hoard. Nothing annoyed the artist more than such watchers; they made him miserable; they made his fast seem unendurable; sometimes he mastered his feebleness sufficiently to sing during their watch for as long as he could keep going, to show them how unjust their suspicions were. But that was of little use; they only wondered at his cleverness in being able to fill his mouth even while singing. Much more to his taste were the watchers who sat close up to the bars, who were not content with the dim night lighting of the hall but focused him in the full glare of the electric pocket torch given them by the impresario. The harsh light did not trouble him at all, in any case he could never sleep properly, and he could always drowse a little, whatever the light, at any hour, even when the hall was thronged with noisy onlookers. He was quite happy at the prospect of spending a sleepless night with such watchers; he was ready to exchange jokes with them, to tell them stories out of his nomadic life, anything at all to keep them awake and demonstrate to them again that he had no eatables in his cage and that he was fasting as not one of them could fast. But his happiest moment was when the morning came and an enormous breakfast was brought them, at his expense, on which they flung themselves with the keen appetite of healthy men after a weary night of wakefulness. Of course there were people who argued that this breakfast was an unfair attempt to bribe the watchers, but that was going rather too far, and when they were invited to take on a night's vigil without a breakfast, merely for the sake of the cause, they made themselves scarce, although they stuck stubbornly to their suspicions.

Such suspicions, anyhow, were a necessary accompaniment to the profession of fasting. No one could possibly watch the hunger artist continuously, day and night, and so no one could produce first-hand evidence that the fast had really been rigorous and continuous; only the artist himself could know that, he was therefore bound to be the sole completely satisfied spectator of his own fast. Yet for other reasons he was never satisfied; it was not perhaps mere fasting that had brought him to such skeleton thinness that many people had regretfully to keep away from his exhibitions, because the sight of him was too much for them, perhaps it was dissatisfaction with himself that had worn him down. For he alone knew, what no other initiate knew, how easy it was to fast. It was the easiest thing in the world. He made no secret of this, yet people did not believe him, at the best they set him down as modest; most of them, however, thought he was out for publicity or else was some kind of cheat who found it easy to fast because he had discovered a way of making it easy, and then had the impudence to admit the fact, more or less. He had to put up with all that, and in the course of time had got used to it, but his inner dissatisfaction always rankled, and never yet, after any term of fasting – this must be granted to his credit – had he left the cage of his own free will. The longest period of fasting was fixed by his impresario at forty days, beyond that term he was not allowed to go, not even in great cities, and there was good reason for it, too. Experience had proved that for about forty days the interest of the public could be stimulated by a steadily increasing pressure of advertisement, but after that the town began to lose interest, sympathetic support began notably to fall off; there were of course local variations as between one town and another or one country and another, but as a general rule forty days marked the limit. So on the fortieth day the flower-bedecked cage was opened, enthusiastic spectators filled the hall, a military band played, two doctors entered the cage to measure the results of the fast, which were announced through a megaphone, and finally two young ladies appeared, blissful at having been selected for the honor, to help the hunger artist down the few steps leading to a small table on which was spread a carefully chosen invalid repast. And at this very moment the artist always turned stubborn. True, he would entrust his bony arms to the outstretched helping hands of the ladies bending over him, but stand up he would not. Why stop fasting at this particular moment, after forty days of it? He had held out for a long time, an illimitably long time; why stop now, when he was in his best fasting form, or rather, not yet quite in his best fasting form? Why should he be cheated of the fame he would get for fasting longer, for being not only the record hunger artist of all time, which presumably he was already, but for beating his own record by a performance beyond human imagination, since he felt that there were no limits to his capacity for fasting? His public pretended to admire him so much, why should it have so little patience with him; if he could endure fasting longer, why shouldn't the public endure it? Besides, he was tired, he was comfortable sitting in the straw, and now he was supposed to lift himself to his full height and go down to a meal the very thought of which gave him a nausea that only the presence of the ladies kept him from betraying, and even that with an effort. And he looked up into the eyes of the ladies who were apparently so friendly and in reality so cruel, and shook his head, which felt too heavy on its strengthless neck. But then there happened yet again what always happened. The impresario came forward, without a word – for the band made speech impossible – lifted his arms in the air above the artist, as if inviting Heaven to look down upon its creature here in the straw, this suffering martyr, which indeed he was, although in quite another sense; grasped him around the emaciated waist, with exaggerated caution, so that the frail condition he was in might be appreciated; and committed him to the care of the blenching ladies, not without secretly giving him a shaking so that his legs and body tottered and swayed. The artist now submitted completely; his head lolled on his breast as if it had landed there by chance; his body was hollowed out; his legs in a spasm of self-preservation clung close to each other at the knees, yet scraped on the ground as if it were not really solid ground, as if they were only trying to find solid ground; and the whole weight of his body, a featherweight after all, relapsed onto one of the ladies, who, looking around for help and panting a little – this post of honor was not at all what she had expected it to be – first stretched her neck as far as she could to keep her face at least free from contact with the artist, then finding this impossible, and her more fortunate companion not coming to her aid but merely holding extended in her own trembling hand the little bunch of knucklebones that was the artist's, to the great delight of the spectators burst into tears and had to be replaced by an attendant who had long been stationed in readiness. Then came the food, a little of which the impresario managed to get between the artist's lips, while he sat in a kind of half-fainting trance, to the accompaniment of cheerful patter designed to distract the public's attention from the artist's condition; after that, a toast was drunk to the public, supposedly prompted by a whisper from the artist in the impresario's ear; the band confirmed it with a mighty flourish, the spectators melted away, and no one had any cause to be dissatisfied with the proceedings, no one except the hunger artist himself, he only, as always.

So he lived for many years, with small regular intervals of recuperation, in visible glory, honored by the world, yet in spite of that troubled in spirit, and all the more troubled because no one would take his trouble seriously. What comfort could he possibly need? What more could he possibly wish for? And if some good-natured person, feeling sorry for him, tried to console him by pointing out that his melancholy was probably caused by fasting, it could happen, especially when he had been fasting for some time, that he reacted with an outburst of fury and to the general alarm began to shake the bars of his cage like a wild animal. Yet the impresario had a way of punishing these outbreaks which he rather enjoyed putting into operation. He would apologize publicly for the artist's behavior, which was only to be excused, he admitted, because of the irritability caused by fasting; a condition hardly to be understood by well-fed people; then by natural transition he went on to mention the artist's equally incomprehensible boast that he could fast for much longer than he was doing; he praised the high ambition, the good will, the great self-denial undoubtedly implicit in such a statement; and then quite simply countered it by bringing out photographs, which were also on sale to the public, showing the artist on the fortieth day of a fast lying in bed almost dead from exhaustion. This perversion of the truth, familiar to the artist though it was, always unnerved him afresh and proved too much for him. What was a consequence of the premature ending of his fast was here presented as the cause of it! To fight against this lack of understanding, against a whole world of non-understanding, was impossible. Time and again in good faith he stood by the bars listening to the impresario, but as soon as the photographs appeared he always let go and sank with a groan back into his straw, and the reassured public could once more come close and gaze at him.

A few years later when the witnesses of such scenes called them to mind, they often failed to understand themselves at all. For meanwhile the aforementioned change in public interest had set in; it seemed to happen almost overnight; there may have been profound causes for it, but who was going to bother about that; at any rate the pampered hunger artist suddenly found himself deserted one fine day by the amusement-seekers, who went streaming past him to other more-favored attractions. For the last time the impresario hurried him over half Europe to discover whether the old interest might still survive here and there; all in vain; everywhere, as if by secret agreement, a positive revulsion from professional fasting was in evidence. Of course it could not really have sprung up so suddenly as all that, and many premonitory symptoms which had not been sufficiently remarked or suppressed during the rush and glitter of success now came retrospectively to mind, but it was now too late to take any countermeasures. Fasting would surely come into fashion again at some future date, yet that was no comfort for those living in the present. What, then, was the hunger artist to do? He had been applauded by thousands in his time and could hardly come down to showing himself in a street booth at village fairs, and as for adopting another profession, he was not only too old for that but too fanatically devoted to fasting. So he took leave of the impresario, his partner in an unparalleled career, and hired himself to a large circus; in order to spare his own feelings he avoided reading the conditions of his contract.

A large circus with its enormous traffic in replacing and recruiting men, animals, and apparatus can always find a use for people at any time, even for a hunger artist, provided of course that he does not ask too much, and in this particular case anyhow it was not only the artist who was taken on but his famous and long-known name as well, indeed considering the peculiar nature of his performance, which was not impaired by advancing age, it could not be objected that here was an artist past his prime, no longer at the height of his professional skill, seeking a refuge in some quiet corner of a circus; on the contrary, the hunger artist averred that he could fast as well as ever, which was entirely credible, he even alleged that if he were allowed to fast as he liked, and this was at once promised him without more ado, he could astound the world by establishing a record never yet achieved, a statement that certainly provoked a smile among the other professionals, since it left out of account the change in public opinion, which the hunger artist in his zeal conveniently forgot.

He had not, however, actually lost his sense of the real situation and took it as a matter of course that he and his cage should be stationed, not in the middle of the ring as a main attraction, but outside, near the animal cages, on a site that was after all easily accessible. Large and gaily painted placards made a frame for the cage and announced what was to be seen inside it. When the public came thronging out in the intervals to see the animals, they could hardly avoid passing the hunger artist's cage and stopping there for a moment, perhaps they might even have stayed longer had not those pressing behind them in the narrow gangway, who did not understand why they should be held up on their way toward the excitements of the menagerie, made it impossible for anyone to stand gazing quietly for any length of time. And that was the reason why the hunger artist, who had of course been looking forward to these visiting hours as the main achievement of his life, began instead to shrink from them. At first he could hardly wait for the intervals; it was exhilarating to watch the crowds come streaming his way, until only too soon – not even the most obstinate self-deception, clung to almost consciously, could hold out against the fact – the conviction was borne in upon him that these people, most of them, to judge from their actions, again and again, without exception, were all on their way to the menagerie. And the first sight of them from the distance remained the best. For when they reached his cage he was at once deafened by the storm of shouting and abuse that arose from the two contending factions, which renewed themselves continuously, of those who wanted to stop and stare at him – he soon began to dislike them more than the others – not out of real interest but only out of obstinate self-assertiveness, and those who wanted to go straight on to the animals. When the first great rush was past, the stragglers came along, and these, whom nothing could have prevented from stopping to look at him as long as they had breath, raced past with long strides, hardly even glancing at him, in their haste to get to the menagerie in time. And all too rarely did it happen that he had a stroke of luck, when some father of a family fetched up before him with his children, pointed a finger at the hunger artist, and explained at length what the phenomenon meant, telling stories of earlier years when he himself had watched similar but much more thrilling performances, and the children, still rather uncomprehending, since neither inside nor outside school had they been sufficiently prepared for this lesson – what did they care about fasting? – yet showed by the brightness of their intent eyes that new and better times might be coming. Perhaps, said the hunger artist to himself many a time, things would be a little better if his cage were set not quite so near the menagerie. That made it too easy for people to make their choice, to say nothing of what he suffered from the stench of the menagerie, the animals' restlessness by night, the carrying past of raw lumps of flesh for the beasts of prey, the roaring at feeding times, which depressed him continually. But he did not dare to lodge a complaint with the management; after all, he had the animals to thank for the troops of people who passed his cage, among whom there might always be one here and there to take an interest in him, and who could tell where they might seclude him if he called attention to his existence and thereby to the fact that, strictly speaking, he was only an impediment on the way to the menagerie.

A small impediment, to be sure, one that grew steadily less. People grew familiar with the strange idea that they could be expected, in times like these, to take an interest in a hunger artist, and with this familiarity the verdict went out against him. He might fast as much as he could, and he did so; but nothing could save him now, people passed him by. Just try to explain to anyone the art of fasting! Anyone who has no feeling for it cannot be made to understand it. The fine placards grew dirty and illegible, they were torn down; the little notice board telling the number of fast days achieved, which at first was changed carefully every day, had long stayed at the same figure, for after the first few weeks even this small task seemed pointless to the staff; and so the artist simply fasted on and on, as he had once dreamed of doing, and it was no trouble to him, just as he had always foretold, but no one counted the days, no one, not even the artist himself, knew what records he was already breaking, and his heart grew heavy. And when once in a while some leisurely passer-by stopped, made merry over the old figure on the board, and spoke of swindling, that was in its way the stupidest lie ever invented by indifference and inborn malice, since it was not the hunger artist who was cheating, he was working honestly, but the world was cheating him of his reward.

Many more days went by, however, and that too came to an end. An overseer's eye fell on the cage one day and he asked the attendants why this perfectly good cage should be left standing there unused with dirty straw inside it; nobody knew, until one man, helped out by the notice board, remembered about the hunger artist. They poked into the straw with sticks and found him in it. 'Are you still fasting?' asked the overseer, 'when on earth do you mean to stop?' 'Forgive me, everybody,' whispered the hunger artist; only the overseer, who had his ear to the bars, understood him. 'Of course,' said the overseer, and tapped his forehead with a finger to let the attendants know what state the man was in, 'we forgive you.' 'I always wanted you to admire my fasting,' said the hunger artist. 'We do admire it,' said the overseer, affably. 'But you shouldn't admire it,' said the hunger artist. 'Well then we don't admire it,' said the overseer, 'but why shouldn't we admire it?' 'Because I have to fast, I can't help it,' said the hunger artist. 'What a fellow you are,' said the overseer, 'and why can't you help it?' 'Because,' said the hunger artist, lifting his head a little and speaking, with his lips pursed, as if for a kiss, right into the overseer's ear, so that

273

no syllable might be lost, 'because I couldn't find the food I liked. If I had found it, believe me, I should have made no fuss and stuffed myself like you or anyone else.' These were his last words, but in his dimming eyes remained the firm though no longer proud persuasion that he was still continuing to fast.

'Well, clear this out now!' said the overseer, and they buried the hunger artist, straw and all. Into the cage they put a young panther. Even the most insensitive felt it refreshing to see this wild creature leaping around the cage that had so long been dreary. The panther was all right. The food he liked was brought him without hesitation by the attendants; he seemed not even to miss his freedom; his noble body, furnished almost to the bursting point with all that it needed, seemed to carry freedom around with it too; somewhere in his jaws it seemed to lurk; and the joy of life streamed with such ardent passion from his throat that for the onlookers it was not easy to stand the shock of it. But they braced themselves, crowded around the cage, and did not want ever to move away.

HONORÉ DE BALZAC

THE UNKNOWN
MASTERPIECE

Translated by Ellen Marriage

I. GILLETTE

ON A COLD December morning in the year 1612, a young man, whose clothing was somewhat of the thinnest, was walking to and fro before a gateway in the Rue des Grands-Augustins in Paris. He went up and down the street before this house with the irresolution of a gallant who dares not venture into the presence of the mistress whom he loves for the first time, easy of access though she may be; but after a sufficiently long interval of hesitation, he at last crossed the threshold and inquired of an old woman, who was sweeping out a large room on the ground floor, whether Master Porbus was within. Receiving a reply in the affirmative, the young man went slowly up the staircase, like a gentleman but newly come to court, and doubtful as to his reception by the king. He came to a stand once more on the landing at the head of the stairs, and again he hesitated before raising his hand to the grotesque knocker on the door of the studio, where doubtless the painter was at work – Master Porbus, sometime painter in ordinary to Henri IV till Mary de' Medici took Rubens into favor.

The young man felt deeply stirred by an emotion that must thrill the hearts of all great artists when, in the pride of their youth and their first love of art, they come into the presence of a master or stand before a masterpiece. For all human sentiments there is a time of early blossoming, a day of generous enthusiasm that gradually fades until nothing is left of happiness but a memory, and glory is known for a delusion. Of all these delicate and short-lived emotions, none so resemble love as the passion of a young artist for his art, as he is about to enter on the blissful martyrdom of his career of glory and disaster, of vague expectations and real disappointments.

Those who have missed this experience in the early days of light purses; who have not, in the dawn of their genius, stood in the presence of a master and felt the throbbing of their hearts, will always carry in their inmost souls a chord that has never been touched, and in their work an indefinable quality will be lacking, a something in the stroke of the brush, a mysterious element that we call poetry. The swaggerers, so puffed up by self-conceit that they are confident over-soon of their success, can never be taken for men of talent save by fools. From this point of view, if youthful modesty is the measure of youthful genius, the stranger on the staircase might be allowed to have something in him; for he seemed to possess the indescribable diffidence, the early timidity that artists are bound to lose in the course of a great career, even as pretty women lose it as they make progress in the arts of coquetry. Self-distrust vanishes as triumph succeeds to triumph, and modesty is, perhaps, distrust of itself.

The poor neophyte was so overcome by the consciousness of his own presumption and insignificance, that it began to look as if he was hardly likely to penetrate into the studio of the painter, to whom we owe the wonderful portrait of Henri IV. But fate was propitious; an old man came up the staircase. From the quaint costume of this newcomer, his collar of magnificent lace, and a certain serene gravity in his bearing, the first arrival thought that this personage must be either a patron or a friend of the court painter. He stood aside therefore upon the landing to allow the visitor to pass, scrutinizing him curiously the while. Perhaps he might hope to find the good nature of an artist or to receive the good offices of an amateur not unfriendly to the arts; but besides an almost diabolical expression in the face that met his gaze, there was that indescribable something which has an irresistible attraction for artists.

Picture that face. A bald high forehead and rugged jutting brows above a small flat nose turned up at the end, as in the portraits of Socrates and Rabelais; deep lines about the mocking mouth; a short chin, carried proudly, covered with a grizzled pointed beard; sea-green eyes that age might seem to have dimmed were it not for the contrast between the iris and the surrounding mother-of-pearl tints, so that it seemed as if under the stress of anger or enthusiasm there would be a magnetic power to quell or kindle in their glances. The face was withered beyond wont by the fatigue of years, yet it seemed aged still more by the thoughts that had worn away both soul and body. There were no lashes to the deep-set eyes, and scarcely a trace of the arching lines of the eyebrows above them. Set this head on a spare and feeble frame, place it in a frame of lace wrought like an engraved silver fish-slice, imagine a heavy gold chain over the old man's black doublet, and you will have some dim idea of this strange personage, who seemed still more fantastic in the sombre twilight of the staircase. One of Rembrandt's portraits might have stepped down from its frame to walk in an appropriate atmosphere of gloom, such as the great painter loved. The older man gave the younger a shrewd glance, and knocked thrice at the door. It was opened by a man of forty or thereabout, who seemed to be an invalid.

'Good day, Master.'

Porbus bowed respectfully, and held the door open for the younger man to enter, thinking that the latter accompanied his visitor; and when he saw that the neophyte stood a while as if spellbound, feeling, as every artist-nature must feel, the fascinating influence of the first sight of a studio in which the material processes of art are revealed, Porbus troubled himself no more about this second comer.

All the light in the studio came from a window in the roof, and was concentrated upon an easel, where a canvas stood untouched as yet save for three or four outlines in chalk. The daylight scarcely reached the remoter angles and corners of the vast room; they were as dark as night, but the silver orna-mented breastplate of a Reiter's corselet, that hung upon the wall, attracted a stray gleam to its dim abiding-place among the brown shadows; or a shaft of light shot across the carved and glistening surface of an antique sideboard covered with curious silver-plate, or struck out a line of glittering dots among the raised threads of the golden warp of some old brocaded curtains, where the lines of the stiff, heavy folds were broken, as the stuff had been flung carelessly down to serve as a model.

Plaster *écorchés* stood about the room; and here and there, on shelves and tables, lay fragments of classical sculpture-torsos of antique goddesses, worn smooth as though all the years of the centuries that had passed over them had been lovers' kisses. The walls were covered, from floor to ceiling, with countless sketches in charcoal, red chalk, or pen and ink. Amid the litter and confusion of color boxes, overturned stools, flasks of oil, and essences, there was just room to move so as to reach the illuminated circular space where the easel stood. The light from the window in the roof fell full upon Porbus's pale face and on the ivory-tinted forehead of his strange visitor. But in another moment the younger man heeded nothing but a picture that had already become fam-ous even in those stormy days of political and religious revolution, a picture that a few of the zealous worshipers, who have so often kept the sacred fire of art alive in evil days, were wont to go on pilgrimage to see. The beautiful panel represented a Saint Mary of Egypt about to pay her passage across the seas. It was a masterpiece destined for Mary de' Medici, who sold it in later years of poverty.

'I like your saint,' the old man remarked, addressing Porbus. 'I would give you ten golden crowns for her over and above the price the Queen is paying; but as for putting a spoke in that wheel, – the devil take it!'

'It is good then?'

'Hey! hey!' said the old man; 'good, say you? – Yes and no. Your good woman is not badly done, but she is not alive. You artists fancy that when a figure is correctly drawn, and everything in its place according to the rules of anatomy, there is nothing more to be done. You make up the flesh tints beforehand on your palettes according to your formulae, and fill in the outlines with due care that one side of the face shall be darker than the other; and because you look from time to time at a naked woman who stands on the platform before you, you fondly imagine that you have copied nature, think yourselves to be painters, believe that you have wrested His secret from God. Pshaw! You may know your syntax thoroughly and make no blunders in your grammar, but it takes that and something more to make a great poet. Look at your saint, Porbus! At a first glance she is admirable; look at her again, and you see at once that she is glued to the background, and that you could not walk round her. She is a silhouette that turns but one side of her face to all beholders, a figure cut out of canvas, an image with no power to move nor change her position. I feel as if there were no air between that arm and the background, no space, no sense of distance in your canvas. The perspective is perfectly correct, the strength of the coloring is accurately diminished with the distance; but, in spite of these praiseworthy efforts, I could never bring myself to believe that the warm breath of life comes and goes in that beautiful body. It seems to me that if I laid my hand on the firm, rounded throat, it would be cold as marble to the touch. No, my friend, the blood does not flow beneath that ivory skin, the tide of life does not flush those delicate fibres, the purple veins that trace a network beneath the transparent amber of her brow and breast. Here the pulse seems to beat, there it is motionless, life and death are at strife in every detail; here you see a woman, there a statue, there again a corpse. Your creation is incomplete. You had only power to breathe a portion of your soul into your beloved work. The fire of Prometheus died out again and again in your hands; many a spot in your picture has not been touched by the divine flame.'

'But how is it, dear master?' Porbus asked respectfully, while the young man with difficulty repressed his strong desire to beat the critic.

'Ah!' said the old man, 'it is this! You have halted between two manners. You have hesitated between drawing and color, between the dogged attention to detail, the stiff precision of the German masters and the dazzling glow, the joyous exuberance of Italian painters. You have set yourself to imitate Hans Holbein and Titian, Albrecht Dürer and Paul Veronese in a single picture. A magnificent ambition truly, but what has come of it? Your work has neither the severe charm of a dry execution nor the magical illusion of Italian *chiaroscuro*. Titian's rich golden coloring poured into Albrecht Dürer's austere outlines has shattered them, like molten bronze bursting through the mold that is not strong enough to hold it. In other places the outlines have held firm, imprisoning and obscuring the magnificent, glowing flood of Venetian color. The drawing of the face is not perfect, the coloring is not perfect; traces of that unlucky indecision are to be seen everywhere. Unless you felt strong enough to fuse the two opposed manners in the fire of your own genius, you should have cast in your lot boldly with the one or the other, and so have obtained the unity which simulates one of the conditions of life itself. Your work is only true in the centres; your outlines are false, they project nothing, there is no hint of anything behind them. There is truth here,' said the old man, pointing to the breast of the Saint, 'and again here,' he went on, indicating the rounded shoulder. 'But there,' once more returning to the column of the throat, 'everything is false. Let us go no further into detail, you would be disheartened.'

The old man sat down on a stool, and remained a while without speaking, with his face buried in his hands.

'Yet I studied that throat from the life, dear master,' Porbus began; 'it happens sometimes, for our misfortune, that real effects in nature look improbable when transferred to canvas –'

'The aim of art is not to copy nature, but to express it. You are not a servile copyist, but a poet!' cried the old man sharply, cutting Porbus short with an imperious gesture. 'Otherwise a sculptor might make a plaster cast of a living woman and save himself all further trouble. Well, try to make a cast of your mistress's hand, and set up the thing before you. You will see a monstrosity, a dead mass, bearing no resemblance to the living hand; you would be compelled to have recourse to the chisel of a sculptor who, without making an exact copy, would represent for you its movement and its life. We must detect the spirit, the informing soul in the appearances of things and beings. Effects! What are effects but the accidents of life, not life itself? A hand,

283

since I have taken that example, is not only a part of a body, it is the expression and extension of a thought that must be grasped and rendered. Neither painter nor poet nor sculptor may separate the effect from the cause, which are inevitably contained the one in the other. There begins the real struggle! Many a painter achieves success instinctively, unconscious of the task that is set before art. You draw a woman, yet you do not see her! Not so do you succeed in wresting Nature's secrets from her! You are reproducing mechanically the model that you copied in your master's studio. You do not penetrate far enough into the inmost secrets of the mystery of form; you do not seek with love enough and perseverance enough after the form that baffles and eludes you. Beauty is a thing severe and unapproachable, never to be won by a languid lover. You must lie in wait for her coming and take her unawares, press her hard and clasp her in a tight embrace, and force her to yield. Form is a Proteus more intangible and more manifold than the Proteus of the legend; compelled, only after long wrestling, to stand forth manifest in his true aspect. Some of you are satisfied with the first shape, or at most by the second or the third that appears. Not thus wrestle the victors, the unvanquished painters who never suffer themselves to be deluded by all those treacherous shadow-shapes; they persevere till Nature at the last stands bare to their gaze, and her very soul is revealed.

'In this manner worked Rafael,' said the old man, taking off his cap to express his reverence for the King of Art. 'His transcendent greatness came of the intimate sense that, in him, seems as if it would shatter external form. Form in his figures (as with us) is a symbol, a means of communicating sensations, ideas, the vast imaginings of a poet. Every face is a whole world. The subject of the portrait appeared for him

284

bathed in the light of a divine vision; it was revealed by an inner voice, the finger of God laid bare the sources of expression in the past of a whole life.

'You clothe your women in fair raiment of flesh, in gracious veiling of hair; but where is the blood, the source of passion and of calm, the cause of the particular effect? Why, this brown Egyptian of yours, my good Porbus, is a colorless creature! These figures that you set before us are painted bloodless phantoms; and you call that painting, you call that art!

'Because you have made something more like a woman than a house, you think that you have set your fingers on the goal; you are quite proud that you need not to write *currus venustus* or *pulcher homo* beside your figures, as early painters were wont to do and you fancy that you have done wonders. Ah! my good friend, there is still something more to learn, and you will use up a great deal of chalk and cover many a canvas before you will learn it. Yes, truly, a woman carries her head in just such a way, so she holds her garments gathered into her hand; her eyes grow dreamy and soft with that expression of meek sweetness, and even so the quivering shadow of the lashes hovers upon her cheeks. It is all there, and yet it is not there. What is lacking? A nothing, but that nothing is everything.

'There you have the semblance of life, but you do not express its fulness and effluence, that indescribable something, perhaps the soul itself, that envelopes the outlines of the body like a haze; that flower of life, in short, that Titian and Rafael caught. Your utmost achievement hitherto has only brought you to the starting-point. You might now perhaps begin to do excellent work, but you grow weary all too soon; and the crowd admires, and those who know smile.

'Oh, Mabuse! oh, my master!' cried the strange speaker,

thou art a thief! Thou hast carried away the secret of life with thee!'

'Nevertheless,' he began again, 'this picture of yours is worth more than all the paintings of that rascal Rubens, with his mountains of Flemish flesh raddled with vermilion, his torrents of red hair, his riot of color. You, at least have color there, and feeling and drawing – the three essentials in art.'

The young man roused himself from his deep musings.

'Why, my good man, the Saint is sublime!' he cried. 'There is a subtlety of imagination about those two figures, the Saint Mary and the Shipman, that can not be found among Italian masters; I do not know a single one of them capable of imagining the Shipman's hesitation.'

'Did that little malapert come with you?' asked Porbus of the older man.

'Alas! master, pardon my boldness,' cried the neophyte, and the color mounted to his face. 'I am unknown – a dauber by instinct, and but lately come to this city – the fountain-head of all learning.'

'Set to work,' said Porbus, handing him a bit of red chalk and a sheet of paper.

The new-comer quickly sketched the Saint Mary line for line.

'Aha!' exclaimed the old man. 'Your name?' he added.

The young man wrote 'Nicolas Poussin' below the sketch.

'Not bad that for a beginning,' said the strange speaker, who had discoursed so wildly. 'I see that we can talk of art in your presence. I do not blame you for admiring Porbus's saint. In the eyes of the world she is a masterpiece, and those alone who have been initiated into the inmost mysteries of art can discover her shortcomings. But it is worth while to give you the lesson, for you are able to understand it, so I will show you how little it needs to complete this picture. You must be all eyes, all attention, for it may be that such a chance of learning will never come in your way again – Porbus! your palette.'

Porbus went in search of palette and brushes. The little old man turned back his sleeves with impatient energy, seized the palette, covered with many hues, that Porbus handed to him, and snatched rather than took a handful of brushes of various sizes from the hands of his acquaintance. His pointed beard suddenly bristled – a menacing movement that expressed the prick of a lover's fancy. As he loaded his brush, he muttered between his teeth, 'These paints are only fit to fling out of the window, together with the fellow who ground them, their crudeness and falseness are disgusting! How can one paint with this?'

He dipped the tip of the brush with feverish eagerness in the different pigments, making the circuit of the palette several times more quickly than the organist of a cathedral sweeps the octaves on the keyboard of his clavier for the *O Filii* at Easter.

Porbus and Poussin, on either side of the easel, stood stock-still, watching with intense interest.

'Look, young man,' he began again, 'see how three or four strokes of the brush and a thin glaze of blue let in the free air to play about the head of the poor Saint, who must have felt stifled and oppressed by the close atmosphere! See how the drapery begins to flutter; you feel that it is lifted by the breeze! A moment ago it hung as heavily and stiffly as if it were held out by pins. Do you see how the satin sheen that I have just given to the breast rends the pliant, silken softness of a young girl's skin, and how the brown-red, blended with burnt ochre, brings warmth into the cold gray of the deep shadow where the blood lay congealed instead of coursing through the veins? Young man, young man, no master could teach you how to do this that I am doing before your eyes. Mabuse alone possessed the secret of giving life to his figures; Mabuse had but one pupil – that was I. I have had none, and I am old. You have sufficient intelligence to imagine the rest from the glimpses that I am giving you.'

While the old man was speaking, he gave a touch here and there; sometimes two strokes of the brush, sometimes a single one; but every stroke told so well, that the whole picture seemed transfigured – the painting was flooded with light. He worked with such passionate fervor that beads of sweat gathered upon his bare forehead; he worked so quickly, in brief, impatient jerks, that it seemed to young Poussin as if some familiar spirit inhabiting the body of this strange being took a grotesque pleasure in making use of the man's hands against his own will. The unearthly glitter of his eyes, the convulsive movements that seemed like struggles, gave to this fancy a semblance of truth which could not but stir a young imagination. The old man continued, saying as he did so –

'Paf! paf! that is how to lay it on, young man! – Little touches! come and bring a glow into those icy cold tones for me! Just so! Pon! pon! pon!' and those parts of the picture that he had pointed out as cold and lifeless flushed with warmer hues, a few bold strokes of color brought all the tones of the picture into the required harmony with the glowing tints of the Egyptian, and the differences in temperament vanished.

'Look you, youngster, the last touches make the picture. Porbus has given it a hundred strokes for every one of mine. No one thanks us for what lies beneath. Bear that in mind.'

At last the restless spirit stopped, and turning to Porbus and Poussin, who were speechless with admiration, he spoke –

'This is not as good as my *Belle Noiseuse*; still one might put one's name to such a thing as this – Yes, I would put my name to it,' he added, rising to reach for a mirror, in which he looked at the picture – 'And now,' he said, 'will you both come and breakfast with me? I have a smoked ham and some very fair wine! . . . Eh! eh! the times may be bad, but we can still have some talk about art! We can talk like equals. . . . Here is a little fellow who has aptitude,' he added, laying a hand on Nicolas Poussin's shoulder.

In this way the stranger became aware of the threadbare condition of the Norman's doublet. He drew a leather purse from his girdle, felt in it, found two gold coins, and held them out.

'I will buy your sketch,' he said.

'Take it,' said Porbus, as he saw the other start and flush with embarrassment, for Poussin had the pride of poverty. 'Pray, take it; he has a couple of king's ransoms in his pouch!'

The three came down together from the studio, and, talking of art by the way, reached a picturesque wooden house hard by the Pont Saint-Michel. Poussin wondered a moment at its ornament, at the knocker, at the frames of the casements, at the scroll-work designs, and in the next he stood in a vast low-ceiled room. A table, covered with tempting dishes, stood near the blazing fire, and (luck unhoped for) he was in the company of two great artists full of genial good humor.

'Do not look too long at that canvas, young man,' said Porbus, when he saw that Poussin was standing, struck with wonder, before a painting. 'You would fall a victim to despair.'

It was the *Adam* painted by Mabuse to purchase his release from the prison, where his creditors had so long kept him. And, as a matter of fact, the figure stood out so boldly and convincingly, that Nicolas Poussin began to understand the real meaning of the words poured out by the old artist, who was himself looking at the picture with apparent satisfaction, but without enthusiasm. 'I have done better than that!' he seemed to be saying to himself.

'There is life in it,' he said aloud; 'in that respect my poor master here surpassed himself, but there is some lack of truth in the background. The man lives indeed; he is rising, and will come toward us; but the atmosphere, the sky, the air, the breath of the breeze – you look and feel for them, but they are not there. And then the man himself is, after all, only a man! Ah! but the one man in the world who came direct from the hands of God must have had a something divine about him that is wanting here. Mabuse himself would grind his teeth and say so when he was not drunk.'

Poussin looked from the speaker to Porbus, and from Porbus to the speaker, with restless curiosity. He went up to the latter to ask for the name of their host; but the painter laid a finger on his lips with an air of mystery. The young man's interest was excited; he kept silence, but hoped that sooner or later some word might be let fall that would reveal the name of his entertainer. It was evident that he was a man of talent and very wealthy, for Porbus listened to him respectfully, and the vast room was crowded with marvels of art.

A magnificent portrait of a woman, hung against the dark oak panels of the wall, next caught Poussin's attention.

'What a glorious Giorgione!' he cried.

'No,' said his host, 'it is an early daub of mine –'

'Gramercy! I am in the abode of the god of painting, it seems!' cried Poussin ingenuously.

The old man smiled as if he had long grown familiar with such praise.

'Master Frenhofer!' said Porbus, 'do you think you could spare me a little of your capital Rhine wine?'

'A couple of pipes!' answered his host; 'one to discharge a

debt, for the pleasure of seeing your pretty sinner, the other as a present from a friend.'

'Ah! if I had my health,' returned Porbus, 'and if you would but let me see your *Belle Noiseuse*, I would paint some great picture, with breadth in it and depth; the figures should be life-size.'

'Let you see my work!' cried the painter in agitation. 'No, no! it is not perfect yet; something still remains for me to do. Yesterday, in the dusk,' he said, 'I thought I had reached the end. Her eyes seemed moist, the flesh quivered, something stirred the tresses of her hair. She breathed! But though I have succeeded in reproducing Nature's roundness and relief on the flat surface of the canvas, this morning, by day-light, I found out my mistake. Ah! to achieve that glorious result I have studied the works of the great masters of color, stripping off coat after coat of color from Titian's canvas, analyzing the pigments of the king of light. Like that sovereign painter, I began the face in a slight tone with a supple and fat paste – for shadow is but an accident; bear that in mind, youngster! – Then I began afresh, and by half-tones and thin glazes of color less and less transparent, I gradually deepened the tints to the deepest black of the strongest shadows. An ordinary painter makes his shadows something entirely different in nature from the high lights; they are wood or brass, or what you will, anything but flesh in shadow. You feel that even if those figures were to alter their position, those shadow stains would never be cleansed away, those parts of the picture would never glow with light.

'I have escaped one mistake, into which the most famous painters have sometimes fallen; in my canvas the whiteness shines through the densest and most persistent shadow. I have not marked out the limits of my figure in hard, dry outlines, and brought every least anatomical detail into prominence (like a host of dunces, who fancy that they can draw because they can trace a line elaborately smooth and clean), for the human body is not contained within the limits of line. In this the sculptor can approach the truth more nearly than we painters. Nature's way is a complicated succession of curve within curve. Strictly speaking, there is no such thing as drawing. – Do not laugh, young man; strange as that speech may seem to you, you will understand the truth in it some day. – A line is a method of expressing the effect of light upon an object; but there are no lines in Nature, everything is solid. We draw by modeling, that is to say, that we disengage an object from its setting; the distribution of the light alone gives to a body the appearance by which we know it. So I have not defined the outlines; I have suffused them with a haze of half-tints warm or golden, in such a sort that you can not lay your finger on the exact spot where background and contours meet. Seen from near, the picture looks a blur; it seems to lack definition; but step back two paces, and the whole thing becomes clear, distinct, and solid; the body stands out; the rounded form comes into relief; you feel that the air plays round it. And yet – I am not satisfied; I have misgivings. Perhaps one ought not to draw a single line; perhaps it would be better to attack the face from the centre, taking the highest prominences first, proceeding from them through the whole range of shadows to the heaviest of all. Is not this the method of the sun, the divine painter of the world? Oh, Nature, Nature! who has surprised thee, fugitive? But, after all, too much knowledge, like ignorance, brings you to a negation. I have doubts about my work.'

There was a pause. Then the old man spoke again. 'I have been at work upon it for ten years, young man; but what are ten short years in a struggle with Nature? Do we know how long Sir Pygmalion wrought at the one statue that came to life?' The old man fell into deep musings, and gazed before him with unseeing eyes, while he played unheedingly with his knife.

'Look, he is in conversation with his *dæmon*!' murmured Porbus.

At the word, Nicolas Poussin felt himself carried away by an unaccountable accession of artist's curiosity. For him the old man, at once intent and inert, the seer with the unseeing eyes, became something more than a man – a fantastic spirit living in a mysterious world, and countless vague thoughts awoke within his soul. The effect of this species of fascination upon his mind can no more be described in words than the passionate longing awakened in an exile's heart by the song that recalls his home. He thought of the scorn that the old man affected to display for the noblest efforts of art, of his wealth, his manners, of the deference paid to him by Porbus. The mysterious picture, the work of patience on which he had wrought so long in secret, was doubtless a work of genius, for the head of the Virgin which young Poussin had admired so frankly was beautiful even beside Mabuse's *Adam* – there was no mistaking the imperial manner of one of the princes of art. Everything combined to set the old man beyond the limits of human nature.

Out of the wealth of fancies in Nicolas Poussin's brain an idea grew, and gathered shape and clearness. He saw in this supernatural being a complete type of the artist nature, a nature mocking and kindly, barren and prolific, an erratic spirit intrusted with great and manifold powers which she too often abuses, leading sober reason, the Philistine, and sometimes even the amateur forth into a stony wilderness where they see nothing; but the white-winged maiden herself, wild as her fancies may be, finds epics there and castles and works of art. For Poussin, the enthusiast, the old man, was suddenly transfigured, and became Art incarnate, Art with its mysteries, its vehement passion and its dreams.

'Yes, my dear Porbus,' Frenhofer continued, 'hitherto I have never found a flawless model, a body with outlines of perfect beauty, the carnations – Ah! where does she live?' he cried, breaking in upon himself, 'the undiscoverable Venus of the older time, for whom we have sought so often, only to find the scattered gleams of her beauty here and there? Oh! to behold once and for one moment, Nature grown perfect and divine, the Ideal at last, I would give all that I possess. . . . Nay, Beauty divine, I would go to seek thee in the dim land of the dead; like Orpheus, I would go down into the Hades of Art to bring back the life of art from among the shadows of death.'

'We can go now,' said Porbus to Poussin. 'He neither hears nor sees us any longer.'

'Let us go to his studio,' said young Poussin, wondering greatly.

'Oh! the old fox takes care that no one shall enter it. His treasures are so carefully guarded that it is impossible for us to come at them. I have not waited for your suggestion and your fancy to attempt to lay hands on this mystery by force.'

'So there is a mystery?'

'Yes,' answered Porbus. 'Old Frenhofer is the only pupil Mabuse would take. Frenhofer became the painter's friend, deliverer, and father; he sacrificed the greater part of his fortune to enable Mabuse to indulge in riotous extravagance, and in return Mabuse bequeathed to him the secret of relief, the power of giving to his figures the wonderful life, the flower of Nature, the eternal despair of art, the secret which Mabuse knew so well that one day when he had sold the flowered brocade suit in which he should have appeared at the Entry of Charles V, he accompanied his master in a suit of paper painted to resemble the brocade. The peculiar richness and splendor of the stuff struck the Emperor; he complimented the old drunkard's patron on the artist's appearance, and so the trick was brought to light. Frenhofer is a passionate enthusiast, who sees above and beyond other painters. He has meditated profoundly on color, and the absolute truth of line; but by the way of much research he has come to doubt the very existence of the objects of his search. He says, in moments of despondency, that there is no such thing as drawing, and that by means of lines we can only reproduce geometrical figures; but that is overshooting the mark, for by outline and shadow you can reproduce form without any color at all, which shows that our art, like Nature, is composed of an infinite number of elements. Drawing gives you the skeleton, the anatomical framework, and color puts the life into it; but life without the skeleton is even more incomplete than a skeleton without life. But there is something else truer still, and it is this – for painters, practise and observation are everything; and when theories and poetical ideas begin to quarrel with the brushes, the end is doubt, as has happened with our good friend, who is half crack-brained enthusiast, half painter. A sublime painter! but unlucky for him, he was born to riches, and so he has leisure to follow his fancies. Do not you follow his example! Work! painters have no business to think, except brush in hand.'

'We will find a way into his studio!' cried Poussin confidently. He had ceased to heed Porbus's remarks. The other smiled at the young painter's enthusiasm, asked him to come to see him again, and they parted.

Nicolas Poussin went slowly back to the Rue de la Harpe, and passed the modest hostelry where he was lodging without noticing it. A feeling of uneasiness prompted him to hurry up the crazy staircase till he reached a room at the top, a quaint, airy recess under the steep, high-pitched roof common among houses in old Paris. In the one dingy window of the place sat a young girl, who sprang up at once when she heard some one at the door; it was the prompting of love; she had recognized the painter's touch on the latch.

'What is the matter with you?' she asked.

'The matter is . . . is . . . Oh! I have felt that I am a painter! Until today I have had doubts, but now I believe in myself! There is the making of a great man in me! Never mind, Gillette, we shall be rich and happy! There is gold at the tips of those brushes –'

He broke off suddenly. The joy faded from his powerful and earnest face as he compared his vast hopes with his slender resources. The walls were covered with sketches in chalk on sheets of common paper. There were but four canvases in the room. Colors were very costly, and the young painter's palette was almost bare. Yet in the midst of his poverty he possessed and was conscious of the possession of inexhaustible treasures of the heart, of a devouring genius equal to all the tasks that lay before him.

He had been brought to Paris by a nobleman among his friends, or perchance by the consciousness of his powers; and in Paris he had found a mistress, one of those noble and generous souls who choose to suffer by a great man's side, who share his struggles and strive to understand his fancies, accepting their lot of poverty and love as bravely and dauntlessly as other women will set themselves to bear the burden of riches and make a parade of their insensibility. The smile that stole over Gillette's lips filled the garret with golden light, and rivaled the brightness of the sun in heaven. The sun, moreover, does not always shine in heaven, whereas Gillette was always in the garret, absorbed in her passion, occupied by Poussin's happiness and sorrow, consoling the genius which found an outlet in love before art engrossed it.

'Listen, Gillette. Come here.'

The girl obeyed joyously, and sprang upon the painter's knee. Hers was perfect grace and beauty, and the loveliness of spring; she was adorned with all luxuriant fairness of outward form, lighted up by the glow of a fair soul within.

'Oh! God,' he cried; 'I shall never dare to tell her –'

'A secret?' she cried; 'I must know it!'

Poussin was absorbed in his dreams.

'Do tell it me!'

'Gillette . . . poor beloved heart! . . .'

'Oh! do you want something of me?'

'Yes.'

'If you wish me to sit once more for you as I did the other day,' she continued with playful petulance, 'I will never consent to do such a thing again, for your eyes say nothing all the while. You do not think of me at all, and yet you look at me –'

'Would you rather have me draw another woman?'

'Perhaps – if she were very ugly,' she said.

'Well,' said Poussin gravely, 'and if, for the sake of my fame to come, if to make me a great painter, you must sit to some one else?'

'You may try me,' she said; 'you know quite well that I would not.'

Poussin's head sank on her breast; he seemed to be overpowered by some intolerable joy or sorrow.

'Listen,' she cried, plucking at the sleeve of Poussin's threadbare doublet, 'I told you, Nick, that I would lay down my life for you; but I never promised you that I in my lifetime would lay down my love.'

'Your love?' cried the young artist.

'If I showed myself thus to another, you would love me

no longer, and I should feel myself unworthy of you. Obedience to your fancies was a natural and simple thing, was it not? Even against my own will, I am glad and even proud to do thy dear will. But for another, out upon it!'

'Forgive me, my Gillette,' said the painter, falling upon his knees; 'I would rather be beloved than famous. You are fairer than success and honors. There, fling the pencils away, and burn these sketches! I have made a mistake. I was meant to love and not to paint. Perish art and all its secrets!'

Gillette looked admiringly at him, in an ecstasy of happiness! She was triumphant; she felt instinctively that art was laid aside for her sake, and flung like a grain of incense at her feet.

'Yet he is only an old man,' Poussin continued; 'for him you would be a woman, and nothing more. You – so perfect!'

'I must love you indeed!' she cried, ready to sacrifice even love's scruples to the lover who had given up so much for her sake; 'but I should bring about my own ruin. Ah! to ruin myself, to lose everything for you! ... It is a very glorious thought! Ah! but you will forget me. Oh! what evil thought is this that has come to you?'

'I love you, and yet I thought of it,' he said, with something like remorse. 'Am I so base a wretch?'

'Let us consult Père Hardouin,' she said.

'No, no! Let it be a secret between us.'

'Very well; I will do it. But you must not be there,' she said. 'Stay at the door with your dagger in your hand; and if I call, rush in and kill the painter.'

Poussin forgot everything but art. He held Gillette tightly in his arms.

'He loves me no longer!' thought Gillette when she was alone. She repented of her resolution already.

But to these misgivings there soon succeeded a sharper

pain, and she strove to banish a hideous thought that arose in her own heart. It seemed to her that her own love had grown less already, with a vague suspicion that the painter had fallen somewhat in her eyes.

II. CATHERINE LESCAULT

Three months after Poussin and Porbus met, the latter went to see Master Frenhofer. The old man had fallen a victim to one of those profound and spontaneous fits of discouragement that are caused, according to medical logicians, by indigestion, flatulence, fever, or enlargement of the spleen; or, if you take the opinion of the Spiritualists, by the imperfections of our mortal nature. The good man had simply overworked himself in putting the finishing touches to his mysterious picture. He was lounging in a huge carved oak chair, covered with black leather, and did not change his listless attitude, but glanced at Porbus like a man who has settled down into low spirits.

'Well, master,' said Porbus, 'was the ultramarine bad that you sent for to Bruges? Is the new white difficult to grind? Is the oil poor, or are the brushes recalcitrant?'

'Alas!' cried the old man, 'for a moment I thought that my work was finished, but I am sure that I am mistaken in certain details, and I can not rest until I have cleared my doubts. I am thinking of traveling. I am going to Turkey, to Greece, to Asia, in quest of a model, so as to compare my picture with the different living forms of Nature. Perhaps,' and a smile of contentment stole over his face, 'perhaps I have Nature herself up there. At times I am half afraid that a breath may waken her, and that she will escape me.'

He rose to his feet as if to set out at once.

'Aha!' said Porbus, 'I have come just in time to save you the trouble and expense of a journey.'

'What?' asked Frenhofer in amazement.

'Young Poussin is loved by a woman of incomparable and flawless beauty. But, dear master, if he consents to lend her to you, at the least you ought to let us see your work.'

The old man stood motionless and completely dazed.

'What!' he cried piteously at last, 'show you my creation, my bride? Rend the veil that has kept my happiness sacred? It would be an infamous profanation. For ten years I have lived with her; she is mine, mine alone; she loves me. Has she not smiled at me, at each stroke of the brush upon the canvas? She has a soul – the soul that I have given her. She would blush if any eyes but mine should rest on her. To exhibit her! Where is the husband, the lover so vile as to bring the woman he loves to dishonor? When you paint a picture for the court, you do not put your whole soul into it; to courtiers you sell lay figures duly colored. My painting is no painting, it is a sentiment, a passion. She was born in my studio, there she must dwell in maiden solitude, and only when clad can she issue thence. Poetry and women only lay the last veil aside for their lovers. Have we Rafael's model, Ariosto's Angelica, Dante's Beatrice? Nay, only their form and semblance. But this picture, locked away above in my studio, is an exception in our art. It is not a canvas, it is a woman – a woman with whom I talk. I share her thoughts, her tears, her laughter. Would you have me fling aside these ten years of happiness like a cloak? Would you have me cease at once to be father, lover, and creator? She is not a creature, but a creation.

'Bring your young painter here. I will give him my treasures; I will give him pictures by Correggio and Michelangelo and Titian; I will kiss his footprints in the dust; but make

300

him my rival! Shame on me. Ah! ah! I am a lover first, and then a painter. Yes, with my latest sigh I could find strength to burn my *Belle Noiseuse*; but – compel her to endure the gaze of a stranger, a young man and a painter – Ah! no, no! I would kill him on the morrow who should sully her with a glance! Nay, you, my friend, I would kill you with my own hands in a moment if you did not kneel in reverence before her! Now, will you have me submit my idol to the careless eyes and senseless criticisms of fools? Ah! love is a mystery; it can only live hidden in the depths of the heart. You say, even to your friend, "Behold her whom I love," and there is an end of love.'

The old man seemed to have grown young again; there was light and life in his eyes, and a faint flush of red in his pale face. His hands shook. Porbus was so amazed by the passionate vehemence of Frenhofer's words that he knew not what to reply to this utterance of an emotion as strange as it was profound. Was Frenhofer sane or mad? Had he fallen a victim to some freak of the artist's fancy? or were these ideas of his produced by the strange lightheadedness which comes over us during the long travail of a work of art. Would it be possible to come to terms with this singular passion?

Harassed by all these doubts, Porbus spoke – 'Is it not woman for woman?' he said. 'Does not Poussin submit his mistress to your gaze?'

'What is she?' retorted the other. 'A mistress who will be false to him sooner or later. Mine will be faithful to me forever.'

'Well, well,' said Porbus, 'let us say no more about it. But you may die before you will find such a flawless beauty as hers, even in Asia, and then your picture will be left unfinished.'

'Oh! it is finished,' said Frenhofer. 'Standing before it you

301

would think that it was a living woman lying on the velvet couch beneath the shadow of the curtains. Perfumes are burning on a golden tripod by her side. You would be tempted to lay your hand upon the tassel of the cord that holds back the curtains; it would seem to you that you saw her breast rise and fall as she breathed; that you beheld the living Catherine Lescault, the beautiful courtesan whom men called *La Belle Noiseuse*. And yet – if I could but be sure –'

'Then go to Asia,' returned Porbus, noticing a certain indecision in Frenhofer's face. And with that Porbus made a few steps toward the door. By that time Gillette and Nicolas Poussin had reached Frenhofer's house. The girl drew away her arm from her lover's as she stood on the threshold, and shrank back as if some presentiment flashed through her mind.

'Oh! what have I come to do here?' she asked of her lover in low vibrating tones, with her eyes fixed on his.

'Gillette, I have left you to decide; I am ready to obey you in everything. You are my conscience and my glory. Go home again; I shall be happier, perhaps, if you do not –'

'Am I my own when you speak to me like that? No, no; I am a child. – Come,' she added, seemingly with a violent effort; 'if our love dies, if I plant a long regret in my heart, your fame will be the reward of my obedience to your wishes, will it not? Let us go in. I shall still live on as a memory on your palette; that shall be life for me afterward.'

The door opened, and the two lovers encountered Porbus, who was surprised by the beauty of Gillette, whose eyes were full of tears. He hurried her, trembling from head to foot, into the presence of the old painter.

'Here!' he cried, 'is she not worth all the masterpieces in the world!'

Frenhofer trembled. There stood Gillette in the artless and childlike attitude of some timid and innocent Georgian, carried off by brigands, and confronted with a slave merchant. A shamefaced red flushed her face, her eyes drooped, her hands hung by her side, her strength seemed to have failed her, her tears protested against this outrage. Poussin cursed himself in despair that he should have brought his fair treasure from its hiding-place. The lover overcame the artist, and countless doubts assailed Poussin's heart when he saw youth dawn in the old man's eyes, as, like a painter, he discerned every line of the form hidden beneath the young girl's vesture. Then the lover's savage jealousy awoke.

'Gillette!' he cried, 'let us go.'

The girl turned joyously at the cry and the tone in which it was uttered, raised her eyes to his, looked at him, and fled to his arms.

'Ah! then you love me,' she cried; 'you love me!' and she burst into tears.

She had spirit enough to suffer in silence, but she had no strength to hide her joy.

'Oh! leave her with me for one moment,' said the old painter, 'and you shall compare her with my *Catherine* ... yes – I consent.'

Frenhofer's words likewise came from him like a lover's cry. His vanity seemed to be engaged for his semblance of womanhood; he anticipated the triumph of the beauty of his own creation over the beauty of the living girl.

'Do not give him time to change his mind!' cried Porbus, striking Poussin on the shoulder. 'The flower of love soon fades, but the flower of art is immortal.'

'Then am I only a woman now for him?' said Gillette. She was watching Poussin and Porbus closely.

She raised her head proudly; she glanced at Frenhofer, and

her eyes flashed; then as she saw how her lover had fallen again to gazing at the portrait which he had taken at first for a Giorgione –

'Ah!' she cried; 'let us go up to the studio. He never gave me such a look.'

The sound of her voice recalled Poussin from his dreams.

'Old man,' he said, 'do you see this blade? I will plunge it into your heart at the first cry from this young girl; I will set fire to your house, and no one shall leave it alive. Do you understand?'

Nicolas Poussin scowled; every word was a menace. Gillette took comfort from the young painter's bearing, and yet more from that gesture, and almost forgave him for sacrificing her to his art and his glorious future.

Porbus and Poussin stood at the door of the studio and looked at each other in silence. At first the painter of the Saint Mary of Egypt hazarded some exclamations: 'Ah! she has taken off her clothes; he told her to come into the light – he is comparing the two!' but the sight of the deep distress in Poussin's face suddenly silenced him; and though old painters no longer feel these scruples, so petty in the presence of art, he admired them because they were so natural and gracious in the lover. The young man kept his hand on the hilt of his dagger, and his ear was almost glued to the door. The two men standing in the shadow might have been conspirators waiting for the hour when they might strike down a tyrant.

'Come in, come in,' cried the old man. He was radiant with delight. 'My work is perfect. I can show her now with pride. Never shall painter, brushes, colors, light, and canvas produce a rival for *Catherine Lescault*, the beautiful courtesan!'

Porbus and Poussin, burning with eager curiosity, hurried into a vast studio. Everything was in disorder and covered with dust, but they saw a few pictures here and there upon the wall. They stopped first of all in admiration before the life-size figure of a woman partially draped.

'Oh! never mind that,' said Frenhofer; 'that is a rough daub that I made, a study, a pose, it is nothing. These are my failures,' he went on, indicating the enchanting compositions upon the walls of the studio.

This scorn for such works of art struck Porbus and Poussin dumb with amazement. They looked round for the picture of which he had spoken, and could not discover it.

'Look here!' said the old man. His hair was disordered, his face aglow with a more than human exaltation, his eyes glittered, he breathed hard like a young lover frenzied by love.

'Aha!' he cried, 'you did not expect to see such perfection! You are looking for a picture, and you see a woman before you. There is such depth in that canvas, the atmosphere is so true that you can not distinguish it from the air that surrounds us. Where is art? Art has vanished, it is invisible! It is the form of a living girl that you see before you. Have I not caught the very hues of life, the spirit of the living line that defines the figure? Is there not the effect produced there like that which all natural objects present in the atmosphere about them, or fishes in the water? Do you see how the figure stands out against the background? Does it not seem to you that you pass your hand along the back? But then for seven years I studied and watched how the daylight blends with the objects on which it falls. And the hair, the light pours over it like a flood, does it not? ... Ah! she breathed, I am sure that she breathed! Her breast – ah, see! Who would not fall on his knees before her? Her pulses throb. She will rise to her feet. Wait!'

'Do you see anything?' Poussin asked of Porbus.

'No ... do you?'

'I see nothing.'

305

The two painters left the old man to his ecstasy, and tried to ascertain whether the light that fell full upon the canvas had in some way neutralized all the effect for them. They moved to the right and left of the picture; they came in front, bending down and standing upright by turns.

'Yes, yes, it is really canvas,' said Frenhofer, who mistook the nature of this minute investigation.

'Look! the canvas is on a stretcher, here is the easel; indeed, here are my colors, my brushes,' and he took up a brush and held it out to them, all unsuspicious of their thought.

'The old *lansquenet* is laughing at us,' said Poussin, coming once more toward the supposed picture. 'I can see nothing there but confused masses of color and a multitude of fantastical lines that go to make a dead wall of paint.'

'We are mistaken, look!' said Porbus.

In a corner of the canvas, as they came nearer, they distinguished a bare foot emerging from the chaos of color, half-tints and vague shadows that made up a dim, formless fog. Its living delicate beauty held them spellbound. This fragment that had escaped an incomprehensible, slow, and gradual destruction seemed to them like the Parian marble torso of some Venus emerging from the ashes of a ruined town.

'There is a woman beneath,' exclaimed Porbus, calling Poussin's attention to the coats of paint with which the old artist had overlaid and concealed his work in the quest of perfection.

Both artists turned involuntarily to Frenhofer. They began to have some understanding, vague though it was, of the ecstasy in which he lived.

'He believes it in all good faith,' said Porbus.

'Yes, my friend,' said the old man, rousing himself from his dreams, 'it needs faith, faith in art, and you must live for long with your work to produce such a creation. What toil some of those shadows have cost me. Look! there is a faint shadow there upon the cheek beneath the eyes – if you saw that on a human face, it would seem to you that you could never render it with paint. Do you think that that effect has not cost unheard of toil?

'But not only so, dear Porbus. Look closely at my work, and you will understand more clearly what I was saying as to methods of modeling and outline. Look at the high lights on the bosom, and see how by touch on touch, thickly laid on, I have raised the surface so that it catches the light itself and blends it with the lustrous whiteness of the high lights, and how by an opposite process, by flattening the surface of the paint, and leaving no trace of the passage of the brush, I have succeeded in softening the contours of my figures and enveloping them in half-tints until the very idea of drawing, of the means by which the effect is produced, fades away, and the picture has the roundness and relief of nature. Come closer. You will see the manner of working better; at a little distance it can not be seen. There! Just there, it is, I think, very plainly to be seen,' and with the tip of his brush he pointed out a patch of transparent color to the two painters.

Porbus, laying a hand on the old artist's shoulder, turned to Poussin with a 'Do you know that in him we see a very great painter?'

'He is even more of a poet than a painter,' Poussin answered gravely.

'There,' Porbus continued, as he touched the canvas. 'Use the utmost limit of our art on earth.'

'Beyond that point it loses itself in the skies,' said Poussin.

'What joys lie there on this piece of canvas!' exclaimed Porbus.

The old man, deep in his own musings, smiled at the woman he alone beheld, and did not hear.

'But sooner or later he will find out that there is nothing there!' cried Poussin.

'Nothing on my canvas!' said Frenhofer, looking in turn at either painter and at his picture.

'What have you done?' muttered Porbus, turning to Poussin.

The old man clutched the young painter's arm and said, 'Do you see nothing? clodpate! Huguenot! varlet! cullion! What brought you here into my studio? – My good Porbus,' he went on, as he turned to the painter, 'are you also making a fool of me? Answer! I am your friend. Tell me, have I ruined my picture after all?'

Porbus hesitated and said nothing, but there was such intolerable anxiety in the old man's white face that he pointed to the easel.

'Look!' he said.

Frenhofer looked for a moment at his picture, and staggered back.

'Nothing! nothing! After ten years of work ...' He sat down and wept.

'So I am a dotard, a madman, I have neither talent nor power! I am only a rich man, who works for his own pleasure, and makes no progress, I have done nothing after all!'

He looked through his tears at his picture. Suddenly he rose and stood proudly before the two painters.

'By the body and blood of Christ,' he cried with flashing eyes, 'you are jealous! You would have me think that my picture is a failure because you want to steal her from me! Ah! I see her, I see her,' he cried, 'she is marvelously beautiful ...'

At that moment Poussin heard the sound of weeping; Gillette was crouching forgotten in a corner. All at once the painter once more became the lover. 'What is it, my angel?' he asked her.

'Kill me!' she sobbed. 'I must be a vile thing if I love you still, for I despise you. . . . I admire you, and I hate you! I love you, and I feel that I hate you even now!'

While Gillette's words sounded in Poussin's ears, Frenhofer drew a green serge covering over his 'Catherine' with the sober deliberation of a jeweler who locks his drawers when he suspects his visitors to be expert thieves. He gave the two painters a profoundly astute glance that expressed to the full his suspicions, and his contempt for them, saw them out of his studio with impetuous haste and in silence, until from the threshold of his house he bade them 'Good-bye, my young friends!'

That farewell struck a chill of dread into the two painters. Porbus, in anxiety, went again on the morrow to see Frenhofer, and learned that he had died in the night after burning his canvases.

VALERIE MARTIN

HIS BLUE PERIOD

FOR ANYONE WHO has met Meyer Anspach since his success, his occasional lyrical outbursts on the subject of his blue period may be merely tedious, but for those of us who actually remember the ceaseless whine of paranoia that constituted his utterances at that time, Anspach's rhapsodies on the character-building properties of poverty are infuriating. Most of what he says about those days is sheer fabrication, but two things are true: he was poor – we all were – and he was painting all the time. He never mentions, perhaps he doesn't know, a detail I find most salient, which is that his painting actually was better then than it is now. Like so many famous artists, these days Anspach does an excellent imitation of Anspach. He's in control, nothing slips by him, he has spent the last twenty years attending to Anspach's painting, and he has no desire ever to attend to anything else. But when he was young, when he was with Maria, no one, including Anspach, had any idea what an Anspach was. He was brash, intense, never satisfied, feeling his way into a wilderness. He had no character to speak of, or rather he had already the character he has now, which is entirely self-absorbed and egotistical. He cared for no one, certainly not for Maria, though he liked to proclaim that he could not live without her, that she was his inspiration, his muse, that she was absolutely essential to his life as an artist. Pursuing every other woman who caught his attention was also essential, and making no effort to conceal those often sleazy and heartless affairs was, well, part of his character.

If struggle, poverty, and rejection actually did build character, Maria should have been an Everest in the mountain range of character, unassailable, white-peaked, towering above us in the unbreathably thin air. But of course she wasn't. She was devoted to Anspach and so she never stopped weeping. She wept for years. Often she appeared at the door of my studio tucking her sodden handkerchief into her skirt pocket, smoothing back the thick, damp strands of her remarkable black hair, a carrot clutched in her small, white fist. I knew she was there even if I had my back to her because the rabbits came clattering out from wherever they were sleeping and made a dash for the door. Then I would turn and see her kneeling on the floor with the two rabbits pressing against her, patting her skirt with their delicate paws and lifting their soft, twitching muzzles to her hands to encourage her tender caresses, which they appeared to enjoy as much as the carrot they knew was coming their way. My rabbits were wild about Maria. Later, when we sat at the old metal table drinking coffee, the rabbits curled up at her feet, and later still, when she got up to make her way back to Anspach, they followed her to the door and I had to herd them back into the studio after she was gone.

I was in love with Maria and we all knew it. Anspach treated it as a joke, he was that sure of himself. There could be no serious rival to a genius such as his, and no woman in her right mind would choose warmth, companionship, affection, and support over service at the high altar of Anspach. Maria tried not to encourage me, but she was so beaten down, so starved for a kind word, that occasionally she couldn't resist a few moments of rest. On weekends we worked together at a popular restaurant on Spring Street, so we rode the train together, over and back. Sometimes, coming home just before dawn on the D train, when the cars came out of the black tunnel and climbed slowly up into the pale blush of morning light over the East River, Maria went so far as to lean her weary head against my arm. I didn't have the heart, or was it the courage, ever to say the words that rattled in my brain, repeated over and over in time to the metallic clanking of the wheels, 'Leave him, come to me.' Maria, I judged, perhaps wrongly, didn't need her life complicated by another artist who couldn't make a living.

I had the restaurant job, which paid almost nothing, though the tips were good, and one day a week I built stretchers for an art supply house near the Bowery, where I was paid in canvas and paint. That was it. But I lived so frugally I was able to pay the rent and keep myself and the rabbits in vegetables, which was what we ate. Maria had another job, two nights a week at a Greek restaurant on Atlantic Avenue. Because she worked at night she usually slept late; so did Anspach. When they got up, she cooked him a big meal, did the shopping, housekeeping, bill paying, enthused over his latest production, and listened to his latest tirade about the art establishment. In the afternoon Anspach went out for an espresso, followed by a trip downtown to various galleries where he berated the owners, if he could get near them, or the hired help if he couldn't. Anspach said painting was his vocation, this carping at the galleries was his business, and he was probably right. In my romantic view of myself as an artist, contact with the commercial world was humiliating and demeaning; I couldn't bear to do it in the flesh. I contented myself with sending out pages of slides every few months, then, when they came back, adding a few new ones, switching them around, and sending them out again.

On those afternoons when Anspach was advancing his career, Maria came to visit me. We drank coffee, talked, smoked cigarettes. Sometimes I took out a pad and did quick sketches of her, drowsy over her cigarette, the rabbits dozing at her feet. I listened to her soft voice, looked into her dark eyes, and tried to hold up my end of the conversation without betraying the sore and aching state of my heart. We were both readers, though where Maria found time to read I don't know. We talked about books. We liked cheerful, optimistic authors, Kafka, Céline, Beckett. Maria introduced me to their lighthearted predecessors, Hardy and Gissing. Her favorite novel was *Jude the Obscure*.

She had come to the city when she was seventeen with the idea that she would become a dancer. She spent six years burying this dream beneath a mountain of rejection, though she did once get as close as the classrooms of the ABT. At last she concluded that it was not her will or even her ability that held her back, it was her body. She wasn't tall enough and her breasts were too large. She had begun to accept this as the simple fact it was when she met Anspach and dancing became not her ambition but her refuge. She continued to attend classes a few times a week. The scratchy recordings of Chopin, the polished wooden floors, the heft of the barre, the sharp jabs and rebukes of the martinet teachers, the cunning little wooden blocks that disfigured her toes, the smooth, tight skin of the leotard, the strains, pains, the sweat, all of it was restorative to Maria; it was the reliable world of routine, secure and predictable, as different from the never-ending uproar of life with Anspach as a warm bath is from a plunge into an ice storm at sea.

Anspach had special names for everyone, always designed to be mildly insulting. He called Maria Mah-ree, or Miss Poppincockulos, a perversion of her real surname, which was Greek. Fidel, the owner of a gallery Anspach browbeat into showing his paintings, was Fido. Paul, an abstract painter who counted himself among Anspach's associates, was Pile.

My name is John, but Anspach always called me Jack; he still does. He says it with a sharp punch to it, as if it is part of a formula, like 'Watch out, Jack' or 'You won't get Jack if you keep that up.' Even my rabbits were not rabbits to Anspach but 'Jack's-bun-buns,' pronounced as one word with the stress on the last syllable. If he returned from the city before Maria got home, he came straight to my studio and launched into a long, snide monologue, oily with sexual insinuation, on the subject of how hard it was to be a poor artist who couldn't keep his woman at home because whenever he went out to attend to his business she was sure to sneak away to visit Jack's-bun-buns, and he didn't know what was so appealing about those bun-buns, but his Miss Poppincock-ulos just couldn't seem to get enough of them. That was the way Anspach talked. Maria didn't try to defend herself and I was no help. I generally offered Anspach a beer, which he never refused, and tried to change the subject to the only one I knew he couldn't resist, the state of his career. Then he sat down at the table and indulged himself in a flood of vitriol against whatever galleries he'd been in that day. His most frequent complaint was that they were all looking for pictures to hang 'over the couch,' in the awful living rooms of 'Long Island Jane and Joe,' or 'Fire Island Joe and Joey.' He pronounced Joey 'jo-ee.' Sometimes if he suspected I had another beer in the refrigerator, Anspach would ask to see what I was painting. Then and only then, as we stood looking at my most recent canvas, did he have anything to say worth hearing.

I don't know what he really thought of me as a painter, but given his inflated opinion of his own worth, any interest he showed in someone else was an astonishing compliment. I know he thought I was facile, but that was because he was himself a very poor draftsman, he still is, and I draw with ease. Anspach's gift was his sense of color, which, even then, was astounding. It was what ultimately made him famous: then Anspach's passion for color was all that made him bearable. It was the reason I forgave him for being Anspach.

His blue period started in the upper-right-hand corner of a painting titled *Napalm*, which featured images from the Vietnam War. A deep purple silhouette of the famous photograph of a young girl fleeing her burning village was repeated around the edges like a frame. The center was a blush of scarlet, gold, and black, like the inside of a poppy. In the upper corner was a mini-landscape, marsh grass, strange, exotic trees, a few birds in flight against an eerie, unearthly sky. The sky was not really blue but a rich blue-green with coppery undertones, a Renaissance color, like the sky in a painting by Bellini.

'How did you get this?' I asked, pointing at the shimmery patch of sky.

'Glazes,' he said. 'It took a while, but I can do it again.' He gazed at the color with his upper teeth pressed into his lower lip, a speculative, anxious expression in his open, innocent eyes. Anspach fell in love with a color the way most men fall in love with a beautiful, mysterious, fascinating, unattainable woman. He gave himself over to his passion without self-pity, without vanity or envy, without hope really. It wasn't the cold spirit of rage and competitiveness which he showed for everything and everyone else in his world. It was unselfish admiration, a helpless opening of the heart. This blue-green patch, which he'd labored over patiently and lovingly, was in the background now, like a lovely, shy young woman just entering a crowded ballroom by a side door, but she had captured Anspach's imagination and it would not be long before he demanded that all the energy in the scene revolve around her and her alone.

318

In the weeks that followed, as that blue moved to the fore-ground of Anspach's pictures, it sometimes seemed to me that it was draining the life out of Maria, as if it was actually the color of her blood and Anspach had found some way to drain it directly from her veins onto his canvas.

One summer evening, after Anspach had drunk all my beers and Maria declared herself too tired and hot to cook, we treated ourselves to dinner at the Italian restaurant under-neath my loft. There we ran into Paul Remy and a shy, near-sighted sculptor named Mike Brock, whom Anspach immediately christened Mac. Jack-and-Mac became the all-purpose name for Mike and myself, which Anspach used for the rest of the evening whenever he addressed one of us. After the meal Anspach invited us all to his loft to drink cheap wine and have a look at his latest work. It was Maria's night off; I could see that she was tired, but she encouraged us to come. She had, she explained, a fresh baklava from the restaurant which we should finish up as it wouldn't keep. So up we all went, grateful to pass an evening at no expense, and I, at least, was curious to see what Anspach was up to.

The loft had once been a bank building. Anspach and Maria had the whole second floor, which was wide open from front to back with long double-sashed windows at either end. The kitchen was minimal, a small refrigerator, a two-burner stove, an old, stained sink that looked as though it should be attached to a washing machine, and a low coun-ter with a few stools gathered around it. Their bedroom was a mattress half-hidden by some curtains Maria had sewn together from the inevitable Indian bedspreads of that period. The bathroom was in pieces, three closets along one wall. One contained a sink and mirror, one only a toilet, and the third opened directly into a cheap shower unit, the kind with the flimsy plastic door and painted enamel interior, such as one sees in summer camps for children. In the center of the big room was a battered brick-red couch, three lawn chairs, and two tables made of old crates. Anspach's big easel and paint cart were in the front of the long room facing the street windows. The best thing about the place was the line of ceiling fans down the middle, left over from the bank incarnation. It was hellish outside that night, and we all sighed with relief at how much cooler the loft was than the claustrophobic, tomato-laced atmosphere of the restaurant.

Maria put on a record, Brazilian music, I think, which made the seediness of the place seem less threatening, more exotic, and she poured out tumblers of wine for us all. The paintings Anspach showed us fascinated me. He was quoting bits from other painters, whom he referred to as 'the Massas,' but the color combinations were unexpected and everywhere there was a marvelous balance of refined technique and sheer serendipity. These days he fakes the surprise element, but his technical skill has never failed him. When Anspach talked about paint it was like a chemist talking about drugs. He knew what was in every color, what it would do in combination with other mediums, with oil, with thinner, on canvas, on pasteboard. He could give a quick rundown on all the possible side effects. Even then he didn't use much in the way of premixed colors; he made his own. His blue was underpainted with cadmium yellow, covered with a mix of phthalo green and Prussian blue, and a few opalescent glazes that he called his 'secret recipe.' The images were recondite, personal. I was pleased to see that he was leaving the Vietnam subject matter behind with the cadmium red he'd given up in favor of the blue. The blue allowed him to be less strident, more interior. He pointed at a section of one large canvas in which a woman's hands were grasping the rim of a dark blue hole – was she pulling herself out or slipping in? The hands

320

were carefully, lovingly painted, extraordinarily lifelike. 'That,' Anspach said, 'is what I call painterly.'

Paul turned to Maria. 'Did he make you hang from the balcony?' he said, for of course, we all knew, the hands were hers.

'Something like that,' she said.

Later, when we were sitting in the lawn chairs and Maria changed the record to something vaguely Mediterranean, interrupted now and then by a high-pitched male voice screaming in agony, Anspach caught me watching her. I was looking at the long, beautiful curve of her neck – she had her hair pulled up because of the heat – and the prominent bones at the base of her throat, which gleamed in the dim lamplight as if they'd been touched by one of his secret opalescent glazes.

Anspach shot me a look like a dagger. 'Miss Mah-ree,' he began. 'Oh, Miss Mah-ree, dat music is so nice. Why don't you do a little dance for us boys, Miss Mah-ree, Miss Poppincockulos, I know these boys would love to see the way you can dance; wouldn't you, Jack-and-Mac? Mr Jack-and-Mac would especially like to see our Miss Mah-ree do a little dance to dat nice music.'

Maria looked up. 'Don't be silly,' she said.

Anspach refilled his glass. Cheap wine brings out the worst in everyone, I thought. Then he swallowed a big mouthful and started up again, this time a little louder and with a wounded, edgy quality to his voice, like a child protesting injustice. 'Oh, Miss Mah-ree, don't say I'm being silly, don't say that. Don't say you won't dance for us boys, because we all want you to dance so much to dat nice music, and I know you can, Miss Mah-ree, Miss Poppincockulos, I know you like to dance for all the boys and you can take off your shirt so all the boys can see your pretty breasts, because she does

321

have such pretty baboobies, don't you know, boys, Mr Jack-and-Mac and Mr Pile, I know you boys would love to see Miss Mah-ree's pretty baboobies, especially you, Mr Jack-and-Mac, Miss Mah-ree, don't say no to these nice boys.'

Maria sent me a guarded look, then raised her weary eyes to Anspach, who was sunk deep in the couch with his arms out over the cushions, his head dropped back, watching her closely through lowered lids. 'I would never do that,' she said. 'I would be too shy.'

Anspach made a mock smile, stretching his lips tight and flat over his teeth. 'She's too shy,' he said softly. Then he closed his eyes and whined, 'Oh, please, Miss Mah-ree, don't be shy, oh, don't be too shy, oh pleasepleasepleaseplease-please, my Miss Mah-ree, don't be shy to dance for us boys here to that nice music, and take your shirt off, oh, please-pleasepleaseplease, I know you can, I know you're not too shy, oh, pleasepleasepleasepleaseplease.'

'For God's sake, Anspach,' I said. 'Would you leave it alone.'

Anspach addressed the ceiling. 'Oh, Mr Jack-and-Mac, look at that, he don't want to see Miss Mah-ree dance, he has no interest at all in Miss Mah-ree's pretty breasts, can you believe that? I don't believe that.'

Paul groaned and set his empty glass down on one of the crates. 'I've got to be going,' he said. 'It's late.'

Anspach leaned forward, resting his elbows on his knees. 'Pile has to scurry home,' he said. 'It's much too late for Pile.'

'Yeah, me too,' said Mike. 'I've got to be downtown early.'

I looked at Maria, who was standing with her back to the record player. She hadn't moved during Anspach's tiresome monologue. She looked pale, ghostly, her eyes were focused on empty space, and as I watched her she raised one hand and pressed her fingertips against her forehead, as if pushing

322

back something that was trying to get out. I too maintained that I was tired, that it was late, and pulled myself out of my lawn chair while Paul and Mike, exchanging the blandest of farewell pleasantries, followed Maria to the door. I stood looking down at Anspach, who was slumped over his knees muttering something largely unintelligible, though the words 'too late' were repeated at close intervals. I was disgusted and angry enough to speak my mind, and I thought of half a dozen things to say to him, but as I was sorting through them Maria, turning from the doorway, caught my eye, and her expression so clearly entreated me to say nothing that I held my tongue and walked out past the couch to join her at the door.

'I'm sorry,' she said when I was near her.

'Don't be,' I said. 'You didn't do anything.'

'He's just drunk,' she said.

I took her hands and looked into her sad face. She kept her eyes down and her body turned away, toward Anspach, back to Anspach. 'You look tired,' I said. 'You should get some sleep.'

She smiled dimly, still averting her eyes from mine, and I thought, He won't let her sleep. As I walked through the quiet streets to my studio I blamed myself for what had happened. I should not have stared at her so openly, so admiringly. But couldn't a man admire his friend's girlfriend, was that such a crime? Wouldn't any ordinary man be pleased to see his choice confirmed in his friend's eyes? Of course the fact that Anspach was not, in any meaningful sense of the word, my or anyone else's friend, gave the lie to my self-serving protest. That and the fact that what I felt for Maria was much more than admiration and I had no doubt it showed, that Anspach had seen it. He knew I wanted to take Maria away from him. He also knew I couldn't do it.

After that night I saw less and less of Maria. Sometimes she still came by in the afternoons when Anspach was in town, but she never stayed long and seemed anxious to be back in their loft before he got home. She had picked up a third, grueling, thankless job, three days a week at an art supply house in SoHo. The pay was minimum wage, but she got a discount on paint, which had become the lion's share of her monthly budget. Anspach was turning out paintings at an astounding rate, and the cadmium yellow that went into his blue was ten dollars a tube. The discount went to his head, and more and more paint went onto each canvas. He was cavalier about the expense, passing on his nearly empty tubes to Paul because he couldn't be bothered to finish them. Paul had invented a special device, a kind of press, to squeeze the last dabs of color from his paint tubes.

It was about that time that I met Yvonne Remy, Paul's sister, who had come down from Vermont to study art history at NYU. She was staying with Paul until she could find a place of her own, and the three of us soon fell into a routine of dinners together several nights a week, taking turns on the cooking. Yvonne was quick-witted and energetic, and she loved to talk about painting. Gradually we all noticed that she was spending more time at my place than at her brother's, and gradually we all came to feel that this was as it should be.

Yvonne was there that afternoon when I last saw Maria. She hadn't visited me in three weeks. She looked exhausted, which wasn't surprising, but there was something more than that, something worse than that, a listlessness beyond fatigue. The rabbits came running as they always did when Maria arrived, and she brightened momentarily as she bent down to caress them, but I noticed she had forgotten to bring a carrot.

Yvonne responded to her with that sudden affinity of kindness which women sometimes show each other for reasons that are inexplicable to men. She warmed the milk for the coffee, which she did not always bother with for herself, and set out some fruit, cheese, and bread. When Maria showed no interest in this offering, Yvonne got up, put a few cookies on a plate, and seemed relieved when Maria took one and laid it on the saucer of her cup. Maria leaned over her chair to scratch a rabbit's ears, then sat up and took a bite of the cookie. 'John,' she said, her eyes still on the docile creatures at her feet. 'You'll always take care of these rabbits, won't you?'

'Of course,' I assured her. 'These rabbits and I are in this together.'

When she was gone, Yvonne sat at the table idly turning her empty cup.

'She seems so tired,' I said.

'She's in despair,' Yvonne observed.

Then a few things happened very quickly. I didn't find out about any of it until it was all over and Maria was gone. Anspach was offered a space in a three-man show with two up-and-coming painters at the Rite gallery. This coup, Paul told me later, with a grimace of pain at the pun, was the result of Anspach's fucking Mrs Rite on the floor of her office and suggesting to her, postcoitum, that she was the only woman in New York who could understand his work. I didn't entirely believe this story; it didn't sound like Anspach to me, but evidently it was true, for within three months Mrs Rite had left Mr Rite and Anspach was the star of her new gallery, Rivage, which was one of the first to move south into Tribeca.

Paul maintained that Anspach told Maria about his new

alliance, omitting none of the details, though it is possible that she heard about it somewhere else. Mrs Rite was not bothered by the gossip, in fact she was rumored to have been the source of much of it. As far as Anspach was concerned, he had seized an opportunity, as what self-respecting artist would not, faced with the hypocrisy and callousness of the art scene in the city. He had decided early on to enter the fray, by bombast or seduction, or whatever it took, marketing himself as an artist who would not be denied.

Maria had narrowed her life to thankless drudgery and Anspach. She had given up her dance classes, she had few friends, nor had she ever been much given to confiding her difficulties to others. She was, as Yvonne had observed, already in despair. However she heard it, the truth about Anspach's golden opportunity was more than she could bear. Anspach told the police that they'd had an argument, that she had gone out the door in a rage, that he assumed she was going to weep to one of her friends. Instead she climbed the interior fire ladder to the roof, walked across the litter of exhaust vents and peeling water pipes, pulled aside the low, rickety wire-mesh partition that protected the gutters, and dived head-first into the street. It was a chilly day in October; the windows were closed in the loft. Anspach didn't know what had happened until the Sicilian who owned the coffee bar on the street level rushed up the stairs and banged on his door, shouting something Anspach didn't, at first, understand.

There was no funeral in New York. Maria's father came out from Wisconsin and arranged to have her body shipped back home. It was as if she had simply disappeared. I didn't see Anspach; I purposely avoided him. I knew if I saw him I would try to hit him. Anspach is a big man; he outweighs me by sixty pounds, I'd guess, and he's powerfully built.

So I may have avoided him because I was afraid of what would happen to me.

Paul told me that a few weeks after Maria's death, Anspach moved in with Mrs Rite, and that he'd sold two of the nine paintings in the group show. At his one-man show the following year, he sold everything but the four biggest, proving his theory that the public was intent on hanging their pictures over the couch. Paul Remy saw the show and reported that Anspach's blue period was definitely over. The predominant hue was a shell pink, and the repeated image was a billowing parachute. This irritated me. Everything I heard about Anspach irritated me, but I couldn't keep myself from following his career, stung with frustration, anger, and envy at each new success.

In the spring, Yvonne and I moved a few blocks south, where we had more room for the same money and a small walled-in yard, which soon became the rabbits' domain. They undertook amazing excavation projects, after which they spent hours cleaning their paws and sleeping in the sun, or in the shade of an ornamental beech. I kept my promise to Maria; I took good care of the rabbits for many years. They lived to be old by rabbit standards, nearly fourteen, and they died within a few weeks of each other, as secretly as they could, in a den they'd dug behind the shed I'd put up for Yvonne's gardening tools and our daughter's outdoor toys. After Yvonne finished school she moved from job to job for a few years until she settled in the ceramics division at the Brooklyn Museum. I took what work I could find and kept painting. Occasionally, always through friends, I got a few pictures in a group show, but nothing sold. Storage was a continual and vexing problem. My canvases got smaller and smaller.

Paul and I were offered a joint show at a new gallery on

the edge of Tribeca, an unpromising location at best. The opening was not a fashionable scene, very cheap wine, plastic cups, a few plates strewn with wedges of rubbery cheese. The meager crowd of celebrants was made up largely of the artists' friends and relatives. The artists themselves, dressed in their best jeans and T-shirts, huddled together near the back, keeping up a pointless conversation in order to avoid overhearing any chance remarks about the paintings. I was naturally surprised when there appeared above the chattering heads of this inelegant crowd the expensively coiffed, unnaturally tan, and generally prosperous-looking head of Meyer Anspach.

'Slumming,' Paul said to me when he spotted Anspach.

I smiled. David Hines, the gallery owner, had come to riveted attention and flashed Paul and me a look of triumph as he stepped out to welcome Anspach. Greta, a friend of Paul's who painted canvases that were too big for most gallery walls and who was, I knew, a great admirer of Anspach, set down her plastic cup on the drinks table and rubbed her eyes hard with her knuckles.

David was ushering Anspach past the paintings, which he scarcely glanced at, to the corner where Paul and I stood open-mouthed. Anspach launched into a monologue about how we had all been poor painters together, poor artists in Brooklyn, doing our best work, because we were unknown and had only ourselves to please. This was during his blue period, a long time ago, those paintings were some of his favorites, a turning point, the suffering of that time had liberated him, he couldn't afford to buy back those paintings himself, that's how valuable they had become.

This was the first time I heard Anspach's litany about his blue period.

It was awful standing there, with David practically rubbing

his hands together for glee and Paul emanating hostility, while Anspach went on and on about the brave comrade painters of long ago. Cheap wine, free love. La Vie de Bohème, I thought, only Maria didn't die of tuberculosis. I couldn't think of anything to say, or rather my thoughts came in such a rush I couldn't sort one out for delivery, but Paul came to my rescue by pointing out with quiet dignity that he and I still lived in Brooklyn. Then David got the idea of taking a photograph of Anspach, and Anspach said he'd come to see the pictures, which nobody believed, but we all encouraged him to have a look while David ran to his office for his camera. Paul and I stood there for what seemed a long time watching Anspach stand before each painting with his mouth pursed and his eyebrows slightly lifted, thinking God knows what. In spite of my valid personal reasons for despising him, I understood that I still admired Anspach as a painter, and I wanted to know, once and for all, what he saw when he looked at my work. Paul eased his way to the drinks table and tossed back a full glass of the red wine. David appeared with his camera, and after a brief conversation with Anspach, he called Paul and me over to flank Anspach in front of my painting titled *Welfare*. *Welfare* had an office building in the foreground, from the windows of which floated heavenward a dozen figures of bureaucrats in coats and ties, all wearing shiny black shoes that pointed down as they went up, resembling the wings of black crows. In David's photograph, two of these figures appear to be rising out of Anspach's head, another issues from one of Paul's ears. Anspach is smiling broadly, showing all his teeth. Paul looks diffident, and I look wide-eyed, surprised. When she saw this photo, Yvonne said, 'You look like a sheep standing next to a wolf.'

After the photograph session, Anspach stepped away from Paul and me and walked off with David, complaining that he had another important engagement. He did not so much as glance back at the door. He had appeared unexpectedly, now he disappeared in the same way. David returned to us with the bemused, wondering expression of one who has met up with a natural force and miraculously survived. He took from his coat pocket a sheet of red adhesive dots and went around the room carefully affixing them to the frames of various pictures. Anspach had bought four of mine and three of Paul's.

I don't attribute my modest success to Anspach, but I guess there are people who do. I attribute it to the paintings, to the quality of the work. I have to do that or I'd just give up. Still there's always that nagging anxiety for any artist who actually begins to sell, that he's compromised something, that he's imitating the fashion. I'm not making a fortune, but I like selling a painting; I like the enthusiasm of the new owner, and I particularly like handing the check to Yvonne. It makes me lazy, though, and complacent. Some days I don't paint at all. I go downtown and check out the competition at the various galleries, drink a few espressos, talk with Paul, who isn't doing as well as I am but seems incapable of envy, of wishing me anything but well.

I sometimes wonder what van Gogh's paintings would have been like if he had been unable to turn them out fast enough to satisfy an eager, approving public. Suppose he'd been treated as Picasso was, as such a consummate master that any little scribble on a notepad was worth enough to buy the hospital where he died. Would that ear still have had to go?

Yesterday, as I walked out of a café in Chelsea, I ran straight into Anspach, who was coming in. I greeted him politely enough, I always do, but I haven't exchanged more than a few words with him since Maria's death. He pretends not to notice this, or perhaps he thinks it's the inevitable fate of the great artist to be tirelessly snubbed by his inferiors. He asked me to go back in with him, to have an espresso. 'You know, I just sold a painting of yours I've had for five years,' he said. 'Your stock is going up.'

It was chilly out, threatening rain, and I'd had an argument with Yvonne that morning. She'd told me that I was lazy, that all I did was sleep and drink coffee, which isn't true, but I had defended myself poorly by accusing her of being obsessed with work, money, getting ahead, and we'd parted heatedly, she to work, I to the café. I was not in the mood to have an espresso with Meyer Anspach. He looked prosperous, expansive, pleased with himself. His breath was warm on my face, and it smelled bitter, as if he'd been chewing some bitter root.

'It must be nice to have an eye for investments,' I said. 'It keeps you from having to buy anything you actually care about.'

He laughed. 'The only paintings I ever want to keep are my own,' he said. 'I'm always trying to find a way around having to sell them.'

'I get it,' I said, trying to push past him. 'Happy to be of service.'

'Looks like I'm the one in service,' he observed. 'When I sell a painting of yours, it makes everything you do worth more.'

This was an intolerable assertion. 'Don't do me any favors, okay, Anspach?' I snapped. I had made it to the sidewalk. 'I know perfectly well why you bought my paintings.'

Anspach came out on the sidewalk with me. He looked eager for a fight. 'And why is that?' he said. 'What is your theory about that?'

'You want me to forgive you for Maria,' I said. 'But I never will.'

'*You* forgive *me*,' he said. 'I think it's the other way around.'

'What are you talking about?' I said.

'You led her on, Jack, don't tell me you didn't. I was wearing her out and there you were, always ready with the coffee and the bunnies, and trying to feel her up on the subway.'

'That's not true,' I protested.

'She told me,' he said. 'She said you were in love with her, and I said, Okay, then go, but by the time she got around to making the decision, you were shut up with Yvonne. You closed her out and she gave up. That's why she went off the roof.'

'If you'd treated her decently she wouldn't have needed to turn to me,' I said.

'But she did,' he shot back. 'You made her think she could, and she did. But you couldn't wait for her. You had to have Yvonne. Well, that's fine, Jack. Maria wouldn't have made you happy. She was always depressed, she was always tired. She was never going to do better than waitressing, and sooner or later she was going to go off the roof. Yvonne is a hard worker, and she makes good money. You made the right choice.'

'What a swine you are,' I said.

He laughed. 'You hate me to ease your own conscience,' he said. 'I was never fooled by you.'

'Shut up,' I said. I started walking away as fast as I could. I looked back over my shoulder and saw him standing there, smiling at me, as if we were the best of friends. 'Shut up,' I shouted, and two young women walking toward me paused in their conversation to look me over warily.

I went straight home, but it took nearly two hours. The subway was backed up; a train had caught fire between

Fourteenth Street and Astor Place. I kept thinking of what Anspach had said, and it made my blood pressure soar. What a self-serving bastard, I thought. As crude as a caveman. I particularly hated his remark about feeling Maria up on the subway. I never did. I never would have. He would have done it, certainly, if he had been with her on those long, cold trips across the river, when she rested her head innocently against his arm; he would have taken advantage of that opportunity, so he assumed I had.

I tortured my memory for any recollection of having brushed carelessly against Maria's breasts. It made me anxious to reach in this way, after so many years, for Maria, and to discover that she was not alive in my memory. I couldn't see her face, remember her perfume. I kept having a vision of a skeleton, which was surely all Maria was now, of sitting on the subway next to a skeleton, and of rubbing my arm against the hard, flat blade of her breastbone.

I spent the rest of the morning trying to paint, but I got nowhere. I could see the painting of Maria's hands clutching the edge of a chute, and behind her, that ominous blue, Anspach's blue period, waiting to swallow her up forever. In the afternoon I picked up my daughter, Bridget, from her school, and we spent an hour at the corner library. When we got back home, Yvonne was there, standing at the kitchen counter, chopping something. Was she still mad at me from the morning? I went up beside her on the pretense of washing my hands. 'Day okay?' I said.

'Not bad,' she said pleasantly enough. 'How about you?'

I sat down at the table and started turning an apple from the fruit bowl round and round in my hands. 'I ran into Meyer Anspach today,' I said. 'He said he sold one of my paintings.'

'That's good,' she said. She wasn't listening.

'He said Maria was in love with me. He said she thought I would wait for her to leave him, but I didn't, and that's why she killed herself.'

Yvonne ran some water over her hands, then turned to me, drying them off with a towel. 'Maria *was* in love with you,' she said. 'Are you saying you didn't know that?'

'Of course I didn't know that,' I exclaimed. 'I still don't know that.'

Yvonne gave me a sad smile, such as she sometimes gives Bridget when she gets frustrated by math problems. Then she turned back to the sink. 'How could you not have known that?' was all she said.

REBECCA LEE

FIALTA

FROM WHERE I stand, on the bridge overlooking the Chicago River, the city looks like a strange but natural landscape, as if it arises as surely and inevitably from the hands of life as does a field of harvest wheat or a stand of red firs. After all, the city was designed by country boys – Mies van der Rohe, Burnham and Root, Frank Lloyd Wright, Louis Sullivan – all wild and dashing, dreaming up the city in the soft thrum of the countryside.

But the buildings that most reflect nature, at least midwestern nature, in all its dark and hidden fertility, are those by Franklin Stadbakken, the so-called architect of the prairies, that great and troubled mess of a man I once knew.

Three years ago, when I was a senior at Northwestern, I sent Stadbakken a packet of drawings and a statement of purpose. Every year Stadbakken chooses five apprentices to come live with him on the famous grounds of Fialta, his sprawling workshop, itself an architectural dream rising and falling over the gentle hills of southwestern Wisconsin. My sketches were of skyscrapers, set down with a pencil on pale blue drafting paper. They'd been drawn late in the night, and I knew hardly anything about how to draw a building, except that it ought not to look beautiful; it ought to be spare and slightly inaccessible, its beauty only suggested, so that a good plan looked like a secret to be passed on and on, its true nature hidden away.

Two months later I received back a letter of acceptance. At the bottom of the form letter there was a note from Stadbakken himself that read, 'In spite of your ambition, your hand seems humble and reasonable. I look forward to your arrival.'

I had been reading, off and on, that year, a biography of Stadbakken, and this moment when I read his handwriting was one of the most liberating in my life – in fact, so much so it was almost haunting, as if a hand had leapt out of the world of art – of books and dreams – and pulled me in.

My first evening at Fialta was referred to as orientation but was really a recitation by one of the two second-year apprentices, named Reuben, of What Stadbakken Liked, which was, in no particular order, mornings, solitude, black coffee, Yeats, order, self-reliance, privacy, skits, musicals, filtered light, thresholds, lightning. 'Piña coladas,' the woman sitting beside me – Elizabeth – said quietly. 'Getting caught in the rain.'

'Fialta,' Reuben continued, 'is dedicated not to the fulfillment of desire but to the transformation of desire into art.' We were sitting in the commons, a beautiful, warm room that doubled as our dining room, our office, and our lounge. There was an enormous fireplace, windows streaming with slanted and dying light, and a big wooden table, whose legs were carved with the paws of beasts at the floor. There was a golden shag carpet and stone walls. It was high up, and the views were spectacular, but the room was intimate. So this statement regarding desire seemed almost heartbreakingly Freudian, since the room and all of Fialta, with its endless private corners and stunning walkways and fireplaces, seemed to ask you at every turn to fall in love, yet that was the one thing that was not permitted. Reuben went on to say,

'Stadbakken does not tolerate well what he calls overfraternization. He sees it as a corruption of the working community if people, well . . .' And there was a nervous moment. Reuben seemed to have lost his footing. Nobody knew what to say until a tall woman in the back, whose name would turn out to be Indira Katsabrahmanian, and whose beauty would turn out to be the particular rocks on which Reuben's heart would be dashed, spoke up: '*Sodo-sudu.*' Reuben raised his eyebrows at her. 'Fool around,' she said, with a slightly British accent. 'It means to not fool around.'

Reuben nodded.

So, no love affairs. As soon as this was declared, it was as if a light had turned on in the room. Until this point, everyone had been so focused on the great absent man himself and his every desire that nobody had really looked around that carefully. But at this mention that we could not fall in love, we all turned to see who else was there. Each person seemed suddenly so interesting, so vital, a beautiful portal through which one might pass, secretly. And this was when I saw Sands, who was, with Reuben, returning for her second year at Fialta. When I try to call forth my first impression of Sands, it is so interpreted by the light of loss that what I see is somebody already vanishing, but beautifully, into a kind of brightness. And as Stadbakken's beloved Yeats said of Helen, how can I blame her, being what she was and Fialta being what it is?

As we left that evening, I talked briefly to Reuben and to Elizabeth, whose nickname became Groovy in those few moments, owing to her look, which had a hundred implications – of Europe and Asia, of girls, of tough guys, of grannies. And I then fell in step beside Sands as she walked outside. It was slightly planned on my part, but not entirely, which allowed me to think that the world was a little bit behind me and my desire. It was mid-September, and in this part

339

of the country there were already ribbons of wintry cold running through the otherwise mild evenings. We had a brief, formal conversation. We discussed Fialta, then Chicago. I had thought I was walking her home, but it seemed that we were actually, suddenly, winding up a pathway toward Stadbakken's living quarters.

'Oh,' I said. 'Where are we going?'

'I'm going up to check on him.' She pointed way up to a sort of lighthouse circling above us.

'Stadbakken?'

'Yes.' There was light pouring out the window.

'Oh sure, go ahead,' I said.

She smiled at me and then walked off. And I turned to walk back to my room, slightly horrified at myself. *Go ahead*, I repeated to myself. *Oh, hey, go ahead*. This is the whole problem with words. There is so little surface area to reveal whom you might be underneath, how expansive and warm, how casual, how easygoing, how cool, and so it all comes out a little pathetic and awkward and choked.

As I walked home, I turned back and saw through the trees again that window, ringing with clarity and light above the dark grounds, the way the imagination shines above the dark world, as inaccessible as love, even as it casts its light all around.

That evening I lay in bed reading Christopher Alexander, the philosopher-king of architects: 'The fact is, that this seeming chaos which is in us is a rich, rolling, swelling, dying, lilting, singing, laughing, shouting, crying, sleeping order.' I paused occasionally to stare out the large window beside my bed, which gave way to the rolling hills, toward Madison's strung lights, and, had I the eyes to see, my hometown of Chicago burning away in the distance. Reuben knocked on my door.

We were roommates, sharing a large living room and kitchen. Reuben was the cup full to the brim, and maybe even a little above the brim but without spilling over, as Robert Frost put it. If one of the skills of being properly alive is the ability to contain gracefully one's desires, then Reuben was the perfect living being.

'I forgot to give you your work assignment,' he said.

The literature on Fialta I received over the summer had mentioned grounds work, which I had assumed meant carpentry or landscaping, but now Reuben informed me that I would be in charge of the cows and the two little pigs.

'There are animals here?'

'Yes. Down in the barn.'

'There's a barn?'

'Yes. At the end of the pasture.'

'Of course,' I said.

He was already bowing out of the door when I asked what I was to do with them.

'Milk the cows, feed the pigs,' he said, and ducked out.

I should never have sent in those skyscrapers, I thought to myself as I fell asleep. Those are what got me the cow assignment. You can feel it as you sketch plans, the drag in the hand, the worry, the Tower of Babel anxiety as the building grows too high. There ought not to be too much hubris in a plan. But this is not a simple directive either, since a plan also needs to be soaring and eccentric and confident. But still humble. A perfect architect might be like a perfect person, the soul so correctly aligned that it can ascend with humility. Humble and dashing, those two things, always and forever.

You could say that Fialta was not quite in its prime. Its reputation was fading a little, and all its surfaces tarnishing, but so beautifully that Fialta was a more romantic place than it must have been even at the height of its influence, something that could be said of Stadbakken as well. Early success as an architect and a slide into some obscurity had given his reputation a kind of legendary, old-fashioned quality, even though he was only in his late fifties. At seven o'clock, at the dimming of the next day, he stepped into the commons for our first session. He had the looks of a matinee idol in the early twilight of his career, and he seemed more substantially of the past than anybody I've ever met, so that even now, when I remember him, it is in black and white. He is wistful in my memory, staring off, imagining a building that might at last equal nature – generative and wild, but utterly organized at the heart.

That night in the commons, Stadbakken entered and said only this: 'We have a new project. It's what we were all hoping for. It's a theater, along a city block in Chicago, surrounded on two sides by a small park designed by Olmsted. I'd like the theater to think about the park.'

Sands and Reuben nodded, so the rest of us did as well. 'Yes, well,' he said, 'you might as well begin.' He put his hands together, in a steeple, as he stared at us – Reuben, Sands, me, Indira, and Groovy – taking each of us in briefly, and then he left.

Reuben immediately then took his position at the blackboard that was usually pushed against the wall. He and Sands began, and the rest of us very slowly joined in until Reuben had covered the blackboard with phrases, what they called patterns for the building – sloping roofs, alcoves, extended thresholds, hidden passageways, rays of light, soulful common areas, the weaving of light and dark, clustering rehearsal rooms, simple hearths, thick walls, a dance hall, radiant heat, filtered light, pools of light, arrows of darkness, secret doorways . . .

I was already developing a rule never to look at Sands, in order not to give myself away and make her nervous. But there was something in her – some combination of joy and intelligence and seriousness – that seemed unrepeatable to me. Her voice had a vaguely foreign sound to it, a rough inflection left over from someplace in the world that I couldn't quite locate. Her clothes were as plain as possible and her hair pulled back in a ponytail, all as if she were trying to overcome beauty, but this would be like lashing down sails in a high wind. You might get a hand on one stretch, but then the rest would fly away, billowing out.

At one point Reuben and Sands got into an argument. Reuben suggested that the building ought to be cloaked in some sense of the spiritual.

'Reuben,' Sands said. 'I'm so tired of all our plans having to be so holy. It's such a dull way to think of buildings. And especially a theater.'

Reuben looked a little amused. 'Maybe we're going to have to divide up again,' he said.

'Divide?' said Indira, who up until now had stayed silent. When she spoke, her earrings made tiny, almost imperceptible bell sounds.

'Last year,' Sands said to her, 'we had to divide into those who believe in God and those who don't.'

'Just like that?' I said. 'You know, people spend their whole lives on this question.'

'It's just for now,' Sands said. 'I don't think He'll hold you to it.' She already knew I'd be coming with her. And I did, risking hell for her, complaining all the way. The two of us worked in a tiny glass balcony, a little limb off of the commons. That first night Sands did most of the drawing, and I stood aside and made my suggestions, sometimes saying them more and more emphatically until she would finally draw them in. 'Fine, fine,' she'd say. We started over many times, a process that previously had seemed to me an indication of failure, but to Sands it was entirely normal, as if each building she called forth introduced her to other buildings it knew, and so working with her could be sort of an unwieldy process and you had to be willing to fight a little to get your way, but ultimately it was like walking into mysterious woods, everything related and fertile but constantly changing, and always there was the exhilarating feeling that one was continually losing and then finding the way.

More than anything, what I wanted was to enter into the rooms she drew, which would be like entering her imagination, that most private, far-flung place. By midnight we brought our draft to the others. It looked crazy, like big Russian circus tents connected by strings of light, like a big bohemian palace, but also very beautiful and somehow humble. I stood there while the others looked at it and felt as though I wanted to disown any participation in it whatsoever, and at the same time I was quite proud.

'It's so beautiful,' Groovy said. Indira and Reuben nodded. And then they showed us theirs, which was austere and mysterious, rising out of the ground like it had just awoken and found itself the last thing on earth.

And we laid out the two buildings on the table and looked at them. They seemed so beautiful, as things can that are of the imagination. One had to love these figments, so exuberant in their postures and desires, trying to assert their way into the world.

'Yours is beautiful,' Sands said, softly.

'*Yours* is,' Groovy said. 'God wouldn't even come to ours. He'd go to yours.'

'Definitely He would go to yours,' Sands said.

'If He existed,' I said.

'Now He's really mad,' Groovy said, and Sands laughed a little, putting her hand like a gentle claw on my elbow. I can feel to this day her hand where it gripped my elbow whenever she laughed. Each of her fingers sent a root system into my arm that traveled and traveled, winding and stretching and luxuriating throughout my body, settling there permanently.

The next morning on our way to breakfast, Reuben and I saw Indira in the distance, making her way down the path to the river that wound about Fialta. There was already a rumor floating among us that Indira was a former Miss Bombay. I couldn't imagine this; she was so serious. She had a large poetry collection in her room and an eye for incredibly ornate, stylized design. Stadbakken had set her to work immediately on the gates and doorways for the theater. Watching her now, slipping down through the fall leaves, one could see the sadness and solitude that truly beautiful women inherit, which bears them quietly along. 'Hey!' Reuben surprised me by calling out, and he veered away from me without even a glance back.

A woman reading is a grave temptation. I stood in the doorway separating the commons from our tiny kitchen, named Utopia for its sheer light and warmth, and hesitated for a long moment before I cleared my throat. Sands looked up. She was wearing glasses, her hair pulled back in a dark ponytail. She said hello.

'What're you reading?' I asked.

'Oh, this is Vitruvius – *The Ten Books of Architecture*. Stadbakken lent it to me.'

'It's good?'

'I suppose. He's asked me to think about the threshold.'

'The threshold. That's romantic.'

She stared at me. Probably men were always trying to find an angle with her. Her face was beautiful, dark and high-hearted. 'What do you mean by romantic?' she said.

This was really the last thing I wanted to define at this moment. It seemed any wrong answer and all my hopes might spiral up and away behind her eyes. 'Well, I guess I mean romantic in the large sense, you know. The threshold is the moment one steps inside, out of the cold, and feels oneself treasured on a human scale.'

'That's pretty,' she said. She was eating Cheerios and toast.

'You know, I never found out the other night where you are from,' I said.

'From? I am from Montreal originally.'

'You went to McGill?'

'Laval,' she said.

I knew Laval from pictures in architecture books. In my books it had looked like a series of dark, wintry ice palaces. 'And how did you get from there to here?' I asked.

'Stadbakken came and gave a lecture. I met him there.'

My mind was at once full of the image of her and Stad-bakken in her tiny, cold Canadian room, its small space heater whirring out warmth, the animal skins on the floor and the bed, the two of them eating chipped beef from a can or whatever people eat in the cold, her mirror ringed with pictures of her young boyfriends – servicemen from across the border, maybe – and then of them clasped together, his age so incredible as it fell into her youth.

'Is he in love with you?' I asked.

'Not in love, no,' she said. Which of course made me think that his feelings for her were nothing so simple or banal as love. It was far richer and more tangled in their psyches than that – some father/daughter, teacher/student, famous/strug-gling artist extravaganza that I could never comprehend.

346

And then Groovy approached, jangling her keys. Her hair had all these little stitched-people barrettes in it. It was bright blond, and the little primitive people all had panicked looks on their faces, as if they were escaping a great fire. 'Stadbakken wants to see you,' she said to Sands.

Sands started to collect her books and her tray, and Groovy turned to me. 'I heard you're taking care of those cows,' she said.

'Yes. And you?'

'Trash,' Groovy said. 'All the trash, every day, in every room.'

'That's a big job. How about you?' I asked Sands.

'She's his favorite,' Groovy said.

'So, no work then?' I asked.

'Oh, it's a lot of work, trust me,' Groovy said, winking a little lewdly, and then Sands smiled at me a little, and then they both left me to my breakfast.

There was a chair in one corner of the commons that was highly coveted. It had been designed by one of Stadbakken's former apprentices, and it was nearly the perfect chair for reading. That night I was just about to sit in it with my copy of Stadbakken's biography when Groovy came out of nowhere and hip-checked me. She sat down. She was reading Ovid.

'Chivalry's dead,' I said, and sat in one of the lesser chairs across from her.

'On the contrary,' she said, settling in. 'I was helping you to be chivalrous.'

'Well then, thank you.'

She was sucking on a butterscotch candy that I could smell all the way from where I sat.

'How's that book?' she said.

347

'It's pretty interesting,' I said. 'Except the woman writing the book seems to have a real bone to pick with him. It's like the book's written by an ex-wife or something.'

'Does he have ex-wives?'

'Four of them,' I said.

'He's hard to love, I bet.'

'I expect so. The book says he loves unrequited love, and once love is requited he seeks to make it unrequited.'

'I see that a lot,' Groovy said.

'Really?'

'Yeah, everybody loves a train in the distance.'

Which is when Sands appeared. 'Choo-choo,' I said. Groovy smiled.

'What's up?' Sands asked. She stood behind Groovy, touching her hair, absently braiding it.

'He's lecturing me on unrequited love,' Groovy said.

'What's his position?' Sands smiled at me. 'Pro or con?'

'Very con,' I said.

'Pro,' Groovy said. 'Look at him. It's obviously pro. It's practically carved in his forehead.'

Fialta did exist prior to Stadbakken. It was originally a large house atop a rolling hill, in which a poet of some significance lived in the late nineteenth century. Apparently Walt Whitman, both Emerson and Thoreau, Jones Very, and even Herman Melville had passed through these walls during the years that America became what it is, when the individual stepped out of the light of its community and every life became, as Philip Larkin later said, a brilliant breaking of the bank. Stadbakken's father had been a member of this circle of friends and had bought the house from the poet in the year 1947; Stadbakken had grown up here as an only child. His parents had cherished him so fastidiously that he had no choice but to grow up to be, as his biographer put it, the ragingly immature man that he was, his inner child grown wild as the thorny vines that clung to the spruce down near the river.

Stadbakken went to school on the East Coast, lived for a while in New York City in his twenties, and then returned to Fialta and built his workshop here, presiding over it in his brimming room, up about a hundred turning wooden stairs, where I joined him every Tuesday afternoon at five. We would speak privately up here about my sketches, most of which involved Sands, about our plans for the theater, and also just about architecture in general. If you read about Stadbakken these days you will learn that as a teacher he can be offhand, blunt, manipulative, domineering, and arrogant, and though this is all true, his faults stood out in relief against the very lovely light of his generosity, like trees along a dimming horizon. He would turn his moony, moody eye on a sketch and see things I had never imagined – sunlit pools, fragrant winding gardens, gathering parties, cascading staircases. He would see people living out their lives. He would see life on earth. I would emerge from these sessions with him wanting desperately to run and run to catch up with his idea of what I might do, and in this way he created within me an ambition that would long outlast our association.

'What I was thinking,' Sands was saying to me, while she leaned over our drafting table to turn on the bent-arm lamp, 'was that we might bring the theater's balcony about two hundred and fifty degrees around. Wouldn't that be beautiful, and just a little strange?'

As she reached for the lamp, her body was crumpling up a map we had laid out of Chicago. 'You're crumpling the map,' I said.

'What?' She turned her face to me. It was riveting – dark

and light in equal measure. Her skin had a kind of uneven quality to it that brought to mind childhood and all its imperfections, sun and dirt.

'Oh, nothing,' I said. Would that the city be crumpled and destroyed by such a torso breaking over it – the Chicago River bursting its banks and running into the streets, the sky-scrapers crashing down, the light extinguished suddenly by that gorgeous, obliterating darkness. We had until morning together to produce a plan that met a number of Stad-bakken's and the client's specifications, which included these words – *bold, rich, witty,* and *wise.*

'It doesn't sound like a building,' she said.

'I know, it sounds like my grandmother in the Bronx.'

By the time we fell out, after finishing three reasonable drafts of interiors to show Stadbakken, it was nearly sunrise, and we went to Utopia, made ourselves cinnamon toast and coffee. I picked up the slop bucket that I set out on the kitchen floor every night with a sign above it for donations. This morning there was warm milk in which carrot shavings and potato peels and cereal and a lone Pop-Tart and some strips of cheese singles floated.

Sands accompanied me down through the field to the barn, which sat at the foot of the campus. We stood in the doorway as the shafts of sun fell through the high windows. The four cows were in their various stages – lying and dream-ing and chewing and standing.

Sands stood quietly, peering at the cows. The standing cow looked back balefully.

'This one is Anna,' I said. And then I introduced the rest – Ellen, Lidian, Marie. 'Groovy named them for Stadbakken's former wives. She's been reading Ovid, where women are frequently turned into heifers when the men can no longer live with them, or without them.'

'And now they're trapped down here forever.'

'Punished for their beauty.'

The cows lived so languorously from one day to the next that their being banished women seemed entirely possible. I was moving aside some hay so that I could set down the milking stool. I looked over to Sands, at her blackened form in the bright doorway. She moved then, and the sun unleashed itself fully into the barn. Daylight. For a moment Sands disappeared, but then coalesced again, this time sitting against the doorframe.

There was some silence as I struggled to elicit milk from the cow, a project that is part Zen patience, part desperate persuasion, and finally I did it. 'Yay,' Sands said softly. Some doves fluttered from their eaves and out the door.

'Stadbakken told me that if I wanted to build well, I should study the cows,' I told her.

'What did he mean?' she asked.

'No idea.'

We both stared for a moment.

'They have those short legs,' I said. 'Under such huge torsos.'

'But good heads,' she said. 'They've got good, well-balanced heads on their shoulders.'

'I suppose.'

'Maybe he meant to make a building the way a cow would, if a cow could, not one that looks like a cow.'

'So, like a barn then,' I said. 'Something nice.'

'Maybe they're quite glamorous thinkers. Maybe something jeweled and spiritual, like a temple in India, or Turkey.'

'Yes,' I said. I shifted my chair to the next cow.

'Are cows monogamous?' she asked.

'Don't know, but I expect so.'

'Why?'

'Look at them. They're so big and slow.'

'Yes, and look at their eyes.'

I patted the cow, and the cow responded by not caring. I looked over at Sands. The sun had risen high enough that it was no longer blinding me. She was slumped sleepily against the doorframe, with her feet kicked up against the other side. Clasped in the V of her body was Fialta rising in the near distance, steam rising from it, brimming over with its internal contradiction.

Stadbakken had in his office an enormous telescope, one of those through which you can actually discern a little of the moon's surface, but instead it was pointed at the earth.

'May I?' I finally asked one October day.

'Please,' he said, and I looked down through it at the river, at the waves breaking softly on the banks, which were made of autumn leaves.

'Your work has been getting better and better,' he said, behind me.

'Thank you.'

'These beams are good. Where did they come from?' He was pointing at one of my drawings.

This was sometimes hard to do, to trace where elements came from in a sketch. It was not unlike pulling apart images from a dream.

'I guess from the barn,' I said, which was true, though I hadn't realized it until now.

'Of course,' he said. 'I saw you walking down there today. How's that going, by the way? How are the cows?'

He must have seen me, trudging in my sleep through the dark field? It made me a little nervous, and anyway the question seemed doubly intimate, since I half believed the cows really were his banished wives. 'They're doing well,' I said.

'Let me show you something,' he said. And from a long drawer he pulled out a series of drawings of Fialta. I had never seen any of his sketches before. It was almost impossible to read them, the lines were so thin and reedy, and they seemed all out of proportion to me, so that Fialta looked like it was blowing in the wind, or maybe going up in flames. He slid out the plan for the barn and laid it out in front of us. 'Here she is,' he said. 'I built it in 1967.'

'The summer of love, sir.'

'Yes, it was.'

One of the things Stadbakken had been struggling to teach us that fall was that a building ought to express two things simultaneously. The first was permanence, that is, security and well-being, a sense that the building will endure through all sorts of weather and calamity. But it also ought to express an understanding of its mortality, that is, a sense that it is an individual and, as such, vulnerable to its own passing away from this earth. Buildings that don't manage this second quality cannot properly be called architecture, he insisted. Even the simplest buildings, he said, ought to be productions of the imagination that attempt to describe and define life on earth, which of course is an overwhelming mix of stability and desire, fulfillment and longing, time and eternity.

The barn, even in this faint sketch, revealed this. It knew. 'It's beautiful, sir,' I said.

'Thank you,' he said.

It seemed only right, I thought, as I spiraled down into the evening air alone, that the cows had such a place to live, since they themselves seemed hybrids of this earth and the next, animals and angels both.

The tradition, Reuben informed us, was that apprentices put on a show for Stadbakken. At first we were going to do a

353

talent show, but nobody could drum up a talent. And then we were going to write skits, but they all ended up involving each of us doing bad impressions of him. And then we landed on the idea of putting on a play. He could be in it, too. We'd give him a part to read at the performance, which was to take place at Thanksgiving. We decided first to do *King Lear*, and then *Measure for Measure*, and then Beckett, and then *Arcadia*, and ruled all of these out as we started to cast them. Finally, Reuben suggested *Angels in America*.

'There's no women in it,' Sands said, when Reuben suggested it.

'There's gay men,' I said to her, 'and one woman.'

'Gay men are not the equivalent of women.'

'Stadbakken likes women better than men,' Groovy said.

'Everybody does,' Sands said.

I frowned. 'So rude,' I said to her.

Still, we decided to do *Angels*, with women playing the parts of the gay men, and then, through some hysterical fair play, I ended up with the part of the woman. Indira would be the angel, hovering above gender, and *sodo-sudu* entirely.

If you did want to know what Stadbakken believed about women, all you had to do was step into the women's wing at Fialta, with its great, circular common room. There were no walls at all. We were all sitting around the enormous wooden table at the room's center. We were drinking sugar gin, and from here it was as if the room seemed to believe that women were so in love with other women that they needed no walls at all. Probably when there were no men in the room they passed right through each other as well.

'What was that you read me from Vitruvius?' I asked Sands. 'That the walls of his Utopia were made of respect and interest only?'

354

'So much for a room of her own,' Sands said.

'My therapist would be appalled at this room,' Groovy said.

'You have a therapist?' I asked. 'Where is he, out in the woods?'

'He's a little gnome.'

'You sit on his mushroom, talk about your boundary problems,' I said.

'You think I have boundary problems?' she said.

I had been joking, but now that the question was put to me, I foolishly answered it. 'Well, a little, I guess.'

Sands looked at me, horrified.

'In a good way,' I said. 'It's charming.'

'I think you have boundary problems,' Groovy said. 'There's such a thing as too-strict boundaries, you know. You're all cut off from everybody.'

'I am?' I felt just the opposite. I felt like I bled all over everything, in an unseemly fashion, and my feelings for Sands were exacerbating this.

The conversation continued, with allegations and drunken accusations, all led by Groovy and me, the two most insecure parties in the group. Finally the phone rang for Indira, and she stepped into the kitchen to speak. None of us could understand the language, but her voice became louder and more upset as the conversation progressed.

Groovy brought out the cake she'd made for us, an Ovid cake. 'It has in it all the foods mentioned in the *Metamorphoses* – cranberries, walnuts, cinnamon, cloves,' she said.

'There are marshmallows in Ovid?' I asked, after I took a bite.

'Oh, those,' Groovy said. 'Those are my signature.'

'She puts marshmallows in everything,' Sands said. And then Indira returned to the room, apologizing as she sat down. 'I'm supposed to be getting married in two months.'

355

'What?' we all said.

'Yes. But I don't want to.'

Reuben looked stricken. 'It's an arranged marriage?' he said.

'Well, sort of.'

'Who arranged it?'

'I did, actually. But it was four years ago, before I went to Princeton and my fiancé to Penn. We planned to return to Bombay and get married, but I fell out of touch with him. Meanwhile, our fathers have joined businesses, and everybody awaits my arrival.'

We talked about this for a while and tried to strategize ways out. By the time midnight rolled around, Sands caught up to me in the kitchen and suggested we peel away, go to the river.

And what is a love affair if not a little boat, pushing off from shore, its tilting, untethered bob, its sensitivity to one's quietest gestures?

'I would love an arranged marriage,' Sands said. I was pushing us away from the edge with my oar, breaking apart the thin skein of ice forming there.

'No you wouldn't.'

'Yes. I'd like to have a family so involved that they were planning the wedding and I just had to show up, the treasured bride.' And then she rose in the boat, and as she stood it was as if the world shifted off course and was just careening back and forth, drunkenly. The trees shook with interest. She stretched and yawned, lifting her arms. Her sweater lifted, so that a narrow strip of her stomach showed. It was like burnished wood, pierced with a ruby. She looked almost psychedelically pretty there, in the tunnel created by the trees over the river.

356

I would have kissed her then, struggled up through the ranks of myself to do this one true thing, except I made the mistake of glancing up first, through the ragged arms of trees. And there was Stadbakken's room alight. A cold wind reared suddenly, and I could feel minuscule shards of ice embedded in it. By the time the river froze, we would no longer be together, and I could feel in the air already the terrible possibility.

The next afternoon, how could I help but think he had seen us, through his telescope, since when I entered for my tutorial, the first thing he did was lift my sketches to the light and say, 'I don't think you and Sands are working well together at all anymore.'

'Why?'

'I used to see Sands all over the page, and now I don't see her here at all.'

I didn't think this was fair, nor particularly true. 'Maybe our work is starting to become similar.'

'Oh.' He looked at me sarcastically. 'The two become one then, is that it?' He actually leaned up against the telescope then. If either of us had looked through it, probably we would have seen the river shrinking, crackling, crystallizing itself into ice.

We had one rehearsal, a run-through in the commons. Reuben was the director. Stadbakken was going to be given the most expansive part in the play, the part of the dying Prior. And Indira was the angel, of course. Sands had made wings. If I hadn't loved Sands before the wings, I would have now, for they were made of the feathers and down of creatures that had to be imaginary – white and brown and long. Picture her in the dewy morning coming off the hill to wrestle down a figment, tear off its feathers, later affixing them with glue to bent clothes hangers and panty hose straps, and there you have Sands and everything about her.

Sands and Groovy played the parts of Louis and Joe, respectively, two gay men. Their interpretations of men were hilarious – strangely deep throated and spliced through with their ideas of gayness, which were like streams of joy running through.

I played a luminous, heartbroken, and uptight woman whom Joe had abandoned. I took her husband's rejection of her quite seriously, tried to imagine exactly how it would feel as I swished in my housecoat along the floor of the commons.

After the rehearsal, I was sitting in the sheepskin chair, minding my own business, when Sands and Groovy came along to deliver their verdict on my performance. 'You don't really have being a woman quite right,' Sands said.

'What do you mean?'

'Well, you need to feel it inside.'

'I can feel it inside,' I said.

'You looked kinda stiff.'

'No, I didn't. That was my interpretation.'

'You gotta loosen up.' Sands reached down to shake my shoulders a little.

'You do,' I said, and I reached for her, and I brought her to me. Her body was such a mysterious rolling landscape in those moments, it turned and turned and turned, and I could feel her falling into my lap. I don't know what I would have done then, some minor consummation of my feelings for her, but Stadbakken stepped into the room. It was very odd to see him in daylight. Sands stood up, not too quickly, but definitely a little shaken.

'Where is Indira?' he said. 'Her father has called me.'

'I'll find her,' I said. I thought she might be back in the room with Reuben, and I knew he would be mortified if Stadbakken knew this.

And I did find them there, sitting across from each other at Reuben's folding table, two beautiful solitudes greeting each other across a little distance, playing cards.

I think it would have been possible to maintain this little world, always on the edge of fruition, if we hadn't spent Thanksgiving together, hours on hours together, if we hadn't consumed so much sugar gin, if we hadn't put on such a beautiful play. It was a snowy day. Dinner was planned for nightfall, which was five p.m. in these parts. Stadbakken would be arriving at four-thirty, at the dimming of the day. So we all met to cook in Utopia at one, after a morning of working alone on our sketches of the theater.

For the first hour we mostly drank. Sands enforced a game of Monopoly, and then we began to cook. Groovy made little pancake hors d'oeuvres, studded with cloves and cinnamon. Reuben and I were in charge of the turkey and the ham and the smaller game hens. Indira was in and out, miraculously cooking gorgeous yams and some exotic bean dish at the same time she was dissolving a multimillion-dollar marriage deal in Bombay on her cell without even breaking a sweat. She just kept rearranging things with her long, bronze hands, which I guess is what cooking is.

Sands relaxed in the commons, reading a book. She had been to town early in the morning to get the drinks and seemed to believe this exempted her from any further participation in the meal, except for leaning against the doorjamb every now and then to read us a passage from her novel, which today was *Justine*, by Lawrence Durrell: 'Certainly she was bad in many ways, but they were all small ways. Nor can

I say she harmed nobody. But those she harmed most she made fruitful. She expelled people from their old selves.'

'That's you, all right,' I said.

'It's me, too,' Groovy said.

'It's totally you,' Sands said, complimenting her.

I was trying to break open the plastic surrounding the turkey, surprised and humbled by all the blood that poured out as it opened. 'How does anybody eat after they've cooked a meal?' I said.

'Welcome to being a woman,' Sands said.

'Well,' I said, 'we have to kill them. That's hard work.'

'Nobody killed that,' she said. 'It wasn't ever really alive.'

'It was,' I said, newly in touch with animals from my months in the barn. I held out the turkey a little. 'It had its days in the sun.'

Sands smiled at me for a few long moments in which I arranged our whole future. We would live out our long chain of days at Fialta, secretly but not so secretly in love, and then we would move together to Chicago, or New York City, and live in our own private warren of rooms together. And our life would be made up of the gentle separations and communion of marriage. A line from a book Indira had given to Reuben ran through my mind, a sad line, I realize now, but it didn't even occur to me then that it was. 'It was good to be alive when you were alive.' My dream, as I stared at Sands, was crosshatched by our friends – Groovy, Indira, Reuben – moving back and forth between us, carrying on.

So, finally, the table was set, and the beloved guest had arrived, exuberant and windswept. He lifted his cup to us, and we drank, our bodies growing warmer as the day grew colder outside, whiter and whiter. The table was laid with the creatures, all burnished a coppery gold. And in the fireplace the log, like another little beast at work on itself, turned and turned as the air filled with the smell of fire. We lifted our cups back to Stadbakken. If you have ever felt that the table at which you sit contains everything and everybody that matters to you, like a little boat, then you know how I felt. It doesn't feel secure at all, but rather a little tipsy. It is unnerving to love a single place so much. There are no anchors to the world outside, the cities in the distance, the country around you. There is just this: the six of you afloat so happily in the temporary day.

After dinner, we cleared away the dishes and then set about the scene from the play. 'Okay,' Sands said to Stadbakken, 'you have a part.' She handed him a Xeroxed copy of the play. 'This chair you're sitting in? It's your bed. You're dying.' She touched his shoulder when she told him this. My eyes settled on her hand, on his shoulder. And his eyes settled on my eyes.

And then the play began. Reuben narrated to Stadbakken what came before: love, disappointment, the crude beautiful drama of sex, Sands and Groovy vamping at love, Sands carrying on like a girl making fun of a boy making fun of a girl, with a painted mustache. She was so ridiculous and beautiful, I thought I might die. Beyond the play, the day darkened. The backdrop was the icy arms of trees, the lift of starlings against the falling sun, the day dying. When Indira's part came, we had to shout for her. She was in Utopia, arguing on her cell. She hung up the phone and came in. She began to cry as she delivered her line, which gave her part a weird veracity: 'Heaven is a city much like San Francisco – more beautiful because imperiled.' We carried on for a few seconds, but then realized she actually was crying, standing there.

'What's the matter?' Sands asked.

'My father, he's sick. They just told me. I have to leave tomorrow.'

361

'Oh no!' Groovy said. And we all murmured. I looked over at Reuben. *What will you do now, Reuben? What display now? What will spill out of you now?* He stood so still, as the heartbroken always do, and then he went to her. He touched her wing, the safest, least intrusive part.

'Let's continue,' Indira said.

And so we did.

'Since you believe the world is perfectible you find it always unsatisfying.' This was Sands, as Louis. And then she kissed Groovy, as Joe. They kissed, as men kiss. I staggered inwardly. And the play wound through its tragedies easily until Stadbakken's final, deathbed lines. 'You are all fabulous creatures, each and every one. And I bless you: More life.' Behind his head thousands of birds took flight. He raised his arms, though dying. He loved the play, you could tell. The wind howled. And then he stood up to go hug Indira.

Since Sands hadn't cooked, it was her duty to clean up. I helped her clear away the dishes. We made an enormous pile of dirty dishes and plates and heaps of food on the silver table at the center of Utopia. There were also the three empty carriages of bones. 'I can't believe that about Indira,' Sands said.

'I know. It's hard to believe.'

'And now she'll have to get married. That's a real primal fear, you know, for women. I can remember as a girl having dreams about having to get married.'

'You're so unromantic, I can't even stand it.'

'Me?' she said.

'You.'

She was leaning against the silver table, looking down at the turkey drumstick that she was tearing apart in her hands, to eat, when I stepped up, finally, and against all better reason, kissed her. Tomorrow, Indira would be gone, and who could predict what would happen then, when one of us was gone? Time was ticking away, the snow was falling. Sands's mouth tasted like ten thousand things – berries and wine and pumpkin and something too human to define. I placed my hand on her spine as it arched back over the table, and then the door swung open. I turned to see Stadbakken, my arm lifting Sands so that we stood before him, my arm around her. He was smoking a cigar, and some of its smoke was spiraling up around his head. He stood still for a moment and then said, 'Oh, is that right? Well, then. Okay. That's fine.'

He walked toward us then. 'First, let's clear away the bones,' he said. 'Let's make some room, then, for you two. Let us clear away the bones!' And with that, he swept his entire arm over the silver lake of the table, so that everything flew – all the bodies breaking up in the air, a flurry of bone and gristle, of life sailing apart.

Later that night I went looking for Sands. She had kissed me, told me to wait in Utopia, and ran after Stadbakken. 'I'll try to solve it,' she said to me. But then she did not come back for over an hour. I went to the women's wing and found Groovy there, helping Indira to pack. And then Reuben came out of Indira's room as well, carrying an empty cardboard box. He wasn't saying anything, so I blurted, 'Indira, why are you going? Please don't go. Please stay.'

Indira looked at me sweetly, indulgently, as if I were a small child. She hugged me.

And then I went to Stadbakken's. The light was falling down out of the building, onto the snow, that's how bright it was. It was too high for me to see anything, but I stood out in the snow for a long time. I must have stood there for close to an hour. It was ridiculous, I knew, and pathetic, but that light was more warm and significant than any I'd ever known in my life, and I knew that when I turned to go there would be nothing, only the cold and the never-ending drifts of snow.

By the next morning, our dinner was dissolving in the slop bucket – the little pancakes, the heads of fish, the turkey breast, the potato shavings. I poured a cup of coffee, picked up the pail, and walked down through the snow and darkness. The beasts were still asleep, and one startled when I opened the door and the cold sun fell over her. Eventually the snow began to fall – enormous lotus flakes that I watched from inside the barn. I milked the one cow for a while and as the sun rose higher I was finally getting warm. The barn was waking up around me, the building itself shifting and ticking away as the light forced itself through the million tiny chinks. As I milked I tried to think of a way to stay in love with Sands and stay at Fialta. In the moment Stadbakken flung his hand across the table, I had known he would never be reconciled to this. I don't believe there was anything illicit particularly in his feelings; in fact, it was probably their very purity that made them so searing, so intolerant. He was her teacher, and she his student, and they met up there in a perfect illumination high above the regular world. Another cow shuddered awake beside me and looked up at me, half in sympathy, half in resignation to all my shortcomings, which is the very look cows always give, which is their whole take on the world.

And then the door opened. The cold, dim day rushed in, and, along with it, Sands. She was wearing a nightgown with a parka over the top, her hair in one long, sleepy braid. She looked like she was fulfilling and making fun of my dreams all at once. 'You look like a farmer's wife,' I said.

'And you the farmer.'

'He wants to see you,' she said. Some doves in the rafters fluttered and made a break for the open door, wheeling then around the corner. Fialta was burning away in the distance. From this distance, it looked already to be stirring – composed, as Auden said all living things were, of dust and Eros. It was clear what would happen. I would leave; Stadbakken would fall – the full, staggering weight of him – in my arms and hug me as he told me I had to leave. But there was still the morning. Her hair and skin were the only moments of darkness in the brightening barn. I kissed her again. One of the cows made a lowing sound I'd not heard before, which sounded like a foghorn in the distance. They'd seen it all before, this whole drama; their large hearts inside them had broken a hundred times before today. The barn smelled exactly like the very passage of time. The cows took their own fertility so practically, as the pigs did joyfully, and the doves beautifully. I already knew then that I'd be forced to leave Fialta; I could practically have predicted my leaving to the hour, but my heart was caught up in the present, whirring away and still insisting that this was the beginning, not the end. And so that's how I felt hardly any grief at all, lying alongside Sands on the crackling, warm hay at the foot of that makeshift paradise, as the cows watched on, remembering human love.

AIMEE BENDER

THE COLOR MASTER

OUR STORE WAS expensive, I mean Ex-Pen-Sive, as anything would be if all its requests were for clothing in the colors of natural elements. The duke wanted shoes the color of rock, so he could walk in the rock and not see his feet. He was vain that way; he did not like to see his feet. He wanted to appear, from a distance, as a floating pair of ankles. But rock, of course, is many colors. The distinction's subtle, but it is not just one plain gray, that I can promise, and in order to truly blend, it would not do to give the duke a regular pair of lovely pure-gray-dyed shoes. So we had to trek over as a group to his dukedom, a three-day trip, and take bagfuls of rocks back with us, and then use them, at the studio, as guides. I spent five hours one afternoon just staring at a rock, trying to see into its color scheme. Gray, my head kept saying. I see gray.

At the shop, in general, we build clothing and shoes – shirts and coats, soles and heels – we treat the leather, shape and weave the cloth, and even when an item isn't ordered as a special request, one pair of shoes or one robe might cost as much as a pony or a month's food from the market stalls. Most villagers do not have this kind of money, so the bulk of our customers are royalty, or the occasional wealthy traveler riding through town who has heard rumors of our skills.

For the duke's shoes, all of us tailors and shoemakers, who numbered about twelve, were working round the clock. One man had the idea to grind bits of rock into particles and then add those particles to the dye-washing bin. This helped a little. We attended visualization seminars where we tried to imagine what it was like to be a rock, and then, quietly, after an hour of deep thought and breathing, returned to our desks and tried to insert that imagery into our decision about how long to leave the shoes in the dye bath. We felt the power of the mountain in the rock, and let that play a subtle sub-textual role. And then, once the dye had reached ultimate intensity, and once the shoes were a beautiful pure gray, a rocky gray, but still gray, we summoned the Color Master.

She lives about a half mile away, in a cottage behind the scrub-oak grove. We summon her by sending off a goat down the lane, because she does not like to be disturbed by people, and the goat trots down the road and butts on the door. The Color Master set up our studio and shop in the first place, years ago; she has always done the final work. But she has been looking unwell these days. For our last project – the duchess's handbag that was supposed to look like a just-blooming rose – she wore herself out thinking about pink, and was in bed for weeks after, recovering. Dark circles ringed her eyes. She is growing older. Also, her younger brother suffers from terrible back problems and cannot move or work and lives with her, lying on the sofa all day long. She is certainly the most talented in the kingdom, but gets zero recognition. We, the tailors and shoemakers, we know of her gifts, but does the king? Do the townsfolk? She walks among them like an ordinary being, shopping for tomatoes, and no one knows that the world she's seeing is about a thousand times more detailed than the world anyone else is looking at. When you see a tomato, like me, you probably see a very nice red orb with a green stem, fresh and delectable. When she sees a tomato, she sees blues and browns, curves and indentations, shadow and light, and she could probably even guess how many seeds are in a given tomato based on how heavy it feels in her hand.

So we sent over the goat, and when the Color Master came into the studio, we'd just finished the fourth dyeing of the rock shoes. They were drying on a mat, and they looked pretty good. I told Cheryl that her visualization of the mountain had definitely helped. She blushed. I said, too, that Edwin's contribution of the ground rock particles had added a useful kind of rough texture. He kicked a stool leg, pleased. I hadn't done much; I'm not very skilled, but I like to commend good work when I see it.

The Color Master approached, wearing a linen sheath woven with blue threadings. Her face hinting at gaunt. She greeted us all, and stood at the counter where the shoes were drip-drying.

Nice work, she said. Esther, who had fronted the dyeing process, curtsied.

We sprinkled rocks into the dye, she said.

A fine choice, said the Color Master.

Edwin did a little dance in place by his table. The goat settled on a pillow in the corner and began to eat the stuffing.

The Color Master rolled her shoulders a few times, and when the shoes were dry, she laid her hands upon them. She lifted them to the sunlight. She picked up a rock and looked at it next to the shoes. She circled both inside different light rays. Then she went to the palette area and took out a handful of blue dust. We have about one hundred and fifty metal bins of this dust in a range of colors. The bins stand side by side, running the perimeter of the studio. They are narrow, so we can fit a whole lot of colors, and if someone brings in a new color, we hammer down a new bin and slide it into the spectrum, wherever it fits. One tailor found an amazing rich burgundy off in the driest part of the forest, on a series of leaves; I located, once, over by the reddish iron deposits near the lake, a type of dirt that was a deeper brown than soil. Someone else found a new blue in a desiccated pansy, and another in the feathers of a dead bird. We have instructions to hunt for color everywhere, at all times.

The Color Master toured the room, and then took that handful of blue dust (and always, when I watch, I am thrilled – blue? how does she know, blue?), and she rubbed the dust into the shoe. Back to the bins, where she got a black, a dusty black, and then some sage green. While she worked, everyone stood around, quiet. We dropped our usual drudgery and chitchat.

The Color Master worked swiftly, but she added, usually, something on the level of forty colors, so the process generally took over two hours. She added a color here, a color there, sometimes at the size of salt particles, and the gray in the shoe shifted and shaded under her hands. She would reach a level and ask for sealant, and Esther would step forward, and the Color Master would coat the shoe to fasten the colors and then return to the sunlight, holding a shoe up, with the rock in her other hand. This went on for about four rounds. I swear, I could start to feel the original mountain's presence in the room, hear the great heavy lumbering voice of it.

When she was done, the pair was so gray, so rocklike, you could hardly believe they were made of leather at all. They looked as if they had been sheared straight from the craggy mountainside.

Done, she said.

We circled her, bowing our heads.

Another triumph, murmured Sandy, who cannot color-mix to save her life.

The Color Master swept her gaze around the room, and

her eyes rested on each of us, searching, slowly, until they finally settled on me. Me?

Will you walk me home? she said in a deep voice, while Esther tied an invoice to the foot of a pigeon and then threw it out the window in the direction of the dukedom.

I would be honored, I mumbled. I took her arm. The goat, full of pillow, tripped along behind us.

I am a quiet sort, except for the paying of compliments, and I didn't know if I should ask her anything on the walk. As far as I knew, she didn't usually request an escort home at all. Mainly I just looked at all the stones and rocks on the path, and for the first time saw that blue hint, and the blackness, and the shades of green, and that faint edge of purple if the light hit just so. She seemed relieved that I wasn't asking questions, so much so that it occurred to me that that was probably why she'd asked me in the first place.

At her door, she fixed her eyes on me: steady, aging at the corners. She was almost twice my age, but had always had an allure I'd admired. A way of holding her body that let you know that there was a body there, but that it was private, that stuff happened on it, in it, to it, but it was stuff I would never see. It made me sad, seeing that, knowing how her husband had gone off to the war years ago and never returned, and how it was difficult for her to have people over because of her brother with the bad back, and how, long ago, she had fled her own town for reasons she never mentioned. Plus, she had a thick cough and her own money questions, all of which seemed so unfair when she should've been living in the palace, as far as I was concerned.

Listen, she said. She held me in her gaze.

Yes?

There's a big request coming in, she said. I've heard rumors. Big. Huge.

What is it? I said.

I don't know yet, but start preparing. You'll have to take over. I will die soon, she said.

Excuse me?

Soon, she said. I can feel it, brewing. Death. It's not dark, nor is it white. It's almost a blue-purple. Her eyes went past me, to the sky.

Are you confusing me with someone else? I asked.

She laughed.

Do you mean it? I said. Are you ill?

No, she said. Yes. I mean it. I'm asking for your help. And when I die, it will be your job to finish.

But I'm not very good, I said, twisting. Like at all. You can't die. You should ask Esther, or Sven –

You, she said, and with a little curt nod, she went into her house and shut the door.

The duke loved his shoes so much he sent us a drawing, by the court illustrator, of him floating, it appeared, on a pile of rocks. I love them, he wrote, in swirly handwriting; I love them, I love them! In addition to a small cash bonus, he offered us horse rides and a feast at the dukedom. We all attended, in all our finery, and it was a great time. It was the last time I saw the Color Master dancing, in her pearl-gray gown, and I knew it was the last even as I watched it, her silver hair swirling out as she glided through the group. The duke kept tapping his toe on the side, holding the duchess's hand, her free one grasping a handbag the perfect pink of a rose, so vivid and fresh the color seemed to carry a sweet scent even across the ballroom.

Two weeks later, almost everyone was away when the king's courtier came riding over with the request: a dress the color of the moon. The Color Master was not feeling well, and had asked not to be disturbed; Esther's father was ill, so she was off taking care of him; Sven's wife was giving birth to twins, so he was off with her; the two others ahead of me had caught whooping cough; and someone else was on a travel trip to find a new orange. So the request went to me, the apprentice. Just as the Color Master had hoped.

I unrolled the scroll and read it quietly by the window.

A dress the color of the moon?

It was impossible.

First of all, the moon is not a color. It is a reflection of a color. Second, it is not even the reflection of a color, it is the reflection of what appears to be a color, but is really in fact a bunch of bursting hydrogen atoms, far, far away. Third, the moon shines. A dress cannot shine like the moon unless the dress is also reflecting something, and reflective materials are generally tacky-looking, or too industrial. Our only options were silk and cotton and leather. The moon? It is white, it is silver, it is silver-white, it is not an easy color to dye. A dress the color of the moon? The whole thing made me irritable.

But this was not a small order. This was, in fact, for the king's daughter. The princess. And since the queen had died of pneumonia a few months before, this was a dress for the most important woman in the kingdom.

I paced several times around the studio, and then I went against policy and tried knocking on the door of the Color Master's cabin, but she called out in a strong voice, Just make it!

Are you okay? I asked, and she said, Come back once you've started!

I walked back, kicking twigs and acorns.

I ate oranges off the tree out back until I felt a little better. Since I was in charge, due to the pecking order, I called together everyone that was left in the studio and asked for a seminar on reflection, to reflect upon reflection. In particular for Cheryl, who really used the seminars well. We gathered in a circle in the side room and talked about mirrors, and still water, and wells, and feeling understood, and opals, and then we did a creative-writing exercise about our first memory of the moon, and how it affected us, and the moment when we realized it followed us (Sandy had a charming story about going on a walk as a child and trying to lose it but not being able to), and then we wrote haiku. Mine was this: Moon, you silver thing / Floating in the sky like that / Make me a dress. Please.

After a few tears over Edwin's story of realizing his father in the army was seeing the same moon he saw, we drifted out of the seminar room and began dyeing the silk. It had to be silk, of course, and we selected from the loom studio a very fine weave, a really elegant one that had a touch of shimmer in the fabric already. I let Cheryl start the dyeing with shades of white, because I could see a kind of shining light in her eyes from the seminar and even a luminosity to her skin. She is so receptive that way.

While she began that first layer, I went to see the Color Master again. I let myself in this time. She was in bed. It was shocking how quickly she was going downhill. I got her brother a glass of water and an apple-cheese snack – Angel, he called me, from the sofa – and then I settled next to the bed where she lay resting, her hair spread over the pillows in rays of silver. She was not very old, the Color Master, but she had gone silver early. Wait, can we use your hair? I said.

Sure. She pulled out a few strands and handed them over.

This'll help, I said, looking at the glint. If we try to make this into particles?

Good, she said. Good thinking.

376

How are you doing? I asked.

I heard word, she said. Moon today, sun soon.

What?

Sun soon. How goes moon?

It's hard, I said. I mean, *hard*. And, with your hair, that'll help, but to reflect?

Use blue, she said.

What kind?

Several kinds. Her voice was weaker, but I could hear the steel behind it as she walked through the bins in her mind. Don't be afraid of the darker shades, she said.

I'm an awful color-mixer, I said. Are you in pain?

No, she said. Just weak. Blue, she said. And black. She pulled out a few more strands of hair. Here, she said. And shavings of opal, do we have those?

Too expensive, I said.

Go to the mine, she said. Get opals, shave 'em, add a new bin. Do you know the king wants to marry his daughter? Her eyes flashed, for a second, with anger.

What?

Put that in the dress too, she said. She dropped her voice to a whisper, every word sharp and clear. Anger, she said. Put anger in the dress. The moon as our guide. A daughter should not be ordered to marry her father.

Put anger in the dress?

When you mix, she said. Got it? When you're putting the opal shavings in. The dress is supposed to be a dowry gift, but give the daughter the strength to leave instead. All right?

Her eyes were shining at me, so bright I wanted to put them in the dress, too.

Okay, I said, faltering. I'm not sure –

You have it in you, she said. I see it. Truly. Or I would never have given you the job.

377

Then she fell back on her pillows and was asleep in seconds.

On the walk back, through the scrub-oak grove, I felt as I usually felt, both moved and shitty. Because what she saw in me could just as easily have been the result of some kind of fever. Was she hallucinating? Didn't she realize I had only gotten the job because I'd complimented Esther on her tassel scarf at the faire, plus I did decent work with the rotating time schedule? Who's to say that there was anything to it? To me, really?

Anger in the dress?

I didn't feel angry, just defeated and bad about myself, but I didn't put that in the dress; it didn't seem right. Instead, I went to the mine and befriended the foreman, Manny, and he gave me a handful of opals that were too small for any jewelry and would work well as shavings. I spent the afternoon with the sharpest picks and awls I could find, breaking open opals and making a new bin for the dust. Cheryl had done wonders with the white, and the dress glowed like a gleaming pearl – almost moonlike but not enough, yet. I added the opals and we redyed, and then you could see a hint of rainbow hovering below the surface. Like the sun was shimmering in there, too, and that was addressing the reflective issue. When it came time to color-mix, I felt like I was going to throw up, but I did what the Color Master had asked, and went for blue, then black, and I was incredibly slow, like incredibly slow, but for one moment I felt something as I hovered over the bins of blue. Just a tug of guidance from the white of the dress that led my hand to the middle blue. It felt, for a second, like harmonizing in a choir, the moment when the voice sinks into the chord structure and the sound grows, becomes more layered and full than before. So that was the right choice. I wasn't so on the mark for the

378

black, which was slightly too light, more like the moon when it's just setting, when the light of day has already started to rise and encroach, which isn't what they wanted – they wanted black-of-night moon, of course. But when we held it up in the middle of the room, there it was – not as good as anything the Color Master had done, maybe one one-hundredth as good, but there was something in it that would pass the test of the assignment. Like, the king and princess wouldn't collapse in awe, but they would be pleased, maybe even a little stirred. Color is nothing unless next to other colors, the Color Master told us all the time. Color does not exist alone. And I got it, for a second with that blue, I did.

Cheryl and I packed the dress carefully in a box, and sent off the pigeon with the invoice, and waited for the king's courtiers to come by, and they did, with a carriage for the dress only. After we laid the box carefully on the velvet back-seat, they gave us a hunk of chocolate as a bonus, which Cheryl and I ate together in the side room, exhausted. Relieved. I went home and slept for twenty hours. I had put no anger in the dress; I remembered that when I woke up. Who can do that while so focused on just making an accept-able moon-feeling for the assignment? They didn't ask for anger, I said, eating a few apples for breakfast. They asked for the moon, and I gave them something vaguely moonlike, I said, spitting tooth cleanser into the basin.

That afternoon, I went to see the Color Master to tell her all about it. I left out the absence of the anger and told her I'd messed up on the black, and she laughed and laughed from her bed. I told her about the moon being more of a morning moon. I told her what I'd felt at the blue, the feeling of the chord, and she picked up my hand. Pressed it lightly.

Death is glowing, she said. I can see it.

I felt a heaviness rustle in my chest. How long? I said.

A few weeks, I think, she said. The sun will come in soon. The princess still has not left the castle.

But we need you, I said, and with effort, she squeezed my hand again. It is dark and glowing, she said, her eyes sliding over to lock onto mine. It is like loam, she said.

The sun? I said.

Tomorrow, she said. She closed her eyes.

When I got to work the next day, there was an elaborate thank-you note from the castle with a lot of praise for the moon dress, in this over-the-top calligraphy, and a bonus bolt of fuchsia silk. The absentees were returning, slowly, from their various tangents, when we received the king's new assignment: a dress the color of the sun. Because everyone felt a little jittery about the Color Master's absence and wanted to go with whatever – or whoever – seemed to work, I was assigned to the order. Esther told me congratulations. Sandy took over my rotating schedule duties. I did a few deep knee bends and got to work.

I liked that guy at the mine a little bit, the Manny guy, so I went back to ask about citrine quartz. He didn't have any, but we had a nice roast-turkey lunch together in the spot of sun outside the rocky opening of the cave, and I told him about the latest dress I was making for the princess.

Whew, he said, shaking his head. What color *is* the sun?

Beats me, I said. We're not supposed to look at it, right? Kids make it yellow, I said, but I think that's not quite right.

Ivory? he said.

Sort of burnt white, I said. But with a halo?

That's hard work, he said, folding up the cloth he used to hold his sandwich. He had a good face to him, something chunky in his nose that I could get behind.

Want to go to the faire sometime? he asked, looking up.

380

The outdoor faire happened on the weekends in the main square, where everything was sold.

Sure, I said.

Maybe there's some sun stuff there, he said.

I'd love to, I said.

We began the first round of dyeing at the end of the week, focusing initially on the pale yellows. Cheryl was very careful not to oversaturate the dye – yellow is always more powerful than it appears in the bin. It is a stealth dominator, and can take days and days to undo. She did that all Saturday, while I went to the faire. It was a clear, warm afternoon, with stands offering all sorts of goodies and delicious meat pies. Nothing looked helpful for the dress, but Manny and I laughed about the latest tapestry unicorn craze and shared a nice kiss at the end, near the scrub oaks. Everything was feeling a little more alive than usual. We held another seminar at the studio, and Cheryl did a session on warmth, and seasons, and how we all revolve around the sun, whether or not we are willing to admit it. Central, she said. The theme of the sun is central. The center of us, she said. Core. Fire.

Careful with red, said the Color Master, when I went to visit. She was thinner and weaker, but her eyes were still coals. Her brother had gotten up to try to take care of her and had thrown out his back to the worst degree and was now in the medicine arena, strapped to a board. My sister is dying, he told the doctors, but he couldn't move, so all they did was shake their heads. The Color Master had refused any help. I want to see Death as clearly as possible, she'd said. No drugs.

I made her some toast, but she only ate a few bites and then pushed it aside.

It's tempting to think of red for sun, she said. But it has

to be just a dash, not much. More of a dark orange, and a hint of brown. And then white on yellow on white.

Not bright white, she said. The kind of white that makes you squint, but in a softer way.

Yeah, I said, sighing. And where does one find that kind of white?

Keep looking, she said.

Last time I used your hair? I said.

She smiled, feebly. Go look at fire for a while, she said. Go spend some time with fire.

I don't want you to die, I said.

Yes, well, she said. And?

Looking at fire was interesting, I have to admit. I sat with a candle for a couple hours. It has these stages of color: the white, the yellow, the red, the tiny spot of blue I'd heard mentioned but never noticed. So I decided it made sense to use all of them. We hung the dress in the center of the room and all revolved around it, spinning, imagining we were planets. It needs to be hotter, said Sven, who was playing the part of Mercury, and then he put a blowtorch to some silk and made some dust materials out of that, and we redipped the dress. Cheryl was off in the corner, cross-legged in a sunbeam, her eyes closed, trying to soak it up. We need to soak it! she said, after an hour, standing. So we left it in the dipping longer than usual. I walked by the bins, trying to feel that harmony feeling, waiting for a color to call me. I felt a tug to the dark brown, so I brought a bit of it out and tossed it into the mix; it was too dark, but after a little yellow-white from dried lily flowers, something started to pop a bit. Light, said Cheryl. It's also daylight – it's light. It's our only true light, she said again. Without it, we live in darkness and cold. The dress drip-dried in the middle of the room. It was

382

getting closer, and just needed that factor of squinting – a dress so bright it couldn't quite be looked at. How to get that?

Remember, the Color Master said. She sat up in bed, her silver hair streaming over her shoulders. I keep forgetting, she said, but the king wants to Marry His Daughter. Her voice pointed to each word, hard. That is not right, she said, okay? Got it? Put anger in the dress. Righteous anger, for her. Do you hear me?

I do not, I said, though I nodded. I didn't say I do not, I just thought that part. I played with the wooden knob of her bedframe. I had tried to put some anger in the sun dress, but I had been so consumed with trying to factor in the squint that all I really got in there was confusion. Confusion does make people squint, though, so I ended up fulfilling the request accidentally. We had sent it off in the carriage after working all night on the light factor that Cheryl had mentioned by adding bits of diamond dust to the mix. Diamonds are light inside darkness! she'd announced at 3 a.m., a bialy in her hand, triumphant. On the whole, it was a weaker product than the moon dress, but not bad – most people don't notice the variance in subtlety, and our level of general artistry and craft is high, so we could get away with a lot without anyone's running over and asking for his money back.

The sky, the Color Master told me, after I had filled her in on the latest. She had fallen back down into her pillows, and was so weak she spoke with eyes closed. When I held her hand she only rested hers in mine: not limp, not grasping.

Sky is last, she said.

And death?

Soon, she said. She fell asleep midway through our conversation. I stayed all night. I slept too, sitting up, and sometimes I woke and just sat and watched her. What a precious person she was, really. I hadn't known her very well, but she had picked me, for some reason, and that picking was changing me, I could feel it; it was like being warmed by the presence of the sun, a little. The way a ray of sun can seem to choose you as you walk outside from the cold interior. I wanted to put her in that sun dress, to drape her in it, but it wasn't an option; we had sent it off to the princess, plus it wasn't even the right size and wasn't really her style, either. But I guess I just knew that the sun dress we sent was something of a facsimile, and that this person here was the real sun, the real center for us all, and even through the dark night, I felt the light of her, burning, even in the rasping heavy breathing of a dying woman.

In the morning, she woke up, saw I was still there, and smiled a little. I brought her tea. She sat up to drink it.

The anger! she said again, as if she had been dreaming about it. Which maybe she had. She raised up on her elbows, face blazing. Don't forget to put anger in this last dress, she said. Okay?

Drink your tea, I said.

Listen, she said. It's important, she said. She shook her head. It was written, in pain, all over her forehead. She sat up higher on her elbows, and looked beyond me, through me, and I could feel meaning, thick, in her, even if I didn't know the details about why. She picked her words carefully.

You cannot bring it – someone – into the world, and then bring it back into you, she said. It is the wrong action.

Her face was clear of emphasis, and she spoke plainly, as plainly as possible, as if there were no taboo about fathers marrying daughters, as if the sex factor was not a biological risk, as if it wasn't just disturbing and upsetting as a given. She held herself steady on her elbows. This is why she was the Color Master. There was no stigma, or judgment, no societal subscription, no trigger morality, but just a clean and pure anger, fresh, as if she was thinking the possibility over for the first time.

You birth someone, she said, leaning in. And then you release her. You do not marry her, which is a bringing back in. You let her go.

Put anger in the dress, she said. She gripped my hand, and suddenly all the weakness was gone, and she was right there, an electric pulse of a person, and I knew this was the last time we would talk, I knew it so clearly that everything sharpened into incredible focus. I could see the threads in the weave of her nightgown, the microscopic bright cells in the whites of her eyes.

Her nails bit into my hand. I felt the tears rising up in me. The teacup wobbling on the nightstand.

Got it? she said.

Yes, I said.

I put the anger in the dress the color of sky. I put it in there so much I could hardly stand it – that she was about to die, that she would die unrecognized, that none of us would ever live up to her example, and that we were the only witnesses. That we are all so small after all that. That everybody dies anyway. I put the anger in there so much that the blue of the sky was fiercely stark, an electric blue like the core of the fire, so much that it was hard to look at. It was much harder to look at than the sun dress; the sky dress was of a whole different order. Intensely, shockingly, bluely vivid. Let her go? This was the righteous anger she had asked for, yards of it, bolts of it, even though, paradoxically, it was anger I felt because soon she would be gone.

She died the following morning in her sleep. Even at her funeral, all I could feel was the rage, pouring out of me, while we all stood around her coffin, crying, leaning on one another, sprinkling colors from the dye bins into her hands, the colors of heaven, we hoped, while the rest of the town went about its business. Her brother rolled in on a stretcher, weeping. I had gone over to see her that morning, and found her, dead, in her bed. So quiet. The morning sun, white and clear, through the windowpanes. I stroked her hair for an hour, her silver hair, before I left to tell anyone. The dress request had already come in the day before, as predicted.

At the studio, under deadline, Cheryl led a seminar on blue, and sky, and space, and atmosphere, and depth, and it was successful and mournful, especially during the week after the funeral. Blue. I attended, but mostly I was nurturing the feeling in me, that rage. Tending to it like a little candle flame cupped against the wind. I knew it was the right kind, I knew it. I didn't think I'd do much better than this dress, ever; I would go on to do good things in my life, have other meaningful moments, share in the experience of being a human being in the world, but I knew this was my big moment, and I had to be equal to it. So I sat at the seminar with half a focus, just cupping that flame of rage, and I half participated in the dyeing of the fabric and the discussion of the various shades, and then, when they had done all they could do, and the dress was hanging in the middle, a clear and beautiful blue, I sent everyone home. Are you sure? Cheryl asked, buttoning up her coat.

Yes, I said. Go.

It was night, and the sky was unlit under a new moon, so it was up to me to find the blue sky – draped over us all, but hidden. I went to the bins, and listened for the chords, and felt her in me. I felt the ghost of her passing through me as I mixed and dyed, and I felt the rage in me that she had to be a ghost: the softness of the ghost, right up next to and surrounding the sharp and burning core of my anger. Both guided my hands. I picked the right colors to mix with blue, a little of so many other colors and then so many different kinds of blue and gray and more blue and more. And in it all, the sensation of shaking my fists at the sky, shaking my fists high up to the sky, because that is what we do when someone dies too early, too beautiful, too undervalued by the world, or sometimes just at all – we shake our fists at the big blue beautiful indifferent sky, and the anger is righteous and strong and helpless and huge. I shook and I shook, and I put all of it into the dress.

Of all people to take back? How impossible to understand that I would never see her again.

When the sun rose, it was a clear morning, the early sky pale and wide. I had worked all night. I wasn't tired yet, but I could feel the pricklings of it around me, peripheral. I made a pot of coffee and sat in the chill with a cup and the dress, which I had hung again from a hanger in the middle of the room. The rest of the tailors drifted over in the morning, one by one, and no one said anything. They entered the room and looked up, and then they surrounded it with me. We held hands, and they said I was the new Color Master, and I said okay, because it was obvious that that was true, and though I knew I would never reach her levels again, at least for this one dress I had. They didn't even praise me, they just looked at it and cried. We all cried.

Esther sent off the invoice pigeon, and, with care, we placed the dress in its package, and when the carriage came by, we laid it carefully over the backseat, as usual. We ate our hunk of gift chocolate. We cleaned up the area around the bins and swept the floor of dust, and talked to a builder, a friend of Manny's, about expanding one of the rooms into an official seminar studio. The carriage trotted off, with the dress in the backseat, led by two white horses.

From what I heard, soon after the princess got the third dress, she left town. The rest I do not know.

The rest of the story – known, I'm told, as 'Donkeyskin' – is hers.

ORHAN PAMUK

I AM RED

(from *My Name Is Red*)

Translated by Maureen Freely

I APPEARED IN Ghazni when *Book of Kings* poet Firdusi completed the final line of a quatrain with the most intricate of rhymes besting the court poets of Shah Mahmud, who ridiculed him as being nothing but a peasant. I was there on the quiver of *Book of Kings* hero Rüstem when he traveled far and wide in pursuit of his missing steed; I became the blood that spewed forth when he cut the notorious ogre in half with his wondrous sword; and I was in the folds of the quilt upon which he made furious love with the beautiful daughter of the king who'd received him as a guest. Verily and truly, I've been everywhere and am everywhere. I emerged as Tur traitorously decapitated his brother Iraj; as legendary armies, spectacular as a dream, clashed on the steppes; and as Alexander's life-blood shimmered brightly from his handsome nose after he suffered sunstroke. Yes, Shah Behram Gür spent every night of the week with a different beauty beneath domes of varying color from distant lands, listening to the story she recounted, and I was upon the outfit of the striking maiden he visited on a Tuesday, whose picture he'd fallen in love with, just as I appeared from the crown to the caftan of Hüsrev, who'd fallen in love with Shirin's picture. Verily, I was visible upon the military banners of armies besieging fortresses, upon the tablecloths covering tables set for feasts, upon the velvet caftans of ambassadors kissing the feet of sultans, and wherever the sword, whose legends children loved, was depicted. Yes, handsome almond-eyed apprentices applied me with elegant brushes to thick paper from Hindustan and Bukhara; I embellished Ushak carpets, wall ornamentation, the combs of fighting cocks, pomegranates, the fruits of fabled lands, the mouth of Satan, the subtle accent lines within picture borders, the curled embroidery on tents, flowers barely visible to the naked eye made for the artist's own pleasure, blouses worn by stunning women with outstretched necks watching the street through open shutters, the sour-cherry eyes of bird statues made of sugar, the stockings of shepherds, the dawns described in legends and the corpses and wounds of thousands, nay, tens of thousands of lovers, warriors and shahs. I love engaging in scenes of war where blood blooms like poppies; appearing on the caftan of the most proficient of bards listening to music on a countryside outing as pretty boys and poets partake of wine; I love illuminating the wings of angels, the lips of maidens, the death wounds of corpses and severed heads bespeckled with blood.

I hear the question upon your lips: What is it to be a color?

Color is the touch of the eye, music to the deaf, a word out of the darkness. Because I've listened to souls whispering – like the susurrus of the wind – from book to book and object to object for tens of thousands of years, allow me to say that my touch resembles the touch of angels. Part of me, the serious half, calls out to your vision while the mirthful half soars through the air with your glances.

I'm so fortunate to be red! I'm fiery. I'm strong. I know men take notice of me and that I cannot be resisted.

I do not conceal myself: For me, delicacy manifests itself neither in weakness nor in subtlety, but through determination and will. So, I draw attention to myself. I'm not afraid of other colors, shadows, crowds or even of loneliness. How wonderful it is to cover a surface that awaits me with my own victorious being! Wherever I'm spread, I see eyes shine, passions increase, eyebrows rise and heartbeats quicken. Behold how wonderful it is to live! Behold how wonderful to see. Behold: Living is seeing. I am everywhere. Life begins with and returns to me. Have faith in what I tell you.

Hush and listen to how I developed such a magnificent red tone. A master miniaturist, an expert in paints, furiously pounded the best variety of dried red beetle from the hottest climes of Hindustan into a fine powder using his mortar and pestle. He prepared five drachmas of the red powder, one drachma of soapwort and a half drachma of lotor. He boiled the soapwort in a pot containing three okkas of water. Next, he mixed thoroughly the lotor into the water. He let it boil for as long as it took to drink an excellent cup of coffee. As he enjoyed his coffee, I grew as impatient as a child about to be born. The coffee had cleared the master's mind and given him the eyes of a jinn. He sprinkled the red powder into the kettle and carefully mixed the concoction with one of the thin, clean sticks reserved for this task. I was ready to become genuine red, but the issue of my consistency was of utmost importance: The liquid shouldn't be permitted to just boil away. He drew the tip of his stirring stick across the nail of his thumb (any other finger was absolutely unacceptable). Oh, how exquisite it is to be red! I gracefully painted that thumbnail without running off the side in watery haste. In short, I was the right consistency, but I still contained sediment. He took the pot off the stove and strained me through a clean piece of cheesecloth, purifying me even further. Next, he heated me up again, bringing me to a frothy boil twice more. After adding a pinch of crushed alum, he left me to cool.

A few days passed and I sat there quietly in the pan. In the anticipation of being applied to pages, of being spread everywhere and onto everything, sitting still like that broke my heart and spirit. It was during this period of silence that I meditated upon what it meant to be red.

Once, in a Persian city, as I was being applied by the brush of an apprentice to the embroidery on the saddle cloth of a horse that a blind miniaturist had drawn by heart, I overheard two blind masters having an argument:

'Because we've spent our entire lives ardently and faithfully working as painters, naturally, we, who have now gone blind, know red and remember what kind of color and what kind of feeling it is,' said the one who'd made the horse drawing from memory. 'But, what if we'd been born blind? How would we have been truly able to comprehend this red that our handsome apprentice is using?'

'An excellent issue,' the other said. 'But do not forget that colors are not known, but felt.'

'My dear master, explain red to somebody who has never known red.'

'If we touched it with the tip of a finger, it would feel like something between iron and copper. If we took it into our palm, it would burn. If we tasted it, it would be full-bodied, like salted meat. If we took it between our lips, it would fill our mouths. If we smelled it, it'd have the scent of a horse. If it were a flower, it would smell like a daisy, not a red rose.'

One hundred and ten years ago Venetian artistry was not yet threat enough that our rulers would bother themselves about it, and the legendary masters believed in their own methods as fervently as they believed in Allah; therefore, they regarded the Venetian method of using a variety of red tones for every ordinary sword wound and even the most common sackcloth as a kind of disrespect and vulgarity hardly worth a chuckle. Only a weak and hesitant miniaturist would use a variety of red tones to depict the red of a caftan, they claimed

– shadows were not an excuse. Besides, we believe in only one red.

'What is the meaning of red?' the blind miniaturist who'd drawn the horse from memory asked again.

'The meaning of color is that it is there before us and we see it,' said the other. 'Red cannot be explained to he who cannot see.'

'To deny God's existence, victims of Satan maintain that God is not visible to us,' said the blind miniaturist who'd rendered the horse.

'Yet, He appears to those who can see,' said the other master. 'It is for this reason that the Koran states that the blind and the seeing are not equal.'

The handsome apprentice ever so delicately dabbed me onto the horse's saddle cloth. What a wonderful sensation to fix my fullness, power and vigor to the black and white of a well-executed illustration: as the cat-hair brush spreads me onto the waiting page, I become delightfully ticklish. Thereby, as I bring my color to the page, it's as if I command the world to 'Be!' Yes, those who cannot see would deny it, but the truth is I can be found everywhere.

ACKNOWLEDGMENTS

Note on all stories for which permission to reproduce has been granted by Random House LLC: Any third party use of this material, outside of this publication, is prohibited. Interested parties must apply directly to Random House LLC for permission.

BARNES, JULIAN: From *Pulse* by Julian Barnes. Published by Jonathan Cape. Reprinted by permission of The Random House Group Limited. 'The Limner' from *Pulse: Stories* by Julian Barnes, copyright © 2011 by Julian Barnes. Used by permission of Alfred A. Knopf, an imprint of the Knopf Doubleday Publishing Group, a division of Random House LLC. All rights reserved.

BENDER, AIMEE: 'The Color Master' from *The Color Master: Stories* by Aimee Bender, copyright © 2013 by Aimee Bender. Used by permission of Doubleday, an imprint of the Knopf Doubleday Publishing Group, a division of Random House LLC. All rights reserved. Bender, Aimee: 'The Color Master' from *The Color Master* by Aimee Bender, © 2013 (published by Random House). Reprinted with permission from David Higham Associates.

BERGER, JOHN: 'A Brush' first appeared in *Harper's Magazine*. Excerpt(s) from *Bento's Sketchbook* by John Berger, copyright © 2011 by John Berger. Used by permission of Pantheon Books, an imprint of the Knopf Doubleday Publishing Group, a division of Random House LLC, and Verso Books. All rights reserved. First published in the UK by Verso Books.

BOYD, WILLIAM: 'Varengeville' from *Fascination: Stories* by William Boyd, copyright © 2005 by William Boyd. Used by permission of Alfred A. Knopf, an imprint of the Knopf Doubleday Publishing Group, a division of Random House LLC. All rights reserved. Boyd, William: 'Varengeville' from *Fascination: Stories* by William Boyd, copyright © 2005 by William Boyd. Reprinted by permission of Penguin Books Limited.

BYATT, A. S.: 'A Lamia in the Cévennes' from *Elementals: Stories of Fire and Ice* by A. S. Byatt, copyright © 1998 by A. S. Byatt. Used by permission of Random House, an imprint and division of Random House LLC. All rights reserved. From *Elementals* by A. S. Byatt. Published by Chatto and Windus. Reprinted by permission of The Random House Group Limited.

CAMUS, ALBERT: 'Jonas, or the Artist at Work' from *Exile and the Kingdom* by Albert Camus, translated by Carol Cosman, translation copyright © 2006 by Carol Cosman. Used by permission of Vintage Books, an imprint of the Knopf Doubleday Publishing Group, a division of Random House LLC. All rights reserved. Camus, Albert: 'Jonas, or the Artist at Work' (approximately 9,600 words) from *Exile and the Kingdom* by Albert Camus, translated by Carol Cosman (Penguin Modern Classics, 2006). Translation copyright © Carol Cosman, 1957. Reprinted by permission of Penguin Books Limited.

FITZGERALD, PENELOPE: 'The Red-Haired Girl' from *The Means of Escape* by Penelope Fitzgerald. Copyright © 2000, 2001 by The Estate of Penelope Fitzgerald. Reprinted by permission of Houghton Mifflin Harcourt Publishing Company. All rights reserved. Fitzgerald, Penelope: 'The Red-Haired Girl' from *The Means of Escape* by Penelope

Fitzgerald. Copyright © 2000, 2001 by The Estate of Penelope Fitzgerald (Rogers, Coleridge & White).

HESSE, HERMANN: 'The Painter' from *The Fairy Tales of Hermann Hesse* by Hermann Hesse, translation copyright © 1995 by Jack Zipes. Used by permission of Bantam Books, an imprint of Random House, a division of Random House LLC.

KAFKA, FRANZ: 'A Hunger Artist' from *The Complete Stories* by Franz Kafka, copyright © 1946, 1947, 1948, 1949, 1954, 1958, 1971 by Schocken Books, an imprint of the Knopf Doubleday Group, a division of Random House LLC. Used by permission of Schocken Books, an imprint of the Knopf Doubleday Publishing Group, a division of Random House LLC. All rights reserved. From *The Complete Stories* by Franz Kafka, published by Vintage. Reprinted by permission of The Random House Group Limited.

LEE, REBECCA: 'Fialta' from *Bobcat and Other Stories* by Rebecca Lee, © 2013. Reprinted with permission from Algonquin Books.

LESSING, DORIS: 'Two Potters' from *To Room Nineteen: Collected Stories*. Reprinted by permission of HarperCollins Publishers Ltd and Jonathan Clowes Limited. © 2002 Doris Lessing.

MALAMUD, BERNARD: 'Rembrandt's Hat' from *The Stories of Bernard Malamud*. Copyright © 1983 by Bernard Malamud. Reprinted by permission of Farrar, Straus & Giroux, Inc. and Lippincott Massie McQuilkin. Malamud, Bernard: Reprinted by the permission of Russell & Volkening as agents for the author. Copyright © 1973 by Bernard Malamud, renewed in 1997 by Ann Malamud. 'Rembrandt's Hat' originally appeared in *The New Yorker*, 1973.

MARTIN, VALERIE: 'His Blue Period' from *The Unfinished*

Novel and Other Stories by Valerie Martin, copyright © 2006 by Valerie Martin. Used by permission of Vintage Books, an imprint of the Knopf Doubleday Publishing Group, a division of Random House LLC. 'His Blue Period' from *The Unfinished Novel and Other Stories* by Valerie Martin, copyright © 2006 by Valerie Martin. Used by permission of The Orion Publishing Group, London.

PAMUK, ORHAN: 'I Am Red' from *My Name Is Red* by Orhan Pamuk, translation copyright © 2001 by Alfred A. Knopf. Used by permission of Alfred A. Knopf, an imprint of the Knopf Doubleday Publishing Group, a division of Random House LLC. Pamuk, Orhan: 'I Am Red' from *My Name Is Red* by Orhan Pamuk, translation copyright © 2001 by Alfred A. Knopf (The Wylie Agency).

YOURCENAR, MARGUERITE: 'How Wang-Fo Was Saved' from *Oriental Tales* by Marguerite Yourcenar, translated by Alberto Manguel. Translation copyright © 1985 by Alberto Manguel. Reprinted by permission of Farrar, Straus & Giroux, Inc. Yourcenar, Marguerite: 'How Wang-Fo Was Saved' from *Nouvelles Orientales* © Editions Gallimard, Paris, édition révisée en 1963, puis revue et augmentée en 1978. Reprinted with permission.